FOR ALL TIME

PART 2

BENEATH

THE

MOON

Janelle Clawson

Fablespinner
Books

U.S.A.

Beneath the Moon

Copyright © 2014 by Janelle Clawson

ISBN-13: 978-0615961620

ISBN- 10: 0615961622

Fablespinner
Books

For information visit
Fablespinnerbooks.blogspot.com
or email Fablespinnerbooks@gmail.com

Printed by CreateSpace in the U.S.A

Acknowledgements

Beneath the Moon was edited and proofread by the following people: Cherri Williams, Janis Carter, Terry Ward, Aubry Thompson, and Jessica Miller.

I want to thank each of you for volunteering your time to edit and proofread this book. Your sharp eyes and input have been invaluable.

Beneath the Moon

One

"He was here," Hadlee MacLean said as soon as Kytan's feet crossed the threshold into her luxurious prison-apartment.

Kytan's eyes widened.

Hers danced, contradicting the blank expression she imposed on her face. She could still hardly believe Ryder had actually been there. However, when she opened her eyes, after only a few hours of sleep, there it was—the blackish stone she'd picked up off the roof. The one her hand fell on as she sat down against the cliff face. On an impulse, she'd tucked the small rock into the pocket of her bomber jacket as a memento of her taste of freedom. She'd forgotten about it in the enchantment of the night and the exhilaration of being out of her prison.

Under a twinkling canopy of stars, she'd shared with Ryder Garrison the dream that was unlike any other she'd ever experienced. Upon waking, it hadn't faded into vague diminishing shadows or splintered into disconnected pieces of a puzzle that could never be put together again to form any solid picture. In fact, the dream had grown in clarity with her increasing consciousness into one of the most intense experiences she'd ever had.

Even now, it was as vivid as when she'd dreamed it. So close to her, she could still feel her parent's love and embrace. Their forgiveness had given her the empathy and desire to let go of her animosity for Ryder, something she'd thought she could never do.

Sharing her dream with Ryder finally freed him from the lingering guilt he'd been unable to escape over the accident that killed her pregnant mother. And forgiving him had filled her soul with tranquility. It had made the glory of the night's brief freedom pale by comparison, and peace like an anthem of joyful praise had sung through her heart.

Afraid she would awake to find her time on the roof with Ryder had only been a dream, she remembered the stone, rooted through her pocket and put the pebble where she would see it as soon as she woke. Proof positive, the experience hadn't been a dream.

Her hand slid into the pocket of her tunic, grasping the stone. Not only was the small rock a token of the spiritual freedom she now felt, but a symbol of hope for the physical freedom she and her fellow conspirators—Ryder, Kytan, and Taya—were working toward. Rubbing its rough edges between her fingers kindled that hope from near dead embers into a bright flame within her.

A smile ruptured her blank expression, which all the conspirators called a slave-face. That empty look was her only possession—a protection and defense against the constant intrusion of King Ateron's guards that now stood inside the door of her apartment whenever Kytan visited, watching their every move.

"Are you talking about"—Kytan shot a look at Lul, his guard and shadow for the day—*"my brother?"*

"Uh-huh, last night." She took his arm and led him over to the sofa as Lul took up his required position by the door. "He climbed up the wall in the guardhouse, crawled through the smoke vent, scaled the palace wall, and crept over the roof just like a cat burglar. Can you believe that?"

"Yes, and I wish I could have seen him do it." Kytan's dimples flared to life as they sat down.

"Well you might not get to see him climb the palace walls, but you *are* going to get to see him and talk to him—without the constant companionship of your guard."

"When?" Kytan gripped her hand.

"Five nights from now—on the night of the new moon—we are going to meet right here at midnight. He thinks the darker it is, the less likely it will be that he'll get caught."

"I am glad he can get out, but how do I get in with the guards stationed in the hall?"

"We are going to slip the guards a mickey."

"What is a mickey?"

"It's what Taya has been doing to me for the past few nights."

Guilt blistered Kytan's face. "Don't be angry with us, we have just been very worried about you. Taya told me you haven't been sleeping, and we thought it might help if you got a few nights of good rest."

"I'm not angry, and Taya is the one that got the good night's rest. I switched mugs with her. She took the herbs and went to sleep like a baby, while I escaped my prison and sat on the roof."

She swallowed a laugh over Kytan's astounded expression, before both of them realized their slave-faces had completely vanished. They shot guilty glances at Lul, who didn't seem to have noticed the breach in their carefully disciplined expressions, and struggled to put their slave-faces back in place.

"I begged *your brother*," Hadlee said, not daring to say Ryder's name, "to take me up to the roof. I just had to get out of this prison for a little while. I can't tell you how wonderful it was to see beyond the terrace walls."

"I can see it did you good."

"You have no idea." Hadlee's face glowed without her consent for one shining moment before she dropped her slave-face back into place, determined not to let it slip again.

"And Taya slept through the whole thing?"

"Yes, but her trick of putting sleeping medication in my herb tea was what gave me the idea about slipping the guards a mickey. *Your brother* thinks it's a good idea. What do you think?"

"Have you talked with Taya about this? Where is she?"

"Still sleeping." Hadlee jumped up. "I better go wake her. She won't want to miss your visit, and we need to tell her about our plan."

Kytan rose too. "I will get things started for breakfast."

"Okay." Hadlee turned the job of putting the kettle on the fire and setting out breakfast to him, while she slipped into Taya's room. They came out together a few minutes later.

While Taya sat at the table with Kytan, sipping her favorite herb tea, Hadlee distracted Lul. It was something she'd gotten very good at doing with all the guards that now stood inside the apartment door during Kytan's visits. With malicious delight, she engaged the gold-toothed guard in conversation. Using a combination of charades and Injanae, she effectively held his attention.

It was a distraction she and Kytan—with the unwitting help of King Ateron—had worked out and one she'd honed to perfection over the past few weeks.

As Kytan explained it to the king, enlisting his support and securing his directive to the guards to cooperate in the effort, "It's important for Hadlee to speak Injanae to as many different people as she can. It will expand her vocabulary and build her confidence. In turn, the guards can help her with proper structure and pronunciation. Their spontaneous conversations with Hadlee will help her develop a more natural form and better inflection as she speaks."

The ruse worked so well, Kytan was able to convey the conspirator's plans to Taya and give her Hadlee's apology for switching mugs with her the previous night. When Hadlee again joined them at the table, Kytan told her that Taya was confident she could find a way to slip the guards a mickey so he could get into the apartment.

"But I still may not be able to make the meeting. Unless the bracing in the tunnel is finished, I will be on tunnel duty that night," he said, referring to the forgotten tunnel that had taken months to clear and was now being braced.

It was an intricate part of King Ateron's plot to end his power struggle with Darvoe, the high priest of Ansuetra— Goddess of the Moon—on the night of the fast approaching Lunar Celebration. Forcing Hadlee to be the Moon Goddess, Ateron planned to stop the ritual sacrifices, using the tunnel as the avenue for Ansuetra's miraculous appearance. From atop a small balcony that was secretly connected to the tunnel, the goddess would materialize, reject the sacrifices, and denounce her high priest.

"How close are you to finishing the bracing? Your *brother* must have thought it would be done or he wouldn't have set the meeting for that night."

"He is probably right, but if anything unforeseen happens and we don't get done, you and Taya should still meet with him. You can tell me about it the next day."

"Okay, but push your crew hard. If both you and Ryder can get here, maybe we can come up with a way to leave here sooner than the night of the Lunar Celebration." Hadlee's eyes darkened with a haunted quality. "That's something I desperately want to do."

Kytan's worried eyes looked into hers. "So do I!"

Two

Four nights later, when their crews traded places in the tunnel, Ryder spoke to Kytan. Of necessity, their conversation was in Injanae. The king had forbidden them to speak to each other in Ryder's tongue. Both knew the penalty for any breach in this command. The king left them with no doubt that the punishment he prescribed would be inflicted should any slip of the tongue be heard from either of them.

"You should be able to finish the bracing in a few hours. We did all but about four feet. That should make it a short shift for your crew. I want to start work on the concealed door tomorrow, and I will need your help with a couple of things. I'll talk to Cartu in the morning. Hopefully, we will have a . . . *planning session tomorrow at twelve o'clock*," Ryder said.

"I will be there."

Only a flash of dimples from Kytan confirmed in Ryder's mind that they were both talking about the meeting in Hadlee's apartment on the following night. He clapped Kytan's shoulder and followed his crew out of the tunnel.

Covered in dirt after their long work shift, Ryder and his seven-man crew headed down to the hot springs bath beneath the palace. They descended a long flight of stones stairs to the mouth of a tunnel, running through the cliff wall. Ryder was obliged to hunch over to enter and navigate this short tunnel. He straightened to his full seven foot, two inch height upon entering the bath cavern. Its domed roof was high enough to allow him to stretch his hands over his head without touching the ceiling.

The floor of the cavern was paved with clay tiles and lit by torches set at regular intervals along the rough walls. The light from the torches reflected brightly off two steaming pools. Tables surrounded the perimeter of the smaller of the two pools. On them sat baskets of dirty laundry and stacks of clean clothes arranged according to the size and rank of the servants and slaves that lived in the palace, and served the needs and wants of the king.

The larger pool was surrounded by chairs and flanked by three tables. One held stacks of woven llama wool towels, herbal soaps in a variety of scents, and pumice stones for scrubbing. The next table was laden with barber's tools. Oswan—the men's bath steward—used a myriad of tools to keep all the male residents of the palace meticulously groomed to the king's high standards. A third table contained the women's grooming tools. Roe, the women's steward, used the tools to keep the female residents of the palace up to par.

The bath was used by both males and females on an alternating day schedule—the day starting at seven-thirty in the morning and ending the following morning at six-thirty. The king's sensitive nose and fastidious standards require all personnel to bathe at least twice a week.

Ryder and the guards stripped off their dirty clothes, dropped them in a basket, and entered the larger pool by a set of stone steps. Sinking into the hot churning water, Ryder decided heaven had to include endless amounts of hot water.

Scrubbed clean from head to foot, he soaked his tired muscles in the steamy, roiling water. Resting his head on the edge, he closed his eyes, letting his spirits soar far beyond the high domed roof of the cavern. *Hadlee is at peace, and now—after all these years—so am I, because she was willing to forgive me.* The burden of guilt he'd carried like a fiery dragon in his soul was finally gone—after twelve long years.

Holding back a smile was impossible. Even being enslaved in the unknown kingdom of Injanae, hidden in the Peruvian Andes, and faced with the impossible task of scaling a five hundred foot cliff—towing three inexperienced climbers—to escape the mad plans of a pagan king, didn't have the power to bring his soul back to earth, take the joy from his heart, or the smile from his face. At that moment, he didn't even regret the amnesia that kept him from remembering how he came into Injanae.

Locking his jaw to keep from grinning like the village idiot, he wondered if Hadlee felt as wonderful as he did. The immediate answer to that question brought utter despair. *She doesn't; and never will.* What he felt far surpassed the peace of forgiveness. He was in love; desperately, irrevocably, everlastingly—in love. It was the most miserable, irrational, hopeless thing he'd ever done. And he couldn't fight it—or deny it—any longer. Even knowing Hadlee would never return his feelings, the longing to scale the citadel of her heart was a relentless ache in his.

Drifting against the side of the pool, letting the churning water buffet him, he lectured his unruly heart. *Without a doubt, my responsibility in Leena MacLean's death will forever keep me from winning her daughter's heart.* His jaw tightened as he squarely faced all the ugly realities that would never go away and would make what he wanted impossible. *So how do I make my heart stop wanting what it can't have?*

He played her smile of forgiveness over in his mind, letting the exquisite peace it brought fill him again. Then he forcefully reminded himself, *Hadlee's forgiveness is a miracle and more than I deserve. I have no right to want, or even expect, anything more from her. She set the boundaries of our relationship—very clearly. Friendship is all there's ever going to be between us.* He nodded imperceptibly, accepting that truth. *I just need to keep reminding myself of what a miraculous gift her friendship is and force my ridiculous heart to stop wanting more.* His lips tightened into a hard line of resolution.

Water splashed his face. Cautiously, he opened one eye. Shur and Gidlo were shoving waves of water at one another. He watched the guard's horseplay with half-closed eyes. Gidlo grabbed Shur and dunked him under the water.

Half a minute passed.

Shur didn't resurface.

Alarmed, Ryder was about to dive under to search for him when a laugh came from the laundry pool. Ryder spotted Shur's dim figure swimming across it.

"How did Shur get into the laundry pool, Gidlo?"

"Through the tunnel of course."

"There's a tunnel between the two pools?"

"Didn't you know?" Numo asked, bobbing up and down in the water.

"No, I've never seen anyone use it. How big is it?"

Gidlo eyed Ryder doubtfully. "You might be able to fit, but if you get stuck you will drown."

"I'll take my chances."

Gidlo crossed the bathing pool to the side nearest the laundry pool, explaining the tunnel's origin. "When this cavern was first discovered, this was the only pool. Then someone—many, many years ago—got the idea to dig the other pool for laundry and tunnel into the bathing pool for the hot springs water."

Ryder nodded appreciatively. "Smart."

"It's actually forbidden to swim through the tunnel." Gidlo flashed him a sly grin. "But when we are down here very late at night, or early in the morning, what Oswan doesn't know, won't hurt him. Just go to the bottom, and you will feel the opening. The tunnel is tiled all the way through. Swim with a hand on the wall so you will know where you are going, but watch your head when you surface on the other end. Some of the tiles have broken off, and it is a little jagged coming out."

Taking a deep breath, Ryder sank to the bottom, running his hand down the wall of the pool until he felt the opening. It was narrow, too narrow to admit his shoulders when he tried to enter moving straight forward. Pointing one shoulder at the top of the pool and the other at the bottom, allowed him to enter the opening. His chest and back brushed the sides as he entered, forcing him to swim the distance on his side. The eerie sensation of being trapped in Davy Jones's locker prickled over him.

Navigating with one hand on the tiled wall and the other one out in front, he frog kicked hard, feeling for the opening into the laundry pool. When he found it, he immediately started to surface—forgetting Gidlo's warning. Propelling himself up and out, he knocked his head against a jagged edge. He came to his feet and pressed his hand against the sting on the left side of his forehead. When he pulled his hand away, it was spotted with blood.

Shur swam toward him, "Are you alright?"

Before Shur reached him, Ryder turned, took a deep breath, dove under the surface of the water again and swam back through the tunnel.

The flickering lights of the torches, surrounding the bathing pool, danced in the water as he came to the end of the tunnel. *A water tunnel, full of light,* the thought pierced him with the brilliant saber of illumination, penetrating the darkest recesses of his mind.

Surfacing in the bathing pool, he emptied his face and let Gidlo look at his head. The cut was minor, but when added to his swim through the water tunnel, the result was miraculous. His slave-face was taxed to the limit as every detail of how he entered the kingdom of Injanae played through his mind.

He dried off and dressed, mentally listing the things that would need to be done and the time it would take to do them. *It will be dangerous too, but it's by far the best chance we have.* He felt like dancing an Irish jig, whooping like a Nahtow brave, and—Hadlee's face materialized in his mind—*kissing a gorgeous blonde.*

Three

The condition of the tunnel ceiling had improved steadily as the work progressed toward the bricked-over door to the small balcony that hung above the palace's rooftop garden. Kytan's pronouncement that the job was done, in the early morning hours, brought a resounding cheer from his crew. After quickly packed up their tools, they spent an additional thirty minutes picking up unused materials and pushing leftover debris to the sides of the tunnel, before exiting it. All expressed the hope they would never have to enter it again.

Kytan lingered after the guards left, doing a careful inspection of the work and evaluating the tunnel's general condition. Taking mental notes to talk over with Ryder, he made his way out. As he came out of the tunnel's mouth, echoed voices reached him from down the stairs and through the hole in the wall that led into the hallway of Hadlee's apartment. He recognized the voices of Toba and Sual, who were still standing night watch inside Hadlee's hall.

He started to close the tunnel door.

"Do you think the king really means to have him killed?" Toba asked.

Kytan's hand dropped away from the door.

"He took a life oath just like the rest of us, didn't he? If the king feels he is being disloyal then what other choice is there?" Sual asked.

Leaving the tunnel door ajar, Kytan crept down the stairs, listening intently to the king's bodyguards.

"Do you think he has done something that proves his disloyalty to the king?" Toba asked.

"That is not up to me to determine. I only know he has made several late night visits to his father's house. And you know Lowanta is no friend to the king."

"Who else—besides me—have you told about this?"

"Only Gidlo and Norr; the king considers the four of us his most loyal bodyguards. The rest are not to be told. Pel is well liked, and many of them will take his death hard. Some might even try to warn him, or protect him—if they know."

Kytan's heart lurched. He pressed himself against the wall and stopped a few steps above the ragged opening Ryder had punched in the brick wall of Hadlee's hall, to access the stairs leading to the forgotten tunnel.

"When will it happen?"

"That will be up to the king, and Cartu. For now, the four of us only need to report to Cartu on Pel's movements when he is off duty. When the opportunity presents itself, Cartu will tell us what we are to do."

"But if he has truly been disloyal, why doesn't Ateron just charge him with treason and have him executed?"

"That would cause the kind of uproar the king wants to avoid. Lowanta is a powerful man. Pel just can't be charged and executed like any common criminal. His father will demand proof. If Pel is charged, he will have to be held for trial. During that time what is to prevent him from telling his father about Ateron's plans for the Lunar Celebration?"

Kytan jumped at the sound of a chair being scraped along the floor. He hugged the wall, his heart racing.

"I see, but who will do it, and how? Pel is a very strong man. Who can defeat him in a contest of arms?" Toba's voice held more than a hint of fear.

"You may lack the skills and confidence, but I don't."

The sneer in Sual's voice sent a chill up Kytan's back.

"Only a mischance allowed Pel to defeat me for the position of captain to begin with. Anyway, I doubt Pel's death will take the form of one on one combat. That would be much too risky, and too obvious."

"Then how?"

"I believe Ateron wants his death to look like an accident, done in a way his father can't possibly trace back to the king."

"Why does Ateron care about that? As king, no one can touch him. Instead of charging Pel with treason, he could just have him executed, and then tell his father he was caught in a treasonable act. Witnesses can always be bribed, and what could Lowanta say?"

"Nothing, but if Ateron openly kills Pel, Lowanta will work against him in the nobles' council. Ateron will lose his power there. You know they rarely vote against Lowanta."

"Then all we have to do for now is—"

The conversation stopped abruptly with the loud rapping of a peculiar sequence of knocks on the hall door. Kytan used the noise to quickly climb back up the stairs. He waited for a few minutes, then shut the tunnel door hard and tromped loudly down the steps. Stretching and yawning, he stepped through the hole in the wall and into Hadlee's hall. He greeted Anlow and Dal who were there to retrieve the hall door key, and take the day's first guard duty shift.

"Sual just told us the work in the tunnel is finally finished," Dal said to Kytan.

"I am sure Ryder will have the last word on that, but other than some minor cleanup, I should say tunnel duty is over." Kytan smiled at the four identical looks of profound relief. "Now if the hall is unlocked, I think I will go take a quick bath before it is given over to the ladies for day."

Four

On the night of the new moon, the guard duty for Hadlee's apartment fell to Orat and Moran. Pel changed the night routine for guarding Hadlee when Cartu found Curlon and Bayo asleep on guard duty. The king took this serious breech in security out on Curlon and Bayo's backs and demanded Pel do something to improve the night security. Pel hoped that by putting both guards inside the hall, they would not only keep each other awake, but vigilant. The new routine required the guards to lock themselves in, only opening the door to a prearranged knocking sequence that Pel changed every night.

Promptly at ten bells, Orat and Moran, accompanied by Pel, relieved Zuph and Tark of guard duty. Pel gave them the knocking sequence, had them both repeat it, and went off to bed.

Moran locked the hall door behind Pel, pocketed the key and sat in the chair across from Orat. Stifling a yawn, Orat pulled out a pair of dice and rolled them across the table. The pair spent the first dreary hour of the nightshift playing a game of dice.

Just after eleven bells, Taya came out of the apartment. The guards looked up from their game. "I need to go to the wine pantry," she said apologetically. "Hadlee is having trouble sleeping, and I thought some wine might help."

Orat raised an eyebrow, "I didn't think Hadlee drank wine."

"No, but I am hoping to persuade her to take just a little for medicinal purposes. She needs the rest, and I don't want to give her any more herbs—they are too addictive."

Orat nodded to Moran. He rose from the table and led Taya down the hallway. Unlocking the door, he went through it with her, locked it again on the outside and stood with his back against the tapestry that concealed it.

Taya hurried off to a large pantry carved into the cliff-side wall. Its recessed doorway was also concealed behind a full-length tapestry of a young Ateron proudly wielding his first sword. Holding a small lamp, she pushed the tapestry aside, pressed the door latch, and entered the cool confines of the pantry.

From floor to ceiling, the wine pantry was lined with shelves. Each shelf held rows of neatly arranged bottles labeled with the wine they contained. Meant for the king's private use, the pantry contained the best wines Injanae could produce.

Taya had access to this pantry because she often used wine in mixing the potions she made for the royal family. Being familiar with the pantry's contents, she made her way through the rows of shelves to the back, where Ateron kept the special wines he used for entertaining. She selected one prized by the king for its strong flavor and potent effect. It was one Ateron only used for his most important guests.

Pulling the tapestry back in place, she quickly returned to Moran, who eyed the bottle with open longing before unlocking the door to the hall. Orat too stared at the wine with a wishful face, forcing Taya to school her own. She hugged the bottle as though the greedy guards might take it from her, nodded her thanks to them and hurried back into the apartment.

She smiled at Hadlee who stood behind the door and clicked the latch firmly in place as soon as she slipped through. Breaking the bottle's clay seal, Taya pulled out the stopper and held it while Hadlee poured in the tasteless, liquid sleeping potion.

Hadlee's nose wrinkled. "Yuck! I don't know how anyone can drink this stuff. The smell alone is enough to make me gag," she said, holding her nose.

Taya giggled, put the stopper back in, and twirled the bottle.

Ten minutes later, she again emerged from the apartment carrying the wine with a dejected expression. "Hadlee won't even try it," she said in a disgruntled tone. "I'm, sorry, but I need to take this back. Hadlee doesn't like the wine's smell. When I took the stopper out, she held her nose and gagged."

Orat licked his lips. "Why don't you just leave it with us? We will see that it is taken care of."

Taya narrowed her eyes, "I can't give it to you, not while you are on duty."

Orat smiled. "But it is already open, and one cup won't hurt us."

"Yes, but there is more than that in the bottle."

"We won't drink it all," Moran said. "We will each just have a little."

Taya looked from Moran to Orat, uncertainty settling on her brow. "I don't know. I don't want you two to get into trouble. Remember what happened to Curlon and Bayo."

Orat touched her shoulder and said in a cajoling tone, "Don't worry. We usually drink a few cups of wine with dinner every night, and I assure you it has no effect on us."

"Well"—Taya hugged the bottle—"it does need to be used now that I have opened it." Her teeth tugged on her bottom lip. "But I really shouldn't let you have it."

"No one will know that you did," Moran said.

She shifted her troubled gaze from one burly guard's imploring face to the other's, shrugged doubtfully, and handed the bottle to Orat. "After you finish it, put the bottle inside the apartment door so no one will find out. I will take it back to the panty in the morning."

Grinning, they agreed.

Kytan slipped through the hall door as the Telquset belfry began to chime midnight. Taya locked it behind him, pocketing the key.

"I see you and Hadlee have done your job well." He looked at the guards, sleeping deeply with their heads resting on the table, the empty bottle of wine sitting between them.

Taya reached for the bottle and the stopper. "I will clean the bottle and take it back to the pantry tomorrow." She gave Kytan a wicked grin. He returned it with devilish dimples.

"You and Taya are very dangerous women," Kytan said, sharing a laugh with Hadlee after closing the apartment door behind him. Linking arms, they settled themselves on one of the apartment's comfortable sofas, propped their feet up on a low gilded table, and listened for any sounds on the roof, or terrace, waiting expectantly for Ryder's arrival.

After waiting for Ryder for a quarter of an hour, it became apparent to Hadlee that Taya and Kytan needed time alone. Excusing herself, she retired to the terrace. Standing in the shadows, she watched them for a moment. They hadn't been alone since the day Kytan took over tunnel duty for Ryder—after the cave in. Kytan wrapped Taya tightly in his arms and tenderly kissed her. Hadlee's heart turned over with a painful sort of joy. *If we don't get out of Injanae soon, things won't end happily for them.*

She turned away and commenced pacing the terrace. The minutes dragged by like hours. Her anxiety grew with each passing one. She finally stopped pacing and fingered the large white blossoms on the trellis vine, now opened and glowing in the light of the starry sky.

The tower clock chimed one.

Disheartened, she dropped onto her favorite bench. "Where are you Ryder?" she said to the roof with a concerned sigh, overlaid with exasperation.

As though saying his name had conjured him up, Ryder swung himself over the lip of the roof, dropped lightly onto the terrace, and grinned at her. "Did you miss me?"

She made a face at him, irritated by the relief she felt he was finally there, and safe.

"Apparently not." He shook his head sadly.

"Where have you been? I—we have been worried."

"I'd like to know that too." Kytan walked onto the terrace and chided, "I could hear your voices very clearly."

"Did you have trouble getting out?" asked Taya, following in Kytan's wake.

"No, I got out just fine, and I see you did too," Ryder said, grinning at Kytan.

Taya giggled. "Yes, the mickey worked very well. Orat and Moran are sleeping soundly, and they should stay that way for a few more hours."

Hadlee got to her feet. "That's right, and they have been that way since the hour you were supposed to have arrived. So if you didn't have any trouble getting out, where have you been?"

"Strolling down memory lane."

Hadlee rolled her eyes, doubled up her fist and shook it at him. "If you don't give us a straight answer right now I'm going to slug you."

His hand shot out, engulfing her fist. With a slight flex of his bicep, he reeled her in.

Caught off balance, she stumbled into him.

Leaning down, he prophesied, "When you know where I've been, you will want to kiss me, not slug me."

Hadlee felt the blush and pulled away. "I will be the judge of that, if you ever get to the point."

Kytan watched this interchange with lifted brows. He gave Ryder a questioning look.

Ryder put on a slave-face.

"What does walking down memory lane mean?" Taya asked.

"It means to go back over your"—Hadlee sucked in a breath and stared at Ryder—"You've remembered something, haven't you?"

Five

Ryder slid down the wall on a rumbling laugh.

"I don't know where you have been, but I do know where we will all end up if you don't stop laughing." Taya tried to hush him. "Even the night watch is going to hear you."

Her warning had little effect on the noise coming out of Ryder.

Hadlee made an exasperated sound, decided the situation called for more direct tactics, and clamped her hand over his mouth.

He raised his hands in surrender, his eyes dancing unrepentantly.

She hissed, "Do you think you could possibly command enough self-control to tell us what you've remembered, sometime before dawn?"

Her reprimand instantly doused the merriment in his eyes.

She removed her hand.

He got to his feet. "Let's get comfortable, and I'll tell you how I came into Injanae and how we're going to leave."

They went inside, shutting out the chill of the night, and settled into the two couches facing each other in the living room.

"When I reached the summit of Farlana," Ryder said, after recounting his climb up the mountain shaped like a dragon, "I started looking around through my binoculars."

There was a pause in Ryder's narrative while he explained binoculars to Taya and Kytan and answered several questions.

"When I spotted Telquset, I had to get a closer look. I walked south along the eastern edge of the mountain until I ran into a crevasse slicing across the top of the dragon's head. The rift starts in the eastern face and runs west. It seemed to go a long way down, but it was too dark to tell if it went all the way to the boulder field on top of the valley's cliff walls. The invitation it offered was too enticing to pass up. I used a rope to drop down the first fifty feet to what looked like a man made staircase."

"A man made staircase off the top of Farlana?" Kytan shook his head.

"It's not man made, but it is a kind of staircase. It was just like descending a steep, ragged set of stairs." Ryder held up Boy Scout fingers. "I promise. There's even a big ledge where I camped after I got too tired to go any farther. We will probably need to camp there too on our way out."

"So we still have to climb the last fifty feet?" Kytan's eagerness was unmistakable. Listening to Ryder's climbing adventures while they were copper mine slaves had given him the desire to learn how to rock climb.

"Yeah, and I brought you a present just for that purpose." Ryder rummaged in his waist pouch. "This is a piton"—he held it up—"and this is a carabineer." He handed both to Kytan. "I thought you might like to see the small and simple means we are going to use to climb the last fifty feet to the top of Farlana."

"Where did you get these?" Kytan fixed Ryder with astonished eyes.

"Out of the knapsack I left in a cavern before I entered Injanae."

There was a collective, inhaled, "Ah."

Ryder grinned like a Cheshire cat.

Hadlee leaned in, "Tell us."

"As soon as I reached the bottom of the steps, I headed for the edge of the boulder field. I wanted to take a closer look at the valley and the city with my binoculars. By then I was close enough to see not only the city clearly, but the people in it too. It was like watching Pucara's story come to life."

He stopped and related the story, Pucara, the Incan guide that led him to Farlana, had told him about the dragon sentinel, and the people and treasure it guarded.

"Of course I didn't believe him," he said, shaking his head.

"I'm not surprised you didn't believe him. It's a pretty far-fetched tale. If I hadn't jumped down this rabbit hole, I never would have believed a place like this existed," Hadlee said, referring to her emergency parachute decent into the valley.

"Me neither. So when I saw it, I had to investigate. I walked along the rim of the valley cliffs looking for a way down until I was right on top of the waterfall. It was mesmerizing. There's no visible river or lake to show where the falls came from. I stayed there puzzling over the waterfall's origin and wondering why there wasn't an easy way—or at least an obvious way—down into the valley. I decided if I wanted to see the city, I would have to climb down the cliff. Only by then it was too late in the day to start. I went back to make camp in the protection of the crevasse for the night. When I got there, I looked around for some kind of overhang I could use for shelter. What I found was a narrow opening into a plunging shaft. It offered protection from the weather, so I climbed in."

Comprehension dawned on Hadlee's face, like a sleuth discovering the critical clue in a mystery. "That shaft is some sort of passageway into Injanae, isn't it?" she asked over the tolling of the city belfry, announcing one thirty.

"Yeah, it is. The shaft drops about ten vertical feet into a tunnel with a steep downward slope." He shrugged. "I wasn't particularly tired, so I went exploring. The tunnel descended for a long way. It finally bottomed out in a large cavern, ending in a pool of water. That's where I spent the night. The next morning I took a bath in the pool and noticed an area of light coming from under the water near the back wall. Being a curious guy, I investigated, swimming under the water into the light. The light led me through an underwater tunnel that came out right behind the Telquset Falls."

This revelation brought a barrage of rapid-fire questions. The conspirators' overlapping inquires, prevented Ryder from answering any of them.

A new question formed in Hadlee's mind when she noticed Ryder's hair was wet. This wasn't unusual. During the months he'd been her interpreter, he'd always bathed before he came. *Still . . . ,* she gave him a quick inspection. *His late arrival, along with his wet hair, and now that I look at him, his damp clothes, can only mean one thing.* Certainty shivered along her arms. "You've been through the water tunnel tonight, haven't you?" she asked over the continuing onslaught of questions Kytan and Taya were throwing at him.

Her question brought a halt to the barrage coming from Kytan and Taya. They sat forward, expectantly.

"How did you find, and follow, the tunnel in the dark?" Hadlee asked.

Ryder gave the conspirators a canny look. "Because I'm not only curious, I'm smart. When I explored the tunnel, I attached a rope to a rock in the cave pool. I decided I would go as far into the tunnel as I could and still get safely back to the cavern pool. I did it in stages going a little farther each time. I was amazed when I came to the opening and could look up at the falls. I found an outcropping of rock at the edge of the tunnel's mouth and secured the rope to it. When I surfaced, I found a big crevice just at the water line directly above the tunnel. I can find that crevice even in the dark. Then I swam back through the tunnel a couple of times to get a feel for it."

"Wait a minute." Hadlee help up a hand. "Why don't the people of Injanae know about this water tunnel? If you could find it, why don't the people of Injanae know about it? Why does everyone say there is no way out of Injanae?"

"I've spent a lot of time thinking about that in the last twenty-four hours, and it's only speculation, but remember what Ateron said about Ansuetra closing up the way the people came into Injanae? If it took time for the waterfall to become as powerful as it is now, the tunnel may have been accessible for some time. I think the spout the falls come out of, along with the water tunnel, and the conduit the river leaves the valley by, as well as the tunnel from your hall to the balcony, are all old lava tubes. I think the cliffs around Injanae are riddled with them."

"So you believe Injanae was once a volcano." Hadlee said.

"I think all of Injanae is sitting on a caldron."

"Do you think the caldron is still active?" Hadlee drew her knees up, hugging them with that disquieting thought.

"The thermal hot springs in the cavern under the palace, and the numerous small earthquakes tell me it is—at least to some extent—and that may be part of the answer to the puzzle. There were three branches in the lava tube from the entrance shaft. I followed the one I did, because it wasn't as narrow or partially blocked, like others were."

"A narrow or partially blocked tube would slow water down, wouldn't it?" Taya asked touching Ryder's knee.

"Right, so maybe it took time and a few earthquakes for the obstruction in the volcanic tube the falls runs through to break up enough to allow the water to flow as freely as it does now. Once it started flowing hard, the river channel wouldn't have been able to handle all the water from the falls, and that's how the pool formed. It eventually submerged the tunnel and filled up the volcanic tube the river uses to leave the valley. I suspect the river tube was also another way to enter the valley in ancient times."

"If the water from the falls that created Lake Quset and filled the river's exit tube, also submerged the tunnel in the first generation after the people came into the valley, it's not surprising no one remembers it's there, Hadlee," Kytan said.

"But wouldn't the history keepers know?" Hadlee pulled an alpaca wool blanket from behind her and handed it to Ryder, shivering from the effects of his still damp clothes.

"No. The early history of Injanae was all oral, and the stories grew and changed over time depending on who held the most power—the priests or the kings—and what they wanted the people to remember, or believe," said Taya.

"One of the oldest stone tablets in Injanae—containing writing—resides in the temple of Ansuetra. It's a decree Ansuetra made directing the pool be untouched. She declared it a sacred place, where she would someday come to bathe because of its purity. To preserve the sacred purity of the pool, no one was, or is to this day, allowed in it," said Kytan.

"With the exception of the high priest, and he is only allowed to touch the water once a year," Taya amended.

"Oh and when is he allowed to do that?" Hadlee asked.

"While he fills ten ritual urns directly from the pool, to use in the washing rites for the victims that are to be sacrificed to Ansuetra during the Lunar Celebration," Taya said.

"So no one, besides me, has touched the pool since the last lunar sacrifices, four years ago?" Ryder asked.

"That's right." Taya nodded.

"Then Ryder should have been arrested when he came out of the pool, not treated like an honored guest," Hadlee said.

"If he had been caught, he wouldn't have just been arrested." Kytan said. "He would have been handed over to the high priest, and immediately sacrificed to Ansuetra. His blood would have been sprinkled in the pool to appease her wrath and cleanse it from his defiling trespass."

"Then it's fortunate I decided to wait and come out of the pool to see Injanae after dark. No one saw me swimming in the pool, or my exit from it." Ryder shivered.

Hadlee got up and brought him a couple more blankets. Ryder wrapped them around his shoulders and legs.

Tucking her feet under her, a puzzled frown grew between Taya's brows. She leaned forward. "Why did you want to come through the tunnel in the dark? You didn't know it was unlawful to swim in the pool."

"No, but I didn't know how my visit would be received either, and I wanted to keep my private exit to myself—just in case."

"So tonight you actually went back through the tunnel in the dark." Taya shrank back against Kytan. "I would be terrified."

"No you won't because Kytan will be with you all the way." Ryder's gold eyes shifted to his brother. "Please tell me you can swim."

Kytan's dimples beamed. "Better than a fish."

Ryder put his hands together and raised his eyes to heaven, "Thank you." He turned his gaze on Hadlee.

"Anything you can do," she said with a lofty look.

"Taya?" he asked.

She shook her head, her chin trembling.

Kytan hugged her tight.

"It doesn't matter, Taya. All you have to do is hold your breath and hang on to Kytan's belt. He will take you through. Can you do that?"

She swallowed, "Yes, but how long is the tunnel?"

"Twenty to twenty-five feet—I think. It sits about eight feet below the surface of the pool on this side of the falls. The tunnel slops downward and comes out about ten feet below the surface of the cavern pool. I'll time how long it takes to do the whole swim the next time I go, then you lovely ladies can practice holding your breath."

Taya nodded, but her eyes were fearful.

Kytan gave her reassuring dimples.

Hadlee's brow drew together. "So how did you lose your memory of getting here, and what brought it back?

"That's the potential danger." Ryder rubbed the hairline scar on his left temple. "A lot of debris; rocks, logs, even dead animals, come over the falls. After I surfaced that night, I was clobbered by something falling through the water. It felt like an anvil and nearly knocked me out. I managed to get out of the pool and reach the edge of the park before I lost consciousness, and the memory of how I came."

"So what brought the memory back?" asked Kytan.

Ryder cleared his throat, "A bath."

"A bath?" Hadlee repeated.

"I didn't know till yesterday that the two pools down in the hot springs bath are connected by a tunnel." Ryder rehearsed the events that led to the unexpected return of his memory, and blew out relief. "I have to tell you, I've been really worried about taking you ladies up a five hundred foot cliff. Going through the water tunnel will be fast, and we will be safe within minutes of our escape."

"You were right," Hadlee said, her expression contrite. "You do deserve to be kissed." She put her hand on Ryder's shoulder, leaned up, and kissed him lightly on the cheek.

He beamed from ear to ear.

"Oh!" Taya sat up straight. "That's what it means, that's what it has *always* meant."

"What?" Kytan asked.

"The name of the falls—Telquset means, the source of life and *freedom!*"

"The source of life and freedom," Hadlee echoed. "Thank heaven!"

Ryder smacked his forehead. "I've heard that said so many times, why didn't I ever put it together, and remember?"

"Because you weren't supposed to leave here without all of us," said Kytan, solemnly.

"I believe that is why you have been here for so long too." Taya reached out and took one of Ryder's enormous hands in both of hers. "I had no hope for my life, and you know I planned to end it, until I met you. You taught me to hope. Even the cruelty you endured under Cartu's hand brought me a gift." Her eyes melted into Kytan's, "You brought me Kytan."

Kytan again enfolded Taya in his arms, adding, "And the gospel."

The truth of that filled Hadlee's heart, and made her wince; thinking of all the brutality Ryder had endured during the nearly two years he'd been in Injanae. He bore the scars of slavery on his wrists and ankles where the shackles he'd worn for so long had left their permanent brands. His back also wore the lingering scars from routine beatings he'd undergone as a mine slave, and the one Cartu administered—because of her unforgiving heart. She'd seen them when she washed his back after the cave-in.

Her eyes welled. *He has suffered so much, and some of it because of me, but where would Kytan, Taya, and I be, if he hadn't lost his memory?* She brushed a hand across her eyes, swallowed the threatening tears, and focused on the sculpted lines of his profile. *I'm thankful you're still here to get us out,* she acknowledged silently. *Even if I were able to escape Injanae without you, I would still be a prisoner of my hate and guilt. You have already rescued me from myself, and all the darkness inside me, by helping me along the path of repentance and forgiveness. For that alone; you will always have my gratitude.*

"They're right, Ryder," she said quietly. "I'm sorry you have endured so much, but I'm also very thankful you're still here. We couldn't get out of Injanae without you." She laid her hand on his arm, giving it a grateful squeeze.

"I can remember anything and everything I choose to," Ryder said, referring to his photographic memory that gave him perfect recall. "Not being able to remember how I came into Injanae has been beyond frustration," he said through his teeth. "Not only that"—he glanced heavenward—"but I have wondered endlessly, why I have been trapped here for so long. If all of you are the reasons, then I don't regret any of it."

The belfry clock struck two.

He gave the conspirators his Cheshire grin, his eyes glowing molten-gold in the amber light of the oil lamps that lit the room. "Let's plan our escape through Freedom Falls."

Six

Ryder followed the king up the steep steps to the balcony jutting out of the cliff face, twenty-five feet above the palace's rooftop garden. He ran a critical eye over the repairs Lunal, the master mason he'd hired, had done. The perilous staircase, built against the cliff face, had needed extensive repairs. Many of the stone steps were so worn and damaged that Ryder made Lunal replace them.

Tugging on the newly installed handrail as he climbed, Ryder tested it for sturdiness. At his insistence, the handrail had been installed along the outside edge of the open staircase. He was afraid the train on Hadlee's gown might hamper her descent and her safety was paramount to him.

Over his shoulder, Ateron praised the new handrail as his own inspiration. Ryder kept his mouth tightly closed on the contradiction that threatened to escape, thinking about the laugh that he'd overheard Ateron share with his chancellor, Cartu, about the purpose of the handrail.

During its construction, the king conducted Darvoe on a tour through the rooftop garden, explaining the details of what he was doing to prepare for the Lunar Celebration. He particularly pointed out the new handrail. With malicious delight, he convinced Darvoe the railing was being installed because of his respect and concern for the high priest's safety. The king and Cartu laughed long and hard over that delicious joke. In fact Ateron was so pleased with it; he shared its full significance with Ryder.

"You see, after the sacrifices, Darvoe is supposed to culminate his triumph over me, by climbing the stairs to the balcony's lofty perch, where all Injanae can watch him complete the sacrificial ritual. That involves leading the common people—waiting below in the courtyard—in a prayer-chant of supplication to the goddess to accept the sacrifices in token of the people's devotion and desire for her continued favor. The chant is then followed by the final prayer of worship and gratitude for all Ansuetra's bounty. It marks the beginning of three nights of revelry and celebration."

"At least that part of the Lunar Celebration will go on as planned." Cartu's gargoyle grin spread across his face, "Sadly, Darvoe won't be there to enjoy it."

Now looking down over the stair railing at the neat rows of carved stone benches, set several yards back from the altar platform, Ryder employed his slave-face to keep his loathing from showing. Stepping onto the small balcony, which had also undergone extensive repairs to its floor and enclosing stone wall, he turned away from the carefully staged sacrificial site, outlining for the king what he proposed to do to make the concealed door, and how he planned to hide Ansuetra's entrance.

"Since this wall is bricked over from one end of the balcony to the other, I can take the old door and frame out from inside the tunnel and enlarge the opening to fit the new door. He patted the bricked over wall. "Then I will scrape the mortar out around the perimeter of the bricks that need to be removed so the revolving door will fit right."

"How can you do that unseen?" Ateron asked

"I don't believe anyone on the ground will be able to see that happen, however, you will need to keep everyone not involved with your plans off the roof while I'm doing it."

Ateron waved an unconcerned hand, "That is easily arranged, but how can you install the revolving door unseen?"

"We won't install the door until the next new moon. As soon as it's dark, I will shroud the balcony wall in heavy black cloth, covering the doorway. Then I can remove the bricks, shutting off the tunnel and set the revolving door in place unseen. The thin brick veneer side of the revolving door will match the bricks we remove from the balcony. That job will require a crew of ten guards to help me remove the bricks. We can distribute them along the sides of the tunnel, like we have the rock."

"Good. Cartu will see you have everything you need."

"Mostly, I need Kytan's metal skills to make the pole and its fittings. Once the door is in, Kytan may need to make adjustments so it revolves smoothly. Also, I want to attach a small copper trough here"—Ryder ran his hand around the inside lip of the four foot balcony wall—"and run it through the wall, into the tunnel. On the night of the celebration, the trough will be filled with some sort of fast burning fuel. Just before Ansuetra comes through the door, whoever is with her will light it. It will flare up, veiling the balcony wall in flames. That should draw everyone's eyes up here. The flames will need to leap up high enough to cover the rotation of the door and Hadlee's entrance. As soon as the flames die down, the silver reflector—I plan to attach to the door at Hadlee's back—should reflect the light of the moon making the white of Ansuetra's gown and all her silver jewelry shine."

Ateron listened to Ryder's detailed explanation, tapping his pursed lips. "I like the revolving door, and the silver disc, but the fire sounds dangerous. I can't afford to have Hadlee burned by flames leaping at her."

"The balcony is wide enough, that if Hadlee keeps her back against the disc until the flames die down, she won't be in any danger."

The wind began to sharpen. Ateron's long braids blew around his head, making their gold clasped ends tinkle together. "What if it is windy?"

"With your permission, I could make a model of the balcony down in the dungeon and test out the procedure to be sure it's safe. We could use bellows to blow the flames to see how close they would come to the door. It wouldn't be exact, but it would resolve the safety issue if wind is a factor. The experiment would also allow me to test different kinds of burning materials to find the right one for the job, judge how much fuel to use to make the flames leap as high as the top of the door, and calculate how long it will take to extinguish them after Hadlee comes through it."

Ateron raised a skeptical brow. "How much time do you need to work this out?"

"With Kytan's help, I would say a couple of weeks. Of course we will need more time to attach the trough to the balcony and the disk to the door, but that shouldn't take too long."

Ryder watched the king's face, trying to see beneath his enigmatic expression, willing him to capitulate to his requests. He knew Ateron didn't want Kytan to work with him, not after the deception they'd pulled—withholding the information about Kytan's ability to speak English. Still at this late date, he felt sure Ateron didn't want anyone new involved in his scheme, and it was important that the door and fire display work properly.

"Alright," Ateron said grudgingly.

Ryder and Kytan walked ahead of their guards, down the dim stairs to the dungeon. Under his breath Ryder said, "Have you noticed that the closer we get to the new moon the more Ateron's anxiety grows?"

Kytan whispered back, "Yes, his temper is getting shorter with each passing day."

"And our work hours are getting correspondingly longer."

"I hope, before the end of this long day, we can determine if the fire will pose a danger to Hadlee," Kytan said as they stepped into a dungeon chamber.

Inside the chamber, Ryder had constructed a model of the balcony wall. Kytan's part of the job had consisted of making and attaching a copper trough inside the wall's edge.

The guards that attended the pair were entertained over the next hour as Ryder and Kytan worked on the fire display. They laughed, doing their best to pump the large bellows, first from one direction and then another, trying to make the flames reach Ryder.

He stalwartly stood the same distance from the flames Hadlee would find herself when she came through the door. When he determined the distance between the door and the balcony wall was sufficient to protect Hadlee, even if it was windy, he nodded his relief to Kytan. "Now we need to figure out what fuel to use."

They went to work experimenting with the different kinds of burning materials Kytan and the guards suggested. It took several tries with different burning agents and quantities, just to get the flames to instantly leap up to the right height for the few seconds Hadlee needed to come through the door.

"Good." Ryder said, after an hour of experimenting. "I think that should do it, don't you?"

"Yes. Now we need to find a way to put it out just as quickly," Kytan said looking over the fire retardants he'd accumulated. He held up a large bottle. "Let's start with this one."

Fifteen minutes later, Ryder shook his head over another failed attempt to effectively put out the fire and keep it from smoking—something that might cause Hadlee to cough or choke. "The flames have to last just long enough to draw the attention of the nobles to the balcony, allow Hadlee to get through the door and begin to speak, before they are extinguished." He picked up a container that held a different fire retardant. "The whole spectacle has to happen in no more than ten seconds."

He knew Ateron wanted it timed to coincide exactly with the most intense moment in the sacrificial drama. His lip curled into a sneer, *just as he and Darvoe raise their knives over the hearts of their victims.*

That looming moment caused Hadlee to spend hours pacing the terrace as the time drew nearer. Her heart pricked her as though it was growing spines like a cactus. *Stop*, she pleaded with her conscience. She circled a bench and started her route over again, pacing to the trellis vine, trying to justify her desire to escape Injanae before she was forced to be Ansuetra at the Lunar Celebration. *We could too if only I could think of a reason . . . ,* she groaned, frustrated.

Their new escape route brought the added challenge of finding a way to keep all their equipment and supplies from being soaked by the trip through the water tunnel. Her brows furrowed as she paced. They'd settled on the means of solving the problem, but hadn't figured out how to get their hands on the required material.

She stopped when she reached the trellis. *What legitimate reason could I possibly have for needing that much oilcloth? If I can think of a reason Ateron will buy, we might still be able to get out of here before the celebration. And for our own safety, it's imperative we leave as soon as we can,* she rationalized.

A drop of rain splashed down her cheek. She dashed for the terrace door as the sky opened up with a brief, but intense, shower. She watched the rain from the shelter of the terrace door. A smile grew on her face.

Seven

On the afternoon of the new moon, Ryder and Kytan found themselves in the familiar position of kneeling before the king, explaining their actions.

"Why isn't it finished?" Ateron glowered from his dais.

"Sire, it will be finished and set in place before the celebration," said Ryder, "but mounting it today isn't possible, or even desirable. It will reflect any light it catches. You wouldn't want it to draw attention to the balcony tonight when Hadlee comes through the door. It will be better to mount the disk after you finish your rehearsals."

Ateron stopped pacing and Kytan took up the explanation. "I have been so busy working with Ryder on the door, the fire display, and making and attaching the trough to the balcony that I haven't had time to work on the disk. With Ryder's help, I am sure it will be done in a week or so."

Ateron scowled, "How long will it take to mount the disk?"

Ryder shrugged. "About two days."

He and Kytan had purposely put off working on the silver disc. Instead, they'd taken as long as they could on the other jobs. They both knew Ryder couldn't afford to find himself in a position where he wasn't indispensable to Ateron.

Concern tightened Ryder's chest. *We're running out of things the king needs me to do, and there are still two full weeks before the celebration. We have to drag out the construction and mounting of the disc for as long as possible.* As soon as it was done, Ryder was sure he would become a permanent resident of the dungeon. That particular fear was becoming a plague in his mind.

Ateron's voice pulled Ryder back into the moment. He grumbled, "Alright, but I want the disc finished and mounted, without fail, in ten days' time. You may go." He flicked an annoyed hand, turning his back on them.

Ryder and Kytan rose, shared a brief look of relief, and walked out the door.

"How is Hadlee holding up?" asked Ryder under his breath, throwing a look over his shoulder at their usual contingency of three guards, who immediately fell in behind them. He picked up the pace, trying to put a little distance between them and their unwanted escort.

He hadn't seen Hadlee in almost a week of self-imposed exile. The last time he made the jaunt over the roof from her apartment, he'd nearly been caught. His heart lurched, thinking about the grueling minutes he'd hung motionless, high on the wall of the guard house, gripping a narrow fissure with his fingers, and balancing his weight on a small ridge of rock.

Norr and Anlow had unexpectedly entered the guardhouse, woke Etin, and sat down to talk with him for a few minutes before going off to bed. After they left he was forced to wait until Etin again slumped over the table and started snoring before he dared to move.

The conspirators agreed it would be better if he didn't come back to the apartment until it was time to take the bags through the water tunnel. Now that the time was getting short, they decided to play it safe. Kytan kept him abreast of things, but the desire to see Hadlee was an unrelenting ache that made him consider risking another visit.

"Not good," whispered Kytan. "Hadlee is too quiet and restless. I think she misses you."

In my dreams. Ryder schooled his slave-face as they hurried down the king's corridor to the door of Hadlee's hall.

The guards were already waiting in the tunnel for their instruction on how to remove the bricks as soon as full darkness settled over the city.

Ryder glanced over his shoulder; then whispered, "I might get to see her tonight, if I am allowed to stay after we put the door in. To do that, I'll have to convince Ateron I should be there in case the door has any problems that need fixing."

"Well, we could always create a small problem that would require your services." Kytan gave him roguish dimples.

The corner of Ryder's mouth twitched. "Yeah, and hopefully I won't lose my hide over it. Ateron is coming apart at the seams. Still, seeing Hadlee is worth the risk," he said as their guards closed in.

"So what shall we do?" whispered Kytan, after they stepped through the hole in the hall and climbed the stairs to the tunnel, while their guards paused to talk with Norr, who was guarding Hadlee's door.

"It can't be too obvious." Ryder quickened their pace again as they entered the tunnel and heard their guards coming up the stairs. "Once we get the door set in, we can work on the problem." He glanced at Kytan, appreciating the fight his brother was having against the reappearance of his dimples as they slowed their strides, letting their guards close in.

Eight

Hadlee peered through the darkness at the heavy green curtain drawn tightly over the mouth of her bedchamber, trying to detect any glimmer of light from beyond it. At Taya's insistence, she'd been laying on her bed for the past couple of hours, trying in vain to get some sleep. *How can I relax and go to sleep when Ateron is due here at midnight to take me to my one and only rehearsal?*

Knowing sleep was a lost cause, she rolled up onto her elbow and listened to the city belfry again chime in its journey to Midnight. *The witching hour*, she mused, a mixture of dread and expectation building inside her.

The part she was being forced to play horrified her, but being allowed out of her prison, under the vastness of the sky, filled her with anticipation. She knew she couldn't afford to let her thoughts linger on either her anticipation, or her dread. Like a hamster going round and round on an exercise wheel, she forced her mind to run her lines over and over in her head. Not only could she say them perfectly, she even understood most of them. Tonight she would learn where Ansuetra was to stand and what she was to do during each segment of the Lunar Celebration.

No doubt, Ateron will be my director. The thought shivered over her. She pulled her vicuna blankets more tightly around her trying to push away this morning's incident. She'd made a small pronunciation error as she recited her lines to him. That prompted Ateron to take her hand and lay his other one on her back as he corrected her error. He'd encouraged her to repeat the mispronounced word correctly, and with the right inflection. But with his hand stroking her back, she'd been so uncomfortable that she found it almost impossible to focus on what he wanted her to do. Struggling to block out the feel of his caressing fingers, she'd tried to concentrate on her pronunciation. After two tries, she'd managed to pronounce the word to his satisfaction. Then, before she could pull away from him, his hand on her back began to slide quickly downward. Jumping away with a gasp, she fled to her bedchamber with as much dignity as her nerves would allow—the sound of his laughter following her.

Fortunately, Kytan hadn't been there, and for that, she felt truly grateful. *He's becoming as unstable as nitro. Every time he sees Ateron's behavior toward me, powerless to do anything about it, he seems to get closer to exploding.*

Kytan thought Ryder should be told about Ateron's advances. With Taya's support, she convinced him not to tell Ryder. "There is no point arousing Ryder's big brother, over protective instincts when there isn't anything he can do about it." She gave him an unconcerned shrug. "Besides, I'm handling it just fine."

At least in front of Kytan, I am, and it won't be for much longer. She clutched her blankets as though they could protect her. *I can get through this—I have to.* She repeated that mantra to herself, but shards of doubt were beginning to scratch away at her confidence. *At least Ateron hasn't truly accosted me—yet. I just need to be vigilant tonight and stay as far from him as I can—or as far as he will let me.*

"Please let there be other people there tonight," she prayed, knowing the presence of others was her best protection against Ateron's advances.

The Telquset belfry chimed eleven forty-five.

She rose from her bed. *A least tonight's rehearsal will allow me to escape this prison, and get a good look at the Telquset Falls.* "The source of life and freedom," she whispered, feeling hope and courage grow with the thought.

The moonless night was overcast and glowering. A brisk cold wind blew off the top of Farlana. The dragon was nearly invisible; its horns and jaws engulfed by dense, billowing clouds. Standing on the platform below the balcony, Ateron watched the sky, hoping it wouldn't rain until the rehearsal was over. Still, he was pleased with the added darkness of the clouds. The threat they posed would keep most of the people of Telquset inside tonight.

He turned to Ryder pointing at the balcony wall. "It looks good. I can't see the outline of the door, but will it still be invisible when the garden is lit with hundreds of torches?"

"It will. Only, on the night of the celebration, the less light there is in the tunnel, the less chance there will be for any light to escape around the edges of the door."

Ateron nodded and preceded Ryder and Kytan up the stairs to make a test run through the revolving door. He pushed hard through the heavy door and came back bristling. "If it's not swung just right it will swing too far and knock Hadlee over—as it almost did me. She could be injured or burned, and that would give everything away. You need to do something about it."

Ryder hastily apologized, "I'm sorry, I didn't think of that. I'll work on it and have a solution by the time Hadlee comes, so I can show her what to do.

"See that you do." Ateron's eyes reiterated the command. "When you have found a solution, wait for us inside the door. I will bring Hadlee through the tunnel, and you can explain how the door works. Kytan," he said turning to him, "stay on this side of the door. When Hadlee comes through, you will explain what is expected of her, and help me guide her through the ceremony." With his usual dismissive gesture, he turned away, descended the stairs, and walked through the door of the rooftop garden.

Kytan dimpled triumphantly from the depths of his hooded robe, which made him one with the night.

Ryder returned it, relieved an act of sabotage hadn't been necessary to accomplish their goal. The weight of the door had done that for them.

His elation diminished with the awareness he was covered in dirt and grease, and he smelled like an ox from removing bricks and setting the heavy door in place. Unfortunately, the door took longer to install than he'd planned, leaving him no time to wash before Ateron brought Hadlee.

At least I will get to see Pilot without having to risk another roof top jaunt. Just the thought of seeing her set off fireworks inside him.

He ducked and pushed through the revolving door into the tunnel. The light of a torch showed him just how filthy his hands, arms, and tunic were. He knew his face must be just as bad. With a glance at Ven—his shadow for the day— he dusted himself off the best he could. Pulling the leather cord off his ponytail, he shook the dirt and brick mortar from his hair, ran his fingers through it, and retied it.

Stop it; he berated himself. *It isn't as though she is going to care if you are cleaned up.* Still, he brushed his clothes off again when he heard Ateron's voice coming down the tunnel corridor.

W̲alking through the tunnel that almost killed Ryder gave Hadlee goose bumps. It was longer and darker than she'd imagined, with a coldness that seeped inside of her. The farther in they went, the more it felt like she was being swallowed by some horrible creature. Ateron's nervous chatter didn't help either, echoing off the walls, surrounding her in an unwanted embrace.

Her eyes widened when Ryder came into view, towering like an apparition at the end of the monster's awful throat. Seeing him brought her immediate comfort. She had to admit that just the sight of him soothed her nerves. *Why is that? Why do I always feel safe when Ryder is near me? Is it just his gigantic size?* She began considering these questions; then abruptly backed away from them. She took a calming breath. *With Ryder here, and Kytan somewhere near, things will be all right tonight.*

As they drew near, she fought to maintain her slave-face. Ryder's hair was no longer its usual chestnut color; instead it was a dull, chalky brown. That same chalky substance made his skin nearly indistinguishable from his hair and covered his clothes. The overall effect made him look like he hadn't bathed in weeks. *Or maybe he just fell into a silo of wheat flour.* She pressed her lips together to keep from laughing. He was the biggest, dirty little boy she'd ever seen. Closing one silver-blue eye, she winked at him.

His face lost its blank expression for a fraction of a second before his mask was back in place. His attention shifted to the king as Ateron began to speak.

When Ateron stopped, Ryder turned to her.

His eyes immediately disconcerted her and nearly undid her careful control. Their amber glow was full of concern, overlaid by the chivalrous duty and responsibility of a Boy Scout. "Are you all right?" he asked lightly.

"Of course," she said, but her response sounded forced even to her ears. *Surely, Kytan hasn't told him about Ateron's advances.* Hoping to alleviate the doubt she saw in his eyes, she quickly added, "I'm just tired, that's all."

He nodded, but even with his slave-face firmly in place, she could tell he didn't believe her.

"Hold on, Pilot, we will be out of here very soon, I promise," he said, his bland tone contradicting the intensity of his eyes. "Now, I am supposed to show you how this door works. Then you will need to go through it a couple of times to practice. It's a revolving door that has a tendency to revolve too far, or not far enough. The king is afraid if it isn't swung just right it will give away the secret of your entrance. I'm going to show you how to make the door go half way around without letting it rotate farther than it should."

The king began to speak. Ryder turned back to him. When he finished, Ven lit a small candle. Norr and Sual, who escorted the king through the tunnel, extinguished the torches they carried, and the one illuminating Ryder's deplorable hygiene.

"The king and his guards will go through the door now," Ryder said to her. "*His Majesty* wants to see the door work from the balcony side, and then from the platform. He wants you to practice your entrance until you are familiar with how the door operates, and can do it perfectly. After you're comfortable with the door, Kytan and the king will take you through the rest of the program."

Ryder again turned to the king and spoke. Ateron nodded and slipped with his two henchmen through the door.

Pressing on the left side of the door, Ryder brought it to a stop in the proper place. He turned to her, stretching out a grubby hand—an invitation to join him at the door. His brows lifted when she put her hand into his dirty one. His fingers immediately closed over hers. His thumb brushed her knuckles, leaving a chalky smudge.

"You need a bath," she said in a laughing tone, faintly wrinkling her nose. "You look like you've been in another cave-in." Reaching up, she erased a dirty smudge that ran the length of his face with her sleeve.

He blushed under his dirt, and retorted, "That's funny coming from the grim reaper."

She was dressed in a floor length, black, hooded cloak that merged with the darkness of the tunnel.

"The only thing I can make out right now is your face floating in the air."

She contorted her face into a ghoulish expression that forced a sputtering cough from Ryder.

Her eyes laughed. "So what are my instructions?"

He recovered from his coughing and leaned down. "You are going to enter through the right side of the door. Push the door hard with your left hand." He placed his on the door demonstrating. "It has to swing all the way to the other side so the silver disc I am going to attach to this side will be at your back when it closes. Keep your right hand down, palm back."

She looked down at the position of his hand.

"When the door comes around you need to stop it with your right hand. If you don't get it stopped, it might knock you down or shove you into the flames. As soon as you go through, put your fingers on the doorframe. That will tell you where the door should stop. When it comes around, stop it with your palm. Whoever is in here with you on the night of the celebration will help by stopping the door on the left side. That should alleviate Ateron's concerns. Any questions?"

"No, let's just try it a couple of times."

He stepped back.

She flashed an impish grin over her shrouded shoulder at him, gave the door a hard push, and slipped through. Doing just as Ryder instructed, she pressed the fingers of her right hand against the doorframe and caught the door with the palm of her hand, preventing it from moving too far, and felt the pressure Ryder put on the left side, making the door come neatly to a stop.

A few minutes later, she came back through the door with the king's verdict. "Ateron says there can't be any light when I come through. Even the dim light of a candle outlines the door as soon as it starts to move. He wants us to blow it out."

Ryder spoke to Ven and reached for her hand. The guard blew out the candle. Darkness encompassed them. He squeezed her hand. She returned it, holding on for a long comforting moment, before again pushing through the door.

Ven escorted Ryder back to the guardhouse after Hadlee finished practicing her entrance. Climbing into his cubbyhole, he poured water from a jug into a large ceramic bowl and gave himself a quick sponge bath. Washing the back of his neck, he relived every moment of the past thirty minutes, playing each one again and again in his mind, like a favorite movie.

Tossing the wet rag into the now dirty bowl of water, he lay back on his bed. He knew he was down for the count, out cold, and destined for bitter disappointment. *How many years will it take to quit replaying all my memories of you, Pilot, let go of my feelings, and forget you?*

Her teasing wink had—for one brief instant—demolished his slave-face. He knew couldn't afford that kind of weakness; or the laughter that nearly exploded from him, at her ghoulish antics. And that smile she'd thrown over her shoulder at him, had lit him up with such irrational bliss he was sure the glow Ateron saw when she went through the door was coming from him—not the candle.

With a groan, he closed his eyes and gave himself up to abject misery. Even being trapped and enslaved in Injanae had never made him feel so helpless, or hopeless.

The falls captivated Hadlee. Even in the darkness, the white water bursting endlessly from the mouth of the lava tube was visible as it roared down into the pool. The cold, clean mist it produced permeated the air. Lifting her face, she inhaled the intoxicating scent of freedom and couldn't keep herself from staring at the falls, longing to be on the other side of them. *All I want is to escape Injanae and be free again.*

Distracted by the conspirators escape route and how they were going to get there unseen, she made a few logistical errors. Ateron growled at her, bringing her mind back to the rehearsal. When she again made one particularly important positioning error, his anger exploded. He grabbed her roughly by the arm. His pinching fingers extracted a painful yelp from her as he jerked her into the proper position.

Her heart pumped fear. Not because of Ateron, or even the pain he inflicted, but because Kytan advanced on him in a threatening way, his fists clinched, anger clearly written on his gentle face. Fortunately, the king's back was to him, and the guards were standing behind Kytan at the far corner of the platform.

She immediately gave Kytan the best sheepish grin she could muster. Resisting the urge to rub her arm, she rolled her eyes and told him to apologize for her blunder.

That stopped Kytan.

Letting her face go blank, she held his eyes until he unclenched his fists, let his face go blank too, and made her apology to the king.

Ateron muttered, "It has to be perfect." He said it so many times; she finally told Kytan he didn't have to keep interpreting the phrase.

The rehearsal continued unwinding and rewinding until she mastered where she was supposed to be and what she was to do as she said each line. Ateron's demand for perfection kept her practicing until she'd gone through the entire program several times without a mistake.

It was just after four in the morning when she again crawled into her bed. She was chilled to the bone from the hours out in the cold wind. Shivering, she pulled her blankets up over her shoulders, snuggled into the warmth of her deep fur mattress, and reviewed her performance with a cold smile of satisfaction. She felt particularly pleased that Ateron had been all business tonight, but it reminded her of her sore arm. Gently, she massaged the spots where the vise of his fingers had gripped it. Already the bruises were forming, ugly and bright.

He's lucky the sleeves on Ansuetra's gown are long, or Ansuetra would be making her entrance wearing big glaring bruises, for all of Injanae to see. That spectacle made her contemplate shortening the gowns sleeves, just to get back at Ateron for that awful moment.

Exhausted, she closed her eyes and curled up on her side. The only other thing that really disturbed her about the rehearsal rose in her mind. Seeing the two altars, knowing what they were meant for, and what she was responsible to prevent, grasped her in an ever-tightening stranglehold. Up until tonight it hadn't been very real. Now it was all too real. Two innocent pawns were caught in the deadly game Ateron was playing with Darvoe, and their fates were in her hands. She thought about what Ryder told her, when she'd asked what kept the victims from jumping off the altars before the knives came down.

"Well," he'd said, running his hand along the back of his neck. "They will be chained hand and foot when they're put on the altars. The guards will stretch them out and attach their chains to the hooks on both ends of the altar bases, keeping them immobile."

After seeing the altars, and those terrible hooks, the image Ryder had painted made her quake. Unable to escape it, she put her head under her pillow, trying to hide from it, knowing if she failed to stop the sacrifices, two innocent people would die. She didn't want to bear the weight of that responsibility.

If we leave before the night of the sacrifices, I won't have to be responsible. Her muscles clenched, fighting to justify that course of action. *But if we do leave before the Lunar Celebration, two innocent people will die, because I won't be here to stop the sacrifices.*

It was a devastating reality, one her conscience wouldn't let her lay aside. She knew in her soul that only a real threat against her life—or to one of her fellow conspirators—would allow her to leave before the night of the sacrifices with a clear conscience. The horror of the responsibility she bore tormented her, denying her the longed for reprieve of sleep.

Nine

"We have come for the oilcloth, Rint," Taya said to the portly steward over the king's storehouse when she and Gidlo entered that vast warehouse of goods.

Gidlo nodded at the steward, crossed his heavy arms, and scowled with obvious displeasure at being used as a pack mule.

"It is a good thing you brought help to carry the cloth." Rint nodded approval at the king's formidable bodyguard. "The amount of waterproof canvas you required is heavy and very cumbersome." He employed his sleeve to wipe the sweat from his forehead and upper lip before snapping his pudgy fingers.

Two slaves brought the heavy roll of canvas.

Gidlo hefted the bulky roll across his shoulders with a grunt, and turned, "I will take it up," he said and strode out the warehouse door.

Taya called after him, "Thank you, Gidlo." She expressed her thanks to Rint and turned to leave.

"Excuse me, Taya." Rint touched her shoulder with his moist fingers, leaving a spot on her tunic. "I was wondering how the queen is doing and if her headache is any better?"

Taya turned back to the sweaty steward—her slave-face carefully in place. "Just what have you heard about the queen's . . . headache?"

"Only that it has made her very ill, and she hasn't been out of her rooms for four days. Her servants and slaves are said to be very worried. I didn't know Her Majesty suffered with such terrible headaches—like my wife. I was wondering what kind of potion you are giving her for it, and if it is beginning to work. If it is, would you make one for my wife?"

"I will send a package of herbs to your quarters for your wife. The next time she has a headache have her steep the herbs in hot water, and then drink the tea when it has cooled. It should help her." Taya forced a smile and left— deeply troubled. The fact she didn't know anything about the queen's condition, and hadn't been called for, was alarming.

Over the past few months, she'd quietly been relieved of her medical duties to the royal family. Ateron told her she had enough to do taking care of Hadlee, and that was to be her only job until after the Lunar Celebration. Taya thought it was more likely the king was trying out her replacement in preparation for giving her to Cartu. Since she knew she would be leaving Injanae soon, she hadn't argued the matter.

Her conscience pointed its accusing finger at her. She'd been so involved with the conspirators, her own life, and hopes for the future, that she hadn't given the Queen—or any of the royal family—a thought in weeks.

If the Queen is really as ill as Rint says, surely the king would have insisted I come, even if Fent is now in charge of caring for the royal family. She knew her talents far surpassed the older doctor's in matters of herbal medicine. Pausing at the staircase to the Queen's fourth floor apartment, she struggled with her conscience.

It was a short fight.

Climbing the stairs, she came out into the queen's hall, and hurried to Telsuea's apartment.

The door opened before she reached it.

The king emerged.

She stopped and bowed. "I have just heard from Rint that the queen is suffering with a severe headache. Do you wish me to attend her?"

Ateron gave her a dismissive wave of his hand. "Her Majesty had a headache that lasted almost two days. Fent has treated her, and she is recovering."

"Then it wasn't four days, as Rint said."

"You know how gossip in the palace grows out of proportion to any event surrounding my family. I am sure Fent made Her Majesty's ailment sound much worse than it was, hoping to make everyone admire his skills by inflating the incident."

"I am relieved it isn't as serious as Rint made it sound."

The king took her arm and propelled her to the slave-operated elevator Ryder had built for his convenience.

"Still, if you wish me to check on her"—Taya dragged her feet—"I am happy to do so."

"There is no need. She is resting comfortably and has assured me she is well enough to resume her normal activities tomorrow. I have every confidence in Fent's abilities, and you have other responsibilities that need your full attention."

Taya's desire to see the Queen intensified, and she offered, "If you will allow me, I could at least visit with Her Majesty and see if there is anything I could do to aid in her recovery."

Ateron paused, still holding her arm. He pursed his lips, pressing a contemplative finger to them. "There is something you can do." He patted her arm. "A sleeping potion would allow the queen to get some much needed rest, and hasten her recovery. She has resisted Fent's sleeping potions, finding their side effects unpleasant. However, I believe she would take one of yours. Bring me a potion for the next five nights. I will see she takes them and let you know how she is feeling at the end of that time."

He again propelled her along with him to the slave-operated elevator that returned them to the king's private level on the fifth floor. As soon as they stepped from the elevator, Taya hurried to the apartment, gathered herbs from her supply closet, mixed a potent sleeping potion, and quickly funneled it into a gauze pouch, while Hadlee inspected the oilcloth Gidlo had delivered. As soon as Ateron permitted, Taya was determined to see the queen and make sure Fent's treatment for her headache had thoroughly eliminated the queen's distress.

Delivering the potion to the king in his private apartment, she again asked if she could administer it. "Please Sire; I am very concerned about Her Majesty's recovery and would enjoy serving her in this small way."

Ateron took the potion from her. "Fent would be deeply offended if you took over treating the queen at this stage of her recovery. "No, it will be better if I personally administer the sleeping potion to my wife. We will keep this secret between us. That way, Fent's pride won't be injured."

She accepted the charge of secrecy with a small bow and reluctantly gave the king the instructions for administering the medicine.

Hadlee was done with her inspection of the oilcloth by the time Taya returned to the apartment, and they began measuring and marking it with chalk.

The rainstorm that drove Hadlee from the terrace inspired her to ask for the oilcloth under the pretense of making waterproof coverings for the apartment's windows and terrace doors—against the onslaught of the rainy season.

The conspirators hailed the idea as an inspired solution to justify the large amount of oilcloth they needed to enclose their knapsacks, and other supplies, in waterproof bags.

When Kytan presented the idea to Ateron, he explained that the oilcloth coverings would allow the windows and doors to the terrace to remain open to the air, which Hadlee always craved, while protecting the apartment from being inundated by rain. Intrigued, Ateron granted the request.

That night, as soon as the night guards were in place, Hadlee and Taya cut the oilcloth into large squares and sewed the bottoms and sides together with rawhide lacing, leaving one side open for inserting the bulging llama skin knapsacks. Each knapsack contained boots, an alpaca fur jacket, a pair of long llama skin pants, a long sleeved tunic, climbing gloves, an additional change of clothes, a heavy blanket, towels, a water bag, and a few personal items.

Over the next few nights they finished the oilcloth bags, inserted the knapsacks, sewed the bags closed, and stitched a strap in place for transporting the bags through the water tunnel. Then they sealed the seams with hot wax, completing the bags' waterproofing.

By the end of the week, four waterproof bags sat in the crowded hiding place inside the box springs mattress Ryder had constructed to store all the supplies for their escape— under the ruse of Hadlee needing a better bed.

"More waterproof bags are under construction for fuel and food," Taya said to Kytan, while Hadlee distracted Bayo with an attempt to converse about the weather. "We will fill them, after the first ones are in the cavern beyond the waterfall."

Kytan passed the news onto Ryder the following morning.

"Good. Then we can leave by the end of the week," Ryder said, drilling a hole into the back, right side of the revolving door to be used as a peephole.

"We could . . . except for Hadlee's conscience," Kytan said.

Ryder stopped drilling.

"She is adamant about the date of our departure."

Ryder groaned. "I know she feels obligated to rescue the sacrificial victims, but going through the water tunnel that night will be more of a risk with all the people in Injanae wandering around than if we do it before the Lunar Celebration."

"She knows that, but . . ."

"She won't be able to deal with the guilt if she doesn't at least try to save their lives. I understand and appreciate what she wants to do, but it means coming up with a plan for escaping the palace after Ansuetra's performance and getting through the water tunnel unseen."

"And we don't have much time to come up with those plans."

"We better meet and talk it over with the girls."

Ten

Waking with regret from a very pleasant dream, Ryder closed his eyes again hoping to resume it. When he couldn't, he relived it, cheering himself with the thought that he would actually get to see the object of his dream at midnight. *And that's even better.* As he yawned and stretched, he became aware of a growing din of voices below him in the guardroom. Poking his head out of his cubbyhole quarters in the cliff face, he heard guards discussing the shocking news—Queen Telsuea was dead.

After breakfast he met Kytan on the tunnel side of the balcony door as they prepared to mount the silver disk. Not daring to say the girls' names or refer to exactly what he meant, he hissed, "Do they know?" He shot a look at Amin, one of their guards for the morning. Their other two guards were lounging in Hadlee's hall, each rotating in to take his turn watching their charges.

Over the weeks, the guards' vigilance had waned due to Ryder and Kytan's careful compliance to the extent they were often left in the tunnel alone, while their escorts lounged in the better air of Hadlee's hall. Today, however, the whole palace was in shock, causing the guards to be more vigilant.

Polishing the round six foot silver reflector, while Ryder tested the strength of the frame it would be attached to, Kytan whispered, "Yes, I told them this morning, but other than announcing it, my shadow for the day had orders not to allow me to stay and discuss it with them."

"How did they take it?"

"Badly—very badly."

"You know what this means," Ryder said under his breath, sinking his chisel into the top edge of the wooden frame, now firmly secured to the back of the revolving door, making a deep groove along it to hold the corresponding medal tongue on the back of the silver disk. "It's what I've been afraid of ever since Hadlee got here."

"We will be gone before Ateron or Cartu can act on their plans."

Catching Hadlee's name on Ryder's lips and the last few English words Kytan spoke to him, Amin barked, "Stop speaking in Ryder's tongue, or I will be forced to report it."

"Sorry." Ryder threw the apology over his shoulder, chipping away at the wood. "Sometimes we just forget."

"It is very sad about the queen," Kytan said, pounding his chisel into the outside edge of the disk's frame.

Both sides of the three-sided wooden frame also needed to be grooved to hold the additional tongues of metal that ran perpendicular from the top one, down the back of the silver disk. The tongues would slide into the groves securing the disk to the wooden frame on the revolving door.

"I didn't know she was ill," Kytan said in a genuinely mournful tone.

"Not many did, but from what I understand of the matter, she had suffered for several days with a severe headache." Amin glanced over his shoulder, lowered his voice as though he was afraid of being overheard, and confided, "I have it on good authority her death was brought on by the herbs she was given to induce sleep and help her recover from that headache."

Kytan's hammer jerked to a stop.

Ryder struck his chisel again. "Who gave her the herbs?"

"Fent claims Taya did, without his consent. Poor girl, her life will be forfeit now." Amin shook his head in a disparaging way. "It's too bad, I liked her."

His reference to Taya in the past tense locked Kytan's jaw. He struck his chisel with brutal force.

Ryder threw him a warning look and carefully cleared the woodchips from the groove he was carving.

After almost thirty minutes, Amin decided his turn was up. With a wave, he moved back down the tunnel, seeking his replacement. Ryder and Kytan waited silently until the sound of the Amin's footsteps receded.

"This was part of the plan all along, wasn't it?" Kytan slammed his hammer into the rock next to the revolving door.

Ryder's face contorted with self-disgust. "Yeah, it was, and I don't know why I didn't see it. The Queen's death makes it easy for the king to have Hadlee, and for Taya to disappear."

"Blaming Taya allows Cartu to have her now without waiting until he thinks she's of age, or even paying the price her uncle is asking. No one will care what happens to the person who poisoned the Queen."

"Things are moving beyond our control." Ryder's eyes locked with his brother's, "We need to leave here—tonight."

"We won't be able to leave tonight or for the next few nights."

"I know the guards are being more careful today, but we've got to risk it. We need to get out of Injanae right now."

"That's not possible. We won't be able to leave until after the Queen's funeral. Her funeral will last three days *and nights*. During that time the streets will be filled with people.

"For three nights?"

"I'm afraid so."

"When will it start?"

Kytan dropped his hammer and sat on the floor of the tunnel, "An hour before sunset, right after a special chiming of the tower bells."

"And it will go all night?"

"Once it starts it won't stop until the queen's body is entombed in the royal crypt beneath the temple's cathedral. A royal funeral is an elaborate ritual. The people will take to the streets and stay there till it is done."

"What in the world will they do for three nights?"

"First there will be a procession of priests that will come to the palace to escort the king, and the queen's body, to the temple. Her body will be on display as she passes through the streets to the temple. The people will cry and mourn through the first night, fasting and grieving at the temple."

"Making it impossible for us to get out."

"Yes. Then tomorrow, poets will tell of her beauty, grace, and good works. She was well loved you know. Then the historians will recite her life history. The people will celebrate her life with music, song, and dance. When the sun goes down the priests will start the funeral rites of preparing her body. It is a long ceremony of chanted prayers, imploring the goddess to receive the queen's soul. It will last all night. The people will camp around the temple burning incense and chanting their own prayers for the queen."

Ryder blew out a frustrated sigh.

"In the morning her body will again be displayed, prepared in the funeral clothing and mask. She will lie in state in the temple cathedral where the people will go to pay their final respects until an hour before the king's arrival. Then the doors will be closed to prepare the temple for the funeral. When Ateron comes, all those who are invited will accompany him into the temple for the funeral rites, and burial ceremony, which will last until sundown. The people will keep vigil outside, waiting for the king. He will address them when the burial ritual is complete. Lastly, there will be a feast that will go all night as the people finish celebrating Queen Telsuea's life."

"Pagans." Ryder slammed his hammer down on the chisel.

"At least Hadlee and Taya will be safe till the funeral is over. Ateron will keep himself secluded with his children until his required public appearances. As his chancellor, Cartu will be kept busy with the priests, seeing to all the arrangements, and details of the queen's funeral."

"Thank heaven for that." Ryder raised grateful eyes to the ceiling then laid a heavy hand on Kytan's shoulder. "The night after the funeral is over—we're getting out of here."

Eleven

A storm shortened the first night of Queen Telsuea's funeral rites. It lit the sky with a vicious display of lighting accompanied by long hours of ear splitting thunder and torrential rain.

Ryder lay in his cubbyhole listening with satisfaction to the storm's violent cacophony. It played like a symphony of opportunity. He waited impatiently for the belfry to chime one, before he left.

The storm rendered this particular rooftop jaunt into a slow and dangerous gamble. Water ran down the cliff face and walls of the palace, making them slippery and perilous. By the time he dropped onto Hadlee's terrace, his clothes were soaked and his hair was plastered to his scalp.

A steam of water followed him from the terrace into the apartment. He stopped at the bottom of the bedchamber stairs and called softly to Hadlee. It took several tries before a sleepy voice behind the curtain responded.

"Ryder?"

"Yeah."

"Umm . . . give me a minute."

It took almost five before Hadlee parted the curtain.

The threat the queen's death was to her made Ryder instinctively reach out his hand to her as she started down the steps.

She hesitated, put her hand in his, and found herself in his arms. She tried to push away from him, but had little success as her feet were no longer on the steps.

"You're soaking wet! And now I am too."

He laughed softly, and said sadly, "Is that anyway to treat a man who has risked his life to come and see you?"

"Risked your life?" She pushed against his chest.

"Absolutely, do you have any idea of how dangerous it is to go crawling up walls in the rain?"

"Why did you?" she asked searching his face in the dim glow of a solitary torch.

"Because I had to know how you and Taya are doing." He put her feet on the floor, took her hand, and tugged her over to the chairs at the dining table.

"Wait. You need towels." She eyed the water running off his clothes and hair; then considered her own wet apparel. "And thanks to you, so do I. We can talk when we're dry."

Ryder stripped off his tunic, wrung it out under the roof's overhang on the terrace, and then squeezed as much water out of his hair and pants as he could. He used all four towels Hadlee gave him to dry his hair and body. Rubbing his arms to chase away his goose bumps, he sat down on a hard dining room chair to wait for Hadlee's return.

She came through the curtain wearing the long sleeved blue tunic and slacks that always made him painfully aware of her sleek figure and magnificent eyes, carrying two blankets. She traded them for his tunic. Hanging that drenched garment over the fire pit, she stirred the ashes back to life, added wood, and waved away the smell of the rising wood smoke.

Ryder wrapped one blanket around his chest and sat on it. Hadlee helped him arrange the other one over his shoulders like a shawl.

"You are going to get a chill sitting in those wet pants," she said to him, sitting in a chair beside him.

He dismissed the warning with a shake of his head and took her hand. "Do you know Taya is being blamed for the queen's death?"

"Yes. She was so upset, I convinced her to take a sleeping potion. I can't imagine why she is being accused of killing the queen. The sleeping potions she mixed for Telsuea were by the king's request, and it was Ateron, not Taya, who administered them. So if anyone killed Telsuea it was Ateron."

"So that's how he did it," Ryder said through his teeth, "and it explains how he can credibly lay the blame for the queen's death at Taya's door. Getting her to make the potions and deliver them to him made it easy for him to claim she poisoned the queen."

"But why would he do that?"

"It's a ploy to put her into Cartu's hands before the agreed upon time, and probably without having to pay for her. And, Pilot"—he held her eyes—"Queen Telsuea's death is meant to put you in Ateron's hands."

"What?"

"I didn't want to scare you, so I haven't said anything about this, but I have suspected it for as long as you've been here. Now that the queen is dead, you are in grave danger." He had both her hands now and her complete attention. "Telsuea was murdered to make way for the Moon Goddess to be Ateron's next Queen."

Hadlee's face went white all the way to her lips. A shudder ran through her.

Alarmed, Ryder pulled the blanket off his shoulders and wrapped it around her. When she continued to shudder and stare at him without uttering a word, he scooped her up and took her to the pillows next to fire pit. After settling her in one, he built the fire up into a solid blaze of heat. She didn't protest or even make a sound when he sat beside her, pulled the blanket tightly around her, and added his arms.

He found her silent, shuddering reaction frightening. It was so unlike her usual defiance. "Pilot, I won't let it happen. On my life, I won't. As soon as the funeral's over—which Kytan says takes three nights—we're getting out of here."

He felt her nod against his shoulder then whisper, "I'm the reason the queen is dead."

"No! Ateron's ruthlessness killed her. You are as much a victim of his evil as the queen."

"Things just keep getting worse. How long will it be before Cartu takes Taya away? Oh Ryder, you can't let that happen. I know what he'll do to her."

"He won't do anything to her. Kytan and I won't let him."

"But you don't know what he's already done." She gasped, and hid her face in the blanket.

Ryder stared down at her. Fear rolled through his gut. "Pilot, what has he done?"

She shook her head.

"Hadlee, tell me what he's done!"

She flinched, and pressed her face into the blanket, still trembling. "I shouldn't tell you. Taya and I were afraid of what Kytan might do if he found out, and telling you is the same as telling him."

"So Kytan doesn't know what Cartu has done either?"

"No."

He pulled her away from his shoulder, letting the blanket fall back.

She averted her face, keeping her eyes tightly closed.

He took a breath, and calmly said, "I promise not to do anything to jeopardize our escape. Now tell me."

She opened her eyes, but didn't raise them to his. With a bowed head, she started to tell him about the visit the king and Cartu made with a rapa, and why, but emotion overcame her. She paused and fought her tears with tight fists.

He drew her close, fighting to calm his own fear, and marveled at what she and Taya had dared to do for him. She began to shake with her effort to control her tears. Wrapping the blanket around her again, he hugged her, waiting for her tears to subside.

When she regained her control, she continued. His arms tightened along with his jaw as she related what had happened. "I was so stubborn and stupid, and I feel so guilty, Taya was injured because of me." She hiccupped on a little sob. "Since then, Ateron has been treating me like some kind of pet." Another strong shudder ran through her.

"Just how does he treat you like a *pet*?

"He finds opportunities, while he is directing Ansuetra's part, to touch me. He runs his hands over my arms, or my face, my hair or—back. It's disgusting.

"Does Kytan know about this?"

"We made him promise not to tell you. It's been all Taya and I could do to keep *him* from doing something stupid. We didn't need the added worry of what *you* might try to do." Ryder's brows glowered, and she hastily added, "Ateron hasn't done anything terrible. His touch just makes my skin crawl."

He knew she was deliberately trying to minimize Ateron's effrontery, and it was obvious she regretted saying anything about it. "I should never have promised not to do something rash. I'm not ashamed to say I'd like to use a rapa on both of them," he said, through his teeth.

His grip on her had been getting protectively tighter, listening to the terror she and Taya had, and were, enduring. Her squeak of protest brought him back from the dark fury building up inside him. Relief at having her safe in his arms made him relax them, slightly. "More than ever, we need to leave as soon as possible, even if we don't have everything we need. We're out of time."

"I think we are too. We can't let Cartu take Taya away."

"He won't have the chance. Kytan and I decided this morning that we're leaving the night after the funeral."

Twelve

"Yes," Kytan said, making them both start. Standing just outside the terrace door, he eyed them with interest.

Hadlee immediately tried to disengage herself from the blanket, and Ryder's arms. The attempt only made him tighten his grasp again.

"I should have known you would come." Ryder stared at his brother. "You and I need to have a long talk," he said, then relaxed his tight jaw and let the anger go. "But at the moment we have more pressing matters to discuss."

Kytan cocked his head. "You are angry with me."

"It's my fault Kytan, I told him about Ateron."

"Good. It has been more than I can stand, and you are welcome to punch me. I stood there and did nothing when he grabbed her arm and jerked her around the night of the rehearsal. I deserve as many bruises as I am sure she has."

Ryder's molten eyes flared into Kytan's before he turned them on Hadlee. "Show me."

"Please don't make this into a big deal. I'm fine."

"Show me!"

"Yes." Kytan backed Ryder up. "If there aren't any bruises, you have nothing to hide."

Ryder loosened his arms and pulled the blanket down.

She lifted her chin and took hold of her left sleeve.

Kytan barked, "Not that one."

Her chin trembled.

Ryder took hold of her right sleeve and pushed it up. Green and yellow bruises encircled her upper arm. Ryder's lips disappeared into a hard, thin line.

Kytan hung his head. "I do deserve to be punched."

"If you had done anything to interfere, you would be dead right now. I didn't want or expect you to interfere. How do you think Taya would feel if you died trying to protect me from something as trivial as a bruised arm? How do you think I would feel for that matter," Hadlee said hotly. "I knew he wouldn't really do anything to hurt me. He can't afford too. His nerves just got the better of him."

Ryder gave his brother a stony stare, but Hadlee's words sank in. He wrapped the blanket back around her, along with his arms. "I know you meant it for the best, and were just trying to keep me from doing something dumb," he said to Kytan. "But then so did Hadlee and Taya, when they didn't tell either of us about Ateron and Cartu's visit with a rapa."

"What?"

"Don't tell him, Ryder," Hadlee begged. "Taya will kill me."

"If you two had just told us what was happening, we could have left as soon as I remembered. It would have been harder without all the gear and supplies we need, but at least both of you would be safe."

Tears sprang to her eyes.

He instantly regretted his harshness and hugged her tight. "Forgive me Pilot. I just can't take any more."

"What happened to Taya?" Kytan demanded.

"It was my fault . . . because I wouldn't work on the lines. Ateron brought Cartu, and he—he . . . ," Hadlee's face puckered, she dropped her head and shook it.

"He threw Taya to the floor and slammed a rapa down next to her, catching her shoulder with one of the strands," Ryder said.

"Taya has a scar because of my stubbornness."

"Hadlee, go get her," Kytan said coldly.

"You ought to beat me with a rapa, Kytan." Hadlee's eyes spilled regret, "I'm sorry, I'm so sorry."

He nodded, but the anger deepened in his face.

Guilt and shame stained her cheeks, "You're wet. Let me get you some towels; then I'll wake Taya."

Ryder reluctantly released her from his arms. She scrambled from the cushion and hurried across the room to the supply closet, coming back out with a few towels.

"Get out of your tunic and dry off. Taya has extra blankets in her room," she said, going through Taya's door.

Ryder eyed his brother. "You've been wall crawling. How did you come?"

"As soon as it started raining, I knew you would be here." Kytan stripped off his tunic and started drying off. "I thought we had better take advantage of the rain."

"Yeah." Ryder nodded his understanding, and agreement.

Kytan squeezed the water from his braid as he continued with his explanation. "I have been studying the row of terraces connected to the servant's quarters. I went from the one in our room, across to the next, and so on, until I got to the wall below the terrace. I remembered everything you told me about climbing, and I climbed. But . . . I can see you have had a much more *interesting* time." There was no mistaking the tone of reprimand and warning in Kytan's voice.

Ryder accepted Kytan's censure with tight-lipped silence.

The door to Taya's bedroom opened. Hadlee shuffled through it, supporting Taya, who swayed groggily against her. Kytan was across the room as soon as she made it through the door, wrapping her in a supporting arm.

Her response to this gallant gesture was identical to Hadlee's. "You are wet," she mumbled in a perplexed tone.

"We have been climbing the palace walls," Kytan said, making her aware of Ryder's presence.

Hadlee handed Kytan a blanket. He took it, wrapped it around himself, and led Taya to the floor cushions.

"Taya are you alright?" Ryder asked, after Kytan settled her in his blanketed arms.

She gave him a foggy smile. "I am now. But what are you two doing here?"

"Getting an education." Ryder looked at Hadlee.

She dropped her eyes, twisting her braid.

"An education?" asked Taya, her voice heavy with the effects of the sleeping potion.

"Hadlee told us what Cartu did to you." Kytan's eyes were black with anger. "Why didn't you tell me?"

Taya hid her face in her hands.

Gently, Kytan pulled them away.

Her eyes filled with liquid guilt. "Anything you might have done would have only gotten you killed, and for what? It was only a minor wound, and Hadlee treated it every day with the herbs I gave her, and it's gone now."

"Hadlee says you have a scar."

"It's nothing. Please just let it go. Now what are you two doing here?" she asked, coming back to her original query.

"I don't think anything could have kept Kytan away after what happened today," Ryder said.

Kytan shot back, "Oh, and I suppose you could have stayed away."

"Neither of you should be here," Hadlee said, settling into a cushion just out of Ryder's reach. "If either of you gets caught, we'll all suffer. I think we should make a few decisions. Then you two need to get out of here."

"You're right, but since we are here, Kytan and I will take the bags and go for a swim. This will be a perfect night for it."

Taya's fingers clutched Kytan's, "Do you really have to?"

"We do. We are getting out of here the night after the queen's funeral is over. You and Hadlee are in too much danger for us to wait any longer."

"I know we should leave as soon as we can, but we still need to make up food and fuel bags. And what about the rope we need from your shop?" asked Taya.

"The need for food and fuel, and the fact it's too dangerous to take you two down rain slick walls, are the reasons we aren't leaving tonight. The food and wood you and Hadlee collect in the next couple of days will have to do. We can pack it out with us the night we leave. Tonight, Kytan and I will go to the shop, get the rope, and take it through the tunnel too," Ryder said.

A look passed between Hadlee and Taya.

"What is the matter?" asked Kytan.

"Taya's not allowed out of the apartment. Cartu came and put her under arrest just after lunch," said Hadlee.

"So that's why I wasn't allowed to come back to the apartment tonight," Kytan said.

A torrent of emotion colored Kytan's face, ending in an angry expression Ryder had never seen. He immediately assured Kytan, "Being confined here is for the best. It will keep her safe."

Kytan's hand caressed Taya's distressed face. "He may be right. You wouldn't be safe, even walking around the palace, with what you are accused of doing."

"Yeah, and since you still have to eat, your food will be brought up by the guards." Ryder leaned forward with a hint of grin on his face. "You both need to develop insatiable appetites for the next couple of days, along with the desire to cook everything you eat. The wood that will require should allow you to make up a couple of fuel bags."

The girls nodded.

"Now, Kytan and I better go." Ryder stood, reached across the fire pit, and retrieved his tunic.

Hadlee jumped up, helping him pull the damp, clinging fabric over his shoulders and down his back. Its contact with his skin made him shiver.

He turned to her after the wet tunic was in place. "We will be back at midnight, the night after the funeral ends."

Hadlee touched his arm, motioning with her head. She led him out onto the terrace, staying under the roof's overhang. They stood in silence, listening to the receding rumbles of thunder, and the rain that had slowed to a steady gentle patter.

"Did you want to tell me something?" he asked when she finally looked at him.

"I just wanted Taya and Kytan to have a few moments alone. They haven't had a private word since the last time you guys were here."

Ryder grinned. "You mean he hasn't been able to kiss her since then."

"Yes, and he wants to reassure himself she's alright. That was a nasty bomb we dropped on him. Can you blame him?"

"No, I understand how he feels." Ryder frowned over the guilt that still marred Hadlee's face as she stared into the rainy sky.

"I wouldn't blame him if he hates me for what happened. He warned me, and tried to get me to change my mind."

"He doesn't hate you. He's just upset. It's understandable. I'm upset too. You shouldn't keep things from me. I can't protect you if you don't tell me what's happening."

"I'm sorry. Really I am, and thank you for trying to . . . comfort me. I'm usually not such a—*girl!* It's just, Taya told me what a kind, gentle person the queen is—was, and knowing she was murdered because of me is so . . . horrible." She turned a tragic, frightened face to him with a lingering shiver. "Ateron murdered his wife, Ryder, *his wife*, because of me. You can't imagine how that makes me feel." Her words were as sodden as the night, and her eyes equally so.

Her anguish made him long to have her back in his arms, and to find the words to take this unwarranted burden of guilt from her. A promise to protect her from everything that would or could hurt her almost leaped from his lips. He clamped them together; revealing that much of his feelings would be a fatal mistake. They would only repel her, and he would lose even the friendship that was so precious to him.

The set of her mouth told him she didn't want his comfort and was already fighting what she perceived as weakness. What she wanted—needed—was strength.

He took hold of her shoulders. "The queen's death isn't your fault, but it changes everything. It means we can't wait any longer to leave."

"Yes, and that means I will be responsible for the deaths of two more innocent people."

"No. That responsibility belongs to Darvoe, and those who empowered him to again practice his evil rituals. Don't you see? Even if we stay, there's no guarantee you could stop the deaths of the sacrificial victims. There are just too many things that could go wrong with Ateron's plan."

Her eyes searched his. "I know you're right, but leaving early means you and Kytan will have to take us down the palace walls on your backs. With guards, servants, and slaves on duty in the palace all night there won't be any other way, will there?"

"Don't worry. If Kytan and I can't figure out a way to take you two out through the palace, we will have no problem carrying you both down the walls. By whatever means I can, I intend to get you out of here before Ateron can lay his hands on you again." He released her shoulders and reached for her hand, "I promised you, no matter what it cost me, I would get you out of Injanae—*and I will.*"

"Don't say that, I couldn't stand it if anything happened to any of us. You, Taya, and Kytan, mean more to me than I can tell you."

Ryder could feel her emotions tremble in her fingers. "I couldn't bear it either, so pray for us, Pilot, pray hard."

"That's just what I came to get you two for," said Kytan.

Ryder turned with an admiring smirk, "Does Kytan by any chance mean sneaky cat. You certainly know how to creep up on people. It's a skill you are going to need tonight, brother."

Thirteen

Ryder knew it was the worst possible night to put Kytan's fledgling climbing skills to the test. He also knew there wasn't any other option as they scaled the wet terrace wall, scurried across it, and disappeared over the slick rooftop, each carrying two oilcloth bags slung across their backs.

The fastest way to the ground lay on the north side of Hadlee's apartment, where the northeast corner met the sheer wall of the cliff face and dropped nearly five stories straight into the palace vegetable garden. Doubled over, they crab walked across the roof to where it met the cliff. Dropping flat on their bellies, they slid to the edge of the roof, and looked over.

Ryder hadn't climbed down this side before. That handicap eliminated the use of his memory. He peered intently down at the rain slick walls of the cliff and palace, while Kytan kept an eye out for the night watch. After several unsuccessful minutes of trying to discern a way down in the darkness, he shrugged his shoulders, and said, "We'll just have to feel our way down the wall."

Kytan nodded.

They flattened themselves against the roof, waiting for the guards to pass. Ryder counted to five after the guard disappeared from view before lowering himself over the edge of the roof, groping for a foothold, and then another.

Kytan waited on the roof until Ryder was two body lengths down before he too lowered himself over the lip of the roof.

Ryder's experience widened his lead. He looked up at Kytan, moving slowly downward, thankful the rough uneven stones of the palace wall held a wealth of places for his brother to tuck in his toes and grasp with his strong, work hardened fingers.

A sound turned Ryder's head. He stopped, and hissed a warning up to Kytan as the night watch approached. Long, tense seconds went by, while the climbers clung to the wall, before the guards turned back the way they'd come.

Kytan's relief expelled itself in a blown out breath when his feet finally found the ground. Ryder exhaled his own relief, and they set off through the rows of soggy plants, heading in a northwestern direction.

The heavy rain had turned the neat furrows between the rows of vegetables into muddy streams. The mud clung to their boots, slowing them down, and making a soft sucking sound as it grudgingly released their boots each time they took a step.

Their direction took them beyond the better-lit part of the palace grounds. Shrouded by deep shadows, they stopped within a few feet of the ten-foot wall enclosing the palace courtyard. Crouching down, they looked for the movements of the night watch.

A lone guard strode along the wall, moving in their direction. They stayed frozen in place. The guard marched to the end of the torch lit area, turned, and marched back the way he'd come. Two seconds later, Ryder and Kytan sprinted to the wall. They leaped for handholds, pulled themselves up, and vaulted into the darkness.

After one brief look, they ran into the shadowy safety of a winding lane of houses on the west side of the palace. Then carefully worked their way south through the wide streets of the noblemen's quarter of the city, watchful for any movement along those dark boulevards until they were beyond the southern end of the sprawling palace courtyard.

The south wall of the palace sat a hundred and fifty yards from the Telquset Falls. Over time, a heavy maze of shops had sprung up between the falls and the palace grounds. Kytan took the lead winding silently through the stone paved lanes to the edge of the park surrounding the falls. They stopped before entering the fifty yards of open ground they had to cross to reach the pool.

The citizens of Telquset used the meticulously manicured park for recreation and socialization. It was dotted with trees, low shrubs, flowering bushes, and stone benches. Scanning every inch of ground within their view, they listened intently for any unnatural sounds. But on this dismal, rainy night, the pathways through the park were empty. Merging into the heavy shadows of the cliff wall, they crossed the empty park to the pool.

Ryder shouted into Kytan's ear to be heard above the roar of the falls. "These bags are going to make it hard to go under, and we won't be able to see once we are submerged, so wrap your arm through one of my bag straps, it will keep us together. Stick tight to the wall of the pool as we move behind the falls. The opening is narrow between the wall and the falls, and you don't want to be caught in its downpour. I will show you the crevice when we get there."

"Right," Kytan yelled.

Ryder stepped to the edge of the pool, and shouted, "We need to take several deep breaths before we go under. Tap me on the back when you're ready. Keep your hand on the wall, and feel along the edge of the tunnel opening to your left. That's where the rope is tied to the rocks. When I find it, I'll put your hand on it. Pull yourself along it with everything you've got. It may feel like a long way. Okay?"

"Okay," Kytan bellowed, and they jumped into the icy water of the pool.

The waterproof bags proved to be very hard to control. They bobbed on the surface of the pool continually being drawn toward the pounding deluge of the falls. With struggling determination, the pair moved along the side of the pool, battling the bags. At almost the center point behind the falls, Ryder's hand found the crevice. He stopped, and put Kytan's hand into it.

"Right!" Kytan shouted.

Ryder heard him inhale deeply and began doing the same thing. Thirty seconds later Kytan tapped his shoulder. Ryder plunged them under the churning surface of the water.

They fought the buoyancy of the bags for the full eight feet going down, taking more time than Ryder wanted. Finding the top of the tunnel, Ryder thrust his hand under it, holding them down. Then he worked his way a few feet to the left, feeling for the outcropping of rock where the rope was tied. He put Kytan's hand on the rocks, and then the rope. Kytan squeezed his shoulder and began to pull himself along it.

Ryder waited a couple of seconds, giving Kytan's kicking feet some space, before he started his own trip along the lifeline.

He surfaced into the blackness of the cavern with Kytan's shout of triumph still echoing through it. His own victory shout mingled with the dying echo of Kytan's as they swam along the rope until their feet found the bottom of the pool and they were able to wade the rest of the way along the rope to the rock where it was tied.

Ryder went around Kytan to the front of the rope. "Hold up for a moment while I light the torch I left on this rock."

His perfect recall allowed his hand to unerringly reach for the torch he'd brought through on his last visit, and the Vesta match safe from his climbing bag. He struck a match and lit the torch. Kytan examined the match, listening to Ryder's brief explanation of this wonder before they turned their attention to more important business.

"Let's get these bags out of the water," Ryder said, feeling the goose flesh ripple over his body from their icy swim, and the chilly air temperature of the cavern.

They waded out of the pool and headed for the area Ryder had camped in so long ago.

"We need to hurry, if we're going to make another trip tonight," Ryder said over his shoulder.

"Right." Kytan shivered, rubbing at his own goose bumps.

Rodents and small animals had ransacked Ryder's camp. Everything that was perishable, including cloth and canvas, had been ruined—with the exception of Ryder's makeshift mess kit, his supply of pitons and carabineers, his climbing hammer, his pocketknife, his compass, and his binoculars—minus their leather strap.

"Thankfully, these invaluable items are rodent proof," Ryder said, picking up his binoculars.

Kytan dropped his bags, and Ryder allowed him a short examination of the binoculars before pulling him away from the remains of the camp.

They secured the torch between two rocks, to provide light on their return trip, took hold of the rope, and plunged back under the water's dark cloak, which now felt slightly warmer to their air chilled bodies.

With as much stealth as the squishy sound of their wet boots allowed them, they crept through the black, rain washed streets to Kytan's shop. Not wanting to draw attention to the shop, they entered, moving through it in darkness. Kytan's familiarity with his surroundings was all the sight they needed. Quickly and efficiently, he collected the supplies he had carefully stowed under the floor of his bedchamber, along with a few precious items of his trade.

Ryder peered out into the empty street, nodded, and slipped through the door. When Kytan didn't follow him, he poked his head back through it.

Kytan stood looking around the dark room.

Ryder stepped back in. "What's the matter?"

"Somehow it feels like I'm saying a final goodbye to my parents. My best memories of them are here."

Ryder clapped his shoulder. Kytan's dimples flickered and died as they went through the door. Ryder noticed he shut it without a backward glance. They slid into the shadows, both carrying long coils of rope, tools, and the pouches of gold Kytan had hidden behind a stone in the fireplace.

Submerging beneath the surface of the pool was easier this time, weighed down by the gold and Kytan's tools. After depositing their supplies in the cavern, Ryder tied a new rope to the large rock in the pool. His fingers had detected many places on the old rope that were worn and beginning to fray due to its long submergence under the water. They swam back through the tunnel securing the other end to the rocks at the tunnel's mouth.

They surfaced behind the falls hungry for air. "You take the lead," Ryder said to Kytan. "I want to be sure you can find the way on your own."

"Right," Kytan said into Ryder's ear, and the pair again dove under the water.

Without error, or pause, Kytan led the way down the wall and to the rope. Ryder congratulated him with a clap to the shoulder. Kytan returned it, and started back along the newly attached rope. Ryder cut the old one away from the rocks, reeling it in as he swam back through.

When they reached the cavern again, they rigged a clothesline with a piece of the old rope around a pair of rocks that looked like aspiring stalagmites. They secured all the bags to the line by looping them over the line and through their handles.

Ryder stowed what was salvageable of his gear in one of Kytan's tool bags, and then gave the line a final inspection.

"Hopefully it will hold off the critters living here until we leave. Now we better high-tail-it back to our prison, before it starts getting light."

Fourteen

Hadlee woke before dawn, listening to the first stirring sounds of the morning birds announcing the start of a new day. She had grown to love their exotic music, and even their frequent discordant quarrels. A twinge of regret touched her, and it occurred to her that they were the only things she would miss when she left Injanae.

We are really leaving tonight. The thought launched a rocket of excitement in her stomach. It hit her heart and exploded, tingling through her with giddy elation. *In just a matter of hours, I will be free again, and on my way home.* Her excitement gave way to a shiver. *But first, I have to make it through the water tunnel.*

Although she had assured Ryder she could swim through the tunnel—and she could—the idea of doing the whole thing in the dark was going to be . . . *a challenge.* Prickles of fear crawled over her skin. The air was her domain. *Truthfully,* she admitted, *swimming blindly beneath the water to gain my freedom is going to be—scary.* She rubbed the goose bumps from her arms and took in a calming breath, reminding herself, *I don't have anything to worry about because Ryder will be with me, and he has been through the water tunnel . . . how many times now?*

She sat up, pushing away the momentary fear that gripped her, threw off her blankets, and began unbraiding her waist-length hair. It needed a good brushing, then she intended to braid it and pin it up. She couldn't risk getting it caught on an underwater obstacle. *I need to do Taya's too. Hers is even longer than mine.*

A knock on the apartment door, followed by the light sound of footsteps told her Taya was awake.

"Breakfast," Taya called, a few moments later.

Hadlee finished unbraiding her hair, hurried through the curtain, and surveyed the huge tray of bread, cheese, meat, and fruit Pel had just delivered. She shared a grin with Taya, knowing several of the guards had commented on the amount of food the two seemed to eat, and their appetite for dried meat, fish, fruits, nuts, and vegetables. Still, they delivered what Taya asked for without question, including the ingredients for making bread and more wood for the fire pit.

The girls had spent long hours during the past two nights making dozens of ashcakes. Additional hours were spent making oilcloth pouches, which they filled with everything the guards brought them, including ones that contained flour, salt, and lard. They sealed the seams of each filled pouch with hot wax, creating a water and airtight container that would keep its contents fresh almost indefinitely. When the waxed seams cooled and hardened, they carefully packed everything away in larger oilcloth bags.

In just two days they had managed to make, and fill, three oilcloth bags of food, and three of wood. Both knew it wasn't nearly enough, but it was the best they could do.

Hadlee eagerly took the plate Taya handed her. "I'm starving."

"Glad . . . you are . . . hungry."

Hadlee smiled. *Taya's English is getting better every day.*

She admired the aggressive way Taya worked to learn the language spoken in the country she hoped would soon become her home. Kytan had been her teacher until the intrusion of an ever-present guard made it impossible for him to continue her lessons. By then, her rudimentary English was sufficient to allow Hadlee to take over the lessons. When they came to a new word or phrase, they often resorted to playing charades until Taya understood. In the give and take of the lessons they both improved their ability to speak in the others tongue.

Using their combined languages, Hadlee explained what she thought they needed to do with their hair, and why, as they settled into the cushions near the fire pit to eat.

Swallowing a mouthful of fresh bread, Taya bobbed her head with ready agreement.

Over breakfast they made a list of last minute things that needed to be done for their escape. Anxious to get started, they quickly finished breakfast, washed their dishes, and started on their most important task.

It took less than thirty minutes to sort the extra food from their meal, stow it in oilcloth pouches, seal them, and put them into the beginning of a fourth food bag they hoped to have filled by the end of the day.

"Now let's do our hair," said Hadlee.

Both searched their rooms and came back armed with brushes, combs, leather ties, and pins. They set everything out on the dining table, sorted it, and discussed what to do.

Hadlee was brushing out Taya's thigh length hair, when the apartment door opened. Their smiles of greeting died instantly. Instead of Kytan, Ateron and Cartu entered the apartment.

In his leisurely way, the king crossed the room and enthroned himself on a gold inlaid bench. He was dressed in formal robes and wearing a gold crown, featuring a silver crescent moon. Cartu trailed him. He too was dressed in his formal attire, his ceremonial sword strapped to his waist.

Hadlee's eyes darted from one to the other. Cartu's unusual smiling stance beside the king sent apprehension's cold fingers down her back. Both the king and chancellor wore expectant looks—their attention fixed on the open door. Hadlee followed their gazes, but from where she stood, she couldn't see into the hallway.

Both girls started when Cartu sharply clapped his hands.

Kytan came through the door flanked by two guards pressing swords against his back, his hands tied securely with rope. Taya gave an audible little squeak. Hadlee gave her hand a warning squeeze. Kytan looked through them with a blank stare.

The guards marched him into the room, and he went without resistance to his knees at the king's feet.

Hadlee flashed ice at Ateron. Then she too, stifled a gasp.

Ryder chained hand and foot in heavy iron shackles walked into the room, escorted by four sword-wielding guards. He too went to his knees next to Kytan, his face devoid of expression.

"Ryder it has been some time since you acted as my interpreter, but it is only right that I allow you that honor today." Ateron's lips twisted in a sardonic grin. "I am sure you will be able to convey my message with more . . . *feeling* than Kytan."

Ryder silently dipped his head then slowly raised it. Keeping his lids lowered, he let his eyes slide between the king and Hadlee.

Ateron turned his attention to her, his ebony eyes boring into hers. She held his stare with her own unflinching one. Her defiant look brought an inward smile that nearly disrupted Ryder's slave-face. *Atta girl, show him you aren't afraid of him.*

The king began his dialog. "This is a very special anniversary for the people of Injanae."

Ryder tore his eyes from Hadlee and forced himself to pay attention.

"As you know, it will feature the offering of human sacrifices to Ansuetra. The high priest has always chosen the victims, but as this celebration marks the return of the sacrifices, Darvoe felt the sacrifices should reflect our mutual consent and commitment to the practice. Therefore, we have chosen the victims by mutual agreement. He and I have talked at great length on the matter. Darvoe has been adamant about a particular victim, and I agreed with him." He paused languidly, gesturing for Ryder to interpret.

Ryder shifted his blank stare to Hadlee's defiant face. Wearing a deliberate look of indifference that extended to the tone of his voice, he let his words express his feelings. "Pilot, put on your slave-face. The king is expecting to be highly entertained by us this morning. We don't want to afford him any more amusement than we can help. As you can see, we've suffered a setback. My brother and I," he said—not wanting to say Kytan's name, "were very neatly ambushed this morning. The king's purpose is to tell us who the sacrificial victims are going to be." He paused. "You ought to slug me. I should have seen this one coming weeks ago. Would you care to lay a bet?"

"No," she said, setting her slave-face in place.

She and Taya took seats on the hard dining room chairs, stiffly facing Ateron, who again began to speak.

Ryder turned his slave-face back to listen.

"It must be a truly terrifying feeling to be chained to an altar, listening to the prayer of the high priest, while he raises his sacrificial dagger high over his head—and of course I will raise mine—knowing that as soon as it ends, we will plunge our blades into the unshielded hearts of our victims."

The tower clock brought a halt to Ateron's narrative. With obvious annoyance, he tapped out its chimes on his knee, waiting for the last chime to die away.

"Of course we all know there aren't going to be any sacrifices." An amused smile made it all the way to the king's eyes. "The lovely Moon Goddess is going to intercede on behalf of the victims. Still, it will be a terrifying ordeal for them, and something I don't want any of the good citizens of Injanae to endure. Therefore, compassion led me to persuade Darvoe to unwittingly choose victims that know Ansuetra will miraculously save them." He chuckled.

Ryder looked vacantly at Hadlee. "He's telling you what you already know. There really aren't going to be any sacrifices because you will stop them. He wants the victims to be people who are in on the scheme. It limits the possibilities, doesn't it? The important thing to remember is the victims won't come to any harm," he said, contradicting the doubt he'd put in her mind three nights ago. His eyes focused on her with reassurance, for a single moment. "Whatever develops right now, just hang on to your slave-face. I think we both know what's coming, and considering this set back, it might even work to our advantage."

Ateron's golden sandals tapped a pleasant little beat on the floor while he waited for Ryder to finish. When Ryder's eyes swung back to him, he sat forward displaying the anticipation of a child about to reveal a thrilling secret.

He fixed Ryder with an unusually animated face. "Today I will deliver to Darvoe the two people chosen to be honored by sacrifice at the Lunar Celebration. They will be escorted through the streets of the city to the temple where they will undergo the purification rites, preparatory to their sacrifice on the first night of the full moon. Of course my most important consideration in helping Darvoe select the victims was to provide the proper motivation for Hadlee's part."

His piranha eyes locked on Hadlee. He smiled at the dead expression they held, before turning his attention back to

Ryder. "From the day you appeared, Darvoe has felt you are to blame for the increased quaking of the earth. As I recall, your arrival was marked by one. So you can see why Darvoe would feel it is essential to sacrifice you." Ateron grinned broadly.

Ryder held his mask of indifference easily intact. "I win." he said dully, turning back to Hadlee, as though they had made the bet. "The king feels you need the right motivation for your part." One corner of his mouth quirked upward. "Too bad he doesn't know our history."

Hurt flared in Hadlee's eyes with an intensity that immediately made him sorry he'd tried to joke about the situation. The look lasted only a single searing second. She blinked, and her eyes went dull.

He'd hoped, by poking fun at their situation, to minimize the seriousness of this new development. If nothing more, he wanted to convey his unconcern, and lessen her tension, something that was evident to him by the fingers she twisted into her tunic.

Her searing eyes told him she wasn't amused by his self-mocking sense of humor.

"I'm sorry," he said, "I just thought—"

"I know."

As he continued, his eyes offered her a lengthier apology than she'd permitted. "Whoever is to be my companion, and I, are to be escorted to the temple this morning for the purification rites—sounds fun," he said flatly, allowing his tone, rather than his words, to express his feelings this time, before he turned back to the king.

The exchange between Ryder and Hadlee drew a baffled expression from Ateron. He frowned as though censuring Hadlee for her lack of concern that robbed him of the entertainment he was expecting. Lines of disappointment grew on his forehead. He tapped his foot for a moment before his visible disappointment receded, replaced by a confident almost smug expression. He leaned forward as though he was certain the next announcement would elicit the sentiments he desired.

"Choosing the second victim was much more difficult," Ateron's brow puckered as though the decision had weighed heavily on him. "Darvoe and I struggled over it, until recently."

He beckoned to Pel, standing in the doorway, while Ryder interpreted for Hadlee. Pel marched across the room with a set of chains in his hands, stopping in front of Taya.

Ryder worked to keep his voice neutral as he relayed Ateron's almost jovial words. "The people's need for justice in the murder of the queen must be appeased."

Hadlee's only visible reaction, as Pel knelt in front of Taya, was the arm she encircled Taya's shoulders with, in a protective gesture.

Taya held out her wrists. Stone faced, Pel slipped the manacles over her small hands and clamped them shut around her delicate wrists. She dropped her manacled wrists into her lap while Pel positioned the heavy shackles. Without hesitation, Taya slipped her feet inside them. Pel locked them around her ankles. She raised her manacled wrists and laid a gentle hand on his cheek, holding his eyes for a moment. He stood, turned on his heels, and marched back to the door.

Taya came to her feet. Hadlee stood too, gave her a ghost of a smile, and squeezed her hand. Taya smiled serenely and took an awkward step in Ryder's direction. She managed three stumbling steps, before the bulky shackles tripped her.

Hadlee leaped forward grasping her around the waist as Ryder's long arms shot out to catch her. Their fingers met behind Taya's back. His closed over hers and held on trying to infuse her with courage, give her comfort, and reassurance.

She clung to his fingers.

"Our lives are in your hands, and I can't think of a better person to entrust them too." He allowed his eyes to smile, but doused the look an instant later. "Whatever you do, after you rescue us from the altars, *don't* send us away like the king's script calls for. You—and my brother—need to find a way to keep us, or at least me, with you. Then," he said quickly, keeping his voice even, knowing Ateron might cut off this conversation at any moment, "try and figure out a way to enable the three of us to leave together, *before* the king dismisses the nobles."

He released her hand. She stepped back with an almost imperceptible nod of her head.

Still holding onto Taya, he rose to his lofty height. He lifted his chained hands. Taya shuffled under them into the circle of his arms. "Taya isn't used to shackles," he said to

Ateron, "I don't think she will be able to walk all the way to the temple. May I carry her?"

"Ryder I—"

A gentle squeeze checked her.

"By all means," Ateron said laughingly. "It will make the procession a most touching and memorable spectacle. Darvoe is sure to be delighted."

Before he could pick her up, Taya brushed her fingertips across Kytan's shoulder. He turned a blank face to her. "I love you," he said softly in English.

She responded with the same words, in the same language, then tore her eyes from him and nodded to Ryder. He picked her up, cradling her against his chest. She lifted her chained arms. He put his head through them. Leaning into his shoulder, she turned her face away.

"I will take care of her," Ryder assured Kytan in English.

"I know you will, and I will take care of—Pilot. Kytan squared his shoulder and held Ryder's eyes.

Ateron boomed, in a theatrical tone, "The people await you! Cartu you may escort the victims out, and wait for me on the roof."

"Of course, Sire." Cartu bowed with a reverence he rarely displayed. He walked passed Kytan, knocking against him with unconcealed malice.

"Stop," Hadlee said in Injanae. Everyone's eyes turned to her. Walking by Ateron, Cartu, and the guards, she stepped to Ryder's side, and laid a hand on his arm. "You won't die, I promise you, I won't let either of you die."

"I know you won't—so don't worry. But . . . if anything does go wrong, my brother will get you out." He dropped his slave-face, and smiled.

She returned it with a trembling one of her own.

At a gesture from Ateron, the guards moved into formation, surrounding Ryder, forcing Hadlee to step back.

Ryder looked back at her over his shoulder as the procession moved through the door.

Fifteen

Hadlee walked back to Kytan's side, dropped to her knees, and bowed her head submissively, proclaiming her compliance. She grasped Kytan's shoulder, "Tell Ateron he has my full cooperation. My performance will be perfect. But," she said coldly, deliberately raising a threatening face to Ateron, "if anything goes wrong—and I mean anything. If Ryder or Taya are hurt in any way—that is where my cooperation ends."

Kytan told Ateron what Hadlee had said, and conveyed his reply. "The king wants me to assure you that nothing is going happen to *our* friends, because you will stop the sacrifices. And of course—*he says*—he will too."

The king rose, smiling broadly.

"He is leaving now to start the procession." Kytan paused, as the king continued to speak then said through clenched jaws, "He thinks it is a *pity* we won't get to see such a touching spectacle."

Ateron paused next to Hadlee, ran a finger down her cheek, smiled when she jerked her head away, and strolled through the door, four bodyguards following in his wake.

When the door closed behind him, Hadlee and Kytan found themselves alone. Still on their knees, they did the only thing available to alleviate their fears and help them find direction. Grasping hands, they prayed.

At the end of the prayer Kytan lifted a determined face. "We have two goals," he said, pulling Hadlee to her feet. "First, is to save Taya and Ryder's lives. Second, we need to create the best circumstances we can for our escape."

She gave him a staccato nod, "I agree, and if everything goes according to Ateron's plans, I should be able to take care of the first goal, but how do we accomplish the second?"

Kytan stared over her shoulder and out the terrace door, seeming deaf to the trilling of a songbird perched on top of the wall. Hadlee watched a parade of dark emotions march across his face, before he focused on her.

"I have an idea."

"I don't think I'm going to like it," she said, disconcerted by his villainous dimples.

"Oh you *are* going to like it. In fact, I think you are going to love it," he said, the villainy infecting his eyes.

"Really?" She stepped back, her brows arching, "and I suppose whatever you're plotting, I'm the one that's going to have to pull it off, huh?"

"Mostly." He glanced at the door. "I don't know how much time we have before someone remembers we are alone, but we need to make some changes in your performance."

"Okay, but first, let's see if I can get you out of these ropes." She reached for his bound hands. "For months I've told myself I wouldn't really have to be Ansuetra." She grimaced, picking at the rope's knot. "I was sure we would be able to escape before the night of the celebration—and we would have—until my conscience got the better of me. If it hadn't, we would already be gone. It's my fault Ryder and Taya's lives are in jeopardy, and now their safety depends on how convincingly I can play the part of Ansuetra." She battled with the knot and the guilt that gnawed at her, managing to loosen the first part of the tightly tied knot.

"Hadlee, only one of their lives will be at stake."

Her head jerked up. "What do you mean? Both of them are going to be at the mercy of a madman with a dagger—"

"Yes, but only one will be under the high priest's dagger. The one under Ateron's—unless things go very wrong—won't be in any danger. But the one under Darvoe's—and I'm sure it is going to be Ryder—won't have that protection."

Her fingers stopped picking at the knot. "Why do you think it will be Ryder?"

"Ateron won't take a chance with Taya's life. She is Cartu's reward for all he has done for the king. Besides, everyone will expect Ateron to execute Taya for the death of the queen."

"Then Ryder's life truly is in my hands"—her trembling fingers pulled at the knot—"and if anything goes wrong . . . he will . . . die." She dropped her eyes to the knot and gave it a hard tug. "I can't let that happen. I couldn't live with myself if anything happened to him."

Kytan stopped her fingers. "Nothing's going to go wrong. You have worked hard, and I know you can do this. Go get a slate so we can write out the new lines I want you to learn."

"But so much could go wrong, and Ryder knows it. He even used it as an argument to soothe my conscience so I would feel better about leaving before the celebration." She pulled apart the last of the knot and unwound the rope.

Kytan rubbed his raw wrists. "Even if the worst happened, Ryder wouldn't blame you. You know he wouldn't."

"But I would blame myself."

"You aren't the one putting him on that altar."

"No. Except . . . I have, Kytan. So many times in my heart, I have. If he dies, it will be as though I willed it to happen."

He gaped at her. "Do you really hate him that much?"

She stiffened, "You know—don't you?"

Taking her hand he led her to the sofa, sat, and pulled her down beside him. "I know you have experienced more pain in your life than I can imagine, Ryder too. It has been obvious to Taya and me that there was something very wrong between you two. I made Ryder tell me."

"Then you must know I am just as responsible for my mother's death as he is."

"I know *you* believe that."

"But *I am*. I knew I was being disobedient when I went out into that street. I thought the only consequence would be a scolding from my mother." She stuttered a breath. "I didn't really understand until then, that once we make a wrong choice, the consequences are out of our hands. We can't control them—but we do have to live with them."

"Yes we do."

A tear slid down her cheek. She dashed it away. "If either Ryder or I had made the right choice that day, my mother would be alive, and neither one of us would have had to live with the terrible consequences we've both suffered."

"I'm very sorry for what you and Ryder have been through. It has been hard for me to watch, but lately I have seen a change in both of you."

"I don't hate him anymore—if that's what you mean. He helped me face my own guilt and find forgiveness for my responsibility in Mama and the baby's deaths, and he has found it too." She paused and met Kytan's eyes. "He's my friend now."

"Then why are you so worried?"

"Because, when I was a child, I wished he would die in some terrible way—like my mother did," she confessed. "Seeing him chained to a pagan altar and watching a knife come down into his heart is about as close to my darkest fantasies as it gets." She bit her lip and drew a breath through her nose. "Maybe, in some terrible way, I have to do this, or need to do it, because it's the only way both Ryder, and I—and heaven—will know for sure, I've forgiven him. If he dies on that altar because I'm a moment too late, I will always wonder if some lingering resentment in my heart made me hesitate just long enough for that knife to—" She sucked in a breath, unable to finish, her stomach churning.

Kytan's hard fingers gripped her shoulders. "Is there some lingering resentment in your heart for Ryder?"

The raucous noise of impatient people gathered in the palace courtyard reached up through the terrace door. She turned, listening to the ruckus, trying to shield her face from Kytan's probing stare. A few nights ago, she'd awoken in a torrent of aggravation. No memory of the dream survived her wakening. The only thing that survived were feelings of frustration, directed squarely at Ryder.

For what? She searched her mind, unable to remember. *Surely, my feelings weren't the result of lingering resentment over the accident, were they?* The heat of a blush crept up her face.

Its betrayal seemed to answer the question in Kytan's mind. "Hadlee." He pulled her eyes back to his fearful ones. "Is there something in your heart you still feel Ryder needs to do to be fully forgiven by you?"

"No! I have forgiven him." She jumped up. "But what I don't need is his guilt, pity, or misguided Boy Scout sense of duty."

Kytan came to his feet. He again took hold of her shoulders, searching her face. "I think there is more in your heart you need to face than you have admitted even to yourself. Don't ignore it until it is too late."

Sixteen

Ateron entered the rooftop garden, giving the signal for the gong to sound. Dal struck the huge copper disk. Its vibrating motion sent a blinding shaft of reflected sunlight across the roof. A deep metallic tone filled the air, reverberating through the city. Dal struck the gong two more times in rapid succession. On the last resounding thrum, Ateron walked with his chancellor at a stately pace to the four-foot wall that enclosed the rooftop garden.

Throughout the palace courtyard, and beyond, a hush moved like a diminishing wave over the gathered multitude when the king came into view. Ateron acknowledged the crowd with a condescending sweep of his hand, before handing a gilded scroll to Cartu.

Bowing formally to the king, Chancellor Cartu unrolled it. His baritone voice boomed down at the expectant people. "This year's Lunar Celebration, marks four hundred years since Ansuetra brought our people into this sacred valley. This historic event will be marked by the return of the blood sacrifices to honor the Moon Goddess. By mutual decree of His Royal Majesty, King Ateron, and Darvoe, the High Priest of Ansuetra; the slave Ryder, and the healer Taya, are to be taken to the temple of Ansuetra. Through the rites of purification, the high priest will prepare them to be sacrificed to the Goddess of the Moon. They will be offered to Ansuetra on the first night of the full moon. The ceremony will start at midnight, when the moon reaches its zenith. The citizens of Injanae are commanded to gather on the palace grounds to witness these sacrifices. All the citizens of Injanae are encouraged to add their petitions to those of the priests, for Ansuetra to temper the quaking of the earth, and grant her continued blessings upon the valley and people of Injanae." Cartu turned, and nodded to Dal, who again struck the huge copper gong, announcing the start of the procession to the temple.

A low rumble swelled through the crowd, as the identities of the sacrificial victims were passed from those within the range of Cartu's voice, to those too far away to hear the official decree. The rumble increased to the timbre of debate when the victims for the coming sacrifices came into view. Each person boisterously voiced their satisfied agreement, or astonished disagreement.

Cartu led the procession down the stairs Ryder had built. He mounted a llama, rode through the courtyard gate, and into the street. Pel followed on foot, with fifteen of Ateron's bodyguards surrounding Ryder and Taya.

Keeping his eyes straight ahead, Ryder whispered urgently to Taya, who hid her face in his shoulder. "Turn your face to me."

Taya turned her head. "Why did you want to carry me?" she asked.

"Because you aren't used to shackles and jeering crowds, and I think every living soul in Injanae is here to see this spectacle," Ryder said into her ear. "It would please them to watch you stumble or fall." She hugged his neck in thanks as he continued, "Mostly I want to talk to you before we get to the temple."

The people began to erupt in loud shouts, drowning out Taya's inquiry about the subject Ryder wanted to discuss. The word ran swiftly through the increasingly hostile crowd that the girl the giant carried was Queen Telsua's murderer. The crowd screamed death chants at her and vile obscenities at the outsider who held her.

Darvoe had convinced them Ryder was Ansuetra's enemy; responsible for the increased quaking of the earth. Still, no one dared touch him or the healer, with the king's bodyguards protecting them—with swords drawn and ready.

Ryder's voice rose allowing Taya to hear him above the hateful chants of the crowd. "Don't listen to them. Listen to me. Do you know what will happen when we get to the temple?"

"The victims"—she tilted her head, raising terrified eyes to his—"us, are drugged to make them compliant. Then we will be taken into the inner sanctuary to begin the ceremonies that consist of long sessions of chanting and prayers. We will also be measured for our sacrificial robes. On the day of the sacrifices we will be ritually washed, dressed in our robes, and brought back to the palace to be—killed."

The procession reached the park surrounding the falls and pressed through the crowd on the road to the bridge. Again, Ryder raised his voice to be heard, this time above the thunder of the falls. "We have to keep them from drugging us, and no matter what else happens—we have to stay together. I don't want you out of my sight."

Taya blushed, "If we insist on staying together, you know what the priests will assume."

"Let them. I won't allow them to separate us. You will be in danger if you're alone. These priests believe you killed the queen. They aren't going to care what condition you're in as long as you are alive to be sacrificed."

"Do you really believe the priests would—"

"Yes I do." Ryder felt her convulsion of fear, and hugged her tighter. "The only way I can protect you is if I stay with you. Don't worry; I'm sure we can work things out to preserve both our modesties."

They crossed the bridge over the river Tel. The mass of people on the other side stood their ground, staring at the victims, stopping the procession.

Pel issued order to his guards, a few of them pressed forward into the crowd. Their swords quickly parted the throng, allowing the procession to proceed.

"Next," Ryder said urgently, "I'm not going to be a part of their purification rites. I'm going to give them a choice. They can kill me—or *try to*—as soon as we get to the temple, or they can simply put us in a room, leave us alone, and take us back when the time is up."

Taya stared at him, "You are going to fight them? Why?"

"Because, I won't compromise myself, or my priesthood, by willingly participating in their pagan rituals."

"But what about being sacrificed?

"That's all a well-rehearsed act, but these purification rites are real to these pagan priests, and I won't do it." The uncompromising set of his face left no room for doubt.

Laying her head against his neck again, Taya took a deep breath, "Alright, we fight."

"I hope it won't come to that. Just follow my lead, and we'll see how good a slave-face I have."

Taya lifted worried eyes to his, "I hope I can find mine before we have to face Darvoe."

Ryder smiled grimly, "I have no doubt, you will. I don't know how things will play out, but if I let you out of my arms, step away from me, and stay away. I don't want you hurt."

"Don't worry about me. I will watch your back."

Surprised, Ryder stared at a face as determined as his. He lightly kissed her brow. "Taya, you are one of my heroes."

The procession stopped at the bottom of the temple stairs. A gantlet of priests lined the stairs leading up to the mouth of the temple, and Natell, the assistant high priest. He stood above Cartu's head, arrayed in the flowing fawn and silver robes of his office. He looked down his nose at Cartu with an expression of contempt.

Ryder inspected the priests lining the stairs, noting their weapons, and calculating their fighting skills. The corners of his mouth lifted involuntarily.

Cartu dismounted and climbed the steps to Natell. He inclined his head with stiff formality. "As Chancellor of Injanae, under the authority of King Ateron, I am authorized to put into your hands the sacrifices the king and high priest have chosen to offer to Ansuetra for the rites of purification."

With a wave of Natell's hand a silver gong at the entrance to the temple sounded. Another wave stilled the crowd. His cold eyes swept over Ryder and Taya. "As guardian of the temple of Ansuetra, and protector of her royal high priest, I am authorized to receive those Darvoe and the king have chosen to be honored by sacrifice for the rites of purification," he said with equal formality, and clapped his hands.

The King's guards backed away.

The twenty priests that lined the stairs marched down them, surrounding Ryder. Again the silver gong sounded.
The spear carrying priests pointed them at the sacrificial victims, marching them up the steps, and into the temple.

Ryder's steps slowed, waiting for his eyes to adjust to the gloom inside the temple. A prod from a sharp point behind him, made him quicken his pace to the length of his shackles. The lack of windows and adequate torchlight made the temple feel cool, and damp. Goose bumps rose on his arms.

The musty smell of fungus, mingled with incense, drifted on the air. He wrinkled his nose, and whispered, "It smells worse than your herbs."

Taya choked, and gave him a reproachful click of her tongue.

He grinned down at her.

Shoulders shaking, she returned it.

The procession walked the length of the dimly lit corridor, and paused. Ryder blinked as a pair of heavy silver doors swung open. Another silver gong heralded their entrance into a large cathedral. It was brilliantly lit with silver ensconced torches evenly spaced along the walls. Silver, candlelit chandeliers also hung high in the vaulted ceiling, sweeping the sanctuary of all shadows.

Ryder stepped into the dazzling light. His eyes moved in an ark, taking in the splendor of the room's towering columns, colorfully glazed tile floor, and ornate stonework, before settling on the walls. They were hung with gory tapestries depicting human sacrifices, featuring the glorious Moon Goddess, and her faithful high priest.

He took note of the treasure trove of silver and gold ornaments that sat on stone tables, lining the walls of the cathedral, wondering if they held religious significance.

"Darvoe is certainly glorious today," Taya whispered calling Ryder's attention to the front of the hall where a towering two level dais sat. Five steps led up to the first level. On it sat a silver throne occupied by a middle-aged man.

Unimpressed, Ryder gazed on the splendor of Ansuetra's high priest. He was elaborately dressed in a raised patterned, scarlet robe. Silver ornamented his ears, neck, wrists, and waist. A silver molded cap crowned his head, sporting an array of colorful feathers that draped around his shoulders.

Directly behind the high priest's throne, an additional three steps led to a platform containing an enormous silver plated altar. The sickly sweet smell of incense rose from the altar, drifting in thin swirling bands through the hall.

Stopping at the bottom of the stairs, Natell commanded in a voice that echoed through the hall, "Put the woman down."

Ryder lowered Taya, keeping her within the protection of his arms.

"Your Eminence." Natell bowed low to the slender, hawk nosed man on the silver throne. "The king has delivered those you have chosen to be honored by sacrifice to Ansuetra." Turning to the victims he commanded; "You will kneel before His Eminence, the Royal High Priest of Ansuetra."

Ryder's arms tightened around Taya.

She leaned against him.

Bright spots of indignation colored Natell's face. "You will—"

"No," Ryder's voice was calm, but absolute. "We won't kneel to the priest of a pagan god, or submit to your purification rights."

Silence as heavy as the incense hung in the air.

Astonishment played across the high priest's pock marked countenance. The look grew when his eyes locked with Ryder's gold ones. He frowned and lifted his hand.

Ryder felt several spear points press against his back. He sent a pray of thanks heavenward for the leather jerkin he wore. Hadlee made it for him, and Taya brought it to him, after the cave-in—hoping to give him added protection against falling rocks—before he went back to work. He wore it almost religiously.

Deliberately, Ryder intensified—what many prison inmates had told him was—the savagery of his predatory eyes. He allowed the look to expand into his face, answering the challenge that grew in the high priest's own. "I have been chosen to die. It matters little to me where I die. Killing me now will spare me the ordeal of your pagan rites. I would much prefer a private death to a public one."

Darvoe made a motion with his hand. The priests pulled their spears back. "Then I will force your participation." He made another gesture.

The spears jabbed Ryder. Their points bit through the leather jerkin pricking his skin, not enough to do any real harm, but enough to make him uncomfortably aware of his vulnerable situation.

He lifted his arms.

Taya stepped out from under them, shuffling her shackled feet until she reached the base of the dais. She lifted her chin defiantly. One chained hand slid into her tunic. "It doesn't matter where or how I die either. Let it be now. You can always ask Ateron to provide you with more compliant victims for the sacrifices. Of course now that the people have seen us, they will be very disappointed. They are delighted with the choices you and Ateron have made. He too is looking forward to putting a dagger through my heart for the death of the queen. I wonder what he will do if you cheat him of that satisfaction."

Ryder suppressed the grin that tugged at his mouth. *Taya has a better slave-face than I do.*

Darvoe shifted in his chair. That small shift in his posture made it clear to Ryder that he wasn't going to kill them here and now, or even do them any real harm. *He can't, not if he wants us for the sacrifices, and he does want us—badly.* Ryder had seen it clearly in his eyes when Natell presented them. That hunger still glinted, unabated.

Darvoe gave his victims a narrow look down the length of his beak like nose, accentuating his hawkish appearance. His eyes shifted. An unspoken message seemed to pass between him and Natell, before Darvoe said, "Take them to their quarters, see they are fed, and remove their chains,"

"We will willingly go to our quarters, as long as we remain together. We *will not* be separated," Ryder said.

Darvoe's astonished eyes dropped to Taya. "Is this your wish also?"

"Yes," she answered, without a blush.

"All we want is to enjoy our last few days together." Ryder gave Taya a broad wink. "We won't make trouble as long as we stay together, and are treated well."

"All you want is your last days together," Darvoe repeated skeptically. "And then you will willingly go back to be sacrificed. Why?"

"Because I can't fight everyone in Injanae. Inevitably, we will be killed. All we want is to be together for these last few days. We aren't afraid to die. Our faith teaches us not to fear death, because in the next life we will no longer be slaves."

Again, Taya rode in Ryder's arms. They descended a long flight of stairs and shuffled down a dimly lit hallway to a door at the end.

"I was hoping we would be taken up to a place that had access to the outside," Ryder whispered, stopping behind the priests, in front of a heavily locked door. "I should have known better."

Natell selected a key from a large ring and unlocked the door with a dour expression. "This chamber hasn't been properly prepared. Being unaware of your attachment to each other, we prepared single rooms, but you will find these quarters have all the basic necessities. I will have food brought, and perhaps you would like water to wash with?" he inquired, solicitously.

"Yes," Taya said. "And we also want fruits and vegetables that are whole and uncooked, dried meat, flour, lard, and salt."

Ryder ducked under the doorframe and followed a torch-bearing priest into the chamber. He put Taya down as a priest lit and set torches in a few wall sconces, while another priest unlocked their shackles.

Ryder rubbed his wrists. "I think that covers our needs for now," he said, dismissing Natell, and his minions.

With a scowl, Natell motioned the priests to leave, turned on his heels, and followed them out, locking the door.

Taya's smile was as big as Ryder's. "We did it!"

"Yeah, we won the first battle, but I'm not sure the war is over."

"I don't think the war is over either. It's too easy to drug prepared food. Believe me, I know. We need to be very careful about what we eat. Whole plant-based foods, and things we cook ourselves will be safer. I will be able to tell if the water or bread ingredients are tainted. I have a very well trained nose, and taste buds."

Ryder grinned. "If that's true, why didn't you know Hadlee switched mugs with you?"

Taya's hands went to her hips, "I was very careful when I prepared that potion. I didn't want Hadlee to suspect what was in it. I made it from a root my mother discovered. Once distilled, it's colorless and tasteless. That's why it worked so well on the guards. But *you* don't have to worry. Anything Darvoe tries on us, I am sure to know about."

Ryder held up his hands in surrender before the storm brewing on Taya's face broke over him. "I believe you, and with you as my taster, I will fear no food." He nodded at the door. "The lock on our door will help protect us too. It will warn us whenever they come. Now let's explore this place."

There wasn't much to explore. The room held four bed shelves. Each had a rather dirty mattress and blanket. There was a battered table, a few mismatched chairs, and a small pile of soiled floor cushions. A smoke blackened fire pit built into the wall, sat below an obviously inadequate vent that disappeared into the ceiling. Next to the pit, a sparse amount of firewood lay in an untidy heap. Across the room from the pitiful cooking facilities, a patched curtain closed off a small chamber for washing and other necessities.

"Well it's . . ."

"Pretty bad." Ryder stuck his finger through a hole in one of the thin blankets. "This is worse than I thought it would be. I'm sorry. The privacy is very minimal."

"At least we are together." Taya gave him a brave face. "We will survive."

"Maybe we can bargain for better accommodations," Ryder said, thoughtfully.

"With what?"

"Cooperation."

"But we aren't going to cooperate, and this"—Taya gestured around the room—"may be the opening skirmish in the second battle. They probably put us here for the express purpose of making us uncomfortable enough to cooperate. Please don't compromise because you think I can't deal with sleeping on a filthy mattress. I can."

"But I don't want you to. Maybe we can get a decent room if we agree to let them measure and make the sacrificial clothes for us. I'm sure Darvoe is going to try to get us to cooperate in some way. All we have to do is use it to our advantage."

Seventeen

After delivering Ryder and Taya to the temple, Pel walked back to the palace with his guards. He pulled Lul aside, put him in charge of the duty assignments for the rest of the day, and retreated through the courtyard gate. He headed north, letting his feet take a familiar path, his mind occupied with the morning's events.

Criminal. That was the word that kept assaulting him, accusing him, labeling him. Delivering Ryder and Taya into the hands of Darvoe made him feel like a criminal. Taya's forgiving eyes, and touch, only intensified that feeling.

Of course, if Ateron's insane plan succeeds neither will be hurt, he tried to console himself. But his conscience argued; *there is no guarantee that will be the outcome. Too much could go wrong.* He had tried to point that out to Ateron, to no avail. He blinked, ridding his mind of his monarch's maniacal eyes.

His feet stopped in front of a large estate, which backed against the cliff face and was enclosed by high walls. A feeling of relief settled over him as he went through the gate of the well-manicured courtyard. It was landscaped with fruit bearing trees and ornamental bushes. He drew in the scent of blossoms. Inhaling deeply, he allowed the fragrance and peace of the garden to soothe him, before going through the door of his parents' home.

Fawla looked up from her sewing and smiled, when her son entered the room. She was an intelligent woman of slender proportions, possessing remarkable insights into human nature, which her husband often sought when he needed counsel. A giving heart, that strove to ease pain wherever she encountered it, also endeared her to everyone who knew her.

"Pel, what a nice surprise," she said, putting aside the decorative tunic she was sewing. "I didn't think we would see you for a few more days."

Enfolding his mother in his arms, Pel held her tightly.

Fawla returned his prolonged embrace, giving the comfort only a mother can communicate with a hug.

"Is that Pel?" a small girlish voice squealed from up the broad stairway.

"Yes, and I am here to challenge you to a game of shewa," Pel said to the young girl as she bounded down the stairs. Her bright black eyes danced almost as much as her long braids. She leaped into his arms, taking her mother's place.

"Do you mean it? Do you have time to play shewa with me?" Dara asked excitedly, her small arms clinging to her big brother with the determined grip of a child unwilling to let go of a favorite plaything.

"I do. Go set up the board. We can play as soon as I speak with our father."

Dara laid her small hands on Pel's cheeks, and pouted, "No! If you do that, we won't get to play. Papa will keep you, and I won't get to have you."

"Alright, little one, we will play first, and then I will talk with Papa."

Dara kissed him, wiggled out of his arms, and went to find the playing board. Pel smiled as she scampered up the stairs.

Fawla watched their interchange almost with a frown. Pel's embrace told her something was wrong, even if his face didn't. Lately his visits occurred long after Dara was in bed. They were often brief, and mostly spent behind the closed doors of his father's study. To see him in the middle of the day was unusual. For him to have time to play with Dara was very unusual.

Dara rushed back down the stairs with the game. Pel helped her carefully set the carved stone pieces on the circular, wooden board and gallantly let her make the first move.

Fawla listened to her daughter's laughing chatter, and Pel's teasing replies. She watched her son visibly relax as he played the childish game with his sister.

"I thought I heard your voice." Pel's father, Lowanta, came in from the garden at the back of the house.

"Oh no, Papa, you can't take him away now, I'm winning."

"Are you? Well then, I better let you finish him off before I have my turn with him." Lowanta ran his hand down one of his daughter's long braids and pinched her chin. He turned to his son, "When you have been soundly defeated, you can find me in the garden."

Pel nodded to his father, gravely considering his next move.

The Telquset belfry chimed the quarter hour twice before Pel got up from the table, soundly defeated for the third time. He kissed the top of Dara's head. She laughed and danced around him in triumph. He hung his head, looking dejected.

Fawla smiled at her son's intentional losses, her heart still concerned with what she saw behind his lighthearted pretense. "Can you stay and eat the evening meal with us?" she asked, knowing it was very unlikely.

"Yes," Pel said, without hesitation.

The answer should have delighted Fawla, and though her face lit with pleasure, her disquiet grew.

"Can you, really?" asked Dara. "Then I can beat you again, and if you stay the night, I will let you win at least one game."

Pel laughed heartily. Something Fawla hadn't heard him do in a long time. The sound unaccountably disturbed her.

He lifted Dara into his arms, and hugged her until she squeaked. "I'm afraid I can't stay the night, little one, but maybe we can play one more game before I go, if you will allow me to visit with Papa until we eat."

"Alright." Dara kissed his cheek.

He set her down, kissed his mother, who hid her concern behind a smile, and went through the door to the garden.

Pel found his father in the midst of the green serenity of his manicured garden. He sat in a comfortably padded chair on his covered patio, listening to the gentle strains of a flute, while he read a scroll.

Lowanta was an unusual man. Built like a warrior, and trained in all those disciplines. He too had been captain of the king's elite bodyguards, for Ateron's father, Porten. Twenty-five years later; he still had the strength and bearing of a warrior, though he now only wielded a sword for sport with Pel and his guards, to keep his skills proficient. He'd gone from warrior to statesman. His outstanding service, and wise counsel to King Porten, as his captain, eventually won him the position of Porten's chancellor. He'd served in that capacity even after Porten's death as his son, Moncara's, chancellor, until the day Ateron took the throne, following Moncara's untimely death—something that still bothered Lowanta.

After Moncara's death, he'd won the chief seat on the council of nobles, and actively pressed for better laws that treated the commoners and slaves with greater equity. He used the disputes between the two ruling powers in Injanae to win small victories in equality for all the citizens of Injanae. His widely known political disagreements with Ateron were largely applauded by the priests, and a source of constant irritation to the king. And although he was a critic of the king, he had no love for the high priest, and the practices he espoused—something Darvoe knew well.

Pel slid into a cushioned chair beside his father, leaned back, closed his eyes, and enjoyed the lilting melody of the flute. He wished he could confide everything going on in the palace to his wise, understanding father, but his oath of loyalty forbade it. *Still he might be able to help me—in one thing.* He opened his eyes to his father's careful scrutiny.

Lowanta dismissed the young musician and silently waited until he left the patio. "It is a pleasant surprise to see you during the day. That has happened far too little in the past few moons," he said, echoing his wife's thoughts. "Even Elta has not seen you."

"I am sorrier for that than I can say." Pel's fingers gripped the edge of his chair. Elta's delicate face rose in his mind. She was lovely, lively, and full of entertaining conversation.

She could make Pel forget his troubles as no one else could. They had been betrothed now for nearly a year.

"For not being here or not seeing Elta?"

"Would it hurt you to know I was speaking of Elta?"

"No." Lowanta chuckled. "That is as it should be." A worried expression grew in his eyes. "Make time for her Pel. If you neglect her too long, don't be surprised if another man steals her from you."

"That would be a very unwise thing for any man to do," said Pel, with a hint of a grin, and more than a hint of steel in his voice. "But my responsibilities have led to her neglect, and perhaps that is why I need your counsel."

Pouring wine from a bottle at his elbow, Lowanta encouraged his son's confidence. "Tell me how I can help."

Pel drank from the cup his father handed him, and straightened in his chair. "Will it give you satisfaction to hear me say you were right about Ateron, and I agree with your assessment?"

He had never spoken openly about his opinion of the king before—to anyone. The revelation brought a look of penetrating scrutiny from his sire.

"I always knew you would come to this painful understanding, though it affords me no satisfaction. How could it, when you have bound yourself by a life oath to serve Ateron in whatever he dictates."

"That understanding is why I want to leave his service."

The edge in his voice deepened the concern in Lowanta's face.

"You are a powerful man. Can you help me do it? Is there an honorable way to do it?"

Lowanta studied his son's troubled countenance, and shook his head. "It is not in my power to have you honorably released from a life oath to the king. Only Ateron can do that. Of course, many kings have given honorable releases to their bodyguards when they have grown too old, or are injured, and can't perform their duties. Some guards have even sought release for family needs, or the desire to pursue another vocation. There is certainly nothing dishonorable in asking for your release, but it will always be in Ateron's hands, because of your oath."

Pel drained the cup in his hand, and reached for the bottle. "Then I will never be released. So perhaps it would be in Elta's best interest to find another man. I don't know how much longer I can tolerate being part of Ateron's guard, and I can't guarantee I won't do something that will give him the provocation he needs to take my life."

Lowanta gripped his son's arm, "No one, throughout all the generations of our family, has ever dishonored it. Don't be the first, my son. We both know Ateron is an evil man, and his chancellor even more so, but you gave him your oath. Now you must honor it."

Pel squared his sagging shoulders, "Forgive me. I won't dishonor you, or our family. No matter what it costs me. I made my choice against your counsel, and I will live, and *die*, with that mistake," he said, his meaning inescapably clear.

"Dying is an easy path, one the weak often take. Living with our choices is a harder course, one that requires great courage and endurance. Your mother and I named you for those qualities, qualities I know you possess."

Pel's eyes fell away from his father's searching gaze. His name meant strong, in both body and spirit. It implied the ability to endure heavy burdens.

"As always, you speak the truth to me, even when it is hard to hear." Pel's eyes came back up, his face set. "You have my oath, I will never dishonor you. My mood is merely the reflection of a very distasteful task. I delivered the sacrificial victims to Darvoe this morning. Neither of them deserves to die. Both are good, honest people."

"You know them, do you not?"

"Yes."

"I take it the healer didn't kill the queen, as Ateron has proclaimed?"

"I don't believe she did. Taya loved Telsuea, and was loved by her. I don't know why Ateron has laid the blame for the queen's death at her door."

"Her death, and that of the big slave, will not accomplish what Darvoe hopes. I do not believe it will stop the trembling of the earth. Nor do I believe that the quaking is caused by Ansuetra's wrath over the king persuading Lontae to allow the council to hold the high priest's power as stewards for so long." He blew out a frustrated breath. "Regrettably, the majority of the nobles' council does believe it. Having reinstated Darvoe's power, and with Ateron's support of the sacrifices, there is nothing I can do."

"I know you tried to get the council to see reason. I'm sorry they have been swayed by Darvoe's lies."

Lowanta picked up his cup and sipped his wine, "Not only am I powerless to stop the return of the blood sacrifices, but my position on the council forces me to attend the grisly spectacle."

Pel grimaced, "I not only have to attend the *spectacle* I have to present the king and high priest with the weapons to accomplish the deed." He straightened in his chair. "The people of Injanae will not be helped by the events of this Lunar Celebration."

"I agree. And the unusual configuration—and location of the celebration—is more about the power struggle between Ateron and Darvoe, than it is about honoring Ansuetra."

"It is. One seeks supremacy by superstition, the other by deception."

"I know you are distressed by this power struggle. All of Injanae is too. The sacrifices will only divide the council and the people further, intensifying the battle between two evil men determined to destroy each other. I am truly sorry you are caught in the middle of this." Lowanta laid a consoling hand on his son's shoulder.

Pel shifted in his chair, silently rolling his cup between his hands.

"Your disquiet tells me there is more going on than you are free to speak of to me, and I won't press you."

"Yes, my lips are sealed as long as my oath subjugates me to Ateron."

"You are not alone in your subjugation. All of Injanae is subject to both the king and high priest—with no release."

Pel smiled grimly, "It is unfortunate that Ateron and Darvoe can't settle their power struggle in honorable combat. If Darvoe killed Ateron in such a contest, I would be free."

Eighteen

Deep within the temple's labyrinth of priest cells, workrooms, slave quarters, and multiple sanctuaries to honor Ansuetra, sat the high priest's luxurious quarters. In the shady arbor of his personal garden, Darvoe spouted his frustration to Natell.

"I can't ask for different victims. The giant must be one of the sacrifices, not only because of the stories I have taken such pains to plant in the minds of the nobles, but because of his obvious value to Ateron."

"Yes." Natell nodded his agreement.

"The coming of the giant, accompanied by an earthquake, played into my hands. It has enabled me to stir up fear in the hearts of the superstitious." Darvoe's eyes narrowed. *But there is so much more in it than that.*

As the quakes increased in frequency, he saw the hand of Ansuetra, and the opening gambit she provided that would give the priests an opportunity—they hadn't had in generations—to take preeminence over the king. Consequently, over the past two years, he had campaigned hard to make the nobles and common people believe the big slave's arrival on the day of a quake was a sign of Ansuetra's displeasure that Injanae had been invaded by this giant. Even the injury she did him upon his entrance into the valley—that robbed him of his memory—proved he was Ansuetra's enemy.

Darvoe smiled over the fortuitous opportunity the giant's murder of the chancellor's wife had given him to expand on this theme. It allowed him to infect the people—and particularly the nobles—with the idea that the earth's quaking continued because Ansuetra demanded the life of the giant for the murder of the chancellor's wife.

Lowanta's support of the king, at that time, defeated Darvoe's petition in the noble's council. The full power of his office was again denied him. That kept Darvoe from sacrificing the giant to appease Ansuetra's a fury, but it also gave Darvoe one more thing he could use against Ateron. *It proved the king's disloyalty to the goddess.*

After every minor quake that rumbled through the valley, Darvoe took the opportunity to put new fear into the hearts of the people. Finally, a majority in the nobles' council rejected Lowanta's advice, and the king's petitions. They returned Darvoe's authority to enact divine directives and exercise his power in performing the sacred rites of the priests.

Darvoe's hawkish face darkened, *As though they ever had the right to take the power of the high priest in the first place.*

With the return of his power, he used his growing influence to force Ateron into giving him the giant as one of the sacrifices. Ateron's capitulation was telling. Darvoe's heart leaped. "The balance of power is definitely shifting in my favor."

"Yes. Even Ateron's *humble* petition to hold the celebration in his garden is proof of your growing power."

"Yes, Ateron is obviously trying to curry my favor, and in so doing, unwittingly providing me with the perfect setting to allow all of Injanae to witness my triumph over him."

With that looming victory, Ansuetra had further inspired his heart with the idea of reordering the government of Injanae. *The goddess will rule Injanae, communicating directly with her royal high priest, eliminating the need for the king, and nobles' council. The endless generations of strife between the high priests and kings will cease. The people will live solely by the dictates of Ansuetra—through me—under a divinely dictated theocracy.*

Darvoe wrapped his royal cloak more tightly around his bony frame, warding off a cold breeze. "I will not lose this chance to further my agenda, and parade my power over Ateron before the people, because of the stubbornness of the sacrificial victims." He knew forcing the giant through the purification rites would be next to impossible. "Somehow, the sacrifices must be purified," he said with frustration.

"We will drug their water, and in a few hours they will be compliant."

"That won't work. My spies tell me the girl is the best herbal doctor in Injanae. She will know if anything we give them is tainted." Darvoe huffed through his beak like nose as though ridding himself of some disgusting smell.

"Then perhaps a night in less than pleasant circumstances will help change their minds."

"Perhaps, but I don't have the time to wait them out. The procession to retrieve the holy water from the pool should already be underway. If word leaks out that I am unable to control the very slaves I wanted for the sacrifices, I will lose the confidence and respect of the nobles. They will see me as weak. I can't afford to lose the backing of those who supported me in reasserting the powers that are mine at this point in my campaign."

"You are the royal high priest, and your priests are loyal to you. To a man, they want the powers of the priests to be preeminent. Only when you control Injanae will we be safe from Ansuetra's wrath, and Ateron's corrupt rule. The priests will do anything you desire to accomplish that. You have only to command them."

Darvoe smiled. "That is true."

He plucked a red blossom from a blood flower bush and rubbed its petals between his fingers. Dropping the crushed flower, he lifted his fingers to his nose, inhaling the coppery scent of blood the sacrificed blossom offered him. *When I rule Injanae, I will plant the blood flower in all the planters on the rooftop garden of the palace. They will remind the people that I hold all the power in Injanae, over both life, and death, because the Goddess of the Moon willed it to be so.*

"Eminence, what do you wish done?"

"We will start the ceremony to bring back the holy-water of the pool." Darvoe's eyes narrowed. "When we return, you will lock up all the temple slaves, and sequester the younger priests in their quarters. The purification rites will be closed to all but the senior priests. I will counsel them and start the ceremonies with proxies. When the people will see the smoke rise from the temple vents and hear the chanting, they will believe the purification rites are underway. No one will suspect we are proceeding without the presence of our sacrificial victims."

"Perhaps tomorrow your sacrifices will be more—compliant." Natell gave the high priest a knowing smile.

Fanning away a bee, Darvoe nodded, and said, "Go gather the priests for the procession to the pool."

"How did this happen, and just when we were so close to escaping too?" Taya asked mournfully.

Finished with a meager meal that didn't begin to take the edge off Ryder's enormous appetite, the sacrificial victim's sat at the battered table, in the rickety, mismatched chairs, mulling over the day's unexpected turn of events, and the problems they now faced.

Ryder groaned. "I think it was always part of the plan. I don't know why I didn't see it."

"Why should you, or any of us, have seen it—or even considered it. The selection of the sacrificial victims has always been the sole right of the high priest. How could we have foreseen Ateron would have a part in selecting them for *this* Lunar Celebration?" She gave him a disheartened face, and changed the subject. "Were you and Kytan together when the guards arrested you?"

"No. The guards put the ladder up to my tomb and called for me. I climbed down just like I do every morning. When I got to the bottom of the ladder, four swords were pressed into my back. For a moment I thought about fighting, but resisting when I didn't know what was happening with the rest of you, wouldn't have helped at that point."

"No, it wouldn't have." Taya patted the hand he slammed down on the table.

"With us as the victims, Ateron is assured of Hadlee's cooperation until the ceremony is completely over, and he is declared the high priest. Even when we are released from the altars, we will be Ateron's hostages to keep Hadlee in line."

"If Ateron always meant for us to be the sacrifices, then why did he include Kytan in this morning's farce?"

Ryder shrugged. "Maybe he didn't want to spoil the surprise of who the victims were going to be for Hadlee."

"Or for me either," Taya said, and then asked, "Do you know where Kytan was when Ateron arrested him?"

"He told me—while they made us wait for our *dramatic entrance*—he woke up with Cartu's dagger pressed against his throat, backed up by two sword wielding guards."

Taya's voice wavered, "That dagger must have been pressed pretty hard. There was blood on his throat."

Ryder shifted in the wobbly chair that squeaked in protest as he gave Taya a comforting hug. "I know. Only Ateron's orders kept Cartu from slitting Kytan's throat this morning. That's what he told Kytan."

Taya sagged against him, her own chair protesting. "It's my fault. I'm afraid my slave-face slips too often whenever Kytan is near me."

"His isn't any better when you're near him." He lifted Taya's trembling chin. "Don't worry. Nothing's going to happen to him. The king still needs an interpreter for Hadlee."

"At the moment, that is my only consolation."

"You know, I think Cartu was hoping for some hysterics from you over the blood on Kytan's throat, and seeing him in bonds. That may be why he was included in this morning's little drama."

"And he was hoping for the same thing from Kytan too, wasn't he, when Ateron announced I was going to be one of the sacrificial victims."

"Yeah, they were both hoping to get a big reaction out of all of us."

"Yes, they certainly enjoyed themselves at our expense."

"To our credit, we didn't provide the level of entertainment they were hoping for. We all wore our slave-faces very well today."

"It was the hardest thing I have ever done, but we did it, didn't we?"

Ryder leaned his elbow on the table, cupping his chin in his hand, "Yeah, and in an odd way—it may turn out to be a good thing that we're the victims."

"Good—how?"

"What I've been afraid of for the past few weeks, is being locked in the dungeon during the sacrifices, unable to help Hadlee if she needs it, or be free to make our escape. At least with us as the victims, the three of us will be together, and I'll be in a position to help Hadlee, if there's trouble."

"Where do you suppose Kytan will be?"

"To begin with, he will be in the tunnel, cueing Hadlee's entrance, setting off the fireworks, and extinguishing them. We convinced Ateron one of us needs to do that since we are the only ones who know how everything works. That's the other reason he is still alive, but after Hadlee goes through the door, I'm not sure where Kytan will end up."

"What if the guards lock him in the dungeon after Hadlee comes through the door?"

"Then I will get you and Hadlee out, and come back for him, but I don't think that will happen."

"Why not?"

"That would take too much time. As soon as Hadlee goes through the door, Ateron will want the guards stationed in the tunnel to get out on the roof as quickly as possible. The one thing Ateron doesn't know, and can't control, is how the priests, or the people—for that matter—will react when Ansuetra divests Darvoe of his power, and bestows it on him. He's going to want all of his guards on the roof to handle any disturbance or protest over Darvoe's dismissal. Kytan may even be brought out onto the roof as an additional hostage."

"Or, if Hadlee can't find a way to keep us on the roof with her, the three of us may end up being locked up together somewhere, effectively eliminating our chance for escape." Taya clicked her tongue. "There are just too many variables, aren't there?"

"Yeah, I'm afraid there are."

"Even in the best scenario we could hope for, with Hadlee able to keep us on the roof with her, and then get us all off the roof before the nobles leave, I just don't see how we can find Kytan—or take him off the roof with us—get out of the palace, and make it to the falls before Ateron and his guards intercept us. Frankly it seems . . . impossible."

"I know, and that's where we are just going to have to pray hard, and have faith. You know Kytan and Hadlee are going to be working and praying over this too. Between the four of us, and with the help of heaven, we will do it."

Taya came out of her chair, dropping to her knees. "Then we better start praying—we need all the divine intervention we can get!"

Nineteen

Pel closed his cloak around him, trying to ward off the penetrating chill of the heavy fog that engulfed him as he left the tranquility of his parent's home.

The city belfry rang eleven times.

It was much later than he'd planned to leave. He pulled the door to the courtyard closed behind him and listened as the steward locked it. He leaned against it for a moment then resolutely turned away. Pushing aside the longing to remain in those peaceful walls, he moved down the lane, away from his dreams, and back into the ugly reality his life had become.

At least I got to spend a few hours with Elta. His heart filled with the serenity she brought him. Her timely arrival for the evening meal was surely his mother's doing. She inevitably knew just what he needed and went out of her way to provide it.

Elta always lifted his spirits. He longed to make her his wife. *If we marry, I would be required to move into quarters in the palace, bringing the evil I want to escape even closer. How can I do that to Elta? I don't want her anywhere near Ateron or his evil; and yet, she is the strength that could make the burden of my life oath to Ateron bearable,* he rationalized, before his conscience rebuked him. *It's not right or fair to draw her into the pit you willingly climbed into because of your pride.* He sulked over his quandary as his heavy boots clattered against the stone paved lane.

It was never wise to be in the streets of Telquset late at night, especially alone. The ranks of life slaves were filled by Injanae's poor, who were driven by desperation to commit criminal acts, using the night and the opportunities it provided, to stay alive and feed their families. Not that Pel feared being robbed or assaulted. He could take care of himself. Still, it required cautious vigilance.

Taking the shortest route back to the palace would be the wisest course of action. His feet moved purposefully in that direction. As a precaution, he took his sword out of its sheath, holding it down at his side as he turned into a mist-choked lane.

Rough hands grabbed his cloak, managing to bind him in it, keeping his sword arm immobile. He pulled hard against the hands that restrained him. A blade slashed through the fabric of his tunic. A burning sensation flared across his chest. He jerked sideways with all his strength. The whoosh of a sword shot by his arm and clanged against the brick wall at his back. He managed to untangle his left arm from his cloak and punch out against the hand that restrained him. There was a muffled grunt. The fingers grasping his sword arm fell away.

He shrugged off his cloak and brought up his sword, still unable to see anything but the dim outline of his assailant through the swirling fog. Swinging his blade in a wide ark at the shadows in front of him, he was surprised when he met the onslaught of two powerful swords. He backed out of the narrow lane, hoping for a better view of the rogues that dared to attack him. He drew another short sword and brought it into play against the forceful press of his attackers.

The ring of metal sang through the streets in a melody dear to Pel's ears. The strokes of his assailants' blades told him these were no ordinary bandits. These two were well versed in techniques few men knew, or could bring to bear when handling a sword.

Kytan's cryptic words clarified in his mind. "Be careful, not all those who surround you are friends," the metal smith had said. He'd delivered that brief warning just after emerging from Hadlee's hall, and shutting the door behind him—on the day the work in the tunnel was finished.

Pel had come to check that Anlow and Dal had arrived on time to take over the morning guard duty for Sual and Toba. Puzzled by Kytan's words, he'd started to ask what Kytan meant when the door to the hall again opened. Sual and Toba came through it. The king's new artisan threw a meaningful glance at the emerging men and walked away from him without another word.

Pel smiled grimly as he got his first glimpse of two hooded heads. Their heights nearly matched his six-foot stance and their swordplay made him almost certain who his assailants were. Still, he couldn't afford the distraction of trying to discern their exact identities in the thick fog—especially if they were members of his own guard. That could prove to be fatal.

His mind focused on countering his assailants' relentless press, while his soul took pleasure in the deadly exchange. It was just what he needed right now to release all his pent up frustration. With a joyous battle roar he wielded his swords with a dizzying flurry, pushing his opponents back into the dark lane.

At one with his weapons, he pressed forward seeking an opening—it came. A cry assured him his blade had found its target and one of the bandits leaped away. The other made a desperate thrust. The blade came out of the mist toward Pel's heart. He caught the thrust between his crossed blades and shoved the bandit's sword up. Holding his foe's blade off with his long sword, he darted in, slashing out with his short one. His blade bit into something. He heard the satisfying sound of pain, followed by the hurried retreat of his attackers' feet. The sound faded into the mist of the narrow lane.

He leaned back against the wall at the mouth of the lane, taking in deep draughts of misty air, waiting for his heart to slow. A laugh rumbled out of him. He touched the slash along his chest. It was nothing more than a scratch, and well worth the price, for the momentary relief his tortured soul received from the encounter.

A hidden door, obscured by a dense covering of vines on the side of the chancellor's palatial estate, opened to a prearranged knocking signal. Two cloaked men ducked through the creaking door. Cartu quickly shut and locked it behind them. By the light of an oil lamp, he silently led them through a secluded garden into the back of the spacious mansion.

The chancellor's mansion was a residence Cartu rarely frequented anymore. Since the death of his wife, Renla, he had taken up luxurious quarters in the palace, a place he preferred. There he was fawned over, his favor courted, his counsel sought. He used this house only for his most private matters. Soon he would be frequenting it more—much more—once he installed Taya in the opulent prison that was now prepared and waiting for her.

"Well?" Cartu demanded of his assassins as soon as they were in the hall.

Norr and Toba glanced at each other, neither one speaking.

They had been chosen for this assignment because of their unwavering loyalty to Ateron—along with being conveniently off duty for the night. No suspicion would be attached to their presence outside the palace grounds.

Cartu scrutinized the pair in the dim light of a lamp. Each held his cloak firmly wrapped around himself, their faces grim and unusually pale. "Well," he demanded again, and then saw the blood dripping onto the smooth tiles of the hall.

Norr leaned against the wall. "I need to sit down."

"And you?" Cartu's eye swung to Toba. "Are you in need of medical attention too?"

Toba flinched. "Yes."

"Fools," hissed Cartu. "I take it he is still alive."

"He is, Excellency. But not without injury," Norr hastened to say.

"Are his wounds fatal?"

Toba and Norr exchanged a glance.

"No, I believe I only grazed him with my blade," Toba said.

"But he obviously did more than that to you two."

Norr tried to excuse their failure. "He isn't the captain of the king's bodyguards without good reason, Excellency. His skill with the sword is only exceeded by your own."

"Please, Excellency, may we sit down?" Toba swayed into Norr.

"Not here." Cartu brushed passed the two. "Follow me."

He led them through a narrow hall and down a short flight of stairs. At the end of the hall, he unlocked the door to a small workroom filled with shelves of dried herbs. Norr and Toba fell onto hard chairs, while Cartu lit additional lamps.

"Remove your cloaks and tunics, while I collect some medical supplies," Cartu said.

He left them fumbling to remove their cloaks and weapons with shaky fingers, while he prepared water, towels, and dressings for their wounds. Returning with the supplies, he set them on a table between Ateron's chosen assassins, letting them care for themselves.

"The king will be very unhappy you have let this ideal opportunity to make Pel's death look like the work of street criminals slip through your fingers. He wanted this assignment finished tonight, before the Lunar Celebration, and you know how he hates to be . . . *disappointed.*"

The grey pallor of Norr and Toba's faces answered him.

Norr defended their failure in a pleading tone, "It was the heaviness of the mist, we couldn't see through it."

"Obviously Pel's vision wasn't as impaired." Cartu inspected their injuries. A quick examination revealed neither had suffered a severe wound, and both injuries could be hidden beneath their uniforms. "Did he recognize either of you?"

"No, of that I am sure," Toba said, pressing a towel against his side.

"Well at least that is something. You need to be sure your wounds are well bound, so your own blood doesn't betray you to Pel. No one must see your injuries. You will have to stay out of the hot springs bath until they heal, and get rid of these clothes—burn them. Also, it is imperative you maintain your normal duties—without excuse."

"Yes, Excellency." Norr peeked under the towel at the deep gash along his upper arm.

"At this moment, the king is waiting for word on the successful completion of your assignment. I don't know how he will take your failure."

Ateron's fury, when roused in the wee hours of the morning only to learn of the inept performance of his henchmen, was explosive. In his usual style, Norr and Toba's faces suffered at his hand. However, his need for their, loyalty, secrecy and further service, kept him from inflicting anything but that mild rebuke. They were dismissed with an angry wave of his hand.

"Undoubtedly, Pel is now on guard. And we have too much at stake to risk another failure and possible exposure, or even the whispers of untimely accusations. The bumbling efforts of my guards have effectively eliminates any further opportunity to deal with Pel until after the Lunar Celebration." Ateron's piranha stare rested on his chancellor. "However, should an opportunity present itself before the celebration, I want you to see to the matter—*personally*."

Cartu smiled and inclined his head.

Twenty

The hours dragged by slowly as Ryder and Taya lay on the dirt floor, head to head next to the fire pit, trying to sleep. A close examination of the mattresses decided the matter. The smell alone would have prevented their use, not to mention the things living in them. The blankets and pillows weren't any better.

Cradling his head in his arm, Ryder stared into their meager fire. His stomach growled, while his mind churned over the problems of escaping the roof, and the palace, before the nobles left. That was vital, because in front of the nobles, Ateron, Cartu, and the guards had to obey Hadlee's directives in order to maintain the charade. However, once the nobles left all the constraints that protected the conspirator's from Ateron and Cartu would be gone.

Hadlee and Kytan know that, and—locked in this dungeon—there's nothing I can do to help them . . . except pray whatever they decide to do will work. Somehow, Hadlee will have to find a way to tell me what Taya and I need to do.

By the time he came to that conclusion, he'd been lying on the cold floor for what seemed like most of the night. When he rolled over, Taya's hand touched his head. "I take it you can't sleep either." He took hold of her hand.

"How long has it been?"

"Almost forever," he grumbled. "As soon as our jailor comes back, we're going to ask to bargain."

"We really don't need to. Once we are both tired enough, we will sleep."

"Yeah, but I may starve to death in the meantime."

Taya stuttered a laugh.

He raised his head and grinned in the dying light of the fire. "What can I say? I will probably always be a slave to my stomach. How do you think I got to be this size?"

She smiled warmly and squeezed his fingers. "I think you had to be the size you are, to have room for your heart. It is a very big heart. Full of faith, honor, kindness, and love."

He kissed her hand, before releasing it. "That is the nicest thing I have ever been told. But I'm not sure you would feel that way if you knew more about me." He paused. "Especially about how much I've hurt Hadlee."

Taya sat up and put the last of the wood on the fire. "I know, Ryder. Kytan told me. I hope you aren't angry, but he doesn't keep secrets from me, and I am not going to keep anymore secrets from him."

"I'm not angry, and I'm not surprised, but I am amazed you can think of me so kindly after knowing what I did."

"You were a brutally treated boy then, one who made a very bad choice, under the pressure of harsh circumstances that resulted in a terrible tragedy. You aren't that boy anymore. You have let the Atonement change you. What I see now is a very good man. Not many men—after being told what Hadlee told you—would have come back and faced what they had done, and taken what you did, to try and help someone who hated them. And you *have* helped her. I can see a definite difference in her."

Ryder sat up, "It wasn't me, Taya. All I did was remind her of the source of forgiveness and peace. She was the one who decided to reach for it."

"But would she ever have done it without your help?"

"I don't know, but she has helped me just as much. I wouldn't have the peace I feel now if she hadn't told me what I didn't know. That allowed me to complete my own repentance. She's also given me what I've wanted most—for twelve long years." Emotion clogged his throat.

"What?" Taya prompted when he didn't continue.

He choked out, "Her forgiveness—for everything I've cost her. I can't tell you what that means to me."

"I am happy for you—and Hadlee too. I believe that is why both of you were brought here. You needed time, and a situation that forced you together, before either of you could fully understand what happened that day and begin to work things out between you."

"I believe that too. And thankfully, we have." Ryder sighed, casting a glance heavenward.

"Have you? Have you really worked out *everything?*" Taya's eyes probed his until they dropped.

"Some things can't be worked out, Taya." He dropped his head and rubbed the back of his neck.

"Are you talking about the consequences of the accident, or your love for Hadlee?"

His head snapped up. "Am I that obvious?"

She shrugged, "To everyone but Hadlee."

A hopeless sound groaned out of him. "Most people, I've found, don't see what they don't want to see. That in itself, tells me she doesn't want to see me as more than a friend, and someone who is trying to help her get out of here."

"Does that mean you intend to keep your feelings hidden and just let her go after we leave here?"

A piece of wood popped, breaking the uncomfortable silence Taya's question induced. It sent a small burst of sparks into the air.

Ryder lay back down, watching them evaporate into the darkness, or float down and burn out in the fire pit. "Yeah," he finally said. "You don't kill a girl's mother, and then expect her to fall in love with you—even when she forgives you."

Natell inserted the key into the lock and turned it. The lock yielded with a hard click. He pushed the creaking door, inward. Two torch-bearing priests preceded him into the cell.

The giant sat in one of the rickety chairs with the healer on his lap. Her head rested on his shoulder, and his arms held her tightly. Their expressions conveyed no dissatisfaction with the night.

Natell's eyes narrowed, looking at them with disgust. *Perhaps the giant and the healer really don't care where they are as long as they are together. That will certainly complicate the high priest's plans.* "You're being granted another audience with Ansuetra's royal high priest," he said. "Perhaps you can think of something that will make your last two days more . . . pleasant. I'm sure His Eminence will listen to any requests you might make."

The victims' next room was infinitely better, but still a cavern. It contained two bed shelves, with clean straw mattresses, llama wool blankets, comfortable pillows for lounging, a well-equipped fire pit, and a sufficient woodpile. Solid chairs surrounded a sturdy table laid out with an abundance of fresh fruit and vegetables, the raw ingredients for bread, and a few dried fish. Best of all the room featured a decent bath chamber, with a door.

In exchange for their new circumstances and providence, they submitted to the high priest's tailor. He methodically measured them for their sacrificial clothes.

Taya's skin was crawling by the time the tailor left. "Being measured for death clothes makes this whole farce too real. It gives me the shivers just thinking about it." She rubbed away the goose bumps on her arms and began patting dough into rounds for ashcakes.

Ryder cocked his head thoughtfully, "Yeah, but what great stories we'll have to tell our grandkids someday." He paused, and ate another mouthful of fish. "When this is over, and we are out of Injanae, I will be very happy to live the rest of my life without any more adventures."

"Me too!" Taya said, and changed the subject. "I can't believe Darvoe gave us all this"—her head swiveled, sweeping the room and its contents—"just for agreeing to be measured for the sacrificial clothes."

"Yeah . . . that was pretty amazing. I'm surprised he didn't press for anything else."

Twenty-one

On the evening of the Lunar Celebration, Darvoe stood alone in the cathedral sanctuary inspecting the priests' preparations for the ritual washing and dressing of the sacrificial victims.

Natell found him there, and bowed.

"What is it?" Darvoe asked turning to him.

"I am sorry, Eminence. But those you will honor by sacrifice refuse to allow the priests to wash and dress them. They say it wasn't part of the bargain they made."

The high priest's shoulders drooped, and he drew in a resigned breath.

"However, they gave me their word—they will wear the sacrificial clothes."

Darvoe finished lighting the incense on the altar." I am disappointed, but not surprised." He huffed out a decisive breath through his hawkish nose. "We will do as we did before, proceeding with the ritual washing and dressing using two priests as proxies for the victims."

Silent anger seethed from Darvoe with every stride he took as the pair left the sanctuary, strode down the long corridor, and up the stairs to the high priest's quarters.

Natell walked half a pace behind the high priest in deference to his office. "It doesn't matter if the victims go through the washing ritual, as long as they wear the sacrificial robes that have been blessed. All of Injanae will assume they've gone through the rituals."

Natell's words did little to pacify Darvoe's annoyance. He glowered, still disgruntled the purification rites had been thwarted by the sacrificial victims, then consoled himself with the knowledge that his triumph was at hand.

Entering his quarters, Darvoe said, "Fortunately the steps we took to maintain the secrecy of the purification rites have proved effectual."

Natell followed, having been granted the honor of helping Darvoe dress for the most important night of his reign.

"My power remains undiminished with the nobles, and dressed in their sacrificial clothes, both sacrifices will appear to have been fully purified—ready to be offered to Ansuetra when the full moon rises over the mountains in just a few short hours. Their deaths will empower me, both in the eyes of the people, and the council. That is of paramount importance."

"And after that?" Natell asked.

"I will begin my campaign to dethrone Ateron as soon as the next quake occurs. Ansuetra will declare her dissatisfaction with the king's hollow display of loyalty to her at the sacrifices. I will point out to the council that his part in the sacrifices was more an act of justice, or revenge, for the death of his wife, than an act of devotion to the goddess."

"Not all of them will believe that—especially Lowanta."

"No, but that is only the first step. Discrediting and dethroning Ateron will take careful, patient steps. I will again wait for another quaking in the earth. When that occurs, I will inform the council that Ansuetra requires a demonstration of Ateron's devotion to her or the quaking of the earth will increase and continue to trouble Injanae."

"What will the goddess require?" Natell asked, his face a picture of admiration for the cunning mind of his superior.

Darvoe's features pulled into a hawkish sneer, "The sacrifice of his sons—under his own hand."

Natell gasped with the audacity of the high priest's plan. "He will never do it."

"Yes he will, because more quakes will prove Ansuetra's dissatisfaction with his reign. I am sure I can convince the council that Ansuetra will reject him as king over the people, if he refuses to prove his loyalty to her. Once he is heirless, he too, will die."

"How?"

"Through the poison in the ritual cup of wine he must drink after the sacrifices of his sons. When he dies, I will proclaim to the council, and the people, that the goddess has arranged his death, and that of his heirs, because she no longer wants corrupt kings to rule Injanae. Instead, she wants me, the Exalted Royal High Priest who communes with her, and knows her will, to rule over this sacred valley."

Darvoe inhaled the heady smell of power coming ever closer. He shared a jubilant, expectant smile with Natell, who bowed deeply to the future reigning power over Injanae.

The long hours of waiting hung heavily upon the sacrificial victims, confined in the bowels of the temple with nothing to do. It made them somber and edgy.

Ryder watched Taya circle their airless cell until he lost count of the number of rotations she'd made. Each one felt like the winding of a watch spring, drawing ever tighter, bringing them inevitably closer to the breaking point. With each revolution, Taya's face became more haunted and fearful. As she walked by him again, Ryder reached out and caught her.

She yelped.

"Tell me," he said gently.

"Tell you what?"

"What you're feeling. I know you're scared. So am I."

"Seven moons ago, I would have welcomed this death without any fear; even embraced it. Being sacrificed would have been a joy in comparison to being given to Cartu, and preferable to meeting death by my own hand," she said, and hid her face, pressing it against his tunic.

"I know." Ryder hugged her, feeling the horror and fear she felt quiver through her petite frame. He stroked her hair, silently praying for the means to comfort her.

She looked up. "I don't want to die. Not now, not when . . . not when I finally have so much I want to live for. Even more than that, I don't want Kytan to watch me die—watch us die. We are all he has. And I don't want Hadlee to live with the guilt if she can't stop our deaths. You know she will feel it is her fault. I can't bear to think of her living with that guilt."

"Neither can I, but what's going to happen tonight isn't in our hands."

"I know." Taya's lips trembled.

"All we can do is pray for Hadlee and leave what happens in the Lord's hands."

Taya's eyes filled with liquid fear, "I wish I had your faith, I want to have it, but I am so afraid right now."

"Would you let me do something for you?" Ryder asked, brushing away her tears.

"What?"

"Let me tell you a story and give you a blessing."

Taya searched his face. "How can a story help, and what will a blessing do?"

"I hope the story will help you see our situation with more faith and perspective; and I know the blessing will bring you a spirit of peace and give you the strength to get through this ordeal. That's something the priesthood can do."

"Then tell me the story, and bless me. I have never felt such blinding fear or so completely helpless. I feel like I am falling apart."

He led her to the pile of large pillows and pulled her down into them, putting his arms around her. She clung to him, her eyes riveted to his, expectantly.

"This story comes from the oldest book of scripture we have."

"The Bible?"

"Yeah, the Old Testament."

"Before the Lord was born."

"Yeah." Ryder smiled. "You have learned a lot in a very short time."

"I believe it too."

"I know, and that's why I want to tell you this story."

"Okay." Taya leaned back, resting her head against his arm.

"Three young boys from Jerusalem were taken by the Babylonians and brought up in the court of king Nebuchadnezzar, the ruler of Babylon. They grew up to be honest and wise. The king trusted them and gave them great responsibilities in his kingdom. But there came a day when they had to choose between the favor of the king and their allegiance to God."

"Was he a pagan king like Ateron?"

"Yeah, he was. He built a huge idol of gold and gathered everyone in his kingdom for its dedication. He commanded that at the sound of music everyone was to fall down and worship the idol. When the signal was given, everyone in his kingdom fell down and worshiped it—except the three young men. They refused to bow down to the idol. They were bound and taken before the king. He told them he would give them another chance. If they bowed to the idol, all would be well, but if they didn't, they would be thrown into a fiery furnace."

"They were thrown in the furnace, weren't they?"

"Yeah. They refused to bow to the king's idol. They said the true and living God could deliver them from the fire—*if* that was his will. *But if not,* if the Lord didn't save them from the flames, they would still only worship, and trust in him."

"What happened?" asked Taya, breathlessly.

"The furnace was so hot it killed the men that threw them in. As the king watched, he saw them walking with someone in the midst of the fire. Astonished, he called them out. When they emerged, not even the smell of the fire was on them. They were perfectly whole."

"Who was with them in the fire?"

"The Lord was with them, Taya. That's what I want you to know. No matter what happens tonight, the Lord will be with us. If we live, he will be with us, *but if not,* he will be with us too. I believe that. I know that. He has been with me, all through the darkest days of my life. I know He will be with us tonight."

"Then bless me, Ryder, so I can feel it, and know it too. So I can accept whatever happens."

He laid his hands on her head, and let the spirit speak words of strength and comfort, filling the room, and their hearts, with peace. When he finished, they wiped the tears from one another's faces.

"Thank you." Taya gave him a serene smile and kissed his damp cheek. "Now I can do this, no matter what happens."

Their final hours of waiting were interrupted with the delivery of their sacrificial clothes. They received them with a kind of morbid relief—the waiting was almost over. Only an hour remained before they were due to be taken back to the palace.

Taya retired to the bathroom to don her attire. Ryder unfolded his costume in the small living room. It consisted of a pair of very short green pants that hit him above mid-thigh, topped by a sleeveless tunic of the same color, trimmed in silver along the edges, and split down the front to his navel. He modeled it with some embarrassment for Taya, who poked her head out the bathroom door.

"Well, it certainly shows off your muscles. And of course your heart has to be exposed, so Darvoe knows where to stab you."

"Oh, thank you for those words of comfort," he said sarcastically, and growled, "Get out here. I've made a spectacle of myself for you, now I want to see what you're wearing."

It took some coaxing before she would come out of the bathroom. When she did, her face was blotchy with humiliation. "Oh Ryder, I can't wear this."

Her outfit was identical to his in color and style, except hers only consisted of the tunic top. Its hemline was shorter than the length of her hair.

Ryder's eyes nearly popped out. Taya always wore loose fitting tunics, over pants or robes. They perpetuated the illusion she was younger than she really was, but the tunic she wore now, clung to a very lovely figure.

Ryder could feel his heart rate jump. "You're right, you can't wear that. Kytan will go berserk seeing you in that."

"He isn't the only one who will see me. All of Injanae is going to see me too. This tunic is going to fall open when they put me on the altar," she wailed, holding the front of that inadequate garment closed.

"Then we better do something about it." Ryder said, through his teeth. "Let's see." His eyes narrowed. "We agreed to wear the clothes in exchange for our room—and you will. But that doesn't mean it's all you'll wear. Bring your clothes out here."

While Taya sat in a chair, holding the front of her tunic together with one hand, and the edge of it over the top of her legs with the other, Ryder examined her clothes. They consisted of a pair of thin, fawn colored pants, and a long sleeved, knee length tunic of the same color.

"Let's see, we don't want to make this too obvious," he mused looking her tunic over, and then at her. "Where's that dagger you always carry?" he asked, hunting for the opening of the tunic's pocket.

"You know about my dagger?"

"With as many times as I've hugged you, yeah, I know."

When he first figured out what she carried in her tunic, he'd thought about confiscating the weapon, afraid the approaching completion of the deal between Cartu and her uncle would drive her to end her life. However, leaving her defenseless against Cartu was too chilling a prospect. Besides, he knew she would only acquire another dagger.

Retrieving the weapon, he drew it from its sheath, and considered the problem. "The first thing we need to do is get rid of these sleeves and make it shorter."

He held the tunic up against her back, and cut over a foot off the bottom. Checking the length, he nodded, and sawed the sleeves out.

"And I suppose, to keep it from being too noticeable, we better lower the neck line a bit."

He cut the scoop neck into a V shape, lowering the overall neckline by several inches. Then he cut the legs off her pants.

"At least you will have some pants on, even if they are very short." He handed her the altered clothes, "Go put these on underneath, and let's see."

She fled to the bath chamber, returning a few minutes later. "I think this will work—with a few more adjustments." She took the knife and retired to the bathroom to work on the armholes and neckline. In a few minutes, she came out, spun around, and grinned. "What do you think?"

"I think Kytan will have every right to kill me for putting you in the position of wearing such immodest clothes. If I had known what they were going to look like, I would never have bargained for this room. There's still far too much of you showing."

"At least I won't have to worry about being completely exposed when I am put on the altar. Do you think Darvoe will let me get away with it?"

"He'd better if he doesn't want a fight on his hands. Now put your cloak on please, before my mind wanders where it shouldn't."

Taya blushed crimson. "Ryder!"

"I'm only human, Taya, and you are a very beautiful woman."

Twenty-two

Ateron sat inside the doorway of his private terrace. For the past hour he'd enjoyed listening to the common people vie for the best places along the path of the priests' procession. They were eagerly awaiting the pageantry of the priests' chanting ritual, and hoping for a display of hysterics from the sacrificial victims being led to their deaths.

Ansuetra had favored the king with a spectacular night. He smiled dreamily at the nearly cloudless sky, gazing up at the stars dancing attendance on the incomparable moon, almost at its zenith. *Finally, all I have so carefully planned will come to fruition. Darvoe will be destroyed. The nobles' council will be abolished, and I will be the only power in Injanae.* He savored the sweetness of his coming victory, reveling in the certainty that this night would endow him with unparalleled power, eager to indulge in that heady reality.

Cartu entered while the king dwelt upon these happy thoughts. He was arrayed in the traditional yellow robes worn by all the chancellors of Injanae. His robes, however, were embellished with the addition of a jewel-encrusted sword, which he wore like the scepter of his office. The sword was, in fact, far more than ornamental. It was a finely balanced and carefully crafted weapon, made just for him. In his expert hands, it was always lethal. He was, without question, the finest swordsman in Injanae.

Born as the youngest son into a minor noble's house, Cartu's only hope to better his station in life had been to become a priest or train in arms. He chose arms, and in that, he had excelled, mastering all forms of fighting and the use of every kind of weapon. Through contests of arms, his talents enabled him to win the place of captain in king Moncara's personal bodyguard, and brought him to Ateron's attention. Their common lust for power immediately made them allies.

Ateron's rule of Injanae was thanks to Cartu's position of trust. His resourcefulness in administering the poison that killed Ateron's older brother, gave Ateron the crown. Cartu had agreed to do the deed for the right incentive. Ateron provided that incentive, and Cartu put on the robes of the king's chancellor the day Ateron was crowned.

"Everything is in readiness for the arrival of the nobles." Cartu dipped his head.

"And the food?"

"The ceremonial dishes are ready to be served, and eaten in thanks for all the providence the goddess has blessed the people with over the past year." Cartu's thick lips twitched. "The nobles will have time to eat and mingle in pleasurable anticipation, before they are seated by their ranks and *honored* with the spectacle of the sacrificial rites."

The king inclined his head in an uncharacteristic show of gratitude; then shared a smirk with his chancellor.

"Darvoe sent a messenger. The procession will start from the temple in just under an hour," Cartu advised.

Ateron consulted the moon. "Good. How soon will the nobles start arriving?"

"The first ones should be here at any moment."

"Then you will need to go up and greet them for me. I'm going to pay Ansuetra a visit before I join you." The hunger of a piranha loomed in his smile. "I have to give Kytan the final lines Ansuetra will say, and I would like a few private moments with the lovely Moon Goddess before her performance." He reached for a matching pair of gold challises. "But first, we will drink to this historic evening. I have no doubt it will become the greatest legend in the history of Injanae. The night Ansuetra visited her people, and bestowed her favor on a mortal man."

Cartu's wide mouth split his face in a gargoyle grin. He held up the delicate cup the king handed him, "To Ansuetra—and her lovely doctor."

The whispered accusations of murder against Taya, which the king and Cartu had carefully propelled toward Taya's

Uncle Tulas, compelled him to complete her sale to Cartu without further delay. Displaying great reluctance to complete the deal, Cartu forced Tulas to accept a pittance of what he had originally demanded for Taya. The whole transaction was settled the night before the sacrificial victims were announced.

Ateron held up his challis, "Yes, and to the end of our . . . *waiting*."

They laughed, touched their cups, and drained them.

The Moon Goddess wove long spirals of silver into dozens of braids, and with Kytan's help, attached them to her crown.

When that was done, Kytan stood back, smiled at the effect, and said, "Now I will go get you something to eat, while you put on your makeup and jewelry."

"I don't want anything," she said, but he insisted, and went out the door. Hadlee knew her stomach was far too unsettled to eat. *There is so much at stake, and so much of what we have planned is going to be a tremendous gamble.* "It will work," she said to her reflection, sitting in front of her mirrored dressing table; applying bright red, oxblood lipstick.

The lipstick, along with an eyebrow pencil, a cake of mascara, and a compact of powder and rouge always resided in the pocket of her bomber jacket. The small makeup kit had been forgotten until the night Ryder took her up on the roof. She felt it then, in the inside pocket of the jacket.

After carefully applying the lipstick, she critically evaluated the total effect of the makeup. Her pale face was brightened by the powder and touch of rouge. The crystal blue depths of her huge eyes, fringed by black lashes, became the focal point of her face. Her pencil-darkened brows added more force and depth to her expressions, and her red lips would undoubtedly focus attention on her words. *The makeup is the perfect finish to Ansuetra's mystique. It really puts the whole costume over the top,* she persuaded herself, deciding it added just the right touch of drama to her character.

Taking a deep breath and letting it out slowly, she closed her eyes and prayed, "Please help me to do this right. Ryder's life is at stake, and I am so afraid." She sniffed, determined not to let another bout of emotion overcome her. She simply couldn't afford it.

If you can jump out of a plane, hundreds of feet above the ground, you can do something as easy as play a part, she told herself, drawing ringlets of hair over one shoulder. *That's what Ryder thinks—but is he right?* Staring at her reflection, she struggled in the no man's land between courage and fear, fighting for confidence, and battling self-doubt.

The outside door opened and closed, bringing her out of her uncertain reflections.

"Are you ready?" Kytan called from beyond the curtain. "I have brought you some bread and cheese. I think it will help settle your stomach, and you need the strength."

She hooked the silver collar around her throat, clipped her earrings on, and attached the silver bands to her wrists. Taking a last look in the mirror, she stood. She needed to know what Kytan thought of the makeup. His immediate reaction to her, when she stepped through the curtain, would tell her if she was right about wearing it. *Maybe it's too theatrical;* she worried—doubt winning the round.

Kytan turned from laying out dishes, looked up and stared, when Hadlee pushed back the curtain and stepped out. The knife he held fell to the table. He tried to speak, swallowed, and tried again. "You look, un"—his voice cracked— "believable. If I didn't know this was all a hoax, I would be on my knees with my face on the floor," he stammered unable to take his eyes off her.

"I hope everyone feels like that!" Hadlee's clasped hands pleaded with heaven. "Because what we are about to do could get us killed."

"No it won't. Just keep Ryder close to you, and do what—" The door flew open.

Ateron stepped across the threshold, and stopped, arrested by the sight of the goddess standing at the top of the bedchamber stairs. He audibly sucked in his breath.

Hadlee lifted her chin with unconcealed disdain. "Will I do?" she asked in Injanae.

Ateron didn't answer, but the unguarded leer in his eyes as he took in every detail of her hair, face, form, gown, and jewels made Kytan struggle with his slave-face. The King's usual lazy smile grew to crocodile proportions. A soft chuckle rose from deep in his chest, changing Hadlee's expression into revulsion.

"Yes, Ansuetra," he said in a caressing tone, "you will do."

Kytan had no need to translate these words. It was evident by Hadlee's tightly compressed lips, and her heightened color that she understood.

The king extended his hand to her, and purred the command, "Come to me."

Again, there was no need for Kytan to interpret. He could almost see the ice in Hadlee's eyes flow down her back and straighten her spine. Rigidly, she descended the stairs, walked across the room, and stopped just beyond the reach of Ateron's extended hand.

"No one will doubt you, Ansuetra." Ateron stepped forward, lifting a long, silvery ringlet of hair that danced over her arm. He caressed it between his fingers, nodding for Kytan to interpret.

Hadlee stood as stiff and still as a statue, seemingly unaware of the king's fingers entwined in her curl. He slid them slowly down it, while Kytan relayed his words.

Ateron's eyes reluctantly left her, moving to Kytan. "There are a few more lines you are to teach Ansuetra. I am sure she won't have any trouble learning them before her entrance. She must say them at the end of her speech to the nobles."

He recited the lines to Kytan and instructed him on what Hadlee was to do. His eyes bore into Kytan's, seeming to weigh his interpreter's reaction.

Unflinching, Kytan nodded his head and recited the words and instructions back to the king—at his request.

"The lives of your friends depend upon Hadlee saying these finishing lines and doing it with genuine emotion. It must be utterly convincing to everyone present. I am sure you will help her understand the consequences if she refuses to say them, or if her performance lacks true feeling."

His fingers continued to play with Ansuetra's long ringlet, as he raised his other hand, and snapped his fingers.

Lul, Yawt, and Etin came through the door. They stopped abruptly, clearly astonished.

Ansuetra stared back at the astounded guards. Fixing them with a withering stare, she commanded, "Kneel."

They fell to the floor, putting their face to the cool stones.

Ateron laughed uproariously. "Now there is no doubt. When they have recovered their wits, they will escort you and Kytan through the tunnel. I will await your entrance with great anticipation—as will your friends."

As Kytan conveyed this message to Hadlee, the king dropped her curl and ran his fingers the length of her arm. When he reached her hand, he raised it and gave her fingers a lingering kiss.

Kytan's hands closed into fists.

Hadlee jerked her hand away, a visible quake of revulsion running through her.

Ateron smiled broadly, and promised, "I will teach you to enjoy my touch." He released her hand and sauntered out the door.

Kytan didn't interpret.

Twenty-three

Covered in green, silver edged cloaks, Ryder and Taya were again shackled for their return trip to the palace. Lifting Taya into his arms, Ryder felt her tremble. "Try not to think about it," he whispered into her ear. "Remember this is the night we leave Injanae. Think about that, and how we are going to do it; if nothing else, practice holding your breath."

"From the moment I am put on that hideous altar that is exactly what I will be doing," she hissed.

Holding her close, Ryder tried to warm and reassure her as they were brought out of the temple and down into the street. Thousands of torches lit their path, held by as many hands. They took their place behind Darvoe's slave held riding chair, watching the flickering light from the torches play over the faces that stared with open enjoyment at them.

Ryder closed out the gawking multitude, fixing his attention on Darvoe. He looked every inch a pagan priest in his garish scarlet and silver robe. A high silver crown with an inlaid jeweled moon, sat on his brow. A heavy yoke of silver encased his shoulders. Silver bands clasped his wrists and ankles. His shoes, too, boasted buckles made from the moon glowing metal. Ryder wondered if he would out shine Ateron in his glory.

Natell signaled for the music and chanting to begin.

Ryder turned his attention to the priestly parade.

Twenty-five, red robed priests, preceding Darvoe, began the march, chanting the prayers of the grizzly sacrificial rites. Some played flutes and rang bells. Others beat the rhythm of the chant on decorative drums of silver and copper.

The crowd added their own petitions to Ansuetra, leaping and dancing with excitement over the gory spectacle to come. They wouldn't be witnesses to the actual sacrifices, but the bodies of the sacrificial victims would be brought down from the rooftop garden and carried through the streets, then left outside the gates of the city on a stone platform until the next new moon, when their remains would be burned.

The horror of their situation grew on Ryder, listening to the priests' imploring chant, but he marched along with an empty face and deliberate calm, surrounded by another twenty-five armed priests. These warrior priests marched with military precision. Beating the ends of their spears in time to the drums, they alternately struck them on the ground and brought them back into position, pointing them at the sacrificial victims.

Ryder looked straight ahead, ignoring the crowd's cheers and jeers as they passed. Only the growing roar of the crowd told him the people were falling in behind the parade, accompanying them to the palace.

Taya buried her face in his shoulder, tightening her grasp around his neck.

He laid his head on hers for a moment. She looked up. He kissed her brow. "Have faith little sister. Remember your blessing."

Taya's eyes filled with peace. She smiled into Ryder's strong confident face. "I wish you could have blessed Hadlee too," she whispered. "She needs it even more than I do."

He wished it too, but there hadn't been an opportunity. *And even if there had, would she have wanted a blessing under my hands?*

The procession reached the bridge over the river Tel. Ryder and Taya couldn't keep their eyes from the endlessly pounding water of the falls.

Taya sighed, "Freedom Falls." She laid her cheek against Ryder's shoulder, "I am praying we will be on the other side of them tonight."

"We will. Just keep praying—and we will," Ryder said, sending his own prayer heavenward.

They crossed over the bridge, and the crowd swelled into a horde. The parade almost came to a standstill before they reached the outer walls of the palace. The common people packed the grounds leaving little room for the procession to pass. Their chanting grew to deafening proportions, and they moved like prairie grass blown by a whirlwind as they vied for one last look at the victims mounting the stairs to their deaths.

The Telquset belfry rang the fatal hour just as Ryder stepped onto the landing below the removable section of stairs that marked the final ascent to the roof.

Natell stood a few paces ahead of the armed escort. He turned to Ryder, "You must remove your cloaks now."

Ryder lowered Taya to the landing. They took off their cloaks. A roar went up from the crowd. Ryder blocked the crowd's view of Taya. Lifting her back into his arms, he faced the palace wall. Holding on to his slave-face with grim resolve, he waited for the command to climb.

W hile Kytan peered through the peephole overlooking the rooftop garden, Hadlee sat on a high stool, trying to slow her racing heart, and calm her churning stomach. She hadn't been able to eat anything after Ateron's visit. "What's happening?" she asked.

"The nobles are on their knees, paying homage to the king. Oh! Come look, Darvoe has just stepped onto the roof."

She took his place peering through the peephole. She felt her face turn to stone. The royal high priest of Ansuetra sauntered across the roof with uplifted hands in the attitude of supplication and adoration of the moon and the goddess he purported to worship. He crossed his arms in the air and brought them down with the grace of a ballet dancer, before turning from the nobles and regally climbing the steps to the platform.

"You deserve what I'm about to do," she said as though he could hear her. "You are as much to blame as Ateron for all we've suffered—maybe more. Your lust for power drove Ateron to create this ridiculous farce I am about to enact."

She glared down upon him. His evil demanded the precious lives of her friends, something she was determined to prevent. Righteous indignation infused her with a burst of courage, thinking of the three people who had become her lifeline, her strength, and her dearest friends.

Each of them has given me something, each has helped me grow, each would do anything to help me, and I won't do anything less for them. It's up to me to get them safely out of the palace, and I will to do everything in my power to accomplish that. "You won't be so proud and puffed up by the time I'm through," she said to Darvoe like an avenging angel.

Her stomach churned with loathing for the high priest. Still, she couldn't pull her eye away from him as he met Ateron at the top of the platform steps.

The king was glorious in his royal purple robes, trimmed in gold. He was weighed down by copious amounts of that precious metal, which ornamented everything from the ends of his braided hair to the elegant boots encasing his feet. The most spectacular ornament he wore was a high crested crown of gold, encrusted with hundreds of twinkling jewels, and arrayed with a billowing plume of exotic feathers that rose from the back of the crown like an open fan.

Smiling, the two rulers of Injanae embraced and inclined their heads, indicating their mutual respect.

Hadlee gagged on their hypocrisy.

Two thrones, one gilded with gold, the other plated with silver, stood side by side in between the altars that sat parallel to the edge of the platform. Ateron and Darvoe walked companionably to their seats and arranged themselves like two old friends about to enjoy a long anticipated evening of entertainment. Each smiled with— what Hadlee viewed as—evil intent.

Ateron inclined his head then swept his arm across the assembly of nobles, indicating they could rise from their knees and be seated.

When the nobles were seated, Darvoe raised his hands, paused dramatically, and then clapped them together twice in rapid succession. It was obviously a signal, but the sound didn't reach through the balcony wall and into the tunnel.

Unwilling to miss any detail of the spectacle, Hadlee waved a hand at Kytan. "Unblock the vent. I want to hear what's going on."

Kytan removed the clay plug that blocked the vent Ryder had punched through the tunnel wall. It was the fuel port connected to the trough that ran around the inside lip of the balcony' wall, and the point of ignition for the wall of fire that would hide Ansuetra's entrance.

The chanting priests that had led the procession and preceded Darvoe onto the roof, rose up from their kneeling position in front of the platform. Their rhythmic chant flowed clearly through the vent. They danced and leaped in an alternately expanding and contracting circle. On the third contraction of the circle, half the priests remained in a tight knot in the center as the circle again expanded. The inner knot of priests formed a new ring and the two circles moved in opposite directions, waving their arms high overhead, paying homage to the moon.

With the spellbound absorption of a child at her first circus, Hadlee watched the writhing, red robed priests. She hung on every note of the complex harmonized chant that grew into a wailing siren of pleading supplication.

Whispering to Kytan—because sound could travel both ways, and they had been warned not to speak in normal voices—she asked, "What are the priest's chanting?"

"They are calling on Ansuetra to hear them and accept their fidelity and gifts."

Knives were drawn from the priests' silver sashes. Their blades flashed in the light of the torches. They whirled them in intricately practiced patterns. When the dance and chant reached a state of frenzy, the priests turned their spinning blade upon themselves, cutting their own arms and legs in token of worship to the goddess.

Hadlee jerked back, choking on a gasp. "You didn't tell me they would spill their own blood."

Kytan took her place and finished watching the grotesque spectacle. "They are pledging their lives to Ansuetra. They believe their blood will draw her to the sacrifices."

The drums stopped, and the wounded priests knelt at the base of the platform.

Kytan turned to Hadlee. Her hand clung to his. He held it reassuringly. "The priests will bring them up now."

Again she peered through the peephole.

More priests swelled over the lip of the roof like a plague of locust. Hadlee waited breathlessly, her heart beating in her ears. Ryder's head loomed above the floor of the garden. He grew in height as he climbed the stairs until he reached the top. Taya clung to him, her face averted.

He stepped onto the rooftop and paused in the blazing light of a hundred torches that lit the garden. His eyes swept the scene with the majesty of a redwood among a grove of scrub oak, condescending to notice all those who dwelled below him. His stance projected an attitude of indifference, and notwithstanding the spears pressed into his back, he appeared almost bored.

With what seemed to Hadlee, cool detachment, he surveyed the rows of nobles seated according to their ranks, on the stone-carved benches he'd designed. For an instant his eyes swung up and across the small balcony above the sacrificial altars. Then—prodded by a spear—he stepped forward.

"Oh." Hadlee squeezed Kytan's hand with relief. "Ryder just looked up here. I think he wants us to know they are alright."

"Let me see."

She stepped aside, putting cool hands to her flushed cheeks.

Kytan's fingers curled around the edge of the silver disk. A hiss escaped him.

"What?"

"What they are wearing."

"Yes, their costumes are kind of . . . skimpy."

"It is meant to enhance the spectacle and accentuate their vulnerability." He stepped back, his dark eyes flashing anger in the meager candle light.

Hadlee laid a comforting hand on his.

He put his eye back to the peephole. "Don't worry. We have a surprise that should—with the help of heaven— ensure our escape," he whispered to his sweetheart and brother in English, as though his unheard words could strengthen them and fill them with his love and faith. He turned to Hadlee. "You better watch now, while I pour the fuel into the trough."

Twenty-four

Ryder marched across the rooftop and up the steps to the altars, without another pause. "Just keep your eyes closed. It will all be over in a few minutes," he whispered to Taya, his own heart beginning to hammer. He stopped at the altar on the right.

Taya hugged his neck fiercely. Putting her lips to his ear, she whispered, *"But if not."*

He hugged her hard, "But if not."

She lifted her chained arms from around his neck. He set her down on the huge altar that dwarfed her, and hesitated for several seconds, before releasing her. Unable to bear the sight of Toba and Ven taking hold of the chains on her hands and feet, preparing to stretch her out on the altar's cold surface and anchor her chains to the metal hooks, he quickly turned away.

Escorted by five spear-wielding priests, he marched across the platform to the altar that awaited him, passing directly in front of the smug king and jubilant high priest. Swinging his legs up onto the altar's bed, he settled himself onto his back, with his head pointing to the center of the platform—as was Taya's. Sual and Norr's deft hands, took hold of his chains, stretching his body to its full length.

Well, you made this bed, now you get to lie in it. Ateron had carefully dictated the dimensions of the altars. At the time, he hadn't even wondered why the king wanted them to be ten feet long. He'd simply designed them, and commissioned Daelo's stone carvers to build them. *Idiot,* he chided himself, a grim, ironic smile twisting his face. It widened Sual's eyes as he secured Ryder's chained hands. Pulling them over the end of the altar bed, he attached the chains to the hook set in the altar's base.

It only took an instant for the cold surface of the stone beneath Ryder to seep through the thin fabric of his tunic. Goosebumps rose on his arms. He twisted his wrists in the manacles until he could grip the chains anchoring him to the altar. *If things go wrong, I need to have one last option.* He knew he could pull the hooks, holding him down, out of the stone, and the chains that bound him, apart.

When he'd first been enslaved, he found he could pull apart any of the chains put on him. He attributed that to the poor quality of the iron produced in Injanae. But the ability to break his chains hadn't made any difference—lost in the depths of the copper mine. All it won him was hauling around more than one set of shackles on his ankles, and too many rapa stripes.

If Hadlee's timing is even slightly off, I'll pull out the hooks, break the chains, and dodge Darvoe's knife—but that won't help Taya. Hopefully, Ateron will be slow with his blade, knowing what's supposed to happen. I won't be able to free myself, and save Taya too, he worried. *Only you can do that, Pilot.* He turned his face away from the nobles' stark fascination, and prayed.

Hadlee tore her eye away from the scene. *It's a nightmare. No, it's worse. This is really happening.* She swallowed, and abruptly sat down, sending another desperate prayer to heaven.

Kytan crouched down and pulled the stoppers from two large clay bottles, ready to pour the fuel into the vent. Hadlee moved the train of her gown away from the open bottles. They couldn't afford to have anything smudge the white gown.

Concerned about keeping the gown spotless, Ateron had Hadlee make a cloak to cover it for the long walk through the tunnel. Then fearing even that wasn't enough; he'd insisted she be carried to keep her hem, train, and sandals, free of dirt. Finally, to ensure the cleanliness of the gown, while she waited to enter, a carpet was put down in the area around the door. And for her comfort, a high stool was placed next to the peephole, so she could sit and watch the spectacle unfold.

Kytan stood and carefully poured both bottles of fuel into the vent. He opened the container of fire retardant, set the bottle down beneath the vent, and put his eye to the peephole. An unearthly growl erupted from him. He spun away, cocked his arm, raised his fist, and took aim at the wall of the tunnel.

Hadlee made a desperate grab for his arm, but her words arrested the progress of his fist, not her strength. "I feel just like you do. It's ghastly to see them chained to those altars, but hurting yourself won't help them, it will only hinder what you have to do."

Kytan's arm jerked to a stop. He unclenched his fist. "I'm sorry. Neither of us can afford to lose our composure now."

A grunt from behind them turned their eyes to the guards. Each rested his hand on the hilts of his sword in a warning manner. Kytan gave them a shrug, blew out his anger, and put his eye back to the peephole.

Darvoe and Ateron stood in unison, turned and bowed formally to each other. Then shoulder to shoulder they solemnly walked in step to the edge of the stage. Behind their backs, Curlon and Shur moved the thrones to the outside corners of the platform, opening a wide corridor between the altars.

Arrayed in the gleaming armor of his commanding rank, Pel ascended the stairs of the platform with steps measured to the beat of priestly drums. His gaze strayed upward to the balcony when he reached the platform. He came to a stop, and went down on one knee before the ruling powers of Injanae. Solemnly, he lifted the silver tray that held two silver handled knives reposing on a golden pillow. Their diamond cut hilts refracted the glowing light of the moon.

Ateron chose one doubled-edged dagger. Holding the hilt against his chest, he pointed the long gleaming blade at the moon. Darvoe did the same. They pivoted on their heels like practiced soldiers and marched in step to the altars.

Pel backed down the stairs and moved to the far left side of the platform. He ascended another set of steps at that end, taking up his position in the corner of the platform as Ateron's sentinel. His directive from the king was to quell any outburst that might come from the priests or nobles once Darvoe was deposed.

In a loud, nasal tenor, bordering on a shriek, Darvoe started his chanting prayer. The soft rhythmic beat of the priests' drums and the mournful piping of a chorus of flutes accompanied him. With the first somber notes the crowd in the courtyard below bellowed their approval, almost drowning out the sound of the high priest's plaintive chant.

The rulers of Injanae marched shoulder to shoulder between the altars. They separated, executing opposite ninety-degree turns with military precision.

The roar of excitement coming from the palace courtyard billowed away on a bitter breeze, replaced by the deadly silence of expectation. All of Injanae strained to hear the royal high priest's dedication of the victims to Ansuetra, and his pleading prayer for her continued favor over the people and valley of Injanae.

Darvoe's imploring voice grew in volume as it ascended to the moon. It reverberated over the valley with priestly fervor on the raw night air. He drew even with Ryder's chest and executed another ninety-degree turn. Looking down on his helpless victim, he smiled through his chanting lips.

Ateron too came to a stop. Turning, he faced Taya, his face devoid of any hope or comfort for his victim.

In unison, the high priest and king slowly raised the points of their daggers high over their heads, lifting their faces to the moon. They held their blades aloft in suspended supplication as Darvoe's voice built to the crescendo in the sacrificial death chant.

Taya closed her eyes against the sight of the dagger still pointing at the moon, but poised above her heart.

Ryder tightened his hold on the chains over his head, the massive muscles of his arms flexing, beginning to pull. He watched and listened with morbid fascination as Darvoe prepared to sacrifice him to the goddess of moon.

"It is time." Kytan pulled his eye from the peephole, helped Hadlee from the high stool, and moved it away from the door. He watched her fingers worry the silver netting on her gown as he pulled back the latch that kept the door immobile. Like Ryder, he'd come to identify that particular action as one Hadlee engaged in whenever she was worried or anxious.

He lit a punk from the wall torch, just before Lul extinguished it, and looked into her eyes by the dim glow of the burning stick. What he saw dropped his heart into his stomach. *She's terrified.* He leaned in and kissed her cheek. "We have prayed hard about this, and I know it is going to be alright, just do what we practiced."

Her brief nod sent all the silver spirals in her hair bouncing. She swallowed hard and put her left hand on the door, but offered him no reassurance she could master the fear he saw in her face or do what they had so carefully planned.

Hoping to infuse her with strength and courage, he took hold of her right hand. It trembled in his. He pressed it to his heart.

She shuddered on a deep breath, drew herself up, and squared her shoulders.

Darvoe's voice reached up through the vent, wailing out the final, prolonged note in the crescendo of the sacrificial chant.

Kytan put his eye back to the peephole. The daggers flashed in the moonlight as their points turned toward the hearts of his sweetheart and brother. He sucked in a sharp breath, dropped Hadlee's hand, whirled away, and thrust the fire stick into the mouth of the vent. It flared instantly. A whooshing sound echoed through the vent as the fuel ignited.

Hadlee remained frozen in place.

"God go with you," he whispered into her ear. Putting one hand on her back, and the other on the door, he propelled both forward.

Twenty-five

Hadlee pushed through the door almost faint with fear and nearly forgot to stop it from rotating beyond halfway. She caught it at the last moment, arresting its progress before it hit her back.

"Stop!" Ansuetra thundered the command through the curtain of fire leaping up in front of her. "Darvoe, Ateron, stay your hands! Do not hurt my servants, Ryder and Taya!"

Nothing was visible beyond the wall of fire. A wave of suffocating heat assaulted her, robbing her of her breath. The acrid scent of the fuel that fed the fire choked her. The wind driven flames leaped at her. She pressed her back against the smooth silver disc. Its cold surface sent a chill up her spine. Drawing a burning breath she counted every beat of her heart, feeling each one thud in her chest harder than the one before—and heard the terrifying silence.

It's over. The death chant is over!

The flames that hid Ansuetra's entrance, now kept her from learning the fate of her friends. Each moment was an endless agony of fear that pierced her with despair. She endured an eternity of doubt before the flames began to diminish. Terror propelled her toward the receding flames. The movement of her silver laden costume ignited flash after flash of refracted white light from the silver disc behind her and the moon above her, blinding her. She blinked against the dazzling brightness and inhaled pure, blinding terror.

Darvoe's dagger was still poised above his head. His body rose upward as though to ensure the maximum downward thrust of the knife.

Hadlee lifted her hands over the heat of the dying flames, and shouted, "I, Ansuetra, *command you to stop*, Darvoe!"

The dagger started its downward plunge.

The nobles leaped to their feet, crying out, pointing to the balcony behind the altars.

Darvoe's arms convulsed back and jerked up. His whole body seemed to wince with the unprecedented sacrilege of the nobles' outburst in the midst of this most sacred rite.

Ansuetra's resounding voice repeated her decree.

Darvoe whirled around, looking up at her as if he hadn't heard her first commands—the fatal blade still clutched in his hands.

In clarion tones Hadlee declared, "I am Ansuetra, Goddess of the Moon." She pointed her finger directly at Darvoe. "You and Ateron will drop your blades." Her other hand swept the occupants of the rooftop garden, "All will kneel in my presence."

The nobles fell to their knees, putting their faces to the stone floor.

Darvoe's fingers released the knife. The blade fell to the platform with a loud discordant clang. His knees buckled; his body folded; his forehead met the stone of the platform.

The high priest's obedience to her command, and the look on his face, almost brought tears. Hadlee looked down upon his groveling posture as a profound sense of peace settled over her. She took a breath of ragged relief, and found Ateron's eyes. The king smiled before he too knelt, put down his blade, and momentarily touched his face to the platform.

Descending the steps of the balcony, Ansuetra commanded, "Pel, Bayo, release Ryder and Taya, remove their chains, and let them come to me."

Ryder's eyes clung to Ansuetra, even while the guards released him from the altar and his chains. The moment he'd heard her voice and saw her through the dying flames, he'd ceased to pull against the hooks that anchored him to the altar. He didn't see, or even think about the deadly blade poised over his heart. What was the point? Darvoe's knife couldn't have stopped his heart more effectively than she did.

She was breathtaking.

The radiant whiteness of her gown was un-earthly in the heavenly light of the moon. Every lovely feature of her face was accentuated, and dazzling. A bowed silver and diamond crown sat on her brow. Within it, most of her silver-white, moon-enhanced hair was pulled into a glistening fountain. Dozens of braids interwoven with spirals of silver wire flowed up several inches then fell in long looping curls down her back. Over her right shoulder, long loose strands of silver woven hair fell to her waist.

Dangling diamond and silver earrings hung to within a half inch of her shoulders. Her long neck was graced with a high thin collar of braided silver. A gossamer web of silver netting fell from the collar as delicate as lace. It spread out like a doily over her skin, above the bodice of her gown, ending in an enormous round diamond that sat in the dip of her sweetheart neckline.

The same delicate silver webbing hung from the bottom of her empire bodice, almost a third of the way down the long flowing skirt of her gown, ending in dangling diamond moons that flashed with each step she took.

A train flowed out from the bodice at the back of the gown. Its billowing edges were brought forward and attached to her wrists by braided sliver bands, matching her collar. It made her look like she had wings.

Ansuetra was on the platform by the time Ryder and Taya were free. Her silver sandals peeked out from beneath her skirt as she stepped between the prostrated forms of the high priest and the king, leaving them with their heads bowed to the cold stone.

Holding her own head high, she walked between the altars. With a warm smile, she beckoned to Ryder and Taya. They came to her and knelt at her feet. She offered them her hands.

Spellbound, Ryder took her hand and look into her glorious face.

She leaned down and whispered into his ear, "I'm going to send you and Taya out. Kytan will meet you and tell you what we have planned."

Hadlee lifted her chin, and became Ansuetra. "Nobles of Injanae you may raise your heads."

Slowly the heads of the nobles lifted from the floor as though they feared to look upon Ansuetra. Her eyes drifted gravely over the nobles' astonished, and in many cases, frightened faces. Her piercing gaze stopped on Cartu, narrowed, and moved on. Not a single person looked at her with doubt.

Squeezing Ryder and Taya's hands, she gave them a brilliant smile. "Listen to my words," she said to the kneeling nobles. "I proclaim Ryder and Taya free citizens of this land. They are free to come and go as they choose."

Taya pressed her forehead to Ansuetra's hand.

Ryder turned her hand over and pressed his lips to the inside of her wrist.

Ansuetra's lips parted on a small, startled breath. She tore her eyes away from Ryder's molten ones, facing the still stunned nobles.

Stepping between Ryder and Taya to the edge of the platform, she proclaimed, "I have heard your prayers and have come to answer them. On this first night of the full moon, I will celebrate life with you, for I am the goddess of life. Did I not lead your ancestors into this sacred valley and give them the falls of Telquset to sustain them and all their children after them? How is it then that you profane my name with offerings of death?"

The goddess's question rang out with accusation. Fear and guilt distorted the faces of many nobles, and more especially the wounded priests, kneeling in cowed submission below the platform.

The icy voice of Ansuetra commanded, "Darvoe, come forth and bring your blade!"

Stumbling over the edge of his robe, the royal high priest of Ansuetra scrambled from behind the altar where he'd listened to the condemnation of the goddess. He prostrated himself at her feet, laying his dagger in front of her.

"I know your heart Darvoe. You would usurp the power of the king—if you could."

Astonishment, rumbled through the ranks of the nobles.

"Indeed, your heart desires the throne of the king, but you shall not have it. You are an evil man, and I strip you of your rank and title. You are no longer my royal high priest or a nobleman of this kingdom." Ansuetra stepped back from the quivering man at her feet. "Zuph, Ven, remove him."

Darvoe reached out imploring hands, trying to touch the hem of her gown.

She stepped beyond his reach with a disdainful glance.

Zuph and Ven's rough hands took hold of the high priest.

A keening plead, wailed out of him.

Ansuetra fixed him with artic eyes as he was dragged down the aisle between the nobles and through the door leading to the king's hall.

The priests, kneeling below the platform, who dared to raise their heads, quailed when Ansuetra's frosty glare focused on them. "Put your faces to the ground you priests who pretend to honor me. You will not look upon my glory until you have learned to do my will." Ansuetra flung her condemnation at the priests as the last pleading cries of despair from their deposed leader fade away.

Her silver-blue stare lifted to the nobles. More of their faces showed fear now. *How many of you sided with Darvoe, and are now trembling in fear of my wrath?* She bit the inside of her lip to hold back the laugh.

"Ryder, Taya"—she turned to them—"bring me oil. I must anoint a new high priest over my people."

Taking Taya's hand, Ryder rose to his feet. Walking by Ansuetra with deep bows, they hurried down the steps of the platform and through the same doorway Darvoe had been taken.

Twenty-six

A breath of fear, colder than the night air, seeped inside Ateron. He shifted on the hard stones of the platform that bruised his knees, panic throbbing in his chest. Ansuetra was supposed to have raised him and brought him with her before she walked between the altars. That omission caught him off guard. He'd instantly considered following her, but recognized the impropriety of doing so, uninvited.

I can't appear impertinent, or impose my attention on the goddess without her permission. But I have to do something. She is confused and getting things out of order. And yet, the pounding in his chest eased, *she did my bidding with even more regal disdain than I put into her lines.* Silent laugher over Darvoe's humiliation shook his shoulders. *Thank you Ansuetra, you deposed the high priest so deftly, and with such flare. But you cheated me of the pleasure of seeing that spectacle.*

That thought instantly increased the pounding in his chest and the ache in his knees. Needing release from the pain of his groveling position, he sat back on his haunches, trying to ease his discomfort. A burning anger flashed over him as he shifted his weight, keeping his head down. He knew he couldn't allow his head to rise above the altar without appearing disrespectful.

Fear became the rhythm that pounded in his chest. Freeing Ryder and Taya, and allowing them to retrieve the oil, wasn't in the script. Ansuetra was supposed to have asked Pel to get the oil, while his guards escorted the rescued victims to seats at the back of the garden.

With the nobles' attention fixed on the continuing drama, the guards' instructions were to hold Ryder and Taya at sword point to ensure Hadlee's continued cooperation. However, by his royal directive the guards were to obey all Ansuetra's commands, eliminating their ability to contradict her orders.

I have no doubt Ryder and Taya will do her bidding and come back with the oil. Pel will see they are secured as soon as they return. That thought brought him a moment of reassurance, and his mind turned to the idea Hadlee had proposed—two nights ago—to use oil to anoint him. It was an inspired idea, adding just the right touch of drama. *It does have a highly ceremonial appeal that is unique and distinctly formal.*

The pain in his knees intensified, and with each passing minute, his humiliation at being left behind the altar as though he wasn't important, or even there, grew. *This is supposed to be my moment of triumph. Ansuetra should be praising me while she waits for the oil.*

He couldn't see anything of what was transpiring. Even worse, he couldn't see Cartu. Crawling to the inside end of the altar, anger and fear took hold of his mind. *What can I do if Hadlee betrays me now?* He stopped, scooted back, and picked up the sacrificial dagger.

Ryder and Taya flew down the torch lit steps of the king's private stairway. The moment they stepped into the hall; Kytan encircled Taya in his arms. He kissed her with the ardor of intense relief. She clung to him, hiding her face against his neck.

"What are you doing here, and unguarded?" Ryder asked, surprised.

Hugging Taya tighter in his arms, he looked up at Ryder. "My directive, after Hadlee went through the concealed door, was to wait here and deliver the urn of oil Ansuetra asked for, to Pel." He grinned, "Or as Hadlee and I planned—to you. My guards were under orders to join the rest of Ateron's bodyguards on the rooftop, in case there was a need to ensure order."

"Good. So what's the plan?"

"I am taking Taya, and the rest of our supplies through the water tunnel, right now. We are hoping the next surprise we have planned will be a big enough distraction to keep anyone from noticing she hasn't returned with you. There isn't time for me to tell you everything. Just follow Hadlee's lead. *Do everything* she tells you to do." He grasped Ryder's arm, peering intently into the golden depths of his brother's eyes, "Trust her Ryder . . . *just trust her.*"

"I will."

Kytan nodded. "As soon as I get Taya and our supplies through, I will come back. If you leave before I get here, take the route to the falls we followed the first night we went, so I don't miss you."

Ryder's arms encircled his friends, "Be careful, and don't come back unless we aren't there in a couple of hours. Now where do I get the oil?"

Kytan picked up a silver tray from a table behind him and handed it to Ryder.

He turned to go.

"Ryder." Taya's hand took hold of his. "Take this, you may need it." She handed him her now familiar dagger.

They shared a grin.

Ryder slipped it through the center split in his tunic, tucking the blade into his waistband. He took Kytan's proffered hand, gripped it hard, then turned and ran back up the steps.

Ryder came back through the door to the rooftop garden in time to hear Ansuetra finish her lecture on the integrity and duties of the high priest. She motioned to him with her hand. He came up the steps, and knelt.

She put her hand on the tray he offered her and slowly examined the urn. Her eyes dropped to her silver sandals.

Ryder's followed.

Her toe nudged the dagger Darvoe had placed at her feet, and she whispered urgently, "Protect me from Ateron and Cartu. Hopefully Pel will be our ally before Cartu can reach me."

His eyes flew to hers, and he couldn't keep his from questioning her sanity. She held his, hers pleading for his trust. Kytan's words ran through his mind. *Trust her, just trust her.* He gave the barest nod, switched the tray to his left hand, and let his right hand hover over the dagger that had been intended for his heart. The muscles in his arms tensed.

Ansuetra's mouth curved upward as she raised her head and took a step forward. "Lowanta, lord over the noble's council, come forth."

An involuntary murmur of surprise ran through the ranks of kneeling nobles. Every eye turned to Lowanta.

The lord over the council of nobles rose to his feet in the front row. Dressed more as a warrior than a noble, he looked down at his wife, released her hand, lifted his head with dignity, and climbed the stairs.

He was a handsome man, and it was easy to see his resemblance to the captain of the king's bodyguards. Ansuetra smiled, holding out her hand to Lowanta. Pel's father took the hand of Ansuetra and knelt at her feet.

"I know your heart Lowanta. You are a good man. Always, yours is the voice of reason, mercy, and justice. Always, you act honorably, with integrity and dignity, seeking the welfare of all Injanae." She lifted the urn of oil from the tray. "Therefore," Ansuetra's voice rang out with power and authority, "I anoint *you*, Lowanta, high priest, *and king—*"

A scream of outrage tore the night.

Ryder looked over his shoulder at the altar.

Ateron shot to his feet, raising his dagger. "You are not Ansuetra, but *I am* the king. No one will replace me."

The tray in Ryder's hand clattered to the platform. Snatching up Darvoe's dagger, he drew Taya's from his tunic, and sprang to his feet, directly in Ateron's path, blocking the king's view of Ansuetra.

Behind him, he heard Cartu scream, "She is not Ansuetra! She is an outsider, come to destroy the people of Injanae by her cunning arts!"

Ryder half turned, holding the king at bay with Darvoe's dagger, his eyes swiveling between Ateron's furious face and the flash of Cartu's sword as he drew it from it sheath.

The chancellor leaped to the stairs.

Just as Ryder turned to face this new threat, Lowanta jumped nimbly to his feet, and pulled his own blade from its scabbard. Bringing it up in a defensive position, he stepped in front of the goddess.

From the wings of the stage Ryder caught the ring of Pel's sword as he drew it from its sheath. He rushed to his father, and met Cartu's charge before the chancellor reached the top of the stairs. The clash of metal rang out as Cartu and Pel's swords collided with deadly intent.

Ryder smiled and glanced back at Ateron. The king seemed stunned by the unexpected turn of events.

The nobles rose as one to their feet, their faces distorted by terrified confusion.

Fear gripped Ryder's heart. *If the nobles side with Ateron, we don't have a prayer of getting out of this alive.*

Ansuetra stepped out from between her champions.

"Pilot," Ryder hissed, reaching for her arm.

She eluded his hand, stepped beyond his reach, gave him a tranquil smile, and turned her eyes to the nobles. In the midst of the battle in front of her and the threat behind her, she stood her ground with majestic calm.

Ryder was astonished by the effect. The people remained immobile. Even the king's guards looked on in bewilderment, watching the progress of the fight.

Pel held the advantage of size and strength over Cartu, but Cartu's expertise made up the difference. He wielded his blade in a complex style, managing to get the point of it through Pel's defenses. A thin red line opened high on Pel's left arm, causing him to stagger back.

Cartu took advantage of his momentary retreat. He drew a small dagger from his belt, neatly parried Lowanta's blade, and pointed the knife at Ansuetra's heart.

Ryder sucked in a hard breath. Dropping Taya's dagger, he scooped up the silver tray, and drew it across his chest.

Cartu's arm drew back to throw the knife.

Ryder hurled the tray like a discus. It spun through the air, crashed into Cartu's hand, and knocked the dagger from his grasp.

Cursing, Cartu wasn't given another opportunity to try an assault on Ansuetra. With a battle cry, Pel jumped back into the fight, adding the additional force of his short sword to the fray, forcing Cartu back. Cartu responded with an unmatched display of swordsmanship that required the best efforts of both Pel and Lowanta to hold him at bay.

Seeing Pel and Lowanta check Cartu, Ryder's eyes swung back to Ateron. The king had raised his dagger, pointing it at Ansuetra's back. Ryder took a menacing step between the altars, aiming Darvoe's blade at the king's heart.

Ateron lowered the dagger, and scuttled backward. Keeping the altar between himself and Ryder, he screamed for his bodyguards. "Sworn protectors of the king's life, defend me! Kill the outsiders!"

Natell rushed to the armed priests crouching below the platform. "If what Ateron and Cartu said is true, then the woman isn't Ansuetra. That means Darvoe is still the high priest, and our hope to become the ruling power in Injanae."

"But how can we know?" one cowering priest asked.

Others added their concurrence with that question.

Natell's eyes narrowed. "There is only one way to know for sure."

The din of battle and cries of the nobles forced the priests to lean in to hear Natell's words.

"One of you must put a spear through her heart. If she is truly Ansuetra, the spear will not be able to penetrate her flesh. But if she is the fraud Ateron claims her to be—she will die, and Darvoe will be vindicated."

The priests looked at each other with fearful faces.

"This is our only hope to undo what has happened, and take back the power that should belong to the high priest— and us," Natell urged.

Half a dozen priests vaulted to the platform and charged Ansuetra.

Stepping in front of Hadlee, Ryder intercepted them.

One of the larger priests lunged at him with his spear. Dropping Darvoe's dagger onto the altar, Ryder caught the shaft hurdling toward his chest, wrenched it from the priest's grasp, and leveled the unfortunate man with one enormous fist. He wrapped his long fingers around the shaft of the heavy spear and swung it like a bat, cracking it against the bodies of three oncoming priests, sending them over the platform edge. The rest of the priests cowered away from him, and the goddess he protected.

Ansuetra again stepped out boldly from behind Ryder. Her voice rang above the din of battle, drawing the nobles' attention to her. "Hear me, nobles of Injanae. Ateron and Cartu killed Telsuea. They must face justice for their crime."

A howl went through the still immobile crowd.

All had loved the queen, but most had little love for their king. There was too much intrigue surrounding his ascension to the throne and too many unexplained deaths connected to him. Many of the nobles who sided with Darvoe did so, not because they believed his tales about the shaking of the earth, but because they wanted the king's power checked.

Transfixed by Ansuetra's calm, undaunted face—in the midst of the deadly threat posed by the king, Cartu, and the priests—the nobles made their choice.

Men leaped forward, swords drawn, to defend Ansuetra, and take the murderers of the queen.

Ansuetra's declaration, and the growing commotion, ended Cartu's battle with Pel and his father. He leaped from the stairs swinging his sword with practiced precision. Two men fell to the fury of his blade. Others backed away from him, guarding their wives. It provided him with a path of escape through the rooftop door. He fled toward it, even as the king's bodyguards rushed forward in answer to Ateron's screaming commands.

Their sworn duty was to protect Ateron. Yet, most of their faces reflected the seeds of doubt Ansuetra had planted. Some hesitated, seeing their captain, and many of their own noble relatives stand against them, fighting for Ansuetra.

Ateron shrieked orders. Toba and Gidlo leaped to the platform in his defense. He stood with his back to the cliff wall. Toba and Gidlo slid around the outside edge of the altar. The two guards stepped in front of the king and started moving him to the far right side of the platform.

Ryder's eyes followed them, but he kept his distance, standing staunchly beside Hadlee. Reaching to take her arm, he whispered, "Move in between the altars. We're going to make a run for the balcony."

"Not yet." She eluded his fingers. "I need to calm things down. Then we will be able to leave without being seen."

He threw her a doubtful look, but immediately turned his attention to Sual who leaped to the platform and engaged him with a sword.

"Put me on top of the altar," Ansuetra said from behind him.

"No, it will make you a better target," Ryder said over his shoulder, parrying Sual's blade with the long broken end of the priest's spear.

"Trust me Ryder. I know what I'm doing."

Using the spear, Ryder parried another thrust from Sual's sword, shoving his blade up. His fist connected in a solid blow with Sual's left eye, sending him flying backward. The guard sailed into the arms of several priests who were again pressing forward. Like dominos, they fell over the edge of the platform.

Ryder spun around, facing Ansuetra.

She repeated her injunction.

He slammed the broken spear down on the altar, swept her into his arms, and placed her on the altar, where Taya had been chained.

Cartu gained the door leading to the king's hall. As he went through it, Ansuetra's voice rose above the din.

"Guards of Ateron, I release you from your life oath to him. By my decree, he is no longer your king. I have rejected him because of his evil. Look to your captain's example, defend King Lowanta, whom I have chosen to serve you, because of the integrity of his heart."

Twenty-seven

Making their way out through the kitchen entrance, Kytan hurried Taya through the ghostly moon lit streets, giving the crowd near the palace a wide berth. They worked their way south, circling the palace through the winding streets of the nobles' houses, struggling with the eight waterproof bags they carried between them.

The chaotic sounds of battle came to their ears.

Taya pulled Kytan to a stop. "How can we leave them not knowing what will happen to them?" She looked back at the palace, but the roof wasn't visible from their position. "Did you know we would be leaving them in the middle of a fight that might cost them their lives?"

Kytan cupped her frightened face in his hands. "Have faith my love. I know heaven will help them, and yes I knew it was very likely there would be a fight. Hadlee knew it too, and we planned for it. Don't worry, if they haven't joined us very soon, I will come back for them."

Faith wrestled with fear, and won. "Alright." She pressed her cheek into his hand.

He kissed her, took her hand, and they rushed on toward the thundering sound of the falls.

The water closed over Taya's head. Its shocking cold, stole her breath. She clung tightly to Kytan's neck, even though his arms held her securely against him. When they broke the surface of the pool, Kytan moved her to his back. She put her arms under his and wrapped them around his chest, letting her feet trail out behind her. Hugging the wall, Kytan began the dangerous journey along the edge of the pool and into the narrow space behind the waterfall.

The frigid water made Taya's teeth chatter. Her breath came in short, sharp gasps. Faith and fear were again at war by the time Kytan found the deep crevice at the waterline, and stopped.

Somewhere beneath the cold, dark surface of the water, laid the only path to a future she longed for with all her heart, but to reach that future she had to be submerged in a liquid coffin for nearly a minute. *I can do it. I have to—it is the only way to reach safety, and freedom.*

Kytan turned his head back over his shoulder. She leaned hers forward. He shouted above the roaring of the falls, "Slide your arms down to my belt. Hold on tightly to it with both hands, and then take several deep breaths. When you are ready, give me a squeeze."

Clutching the fabric of his tunic, she worked her hands down his chest to his belt. Her chin was barely above the surface of the water by the time she secured a solid grip.

In an effort to close out fear, her mind returned to the blessing she'd received. *Already the promises of protection and safety Ryder blessed me with have been given—no, it wasn't Ryder. The Lord blessed me and fulfilled those promises. He has been with me this whole time, just as Ryder said He would. And with His help—I can do this. I have to take this path to reach my future, and Kytan will get me through as fast as he can. All I have to do is hold my breath.*

She willed her breathing to slow, concentrating on taking slow, deep breaths. *This can't be any worse than being chained to an altar, with a knife plunging toward my heart,* she told herself. Taking one last tremendous breath, she squeezed Kytan's waist.

Kytan inserted his fingers into the deep crevice and pulled them upward. She felt the sculpted muscles of his arms flex, drawing them high out of the water. He let go, plunging them under the surface.

Taya kept her eyes closed tightly, feeling the taut muscles of Kytan's back, and legs move them down and then across. Her hip bumped against the rough rock above the mouth of the tunnel, before she felt Kytan grasp the rope. They surged along the bouncing line under the power of Kytan's reach and pull action. She counted the seconds long past the time she had ever been able to hold her breath, and still Kytan pulled them along the rope.

Panic tingled in her fingers and crawled up along her arms. Finally, Kytan's hand wrapped around both of hers, broke her grasp on his waist, and lifted her into the air of the cavern. She choked and gasped as he transferred her to his back. Her arms clung to his neck with a death grip.

"It alright now, we have made it." He ran a gentle hand over her shaking arms.

Her grip eased as Kytan followed the rope through the utter blackness to the boulder that anchored it. He lit a torch wedged into the boulder's fractured surface and carried her out of the water.

She lay limply in his arms, her chest still heaving, trying to inflate her completely depleted lungs. In those final desperate seconds, before he pulled her to the surface, she'd used the last whisper of air left inside them.

With trembling fingers, she reached to push the wet hair from Kytan's face. "I don't know how you can go through that tunnel time after time," she said, gulping breaths. "I have never been so terrified. Even being chained to an altar with a knife pointed at my heart, wasn't as bad."

He hugged her tight, his dimples adoring her. "You have been very brave tonight, my angel." He gave her a gentle, lingering kiss. "Rest, while I go back and get the bags."

She clung to him for a long moment, taking comfort from his arms, letting them strengthen and calm her. He kissed her again, before he set her down on a rock at the edge of the pool, and disappeared beneath its surface.

It took another four trips for Kytan to bring the fuel and food bags through. Taya was surprised at how quickly he returned and left again. She marveled over his swimming ability. The trips back and forth through the tunnel didn't seem to tire him, and they certainly didn't frighten him.

She stood up, hearing, more than seeing him break the surface of the pool. He waded out of the water with the last two bags. "Let's get our camp set up."

"Yes." She shivered. "Hadlee and Ryder will be cold and tired when they come through."

"Ryder said there is a good room we can make camp in through the tunnel at the back of this cavern. Let's light a couple of torches and go find it. Then I will bring up all our gear."

The cool cavern air on their wet bodies made them shake with cold. They worked their way up a rocky incline and into the tunnel at the back of the cavern. Several yards in, an opening yawned to their right. They took careful steps into the room sweeping it with their torches. It wasn't as big as the pool cavern, but the ceiling was tall enough for Ryder to stand up straight, and the floor was flat and fairly smooth.

"This will be perfect," Taya said, walking to the middle of the room. I will start digging a fire pit." She reached into her tunic for her dagger, before she remembered. "Oh, Ryder has my knife."

"Why don't you gather some rocks to ring the fire pit while I dig?"

Digging out a shallow pit in the hard packed ground with only a knife was slow work. Taya had the rocks ready by the time it was done. She quickly encircled the pit with them, before they laid the wood for the fire.

Kytan rubbed her arms vigorously. "You need to dry off, and get into warm clothes, before your teeth break from chattering."

"I will, but first I would like to take a bath. It may be the last one I get for a while."

"Alright, let's go bring up the bags. I will get everything laid out while you wash." He frowned as another shiver shook her, but said, "I think we better wait to light the fire until Ryder and Hadlee come. We don't have very much wood."

"I agree. Now I better go bathe before I am in danger of being interrupted."

Kytan's face darkened. "Yes I think Ryder has seen quite enough of you, along with most of Injanae."

She blushed. "You ought to thank Ryder. It was his idea to modify my clothes and have me wear them under my costume to keep everyone from seeing all of me."

Kytan grumbled, "He shouldn't have modified them quite so much."

Taya turned and walked stiffly out of the cavern.

He hurried after her. "I'm sorry."

She turned and gave him a hurt look.

He took her hand, and smiled pleadingly, "I am sure you and Ryder did your best."

She gazed at him from under her thick lashes. His pleading eyes lifted the corners of her mouth. He let out a relieved breath, and they walked back to the pool.

It took five trips before all the baggage and equipment were stowed in camp, and another to fill the water bags the conspirators would have to rely on, once they started their trek out. Lugging everything up the incline to reach their camp helped warm them slightly, but Taya's teeth were chattering again by the time she opened the oilskin bag that held her knapsack, and quickly drew out towels, dry clothes, and soap.

Kytan stood watching her with a far off look, "I can hardly believe we are finally free, and going to America."

His comment brought a teasing twist to Taya's lips. She pressed them together frowning. "Sometimes I think you love America more than you love me," she said tragically.

His eyebrow shot up. "I don't."

"Good," she said sternly, and laughed. "Then before you start dreaming, get everyone's knapsacks and beds set out around the fire pit. When Ryder and Hadlee get here, we will celebrate. Then you can tell us all the things you want to do, have, and see in The United States."

Twenty-eight

Cartu wove his way north through the empty moon lit streets, listening to the voices of alarm from nearby rooftops, where many sat watching the spectacle unfold. More voices rose from the people inside the palace courtyard. Their cries of astonishment and fear rent the night, growing in volume even as he put more distance between himself and the scene of his defeat.

I had no choice, he rationalized. Ateron might trust his bodyguards to rescue him, but Cartu didn't share his confidence. Far too many of Ateron's bodyguards—not to mention the nobles—admired Pel and Lowanta. Considering the probability they would believe what Hadlee said about the death of Telsuea, and turn on the king, he knew the odds were stacked against him, and he never took on odds that didn't favor him.

Rage lengthened his short stride. Everything he had worked so long to protect and possess had been destroyed by a few words out of the mouth of a girl Ateron thought he could control. *By morning I will be a hunted man, maybe sooner. Why did I believe in Ateron's mad scheme?* He broke into a run. *No, it wasn't the scheme that was at fault, it was the soft methods Ateron employed. If he had been more brutal with Ryder, Kytan, and even Taya, Hadlee would never have dared defy him.*

He merged with the shadows of a building, watching a group of late comers to the celebration saunter down the street, talking and laughing. *Drunk, he decided. A state I would like to be in—not that it would help. Where in Injanae can I hide that I won't be found?* For the first time in his life, he felt trapped.

The courtyard doors to the chancellor's mansion were locked. In the darkness, Cartu fumbled with the lock, opened it, and slipped through the gates without a sound. Abandoning stealth, he slammed through the door of his residence. *This will be the first place Lowanta will look for me.* He knew he couldn't stay. *Where can I go? There isn't any way out of this valley.*

His temper exploded in a loud screech. He smashed several decorative pots and overturned an elegant table. His whole body vibrated fury. *Is there a way to reverse what just happened?* He needed time to think, and that was something he didn't have.

He bounded up the stairs to his bedchamber, pulled off his ceremonial robes, and dressed for battle, strapping two swords around his waist. Three slim daggers slid into sheaths at his boot, waist and wrist. Smiling grimly, he hefted the weapon delivered to him just the previous evening. The handle was heavy but well balanced. He ran appreciative fingers over the weapon before hanging it across his shoulder. Then he added a quiver of arrows and a bow to his arsenal, securing them to his back.

Lowanta and Pel will have to kill me. I won't suffer the indignities of becoming a slave. I would rather die in battle, killing as many of my enemies as my skills will allow me. His only choice now was the battleground. He pulled a floor length black cloak over himself, his mind whirling with dark emotions.

All my troubles started the day Ryder appeared in Injanae. He thought he'd solved them when he blamed Ryder for Renla's death. His face contorted with the memory, as he unlocked the vault that held his most prized possessions.

Renla, whose beauty rivaled the queen's, had possessed a heart as devoid of conscience as his. It made her the perfect confidant. Together, they had conspired over so many things. Their fondest scheme involved the death of Ateron, with Cartu succeeding him.

He laughed bitterly at the memory.

He'd been under no illusions as to why Renla married him. As the chancellor's wife, she was courted and fawned over. Only the queen commanded more attention. Even knowing she didn't love him, she was a prize he'd delighted in flaunting in the faces of many who had sought her favor.

Then her eyes turned to Ryder. His jealousy had known no bounds when he found her waiting for Ryder in his room. *Wearing her most enticing . . . .* He pushed the memory from him. Anger blurred his vision, diverting him from his purpose. More than anything else, at that moment, he wanted Ryder's life. He nursed his hate, filling a large leather bag with gold. Leaving the vault open, he left the room, moving swiftly to the stairs.

Not only had he lost Renla, but now the opportunity to have the one woman he'd always coveted was gone. The first time he walked into Petra's shop, and saw her little daughter, he decided nothing would stop him from owning Taya. Her beauty exceeded both Renla's and the queen's. Her delicate, diminutive size made him feel large and powerful, a feeling he rarely experienced around women. He assumed killing Petra would easily put Taya into his hands through the orphans slave auction, until Tulas, Taya's uncle, exercised his legal rights, and took her into his home. *At least Petra's death silenced the only person who knew by what means King Moncara died.*

Cartu's fingers caressed the hilt of the jeweled dagger at his waist. He longed to put it into Tulas's heart for thwarting him, and forcing him to wait until Taya was of age, before he could bargain for her. She should have been his for the past six years. Now even though she belonged to him legally, he would never have her.

Fury howled from his lips. He tore an elaborate tapestry from the wall next to the stairs before he started down them. A venomous cocktail of bitterness, anger, and hate pumped through his veins, filling his heart with vengeance.

Everything I have accomplished is meaningless now. Everything I want is now beyond my reach, and it is all Hadlee's doing. There are things I would like to do to her . . . , he froze on the stairs, his thoughts clarifying with stunning force. *There is a way to turn this around, but I will have to act quickly. All I have achieved, all I want isn't lost—not yet.*

He leaped down the remaining steps, threw open the door, and embraced the darkness.

Twenty-nine

Pel and Lowanta stood with Ryder, guarding the goddess. Lul, Tark, Zuph, Numo, and half a dozen more of the king's bodyguards, joined them, nodding their support of Lowanta.

Pel looked up at Hadlee, "Did Ateron have Telsuea killed?"

"Yes, just as he had Cartu kill his first wife, and his brother, so he could be king."

Lowanta roared, "He killed my sister's daughter? Why?"

"Because he tired of her and wanted a new queen," said Ansuetra, without hesitation.

"Then he will die by my hand." Lowanta took a step toward Ateron and his defenders that now numbered over two dozen.

Half a dozen of his personal guards defended Ateron, along with many of the priests. Gidlo, Toba, and Sual stood in front of Ateron on the far right edge of the platform guarding him, while Norr, Anlow, Moran, with a number of priests, thrust their swords and spears down at the nobles fighting them from the floor of the garden.

Pel took hold of his father's arm, "You will be the king. Your justice will deal with him."

"No!" Ansuetra's voice rang out. "I will deal with him!"

Handing the urn of oil she still held to Ryder, she drew herself up to the majesty of her six foot, one inch glory. Turning to face Ateron and his followers, she clapped her hands together.

Fire blazed from her finger.

The priests, defending the king, cried out, and fell to the platform, averting their faces.

The goddess brought her hands together again, as though she was praying, touched them to her lips, then pushed her palms out hard, directly at the king. Fire spewed at Ateron from her mouth.

The astonished screams of the nobles shattered the night. They too dropped to their knees.

Those who were sitting on nearby rooftops, far enough away to see what was happening, shouted what they saw— the enraged goddess was spitting fire at the king.

The common people and slaves crushed into the palace courtyard, howled. Some tried to push their way to the rooftop stairs. Others jostled in the direction of the gates, seeking escape. But the vast majority was caught in the paralysis of indecision.

Ansuetra drew three silver rods from her hair. She touched their tips. They exploded in flames. She hurled one with the accuracy of Thor, at Ateron. His robe caught fire. The other two followed, striking true.

Ateron screamed.

Sual and Gidlo dropped their swords, frantically beating out the flames on Ateron's robes.

"Enough!" Fire again erupted from Ansuetra's mouth. "My patience is at an end. Drop your weapons!"

Swords fell in clanging chords to the stone floor from the nobles and guards alike. All those engaged in the fighting fell to their knees cowering before the infuriated countenance and wrath of Ansuetra.

Toba pushed Ateron to his knees. Gidlo clamped his hand over the king's mouth.

Ansuetra's eyes swept the rooftop garden, promising swift retribution against all who dared oppose her. Her silence was terrible. She let it grow until the hush reached down, subduing even those in the courtyard.

Looking at Lowanta's son, she commanded, "Pel instruct your men in their allegiance to their new king."

He stood, calling to each one. "You have been loyal to Ateron even though you suspected his evil. It is time for it to end. My father is a good man; give him your allegiance."

Ateron's head jerked, escaping Gidlo's restraining hand. He screamed, "I will have your life, Pel. No one will take my kingdom from me. I have the pure royal blood of generations of kings in my veins, and the right to this kingdom."

With the fury of a mad man, he threw off Toba's hands, and leaped to his feet. Lost in a blinding rage, he shouted abuse and commands at his guard. Toba and Gidlo jumped to their feet and pressed their swords to his chest. Sual yanked the sacrificial dagger from his grip, preventing him from hurling it at Ansuetra. Despite their swords, he screamed threats and spit into their faces.

Ansuetra leaned down and picked up Darvoe's sacrificial dagger from the altar. Her long fingers ran down the blade. She pointed it at Ateron. The blade burst into flames. "Silence him now, or I will!"

Toba and Gidlo clamped their hands over Ateron's mouth. He writhed in their unyielding grasp, unable to escape.

"Take him from my presence. There has been enough violence at the hands of this evil man. By my decree, he is no longer your king, nor will his posterity ever rule Injanae."

Again, her eyes flared with challenge. She swept the assembled company with her flaming blade.

No one objected.

"Let no more blood be spilt this night. Pel, direct your guards to see to the wounded." She dropped the flaming dagger behind the altar. "My time with you draws to a close, and I must anoint your new king."

Pel stepped forward directing Toba, Gidlo, and Sual to take Ateron to the dungeon. "Ven take Shur and Orat, and go search for Cartu. Tark, Yawt, Dal, take the wounded into the king's quarters, and find Fent to treat their wounds. The rest of you, help the nobles back to their places."

Ansuetra looked down on Ryder with a smile as luminous as the moon. He looked back with an astounded one. She shifted her gaze and gave Lowanta her most spectacular smile. He lifted his sword from the floor of the platform, saluted her with the blade then bowed his head and offered it to her, hilt first.

Ansuetra put her hands on Ryder's shoulders. His encircled her waist, and he carefully lifted her off the altar.

The goddess accepted Lowanta's sword with serene poise. She raised it above her head, her face glowing with the glory of her victory. Laying the sword on the altar, she picked up the urn of oil Ryder had placed there, held her hand out to Lowanta, raised him from his knees, and walked with him to the center of the platform.

The silence over Telquset was so complete that the voices of night birds and insects sang on the air.

Lowanta again knelt at the Moon Goddess's feet. Holding the urn above Lowanta's bowed head, Ansuetra's voice trumpeted, "Lowanta, I anoint you king, and high priest, over the people of Injanae." She poured a few drops of oil onto the top of his head. "The right to rule in all things, as king and high priest, is yours, and your posterity's, as long as you—and they—rule with honor and integrity."

She held the urn out to Ryder. He took it from her. Placing her hands on the sides of Lowanta's bowed head, she tilted it up, leaned down and kissed the new king's brow, leaving the imprint of her oxblood lipstick.

Holding out her hand to Ryder, she nodded at the altar. He picked up Lowanta's sword and brought it to her. She took it and bent to speak to Lowanta in a voice only he could hear. He bowed his head to the platform when she finished speaking and reverently kissed the hem of her gown.

Once more Ansuetra held Lowanta's sword over her head. "This sword is now a scepter of justice and mercy." Lowering it slowly, she placed it in the new king's hand.

Again he saluted her, before he sheathed his sword.

The goddess raised him to his feet and turned to the nobles. "Give King Lowanta your loyalty and trust, for he is worthy. Listen to his counsel in all things, and the people of Injanae will prosper."

The nobles broke into a prolonged cheer, before they lowered their heads to the ground pledging their allegiance to their new king.

Pel and Ryder shared stunned, triumphant grins.

Ansuetra laid her hand on the arm of King Lowanta. They descended the stairs of the platform. Pel and Ryder followed in their wake. Crossing to the rooftop wall, they looked down on the people crowded into the courtyard, sitting on the walls, spilling out the gates, and standing on nearby rooftops.

The house guards had kept a surge of distraught people from charging the roof when the fighting broke out. Helplessly, they had heard and seen only part of what happened, leaving them in a state of fearful agitation.

A deafening cry went up as Ansuetra came into full view. All Injanae fell to their knees with hands and voices raised in supplication.

Ansuetra extended her hands to them, and smiled. She allowed them to express their wonder and joy at her presence. Then lowering her hands, she called them to silence. Like the fading ring of a bell, the crowd stilled.

Her voice rang out through the clear night air. "I am Ansuetra. I have felt your pain and seen your suffering at the hands of wicked men. Therefore, I have reordered the affairs of this kingdom." She raised Lowanta's hand. "Lowanta is your new king, and high priest. Serve him faithfully, and he will serve you with justice and mercy."

The crowd exploded in wild acclamations of joy that lasted until the king held up both his hands for silence.

"I pledge to rule as Ansuetra has directed me. No more will this people suffer the evils of a corrupt king, and high priest. Ansuetra has instructed me to lead you in prayer and solemn reflection. We will pray long into the night for her forgiveness in offending her with our sacrifices and sue for her favor. Never again will the people of Injanae stain the worship of Ansuetra by human sacrifice. She is the goddess of life, and will not accept death offerings."

Another resounding cheer rose up from the crowd. Ansuetra waved a graceful hand at her adoring people and turned away. Lowanta led her back to the top of the platform.

"It is time for me to leave you," she said to him, transferring her hand to Ryder's arm. "My servant Ryder will accompany me, after I have listened to the prayers of my high priest."

She walked between the altars and put her foot on the stairs.

Lowanta directed Pel to command his people below in the courtyard to kneel and place their faces to the ground. He turned to the nobles and gave them the same command. Kneeling down, he faced Ansuetra who again stood on the small balcony above the platform.

Laying his face to the cool stones, King Lowanta began to pray and praise the incomparable Moon Goddess, in the first of many long and heartfelt prayers that would rend the air until the sun rose over Telquset.

When Lowanta finally raised his head, Ansuetra and the big slave were gone.

Thirty

Ryder held on to Hadlee's arm, trying to help her pick her way over the rocky, uneven floor of the tunnel. Ansuetra's delicate sandals kept Hadlee from being able to move quickly over the rough floor.

"Ow," she said again after stubbing her toes for the second time in ten feet.

"We have to move faster," Ryder said when she stopped to massage her toes and work a pebble out of her sandal. "I don't believe everyone is going to stay all night for the prayers. We need to be through the water tunnel before Lowanta finishes too many more, and the people start wandering off."

"Then you will just have to carry me—like Kytan did."

He lifted a questioning brow.

"Ateron didn't want the edge of my gown or my sandals to get dirty by walking through the tunnel."

"Well then," he said, handing her the torch he held, and sweeping her into his arms. "Hold the torch out so I can see."

She pushed the torch out in front of them, lowering it slightly. His long strides propelled them forward at a brisk pace. He felt her relax into the relief of victory.

She idly draped the gown's train over his head and across his shoulders. Resting her arm around his neck, she grinned. "We look like a couple of characters from Grimm's Fairytales that have just escaped the pages."

"You definitely look like the goddess all of Injanae believes you to be."

"And you look like you just fell from mount Olympus."

His neck flared with heat. "Darvoe's dagger in my heart would have ruined that illusion."

She pulled the cloth off his head, letting it fall back onto his shoulders, and sobered. "I have to tell you, seeing you and Taya chained to those altars"—she shivered—"was so horrible, I had to sit down."

"You sure hid whatever fear you felt very convincingly. In fact you were magnificent," he said, carefully watching the ground; afraid the bewitchment he had been under since she stepped onto the balcony might now, that he was holding her in his arms, get the better of him, and make him trip over his feet.

His mind was still reeling from the events of the past hour. She had done the impossible. Through the most brilliant display of courage, grace, and majesty, he knew he would ever see, she'd convinced the nobles and Ateron's bodyguards—who knew the truth—that she was Ansuetra. She had even won their support in dethroning Ateron.

Of course the miraculous fireworks she'd done hadn't hurt either. Even her language skills amazed him. She'd answered Pel and Lowanta as though she understood every word. And the lines she delivered while dethroning Ateron— he couldn't imagine where they had come from. But she delivered every one with the assurance of someone who knew the language well.

"How did you and Kytan dream up that impossible scheme? How did you learn those new lines in just three days, and keep your composure through everything?" He shook his head, "I especially want to know how you did those fire stunts. They were unbelievable." He gave her a squeeze of admiration, drawing in the heavenly feel of holding her in his arms.

"It was a miracle." She smiled serenely. "Kytan and I prayed so hard, and—you know—I'm really not sure I did any of it. You have no idea how close I was to fainting with fear when I came out onto the balcony and couldn't see anything because of the flames." She stiffened with the memory. "I was actually dizzy with relief when Darvoe finally turned and dropped that awful dagger. Then the most amazing peace came over me." Reverence glowed from her eyes. "I think heaven did all the rest." Closing her eyes, she rested her head on his shoulder.

He felt her again relax, releasing the tension from her muscles. His steps slowed. *She really was concerned about me.* He drew the feeling in, holding it in his heart like a treasure.

Their faces were only inches apart. The siege of longing his heart had resolutely withstood was breeched by her nearness. *I shouldn't. It wouldn't be right—or fair. Not while she's still dependent on me to get her out of Injanae, and home.*

He came to a stop, torn between his resolve never to tell her his feelings, and the compelling desire to kiss the lips that were so alluring and close to his. The feel of her cool fingers clinging to his neck, her head resting on his shoulder, the fragrance of her hair that he inhaled with every breath, and the feel of her in his arms all undermined his resolve.

He lowered his face to hers.

The torch twitched in her relaxed hand, wobbled, and dropped slightly.

He jerked back as her eyes fluttered opened.

"Oops." She turned her head, and lifted the torch back up.

"It's okay. You have a right to be tired after everything you've been through tonight. And even if it was with heaven's help, you were absolutely amazing," he said, recovering himself.

He forced his feet to move again, keeping his attention on the rocky floor. They emerged from the tunnel, descended the steep stairs, and came out into the soft light of the hall. He didn't put her down until after they entered her apartment.

"I need to get out of this dress." She turned her back to him. "You will have to help me."

"What?"

"It took Kytan's help to get into this getup, and it's going to take yours to get me out of it."

"Just how much help did Kytan give you?"

She whirled to face him, surprised by the suggestion of impropriety in his tone. "There aren't any zippers or buttons in this kingdom, in case you haven't noticed. To get into this dress, and make it fit properly, I had to design it with a gusset in the back that is cinched together with lacing. I just need you to untie the lacing so I can get out of it."

"Oh."

She turned her back on him again, lifting her hair away.

He took a breath, held it, reached for the lace and tugged. It didn't budge. He tugged again. It still didn't move. "It's not coming loose." Beads of sweat broke out on his forehead. He stooped to examine the lacing. It was small and tightly knotted. "Kytan double knotted it." His fingers felt unusually clumsy as he fumbled with the knot.

"Use your dagger," she urged, "We haven't got all night."

"But I might hurt—"

"Oh for goodness' sake—just do it."

He pulled Darvoe's dagger from his waistband. Carefully inserting the flat side of the blade in between the gusset pocket and the lacing, he turned the blade's edge toward the laces, and gave it a hard sawing jerk.

The lacing spilt.

The force of the cut pulled her into him. His arm encircled her waist, steadying her.

The abrupt release of the gusset, and the weight of the gown's silver netting, slipped the gown from her shoulders. She grabbed the front of it, pressing it tightly against her chest.

Ryder sucked in a breath.

"Thanks," she said, "now undo my necklace please."

His big fingers struggled for a moment with the clasp, but managed to undo it.

She let go of her hair.

It tumbled across his arm like silk. He swallowed and put the necklace into her outstretched hand.

She took it, scooped up the long train of her dress with the same hand—her other one still holding up the front of her dress—and ran up the steps of her bedchamber. "I'll be quick." She threw over her shoulder, disappearing behind the curtain.

He hadn't begun to breathe again, when she screamed.

Thirty-one

Taking the steps in one flying leap, Ryder burst through the curtain.

"Stop! Or I will cut her throat."

Ryder skidded to a breathless halt. The sight that met his eyes, suffocated him in fear.

He held a knife, pressed firmly against Hadlee's throat. His other arm encircled her waist, holding her tightly against him.

Hadlee's eyes were enormous, radiating the same fear disabling Ryder. Her face was as white as her gown, and so were the fingers of her hand. They strained against his wrist, shaking with the effort to keep the deadly blade from biting into her throat. Her other hand still faithfully held up the front of her gown.

He willed her to relinquish her hold on the gown and fight for her life with both hands. Her commitment to her modesty was admirable, and he loved her for it, but felt it wasn't worth her life. To reach her, he needed the fraction of a second the strength of both her hands against the knife would give him. However, her white knuckled clutch on the silver weighted fabric, told him she wouldn't do it.

Adrenaline filled Ryder's veins like air expanding a balloon, stretching its limits. His muscles demanded the release of immediate action, but the situation allowed him no relief. All his physical prowess, all his astonishing speed, and lightening reflexes—so acclaimed on the battlefields of athletics—couldn't outpace the knife pressed against Hadlee's throat.

Ryder's toes inched forward as his pent up adrenaline continued to build. Cold sweat trickled down his back and broke out on his forehead. He tore his eyes from Hadlee's frantic, pleading ones, concentrating on the knife at her throat.

"I can see you didn't expect me." The trembling of Ateron's voice bordered on hysteria. "Drop your dagger, or I will spill her blood."

The trickle of sweat running down Ryder's back increased. He released Darvoe's dagger. It hit the floor with a pinging clang. He'd never felt so powerless, terrified, or desperate. One quick motion of Ateron's hand would end the dearest life the world held for him.

Ateron giggled nervously as though the whole thing was a joke. "Did you really believe all my bodyguards would renounce their oath of loyalty to me?"

"Where are your—*faithful guards*?" asked Ryder with quiet calm, even though the force of his heartbeat threatened to crack his sternum.

"They will be back shortly." The humor died in Ateron's face. "They are gathering supporters to my cause."

Ryder shuffled a step closer. "Your rule is over Ateron. Hurting Hadlee won't help you."

"It isn't over. One way or another, *Ansuetra* is going to help me reclaim my throne. I am going to take her back out onto the balcony. She is going to change her mind. If she doesn't, I will slit her throat in front of all her devoted subjects, proving she is no goddess, and what she said was a lie. I have the royal right of ancestry. My reign will continue."

"That won't happen now that the people know you killed the queen. Not even killing Ansuetra will change that."

The hand that held the blade to Hadlee's throat trembled with Ateron's barely controlled insanity. He pressed the blade against her neck, steadying his hand.

She stuttered a gasp. A drop of red splashed onto Ansuetra's white gown.

Ryder's hands became fists.

"We will see." Ateron's eyes narrowed. "Stop moving, Ryder! Your next step will kill her. It doesn't matter to me if I take her out of here alive or dead. In fact it would be far easier to just take her head," he said, on an unsteady chuckle. "Either way the people will see the trick that has been played on them. When I tell them Pel and Lowanta conspired to use her to overthrow me, and she is really an outsider, the people will turn against Lowanta. My crown will be restored."

All through his tirade, Ryder had been inching forward. He stopped. The grizzly image Ateron put into his mind, tore at him like the razor sharp teeth of a piranha. That ravenous killer was now openly reflected in the king's dead, unfeeling eyes. They left no doubt in Ryder's mind—Ateron would prove good on his threat.

A pulse at Ryder's temple became a metronome, beating out time they didn't have and couldn't afford for this standoff. He had to do something—fast. He studied their position in the room. Ateron and Hadlee were standing a few feet from the bathroom wall. There was nothing close enough for Hadlee to grab and use as a weapon.

"The truth is you did kill Telsuea," Ryder said, trying to buy more time while he worked on a solution.

"That can't be proven, but I can prove Ansuetra is a fraud. Once the people know that, it will call into question her accusations against me, allowing me to reverse what she has done." His arm tightened around Hadlee's waist.

She sucked in a sharp breath, tugging up the gown.

"Back away, Ryder."

He took one small step back, and saw it. "Pilot, get him to back into the wall," he said urgently.

"One more word in your foreign tongue and my blade will slice her throat. He drew his elbow back an inch. Hadlee's head moved with the motion, keeping the blade from sinking into her neck. "Do what I said."

Ryder took a step back.

Hadlee shifted her feet and stepped clumsily on Ateron's foot. He winced and shuffled back with a curse, dragging her with him. She stumbled over the gown's train, gasping with fear.

The sound tore through Ryder's heart. His muscles tensed and his fists tightened.

Ateron stepped back again to keep them both from falling. His shoulders hit the wall. Angry hissing blared out behind him. With a startled yelp, he shoved away from the wall.

Ryder streaked across the room.

The blade in Ateron's hand jerked and skidded.

Hadlee gasped.

Ryder's long arm shot out, his hand seized Ateron's arm, wrenching it away from Hadlee's throat. A bright crimson stream flowed down her neck.

Rage exploded behind Ryder's eyes.

Hadlee clutched her neck and fell to the floor.

A predatory sound growled out of Ryder. His steel fingers tightened on Ateron's arm, jerking it down and back.

Ateron screamed. The knife fell from his fingers.

Ryder released Ateron's now useless arm.

Wailing in pain, Ateron tried to defend himself with his other arm.

Ryder's huge hand closed over the fist that flew at his stomach. He wrenched it backwards, pinning it behind Ateron's back. His other enormous hand encircled Ateron's throat, jerking him off the floor.

Ateron's face drained of color. He writhed, gasping for air.

Ryder's fingers closed tighter.

Ateron kicked out feebly with his dangling feet. They stilled as his eyes rolled back in his head.

Cold, trembling fingers tugged on Ryder's arm.

"Ryder, Don't . . . don't do it. Don't lose yourself because of him. He's not worth it. I'm—I'm alright."

Hadlee's fearful pleading broke through the predatory madness that gripped him. He inhaled through his teeth, and threw Ateron into the wall. The king hit with a dull thud and slid to the floor.

He took hold of Hadlee's shoulders, pushed her hair back, and looked at her neck. She held the blood stained train of her gown across it, hiding her wound. Her other hand still faithfully pressed against the front of her gown. His arms came around her, crushing her to him. She let out a little squeak; he eased his grip.

Her head drooped against his chest. She was shaking hard, and so was he. He never imagined he could feel the level of fear or anger he had just experienced. The terror he understood. Thinking Hadlee was dead, made him feel like every reason for his existence had just been sucked out of his soul. The rage that followed was the darkest thing he had ever known. It hadn't been hot or irrational. No, it had been icy cold, almost without feeling, but with a clear, deadly purpose.

"He came out of the bathroom as I was pulling off my earrings," she mumbled into his chest. "I tried to run—and he wouldn't have caught me—except I got tripped up by the stupid train on my gown."

She swayed unsteadily against him. He lifted her into his arms, afraid she might faint. She released the covering on her wound and clung to his neck as tightly as he was holding onto her.

The cold tentacles of the rage began to grasp at him again at the sight of her blood, and he knew if she hadn't stopped him, he would have killed Ateron. Maybe he had. He glanced at the king's limp, prostrated body.

"Towels," he demanded in his dictator voice, the red stream flowing down her neck, spiking his fear.

"Bathroom."

He laid her gently on the bed, and fetched towels and a bowl of water from the bathroom. After tearing a towel into long strips, he folded another into a thick pad, sat on the side of the bed, and pressed it firmly against her bleeding neck. "Hold this tight against your neck."

"What happened when we hit the wall?" she asked, sitting up and pressing the towel against her wound.

"A very useful citizen helped us out."

"Thank heaven for sunqaras."

"I'm so sorry." His arms enfolded her. "My half-baked idea almost got you killed, but I couldn't see any other way."

Watching Ateron's knife skid across her throat was a memory he knew he wouldn't be able to banish for a long time. *No doubt it will come back to haunt me—maybe even give me nightmares.*

He took several unsteady breaths, still shaking. Only the comfort of holding her calmed him. He closed his eyes and leaned his cheek against her silver crown, trying to slow his heart, feeling hers pounding heavily against his.

She moved her head, and he lifted his away. Her eyes looked up at him earnestly. "If you had backed off, I would be dead. He wanted to kill me for dethroning him, and I know he would have cut my throat as soon as he had me out in front of the people again." A tear trickled down her cheek. "Your half-baked idea saved my life."

"And your brilliant performance saved mine." He dunked another towel into the bowl of water.

Her smile was tremulous. "I guess that's just what friends do for each other."

The words were true, but hit a raw nerve in his heart. He forced a smile; wrung the water from the towel, and wiped the blood off her shoulder and collarbone, while she continued to apply pressure to her injury.

"It's too soon to release the pressure, but we're short on time, and I need to look at your wound."

"It's only a scratch," she said pulling the towel away.

But Ryder instantly saw that it wasn't. Silently, he blistered himself with a scathing assessment of his intelligence. A two-inch laceration marred the left side of her neck. It was still bleeding freely, making it difficult for him to tell how deep it was, but he was certain the knife had bitten into the muscle of her neck. He was sure it was very painful, and even more so, with every movement of her head. Thankfully, the blade hadn't moved across the front of her throat to her windpipe, or the carotid artery. A profound prayer of gratitude rose up from his heart.

He folded a doublewide strip of toweling and placed the pad over the cut. She sat up woozily, while he secured it with another strip of toweling, tying it carefully on the other side of her neck.

"We need to get out of here before Ateron's loyal guards show up." He searched her pale face. "Are you strong enough to get changed?"

"I think so," she said, still holding tightly to the front of her dress.

"Okay, I'll take Ateron out so you can get started." He let her go, picked Ateron up, and tossed him across one broad shoulder. "Hurry," he said, going through the curtain.

Dumping Ateron into a pile of cushions, Ryder reached down and took his wrist. The pulse was weak, but steady. He sighed feeling something between regret and relief, and growled at Ateron's inert form, "As long as you're alive, I better secure you in case you wake up before we leave."

He was pacing anxiously up and down with Ateron neatly trussed up and lying comfortably in the cushions when Hadlee came through the curtain. She was dressed in fawn colored pants and a tunic, with a leather bag hung over one shoulder. He looked up with relief at her washed face, and long thick braid, encompassing dozens of smaller ones, swinging behind her back, but frowned at the blood oozing through the makeshift bandage.

"Forgive me for failing you." He reached up and took her hand, holding it along with her eyes. "I promised to keep you safe, and that wound on your neck is proof I wasn't as good as my word. I knew Cartu was running around somewhere. That alone should have put me on guard. I should have checked your room before I let you put one foot in it."

"You aren't responsible for my every breath." She squeezed his hand. "What happened was my own fault. I knew Cartu was on the loose too. That should have made me stop and think about what might have been behind the curtain before I flew through it. I was just so relieved and anxious to be gone that I got careless."

"So did I," he said, unable to take his eyes from the bandage on her neck.

Hadlee glanced at Ateron. "I take it by his hogtied condition, he's alive."

"He is, although he doesn't deserve to be. His kind of evil will continue to find ways to destroy people as long as he is alive. Not even what I did to him will change him, but thank you, for keeping me from being his executioner."

"I agree. His evil runs so deep, nothing will ever change him, but his death at your hand wasn't something I wanted to witness." She started down the steps.

"Wait. You need to cover your hair. It will stand out like a beacon in the moonlight."

"You're right." She went back through the curtain, and returned wearing a short cloak with a hood. Her eyes traveled over Ryder's costume. "Maybe we should find you a change of clothes before we leave."

"Believe me, I wish there was time, but we've been here much too long." He reached for the bag over her shoulder. "What in the world is in here? It weighs a ton."

"Kytan and Taya are going to need money to get started when we reach the states. Shoot, we are going to need money just to get there. This is the money."

He loosened the strings and looked inside. All Ansuetra's diamond and silver jewelry, including the gossamer netting from around the bodice, was inside the bag. He pulled the strings tight again. "Good thinking. Ateron owes us at least this much for all the work Kytan and I have done. Now let's get going. It's been well over an hour since Kytan and Taya left. If we don't hurry, we will all have to go looking for Kytan, who will be wandering around the palace looking for us."

Thirty-two

With all of Injanae still bowed in prayer, Ryder took Hadlee out through the kitchen. Pausing inside the dark doorway, they watched several of Ateron's former bodyguards patrol the entrances to the palace.

Hadlee whispered, "Why aren't they praying like everyone else?"

"I don't know, but we have to get by them without being seen. There's no way to tell if they are loyal to Ateron or Lowanta."

Long minutes went by while they waited and watched for an opportunity to escape the palace. The guards finally converged at the common people's gate about fifty yards from them.

"I have an idea." Ryder went back into the kitchen and returned with a small iron pot. In a high arching shot, he threw the pot at the palace wall to the south of them.

The startling crash of the pot against the wall, brought the guards head's up. They ran toward the sound.

"Come on." Ryder grabbed Hadlee's hand. They slipped out the door, hugged the palace wall, and slunk their way north. Rounding the northwest corner of the palace, they pressed east until they came to the cliff face. They trudged their way through the vegetable garden until they were well into its depths.

When they were far enough from the glow of the palace torches, Ryder turned west, directly into the revealing light of the moon. He pulled Hadlee along as fast as he could, through the neat rows of vegetables, to the wall surrounding the palace, and boosted her up and over, into the dense shadows offered by the buildings on the other side of the wall. A moment later, he joined her.

They sped down a lane on the west side of the palace. Their thick moccasin boots made a muffled clapping against the stones beneath their feet that echoed through the stillness of the empty lane. The moon's westward trek allowed them to hide from its betraying light, by keeping to the west side of the winding lanes as they worked their way south. Turning east toward the cliff, the moon became their enemy, again spotlighting them in its piercing beam.

Hanging on tightly to Hadlee's hand, Ryder turned into the cliff side lane, moving south again, heading for the falls, picking up the pace. Hadlee ran in an effort to keep up with his expansive strides.

The thundering of the falls grew louder with each step. Halfway down the lane, a shout at their backs brought Ryder to an abrupt halt. He whirled, dropping Hadlee's hand.

Three of Ateron's bodyguards were running toward them.

Ryder calculated the distance. *We might be able to outrun them, but we won't be able to get into the pool, and behind the falls, without being seen.* He barked out, "Keep going, Pilot. Kytan will be here any minute. He can take you through."

"No, we're sticking together." She took his arm.

"I see we have company," a familiar voice observed from behind them.

"Kytan, thank heaven!" said Hadlee, as he emerged out of the night.

"Yeah," Ryder agreed, not taking his eyes off the approaching men who had slowed and were moving more warily now. Without looking at Kytan, Ryder handed him the leather bag of silver, and spoke in Injanae. "It's time to fulfill your oath. I'll hold them off while you take her through."

Kytan's eye's narrowed, watching the guards' calculated approach. "As soon as I take her through, I will come back to help you."

"No. You can't come back for me. One of us has to stay with the girls. They won't be able to find their way out through the tunnels on their own. I've only told the route to you."

Kytan moved to Hadlee's side. "Alright, you are on your own."

Ryder's eyes turned to him. "I'll be there."

"I am going to hold you too that, brother." Kytan grabbed Hadlee, threw her over his shoulder, and bolted.

"No!" she wailed. "We can't leave him." Her voice rang through the empty street until it was lost in the roar of the falls.

Ryder stood in the middle of the lane. *I can't let the guards get around me and follow Kytan and Hadlee. I have to give them the time they need to get behind the falls.* He drew himself up, his resolve fixed, his determination absolute.

Hadlee had learned how strong Kytan was when he carried her through the tunnel, but his hold on her as he raced for the pool was almost lethal. Trying to yell at him, she found it next to impossible to draw a sufficient breath with his shoulder digging into her stomach. She settled for beating on his back with her fists.

It did nothing to slow him down. He pressed on at an easy lope as though he was unaware of her pounding, and the hard knocking of the heavy bag of silver she felt banging against his side.

He dropped her to her feet only long enough to yank off her short cloak, grab her hand, and pull her with him into the freezing water of the pool. When they came up, he yelled for her put her hand on his belt.

She hesitated, looked up at the edge of the pool, and knew she couldn't get out without help. With no choice, she grasped Kytan's belt, and followed as he started to move along the wall.

A few minutes later, she came up in the cavern pool behind the falls, furious and breathless, the pain of her wound forgotten by the fear that replaced it.

Kytan's head bobbed above the water just in front of her. As he turned to her, she lashed out at him. "How could you? How could you just leave him to face those guards?" she yelled into his face, drawing rapid breaths.

"I didn't have a choice."

"Of course you had a choice. I thought you two were brothers!"

"Hadlee, Ryder and I made an oath to each other to—"

"Run off and leave him?"

"Yes, if it came to that, or me, if it was necessary. You and Taya are more important to us than our own lives."

She shrieked, slamming her hand against the surface of the water, sending a wave into his face. "Boy Scouts! I'm surrounded by self-sacrificing Boy Scouts! Well, first class scout Kytan, you can just go back and help him, now that I'm through."

"I am truly sorry, but I can't. One of us has to be here to get you two out through the cavern tunnels, over Farlana, and home. If I go back to help him, there is no guarantee either one of us will make it back." He laid his hand over hers on the rope, holding tightly to it when she tried to pull away. "It was the last thing he made me promise before I ran off with you."

"So you're telling me, you're fine with leaving him at the mercy of those armed men!"

"No." He bristled. "I hate it as much as you do, but it is the only way to ensure you and Taya get out of here safely."

"Go back and help him!"

"Listen to me, Hadlee. He doesn't need my help. There were only three of them. I have seen him take on more and win. In the copper mine, clothes were precious. The clothes I wore in were the worst ones I had, but they were better than anyone else's clothes. Five slaves attacked me when I was alone. They nearly stripped me naked before Ryder came. He was as wild as a madman and more ferocious than a jaguar. Even I was terrified. He had my clothes back in no time. Believe me, he can take care of himself, and before you know it, he will be here with us."

What he said gave her pause. She had seen Ryder fight—twice. He'd kept everyone away from her on the platform and had easily taken care of Ateron. "But the men up there are Ateron's elite bodyguards. They are trained warriors, armed with swords."

"What is the matter?" Taya called, from the edge of the pool. "I could hear your voices all the way into the next cavern." She picked up the torch wedged between the rocks, and swept the pool. "Where is Ryder?"

"Good luck explaining *that* to Taya." Hadlee let go of the rope and swam across the pool.

Again Taya demanded, her voice rising, "Where is Ryder?"

Kytan followed Hadlee, waiting until his feet found the bottom of the pool, before he told Taya what had happened.

Her face became a thundercloud. Her voice rose, and by the time they were out of the pool, Hadlee thought she might hit him. She smiled at Kytan's discomfort, taking the towel Taya handed her.

"Go back for him! I don't care what promises you two made. I won't leave here without him." Taya's black eyes snapped. She handed the torch to Hadlee, put her small hands on Kytan's chest and tried to push him back to the pool.

He looked from one angry face to the other, dropped the bag of silver, and waded back into the water.

Thirty-three

Ateron's bodyguards drew their swords, and came to a stop, thirty feet from Ryder.

"I don't want to fight with you," Ryder said truthfully. "Turn around, and no one will get hurt. Ansuetra freed me. I can go where I want."

A derisive choral of laughter answered him. "You and Hadlee are needed for an encore performance. Come quietly, and *we* won't hurt *you*," Sual said.

The guards moved closer. The moon revealed the faces of Sual's companions. Gidlo and Toba slowly fanned out, trying to out flank him in the narrow lane.

Good, Ryder relaxed, when they didn't rush him. *At least they have decided to deal with me, before going after Kytan and Hadlee.* "I'm not going back with you." The moon accentuated the hard, unyielding set of his face. The jaguar flared to life in his eyes, halting the advance of the guards.

He'd watched them practice their fighting skills, studied their techniques—both collectively and individually. He knew their strengths, and their moves, but they didn't know his. The way he fought wasn't pretty. It was junkyard dog, down and dirty. His fighting skills were an endowment from his prison years and something he hadn't used since then, but under the circumstances, he felt no qualms. Instead, he offered a silent thank you to Jimmy O'Hara, the toughest guy he'd met in prison.

During his first year of incarceration, when bitterness and self-hate filled him, Jimmy not only protected him, but also taught him every dirty trick and strategy he knew for fighting. He taught Ryder to use their intensive manual labor to build his muscles. Ryder was amazed at the amount of muscle he put on in a very short time under Jimmy's careful tutelage. By the end of his first year, no one wanted to take him on, at least not one on one. By then, he stood six foot seven, and had put on thirty pounds of muscle.

Ryder smiled sardonically. This wasn't the first time he'd faced multiple assailants with weapons drawn, but this was different. These three were professional soldiers with swords. It made the situation more deadly than facing a handful of inmates with shanks in their hands.

His assailants began to move.

Jimmy O'Hara's voice whispered in his mind. *"The first thing ya gotta know about fightin a gang, kiddo, is not to let um surround ya."* Slowly, Ryder angled his way back toward the rock wall of a building on the west side of the lane, keeping the moonlight at his back. He stopped about four feet from the wall.

"Den you gotta keep um from attackin ya all at once, see. Try to make um come at ya one on one. Dat's the best way to even yer odds. Dere's lots of ways to do dat, but da one dat almost never fails—specially if ya know da jerks dat wanna piece a ya—is to challenge deir individual fightin skills. Sure dey can take ya on altogether, but dat only proves dey can't take ya alone. So ya gotta make um wanna prove dey're as tuff as you. Ya know, show off for deir pals, score some respect for demselves."

Ryder's teeth flashed a mocking grin, at his opponents' wary approach. "I'm surprised Ateron sent you after me Sual." The moon revealed Sual's left eye was swollen shut. "You can't even see out of that black eye I gave you." Ryder's grin widened, and he sneered, "I'll bet you thought Gidlo and Toba would even your odds, but the three of you aren't a match for me."

Sual stopped, and barked orders to his companions. "Stay back. I want to take him on my own. I owe him for this eye, and now that he doesn't have a spear in his hands, we will see how his odds stack up against my sword."

Ryder laughed scornfully. Jimmy certainly knew men. He took a defensive stance, beckoning with his hand for Sual to come at him, adrenaline pumping like high octane through his veins.

With a savage roar, Sual rushed him, his blade gleaming wickedly in the moonlight.

Ryder stood still until the last possible moment, his eyes fixed on Sual's blade. He faked a step left, like the All American tackle he was. Sual's battle cry tore the night as he lunged in that direction, thrusting out his sword. Ryder leaped right, feeling the swish of the blade as it went by him.

The momentum of Sual's lunge drove him beyond Ryder. Spinning, Ryder became the fighter Jimmy O'Hara taught him to be. Clasping his hands together, he swung them like a bat, hitting Sual hard right between his shoulder blades, propelling him face first into the wall. Sual's sword clanged against the stone building, and fell from his hand. His body bounced off the wall.

Ryder rammed one massive shoulder into Sual's back, putting all his weight behind the move, slamming him again into the wall. Sual collapsed in a heap to the ground. Ryder jumped away, reached down and brought up Sual's sword.

With their own battle cries, Gidlo and Toba came at him, but with a slower, more wary approach.

Gidlo was in the lead by several paces. He brought his blade up then down in a sweeping arch.

Ryder stepped in catching Gidlo's sword with the broad side of Sual's blade. The muscles of his arm hardened to steel. He shoved Gidlo's blade up and back, leaving the guard's face open. His fist connected neatly under Gidlo's jaw in a brutal upper cut. The blow lifted Gidlo up off his feet, and sent him flying back into Toba's oncoming shoulder.

Toba stumbled, with the impact of Gidlo's falling body cashing against him.

Ryder twisted sideways and kicked out, planting his boot hard in Toba's stomach. Toba doubled over. Ryder dropped Sual's sword and slammed both fists down between Toba's shoulder blades. The guard crumpled in a heap on top of Gidlo.

Without a glance at his downed assailants, Ryder took off for the falls like a thoroughbred coming out of the starting gate, his legs pumping as hard as he could make them. The stone paved street and shops quickly gave way to the soft dirt and trees of the park surrounding the falls. Weaving like a running back, he moved through the trees, and broke into the open ground around the pool.

Ten yards from his goal a bolt of lightning tore through the thin fabric of his tunic, running like a blade of fire across his back, sending him to the ground.

The pain was astonishing, unlike anything he'd ever experienced. It ripped without pity through his entire body.

The heinous laugh that erupted behind him, told him what had happened.

He tried to get up, but the crack of the whip came again, landing next to his head. He flinched, jerking away from the dirt kicked up by the lash that sprayed his face.

"Stay where you are, slave!" Cartu's triumphant voice commanded. "I have waited a long time for this moment." He cracked the whip menacingly in the air. "This whip was made just for you. I am going to teach you how easily it can humble a man, even one as large as you."

The whir of the whip cutting the air came at Ryder again. His whole body bucked with the impact, and the pain. It shredded what was left of his thin tunic, opening another long bloody line across his back. The intensity of the pain immediately made him long to retreat into his mind—into a memory—to escape it.

Long ago, he'd learned he could escape pain by pulling himself out of the moment, and into a memory. His perfect recall could retrieve an experience, and replay it, making it so real he could not only see it, but also touch it, taste it, smell it—and most importantly—feel it.

"I am going to kill you," said Cartu, calmly, "but you will decide if it's slow and painful, or quick and merciful. I hope you choose the slow way. I know you won't be able to make it through this lashing in silence, and I am going to enjoy the sound of your suffering."

For an instant, Ryder gave into his mind. He was back on the roof with Hadlee, enjoying her smile of forgiveness, which was his most prized possession. *If I am going to die, I want that smile to be the last thing I see, and feel.*

Ryder gave Cartu what he yearned for, and moaned, forcing himself back into the present, into the pain. He couldn't afford to escape this situation. This time he had to stay in the moment. If he wanted his life, he had to live the pain, and find a way to survive.

"What . . . do you want?" He groaned, knowing Cartu was right. He couldn't endure much more of this kind of torture.

He had to do something, before Cartu completely disabled him, but he couldn't think. The pain screaming across his back consumed him, body and mind.

Desperately, he tried to focus on his surroundings. His eyes searched the area, hoping for some kind of weapon. There was nothing within his immediate reach. Then he felt something digging into his hip, cautiously he moved his hand.

"Where is Hadlee?" Cartu's question held a smile of malice. "I know she was with you up until the guards attacked you. I have been following you since you left the palace. Tell me where she is, and I will kill you quickly. But, for every moment you hesitate, I will add to your pain. Now tell me."

Ryder's fingers closed around the rock under his hip. The pain, caused by landing on the fist-sized rock, had gone unnoticed in the agony the whip inflicted. He ignored it now, and took a deep, shaky breath. "She went with—"

He rolled, sat, and threw the rock in one excruciating, fluid motion, putting everything his tremendous arm was capable of into the throw, like a pitcher delivering a hard ball for the strikeout.

Cartu's arm was drawn back, ready to swing the whip, when the rock slammed into his chest. The whip flew from his hand. His bug eyes popped opened wide with surprise. His body careened backward, smacking the ground in a skin shredding skid, and slid to a stop.

Ryder struggled to his feet. He leaned his hands on his knees, panting with pain, keeping his eyes on Cartu, sprawled motionless next to a stone bench.

The sound of running feet straightened his back.

The Guards! Ryder hurdled toward the pool, launching himself out over the water.

Even before he hit, he knew he was too far out.

His body collided with the water like a block of cement. The trauma inflicted on his back was immediately numbed in the frigid grip of the churning water. The tremendous power of the falls plunged him downward into the black depths of the pool, as though he was no more than a puny pebble swept away in its mighty torrent.

He battled helplessly, humbled by the vastly superior strength of the falls. It smashed him against the rocky bottom of the pool, pinning him down, holding him prisoner by the weight of its pounding fist. He struggled against it for endless, lung draining seconds, before its mighty hand swatted him outward, releasing him from its crushing grip.

He floundered, trying to orient himself. With the air in his lungs waning, he propelled himself in an upward direction. Rising only a few feet, his hands bumped against a hard rocky surface. Confused, he pushed himself downwards, his lungs smoldering, aching for breath. His feet tangled in a rope, and he immediately knew where he was.

Taking hold of the rope, he fought his way forward, toward what he hoped was the safety of the cavern. The smoldering pain in his lungs became a fire, demanding to be quenched. He resolutely pressed on, but it felt like he was no longer swimming in water.

Instead, his feet kicked through thick molasses that tried to hold him fast, and bound his fingers as he tried to slide them along the rope. Frantically, he lurched forward, certain he was still holding onto the rope, but felt nothing.

The fire in his lungs became an inferno. Blazing up his throat, it exploded from his mouth.

Thirty-four

Kytan was already waist deep in the pool when Hadlee shouted, "Look." She pointed to the rope, pulled taut and bouncing hard. "It's alright, he's coming."

They waited in hopeful anticipation, watching the rope bounce.

It stopped. Seconds slipped by, but the rope didn't move.

"What happened?" asked Taya.

"I have a very bad feeling." Kytan dove for the rope, grabbed it, and was gone in a moment.

As fast as his agile body could swim, he propelled himself along the lifeline. Only a few feet into the tunnel, his foot hit something unusual below him. He stopped, hooked his feet around the rope, and reached down, flailing his arms blindly in front of him. His fingers brushed against flesh. He reached as far as he could, took hold of an arm, and pulled with all his strength.

There was no mistaking that massive arm. Drawing him in, Kytan wrapped his own arm over Ryder's shoulder, across his chest and under his other arm, while his feet kept their tenuous hold on the rope. Praying fervently, he put his hand to the rope, and pulled. Struggling to keep hold of both Ryder and the rope, he inched along its path, frantically trying to reach the air they both desperately needed.

He broke the surface with a tremendous gasp, his lungs ablaze. With his first ragged breath, he pulled Ryder's head above the water, and tried to yell, but only managed to choke, "Help me."

Hadlee swam straight for the heads bobbing next to the rope. She reached them and took hold of Ryder's chin, keeping his head above the water. Lying on her back, she drew him across her body, holding him like a lifeguard. Kicking hard, and with Kytan's help, she towed Ryder's limp body across the pool.

Taya was knee deep in the water by the time Hadlee and Kytan's feet found the bottom. She moved out to meet them. It took all of them to drag Ryder out of the pool and lay him on the rocky ground.

Dropping to her knees, Hadlee felt for a pulse, her own pounding against her temples.

Taya dropped to her knees too, putting her cheek close to his mouth and nose. "He is not breathing!"

"But his heart is still beating. Help me! I know what to do." Hadlee looked at the incline that rose from the pool. "We've got to roll him onto his stomach, and let's turn him around so his head is lower than his body," she said, fighting the panic she felt, looking at his bluish-gray face. Tugging on his arm, she began to pray, "Please, please help me do this. Please let it work."

They rolled Ryder to his stomach, and recoiled. The power of the waterfall had stripped away what was left of his tunic. Blood poured from two long slashes.

Instinctively Taya reached for a towel to stop the bleeding.

Hadlee snapped, "Not now, Taya. Help us turn him. If we don't get him breathing, his back won't matter."

Nodding mutely, Taya helped them turn Ryder's body so his head was pointed down toward the pool.

Hadlee stretched one of Ryder's long arms above his head, bent the other, and placed his head on it, facing out. Opening his mouth, she swept it with her fingers. Then facing his head, she straddled his back, and dropped to her knees. Placing both hands on the small of his back—wrists facing in, fingers pointing outward and slightly over his sides, thumbs parallel to and brushing his lower ribs, little fingers just above the pelvis—she took a deep breath, rocked forward and pushed down.

Trying not to think about the blood splaying up through her fingers from his wounds, she released the pressure, and commanded in a dictator voice, "Breathe, Ryder."

Rocking forward, she pressed down again, released, and repeated the motion again, almost raising herself off her knees with the effort. "Please," she pleaded, the dictator replaced by a desperate petitioner. "Please, breathe."

A sob tore from her with the memory that accused her. *I promise you—even if it takes my life—I will get you out of here. That's what he said, and I heartlessly replied, I'm going to hold you to that promise, Garrison.*

Pushing forward and down hard, she wept, "I didn't mean it. Please, I didn't mean it. Don't die! Don't leave like this. You still have to get us home."

Kytan gripped her shoulder, his fingers telling her what he couldn't bring himself to say.

"No!" She pulled away from him, pushing down on Ryder's back with more determination. *Surely, it hasn't been that long. It seems like forever, but it can't be more than a minute since I started.* She rocked forward, pushing again, fighting her panic.

Sitting down beside him, Taya took Ryder's outstretched hand, and wept uncontrollably, mumbling, "But if not."

Kytan dropped down next to her and wrapped her in his arms, tears like a silent waterfall, flowing down his face.

Tears coursed down Hadlee's face too. Exerting all her strength she rocked forward and pushed down, lifting herself off her knees.

Water spewed from Ryder's mouth, his body convulsed in a long rolling shudder under her hands, she pushed down again groaning with the effort. More water gushed from his mouth. He drew in a deep gasp of air that ended in a series of hard rasping coughs. He labored against the coughing, and drew another gagging breath into his lungs. Shuddering, he pushed himself up.

Hadlee jumped from his back.

He came to his elbows and knees, vomiting water.

With strength she didn't know she had, she caught him as he fell to his side, dragging his quaking body across her lap, and into her arms. His head crashed onto her shoulder. Wrapping her arms around his chest, she laid her hand over his heart, and leaned back against the rough, biting surface of a boulder. Relief gushed from her eyes, feeling the solid, rhythmic beat of his heart, and the heaving rise and fall of his chest with each tremendous breath he inhaled. Brushing his long hair away, she put her lips against his ear, and murmured, "Breathe, Ryder, just breathe."

Pain shrieked through him. Cold shivered over him. The strength to control any part of his body eluded him. All he could do was obey the demands of the voice in his ear, dragging one breath after another into his depleted lungs.

He wrestled with the persistent coughing for each gulping breath he drew. It felt like the terrible coughing would never end, but finally it slowed, and gradually subsided. The arms holding him rode out the coughing with him, supporting him while he struggled to breathe.

The voice in his ear demanding that he keep breathing sounded so much like Hadlee's, he gave himself up to it. Content to believe his head was resting on her shoulder and that it was her arms he felt around him, he obeyed—inhaling and exhaling.

His strength returned. He forced his eyes open, and saw a bloody red wound, marring a lovely white throat.

Hadlee lifted her cheek from his forehead and smiled down into his eyes.

His opened wide. *I am in her arms, and she's—soaking wet.* Her face was wet, so was her hair. Her thick heavy braid hung over his shoulder and dripped down his arm. *This should feel like heaven,* his heart insisted, but instead his whole body continued to shiver and shriek.

The events of the past hour rushed at him, with one gaping hole. He couldn't remember making it through the water tunnel. *Was I the last one?* Uncertainty forged a frown between his eyes.

Searching for Kytan, Ryder found his anxious face, and croaked out, "The rope."

"Oh! I better go take care of it." Kytan gave his arm a reassuring squeeze. They had decided the last person through would cut the rope and reel it in to keep anyone from following them.

Ryder heard Kytan's splashing dive back into the pool, and closed his eyes again. "How did I get here? I don't remember making it through the tunnel."

With his return to the living, Doctor Taya took charge. "You can hear about it later." She leaned in, hugged his hand, and kissed his cheek. "Right now, you should be quiet and rest. Your back needs treating." She got up, and said over her shoulder as she started for their campsite, "I will be back with my medical bag in just a moment."

Ryder looked up at Hadlee and groaned, "Not again."

Hadlee hugged him tight, and laughed.

He sucked in a painful moan.

She winced. "Sorry. I'm afraid we neglected your wounds while we were trying to get you to breathe. Hold on for a few minutes. When Taya and Kytan come back, we will move you so Taya can treat you."

"I wasn't breathing?" he asked, and then noticed her blood stained hand on his heart. He took hold of it. "Mine?"

"Ah—yes," she said and changed the subject. "What happened after Kytan hauled me off?" Her face changed from concerned to irritated, and before he could answer, she said in a frosty tone, "That, I have to tell you, is a very sore subject with me. So maybe we better save it for later."

He gave her a less than penitent grin. "Yes, ma'am."

"And you should know that if Kytan hadn't gone back after you, when we saw the rope stop moving, you would be dead right now."

"He seems to be my guardian angel." Ryder drew in a long breath, and let it out slowly.

"But not the only one," Kytan said from the depths of the pool. "What Hadlee did was like magic. Taya and I thought you were dead. I tried to make Hadlee stop, but she wouldn't." Kytan walked out of the pool, dropped a wet coil of rope, and stooped down next to them.

"What were you doing?" Ryder asked.

"Artificial respiration. I saw the procedure on a cigarette card one of the guys at work had. It caught my eye because a Boy Scout was demonstrating it. That sparked a discussion of the procedure and its merits. David Willard demonstrated it for me. He said he'd seen it done three times while he was in the Navy, but it only worked in one case."

Ryder stared at her in amazement. *If she hadn't known how to do that lifesaving procedure, I would be dead. That makes twice she's saved my life—no three times. She also saved me with her forgiveness.*

His eyes were lost in a swamp as he struggled with his feelings. Squeezing her hand, and taking Kytan's, he choked out, "Saying it isn't enough, but thank you, both. What would I do without friends like you?"

Hadlee growled with exasperation, "Maybe if you let them help you, you wouldn't get yourself into so much trouble."

Kytan grinned. "So what happened?"

"First, I think we need to wash him, and take care of his wounds," Taya called, coming down the slope from the tunnel with a small bag of medical supplies and a cup in her hands. "I don't have much with me, but it will do. Let's start by getting these herbs into you. They will help with the pain.

Ryder took the cup she offered him without protest, drinking the bitter tasting liquid in one long swallow, knowing and needing the effect it would have.

"Kytan, help him up. Then you and Hadlee better get him into the pool. He needs washing."

"Here we go again," Ryder muttered, feeling Hadlee's shoulders shake with silent laughter. "Alright, but no one's touching my pants."

Hadlee and Taya sputtered, choked, and then winced when he sucked in a painful breath.

Kytan took his arm and gently pulled him away from Hadlee, who crawled out from behind him. With Kytan supporting him, Hadlee crouched at his side, draped his arm across her shoulders, and hung on tightly to his hand.

Ryder looked at his blood, soaking the front of her tunic and pants. "You need washing just as much as I do," he said through his clenched teeth, and shivered.

Mimicking his voice, she sternly said, "You're right, and no one's touching my pants either."

The laughter that erupted helped release the tension of the night's frightening experiences. Ryder followed it with another moan.

Kytan took the same hold Hadlee had on Ryder's other side. Together they helped him to his feet. Gratefully, he accepted their support, and help down into the pool.

When they were nearly waist deep, Hadlee said, "Why don't you float on your back while Taya and I wash you?"

"Kytan can support you while we do the scrubbing, and we will make this the fastest bath you have ever had," Taya added.

He gave them a resigned look, and stifled a groan, lying back in the water. *Even the water hurt*s.

Taya and Hadlee went to work quickly with the soap, washing as much of him as decency allowed. Helping him back up, Hadlee and Kytan again supported him, letting Taya wash his back. His body tensed, and his muscles jerked when she gently soaped and sponged water over his wounds.

She closely examined the two bleeding slashes, describing them to him. "One runs from the middle of your back, under your right shoulder blade out to your right side. The other starts just below your right shoulder, and runs diagonally to the left. It intersects the other one in the middle of your back, and runs almost to your waist."

Ryder's grip tightened on his supporters, nearly crushing the hands that held on to his, silently enduring Taya's careful treatment. She applied an herb paste, causing him to breathe heavily and shake visibly, then wrapped a towel around his back, under his arms, and tucked it together over his chest.

"Well," Taya said, after he was out of the pool and sitting stiffly on a rock. "What you need right now is to be dry, warm, and in bed. I am afraid it is going to take some time to get the bleeding completely stopped. That will be easier to do if you are lying down." She pointed at a nearby rock, "I brought you some dry pants." Her eyes swung to Kytan. "Yours are there too, along with a couple of towels. You still need to bathe, but be quick, I want Ryder fed, and in bed, as soon as possible."

Hadlee scrutinized Ryder's face, and asked, "Are you going to be able to manage?"

He mustered a smile and nodded.

She gave his hand a squeeze, and said to Kytan, "If you need help getting him to camp, just give me a yell."

He nodded, and she followed Taya up the incline leading to the campsite.

"I want to hear about what happened," Ryder said to Kytan, watching his angels of mercy pick their way to the back of the cavern by the light of a torch. "But right now, I just want to put on dry pants and lie down for about a year."

"I want to hear what happened to you too—but let's wait till we are all together." Kytan's dimples cringed. "You are going to get the tongue lashing I took a while ago. I want to see how you handle it. I didn't do very well."

"Hadlee already gave me an idea of what I'm in for. I'm sure I won't fare any better than you did."

"You were right about those two. They are the most stubborn women in the world." Kytan frowned when Ryder shivered. "Do you need my help with the pants?" he asked, stripping off his wet tunic.

"No," Ryder said, drying his arms with a towel. "Just hand them to me."

Thirty-five

Sitting next to the fire in her wet clothes, waiting for her turn to take a bath and change, Hadlee hugged her knees to her chest to keep from looking at Ryder's blood that saturated the front of her clothes. Resting her chin on top of her knees, she shivered in the cool cavern air.

Taya stood behind her, carefully undoing all the braids that had been woven with silver wire until her hair was completely loose. Running her hand over Hadlee's wet hair, she asked, "Okay?"

Hadlee forced a flickering smile hoping to eliminate Taya's concern. "Okay," she said not quite truthfully, trying to still the internal quaking that had nothing to do with being wet or cold.

She'd been running on adrenaline and pure nerve since stepping out on the balcony above the altars. Now the aftermath of standing up to all the horror and trauma of the night was catching up with her. Drained of every reserve of emotional and physical strength, she felt like an empty shell, one so fragile that the tremors quaking over and through her threatened to make her shatter into her own emptiness.

Why are you falling apart now that it's all over? She berated herself, struggling to shore up the deteriorating armor of her self-control. Gripping her knees tighter, she fought the trembling, trying to keep herself from shattering into pieces. Focusing on the fire, concentrating on the feel of its warmth on her skin, she pushed away the terrible images running through her mind, allowing only the dancing of the flames to remain.

Muffled sounds from beyond the cavern brought her out of her trance. In unison, she and Taya looked at the cavern entrance, hearing the men's voices grow louder with their approach.

She stood, reached for her clothes, a dry towel and the still damp one that Taya had hung near the fire. Its light revealed the exhaustion in both men's faces, and the pain Ryder seemed unable to control, as they entered.

"I thought you two would never get out of the bathroom," she said lightly, taking the torch and the soap from Kytan's hands. "It's time Ansuetra fulfilled her promise to bathe in the fall's pool, don't you think?"

"Too bad the people of Injanae will never know you fulfilled that promise," Ryder said.

"A pity," Kytan agreed.

Taya called after her as she went into the tunnel, "Hurry. I'm going to make soup."

Walking away from the campsite, and down the tunnel, Hadlee felt grateful for the darkness that closed in around her. It veiled her in longed for solitude, hiding her weakness from her friends.

Stepping into the cavern, she picked her way carefully down the rocky incline leading to the pool, stubbornly refusing to let the flood of emotion now filling up the emptiness inside her overflow the reservoir of her will, which held it back.

Without the fire's warmth, the cold air made her shiver violently. She clenched her teeth together to keep them from chattering, without success. When she reached the pool, she put down her dry clothes and towels, anchored the torch between two rocks, and then waded into the cold water.

Rubbing the soap over the front of her tunic and pants, she scrubbed vigorously until Ryder's blood was no longer visible in the limited light of the torch. She struggled out of the wet, clinging garments, tossed them onto a rock, and thoroughly washed from head to foot. Diving under the water, she swam to the far wall of the pool, letting the motion of her strokes rinse away the soap.

The cut on her throat still burned. Pain radiated down her neck each time she moved her head. She knew the ugly wound would heal, and eventually be gone. *But it's sure to leave a scar, and probably an even deeper emotional one in my memory. If only I could rinse away the terror and memories of the past hours as easily as I can the soap.*

She broke the surface on a sob, began treading water, and turned to face the wall. Her reservoir of determination crumbled and gave way to the overflowing flood of emotion she could no longer contain. It forced her to tread hard in order to keep her head above the water as tears poured down her face, and gasping sobs cut off her breathing, echoing through the cavern in ghostly moans. Not wanting the sound of her distress to reach her friends, she choked down the sobs until their ghostly echoes diminished to mere mutters. *We're finally free, but the price of our freedom came within a breath of costing more than I would ever have been willing to pay.*

Several minutes slipped by before her torrent of tears gradually subsided into the eerie echoes of sniffing and hiccupping murmurs, but it felt good to release her pent up feelings over the horrendous events of the night. With that acknowledgement, a powerful spirit of gratitude unexpectedly enfolded her. She let its calming warmth fill her, and found she was no longer shivering.

Every one of us received heaven's help tonight. At every turn, the hand of the Lord intervened. She drew that infinitely peaceful understanding into her heart, and held it there, letting it grow and comfort her. Then inhaling her first truly comforting breath of freedom, she sank back under the water and swam beneath its surface, coming up a few yards from the edge of the pool.

When she was dry, with her hair turbaned in a towel, she applied the herbs, and Taya's makeshift bandage, over her still seeping wound. Dressed, she fell to her knees and poured out her gratitude to a very kind and caring Father. *I know you held all of us in your hands tonight, and we are alive—and free.*

Ryder stood in the mouth of the campsite cavern, and shouted through the tunnel, "Pilot, are you about done?"

"Yes," her voice echoed through the pool cavern and into the tunnel.

"Good, the soup's nearly ready," he shouted back, moving through the short tunnel, watching her progress by the steadily increasing light of the torch she carried.

When she reached the tunnel's mouth, he relieved her of the torch and peered down at her. "Are you alright?"

"Sure," she said not meeting his eyes. "How about you?"

"Terrific," he said heartily, modeling the towel strip bandages Taya had constructed and applied to his back in her absence. "The bleeding has almost stopped, and Taya's herbs have kicked in."

"That's good, but aren't you supposed to be lying down?"

He took her elbow, leading her over the last few feet of rough stones. "Well, it's hard to keep a good man down," he said in a self-mocking tone.

She stopped, and took his hand. "You are a good man, and I am very grateful you're my friend."

He managed a strained smile. *Why does that word feel like Cartu's whip, instead of the priceless gift it is?*

"Let's go eat; then you need to get some sleep." She squeezed his hand, let go of it, and walked into the cavern.

He stayed in the tunnel, wishing Taya had a strong herbal remedy for the emotional distress he felt. *There may be a remedy*, he acknowledged, *but how long will it take to build the defenses I need against my heart, and memories.* Huffing out a disheartened sigh, he followed Hadlee into camp.

Watching her platinum hair tumble out of the towel as she pulled it from her head, he acknowledged, *If I'm ever going to be able to school my mind and heart, I've got to have Zedekiah's help, and then employ endless amounts of prayer.*

Kytan looked up from the edge of the fire pit. "I don't know about you two, but I am starving."

Standing over the bubbling pots, Hadlee and Ryder inhaled the fragrant stew Taya was stirring, made from the dried meat, vegetables and herbs they had brought. Ryder's stomach growled, protesting its emptiness.

Hadlee smirked, but admitted she was finally hungry too.

"Let's pray so we can eat," Kytan said.

They knelt on Ryder's bedroll and held hands. Ryder prayed, pouring out his heart, and theirs, in gratitude for the Lord's intervention in their behalf. The fronts of their tunics were liberally spotted with the tears that fell freely from everyone's eyes by the time he finished blessing the food.

Without a word, they moved together and held on to each other, while the stew continued to bubble in the pots from Ryder's makeshift mess kit. When they finally broke their hug, they sat down in a tight circle with the soup pots in the middle.

Taya passed out ashcakes and handed out spoons. "I hope it is alright. At least it is warm," she said.

They ate in silence for a few minutes, breaking it only to complement Taya on the stew until she waved a dismissive hand, and said, "I would like to hear about everything that happened tonight." She paused, considering Ryder with worried eyes. "That is, if you aren't in too much pain.

Kytan took another ashcake, and said to Ryder, "So would I, but only if you are feeling well enough."

"Ryder looks exhausted," Hadlee said, glancing at him. "We probably ought to wait until tomorrow."

Ryder summoned a smile, touched by everyone's concern. "I'm fine." His lacerated back was throbbing with a dull, but manageable pain. "Taya's herbs are working, and there are some things I would like to know too. So, Taya, why don't you tell our fellow conspirators about our stay in the temple?"

Kytan's eyes grew to saucer size, as Taya ran through the highlights of what had happened in the temple. "I can't believe you two had the courage to defy a whole temple of spear wielding priests."

"I'm glad the bargain you made got you out of that first bug infested chamber," Hadlee said.

Kytan flashed Ryder a look that made him hang his head. "I told Taya you would have every right to kill me over that outfit, but I couldn't let her stay in that dungeon." He rubbed the back of his neck. Kytan patted his shoulder, and gave him forgiving dimples.

"I think Kytan would have punched the wall regardless of what Taya was wearing when he saw her chained to that horrible altar," Hadlee said.

Taya gasped, and reached for Kytan's hands.

"Don't worry, Hadlee kept me from doing it. I lost my temper for a moment," he said. "It was more than I could bear to see the two of you chained to those altars."

"I know. When I put Taya down on that pagan altar, I had the wildest urge to just grab her up again, and make a run for the balcony."

Taya patted his hand, "I only made it through that awful ordeal, and going through the water tunnel because of the blessing you—I mean the Lord—gave me."

Kytan kissed her cheek; then gripped his brother's hand. "Thank you for doing that. I know how frightened she was about coming through the water tunnel, and I can't even begin to imagine what you two went through on those altars."

Taya took Hadlee's hand, "Thank you for saving us."

"You were incredible, Pilot," Ryder whispered. "I even forgot about Darvoe's knife, when I saw you."

"So did everyone else," Kytan said. "My eye was glued to the peephole, and I didn't start breathing again until he and Ateron dropped their daggers and fell to their knees."

"Those were definitely my worst moments." Hadlee tensed as though warding off a shiver and found Ryder's eyes. "I wish you could have given me a blessing too," she whispered.

Ryder's heart gave a particularly hard thud of surprise. "So do I, but I was fasting for you."

"Me too," said Taya.

"That makes three of us," Kytan said.

Hadlee's eyes brimmed. "That certainly explains the incredible peace I felt. Thank you. I can't tell you how much your fasting helped me. I couldn't have made it through everything without it. I just wish that feeling of peace would have arrived before Darvoe dropped his dagger, and I almost passed out with fear," she said, and then laughed. "But you should have seen the look on his face when he saw me."

"Yes, and you should have seen the look on Ateron's face when he came to see her, just before the ceremony," Kytan said to Ryder.

"Oh?" Ryder turned to Hadlee.

She shrugged and sipped another spoonful of soup.

"I was so proud of her. She handled herself like a goddess while he leered at her. It took every bit of self-discipline I had not to punch him; especially when he told me there were new lines he wanted me to teach Hadlee, what they were, and then kissed her."

Ryder dropped his spoon. "What?"

"He just kissed my hand. It was so disgusting, I shivered—and he laughed." Hadlee dismissed the incident with a wave of her hand and reached for another ashcake. "So what were the new lines I was supposed to say? They must have been pretty awful because your face went completely dead, Kytan."

"At the end of your speech to the nobles, you were to lovingly take Ateron's hand, kiss him—and I mean *really* kiss him. Then declare your desire to comfort him over the death of Telsuea, by staying with him until you gave him the consolation of a son—who would be his heir."

Hadlee choked on her ashcake.

"I should have broken his neck," Ryder muttered under his breath, patting her on the back in an effort to ease her choking.

Hadlee took a gagging breath and caught Ryder's hand, warding off his continued thumping on her back. "I'm okay," she gasped. "Thank you, Kytan, for not telling me any of that. My stomach was sick enough just worrying over you sacrificial victims"—she nodded at Ryder and Taya—"and all the havoc I was hoping to wreak."

"Havoc is exactly what you did wreak, and I want to know how you two came up with that amazingly, impossible plan. I still can't believe it worked," Ryder said.

Taya gazed at Hadlee with wide-eyed curiosity. "Yes, tell us about the three days you two spent together."

Thirty-six

"Together is exactly what we were," said Hadlee. "After you two were taken to the temple, Ateron moved Kytan into your room, Taya."

"He needed someone involved in his plot to look after Hadlee's needs, and since I could also interpret, and help her practice her lines, the job fell to me."

"His decision to have Kytan move into the apartment played right into our hands." Hadlee grinned like a shark. "The arrangement was exactly what we needed to be able to work on our own plot."

"But how could you work on your plot with a guard always there?" asked Taya.

"As soon as you two were taken to the temple, Ateron quit making the guards stand inside the door," Hadlee said.

"Why?" asked Taya.

"I think he thought you two were enough insurance to keep us in line," Kytan said.

"Along with the fact none of the guards could understand what we were saying anyway, so there really wasn't any point. When they did poke their heads in, I simply started repeating Ansuetra's lines."

"They got pretty tired of hearing them, and eventually didn't poke their heads in at all." Kytan's dimples smirked. "The arrangement also allowed me to protect Hadlee from any unexpected visits from Ateron."

Ryder and Taya nodded their approval.

"I felt a lot safer with Kytan close at hand. He is the one that came up with the plan and he worked me like a slave for those three days, teaching me my new lines. I have to tell you, as much as we prayed about it—and felt like it was what we should do—I was still scared to death I was going to say something wrong, miss a line, or just pass out from stage fright."

"I have to admit, I was scared too and . . . not completely sure the plan would work," Kytan said with a sheepish display of dimples.

Hadlee made a face and threw a piece of her ashcake at him.

"But the idea came with such force, I couldn't dismiss it. Besides, it was the only thing I could think of to get you both out of there, without letting you fall back into Ateron's hands. And I admit; I did want to pay him back for all the trouble and pain he has caused us."

"Well it was an inspired idea, but how did you come up with it?" Ryder pressed.

Kytan rehearsed the plot he'd overheard to have Pel assassinated—because Ateron felt his loyalty was faltering and was afraid he might tell his father about the Moon Goddess deception.

"I think Ateron may have been right about that," Ryder said. "Whenever I saw Pel with the king, the tension between them was almost explosive."

"I tried to warn Pel, but I only got out a few words before we were interrupted. I kept trying to find another opportunity to tell him what I had overheard, but I was never alone with him."

"Poor Pel," Taya said, reaching for another ashcake.

"Yes, but he obviously didn't tell his father about the Moon Goddess deception. Lowanta would have put a stop to it. He wouldn't have allowed Ateron to deceive the people," Kytan said.

Hadlee smiled. "I knew I liked Lowanta, the minute I laid eyes on him."

"You and almost everyone else," Kytan said. "He is known as an honest, practical man, and his family is a prominent branch in the royal line of kings."

"Do you think that's why the people accepted Lowanta so readily?" Ryder asked.

"Yes. And it was his royal lineage, along with Ateron's plan to kill Pel that got me to thinking about the contrast between Ateron and Lowanta, and how different life in Injanae would be if Lowanta were the king."

"It sure would have been better for all of us," Ryder said.

"Yes." Hadlee's wet ponytail bobbed up and down.

"I don't understand what all of you are talking about? What did you and Hadlee plan, and what happened after we left? " asked Taya.

Ryder's lips twitched. "Hadlee dethroned Ateron—that's what happened."

Taya stared, at three maniacal grins. "How could you have possibly dethroned Ateron with Cartu and all his bodyguards right there?"

"Actually, Ateron's script made it easy. You know I was supposed to call Lowanta up and disband the noble's council. So when Ryder came back with the oil, I simply called Lowanta up, but instead of disbanding the council, I started to anoint him high priest and *king*—"

"That's when the fun started," Ryder interrupted, describing the battle between Ateron and his supporters, and Ansuetra and hers. "It looked like it was going to be a long fight until Hadlee used some of the most amazing magic I have even seen."

"Fire magic," Kytan said.

"Do you know how she did it?" asked Ryder.

Hadlee and Kytan exchanged looks.

"He knows," Taya said. "I can tell by his face." She poked her finger into Kytan's chest. "I want to know what Hadlee did, and how she did it."

"Forgive me, but I promised not to reveal the secrets."

"You can at least tell me what she did," Taya said.

With wicked delight, Ryder explained to Taya, what Ansuetra had done.

"I don't believe it," she said, when he finished.

"It's true. I watched her do it and I still don't have a clue how she did it."

"I watched her do it too. She had to practice it a few times to be sure she remembered how it worked, and could make it look convincing," Kytan said.

Ryder and Taya pleaded with Hadlee to share the secret of how she did the fire magic.

She gave them an elusive smile. "I'm not going to tell you. A magician never reveals how the tricks are done. I had to tell

Kytan, only because I needed his help with a couple of things. He gave me his solemn oath not to reveal how the magic works."

Taya pouted, "I think you are being very unfair."

"So do I," said Ryder.

When they continued with their pleading, Hadlee conceded, "Alright." She held up her hands. "I will give you two hints. First, the urn of oil I had you bring to me wasn't just for anointing a new king—there were a couple of tricks hidden in there."

Questions sprang off Ryder and Taya's lips.

Hadlee held up her hand dismissing them. "Secondly, I'll show you what I used to produce the fire, but that's all."

She got up, and came back with the bag of silver from her gown. After a few moments rummaging through it, she pulled out a rectangular, silver object, and tossed it to Ryder.

He caught it, rolled it over in his hand, and whooped, "Where did you come up with this?"

"David Willard gave them to all his pilots for Christmas last year. Most of them smoke, so they use them regularly. He wasn't going to give me one, but I told him I wanted one too because you never know when a little fire will come in handy—especially for a magician." She bowed with a flourish. "I forgot I had it with me, until I felt it in the pocket of my bomber jacket, the night we were on the roof."

"What is it?" asked Taya, touching the object in Ryder's hand.

"It's a Zippo lighter," said Ryder.

"What is a Zippo lighter?" Taya asked.

Ryder grinned, flipped the lid open, and brought the flame to life. Taya's eyes grew round with wonder. He handed her the lighter while Kytan explained. "A lighter holds fuel that can be ignited by quickly rolling your thumb over this little wheel." He pointed to it.

"May I try?" asked Taya.

"Go ahead," Hadlee said.

It took a couple of tries for Taya to roll her thumb down the wheel hard enough and fast enough to ignite a spark. When she succeeded, everyone cheered.

"So now you know the two basic secrets of the magic, and that's all I'm going to tell you."

"Aren't you going to show me the magic?" asked Taya.

"It takes a lot of preparation to do the magic, and I don't have the things I need, but when we get home I'll round up the stuff I need and do it for you—I promise."

"So how did you learn to do it?" Ryder asked.

"My cousin, Sky, taught me. He was fascinated with magicians in his early teens, and spent a lot of time going to magic shows. He volunteered to help pass out handbills, advertising the shows, and worked back stage with the props. In return for his free labor, the magicians taught him some of their tricks."

"Smart boy," Ryder said.

Hadlee smirked. "Not smart enough to keep from getting burnt several times while he learned the tricks." She paused, and confessed, "Actually we both singed our eye brows and lashes while we were learning to do the fire tricks, but it was so much fun."

Ryder chuckled. "You two sure must have been a handful to raise."

Hadlee's ponytail swung back and forth, "My poor aunt, you can't imagine what a disappointment I was to her. I was never interested in the girly things she wanted me to like. I was happier burning my eye lashes than putting mascara on them."

"How did you get your cousin to tell you the secrets of the fire magic, if a magician never tells?" Taya challenged her.

"I blackmailed him of course, with all the dastardly deeds I knew he'd done."

Ryder's shoulders shook with laughter that made him groan. "You know the more I hear about Sky, the more I would like to meet him. He was definitely a very bad influence on you."

Hadlee grinned. "Not as much as I was on him."

"So you used your magical powers to dethrone Ateron." Taya brought them back to the subject at hand.

Hadlee finished recounting the rooftop drama, and their exit through the revolving door.

"We thought we were home free. Ryder shook his head with disgust. "But when Pilot went into her bedchamber to change, Ateron was lying in wait for her. He held her hostage."

"How did you escape him?" Taya asked with a shiver that sent Kytan's arms around her.

Ryder's jaw hardened. His eyes darkened with a dangerous light as he recounted the sunqaras distraction and his leap for the knife.

Hadlee leaned up and kissed his cheek. "Thank you again for saving the life of a person that spent too many years hating you, and who intentionally hurt you. I'm sorry it took me so long to forgive you and see what a good man you are."

"So how long was it after you left the palace before you knew you were being followed?" asked Kytan.

It took Ryder a few seconds to recover himself. What Hadlee said, and the kiss she'd given him, made his heart pound in his ears. He came back with an effort, and focused on what Kytan had asked. Disgust hardened his face. "There again I was an idiot. I didn't see or hear anything until Sual yelled at us, and that was just before you showed up."

"And now we have arrived at my sore spot." Hadlee glowered at Ryder. "Suppose you two tell us about your Boy Scout complexes."

Taya nodded and scowled reproachfully at Kytan.

Undaunted by the girl's glowering looks, Ryder and Kytan exchanged an impenitent one of their own.

"If a Boy Scout complex means you two are overprotective and self-sacrificing, I have to tell you, women only appreciate that up to a point," Taya said.

"And that point comes when you try and get yourself killed to spare the not so helpless females," said Hadlee. She fixed Ryder with a frustrated expression, and demanded, "Do you have any idea how traumatizing it is to be left waiting, wondering, and worrying?"

Ryder shrugged. "If I had it to do over again, I'd make the same choice. Because you have no idea what it does to a man to see a woman he cares about in grave danger."

"Exactly," Kytan agreed. "It's part of our nature to defend women. You are asking us not to do what men have always done, and will continue to do, for women they care about."

Hadlee and Taya glared at their unrepentant faces.

"I can see it's useless to argue with you two," Hadlee finally said. "But my stomach is still angry with you Kytan—hauling me around like a sack of flour, and dragging me into the pool."

Ryder shared a broad smile with Kytan. "I knew you wouldn't fail me."

Hadlee rolled her eyes. "Okay, *first-class scout* Ryder, tell us what happened after *first-class scout* Kytan hauled me off. How did you escape those three guards? It must have been quite a fight for you to end up with those sword slashes on your back."

His lips twitched. "The hardest part of that fight was disabling those three clowns, without really hurting them. After all, they did help dig me out of the tunnel. I didn't want to do them any lasting damage."

"I hope you didn't lavish too much kindness on them. I'm sure they had every intention of killing you," Hadlee said.

"Well ma'am," Ryder said in his best western drawl, "I don't suppose they took what I did to them any too kindly." He tipped an imaginary cowboy hat to her and recounted the details. His recital was met by three astounded faces. He shrugged, "I didn't have time to be nice."

"Wait a minute, if they didn't give you those slashes—who did?" asked Kytan.

Ryder spat out the name like a curse, "Cartu."

Astonishment chorused out of the mouths of his companions.

"Yeah, he was following us too." He turned hard eyes on Hadlee. "And it wasn't me he really wanted."

Hadlee paled.

"Are you still sorry Kytan hauled you off?"

She opened her mouth to answer, her face set with defiance.

He held up a hand, "Before you say you still think I shouldn't have made Kytan get you out of there, I'll give you one guess how I came by my—slashes."

"A whip." Taya shuddered. "I thought so."

"Yes ma'am," he drawled. "The one Cartu had specially made, just for me."

The defiance on Hadlee's face turned to horror. "What happened?" she asked, massaging her brow as though it ached.

As Ryder described Cartu's unexpected attack, Hadlee's eyes became increasingly haunted. He finished with, "I think he had the same idea Ateron had about using you to regain power."

Hadlee wrapped her arms around her knees, shaking hard. Her reaction made Ryder feel like kicking himself. He'd seen that same reaction on the night he told her Ateron killed the queen, because of his desire to have her. Unwarranted guilt filled her face. He knew she was feeling responsible for what Cartu had done to him, to try to get to her.

Impulsively, he pulled her into his arms.

She sank into his embrace, and moaned, "You should be dead. How did you get away?"

He chuckled with sardonic amusement. "Cartu has never played baseball."

"Baseball?"

Grinning with real enjoyment down into her upturned face, he recounted his perfect pitch, and the result.

Kytan cheered, and Taya clapped. They hugged each other and laughed until tears rolled down their faces.

Hadlee sagged against his chest, relief trickled down her face. "I'm grateful Goliath won that round, but why did you drown?"

He wiped a tear from her cheek with his thumb, and told her about his hurried entrance into the pool. "You will have to tell me how I got out. I don't remember anything after I started pulling on the rope. That is, until I heard *your dictator's voice*"—he smiled down at her—"in my ear commanding me to breathe."

Hadlee tried to respond, fought her emotions, and shook her head.

A small sob from Taya brought his eyes to hers. "But if not," she whispered, wrapped in Kytan arms, "that's what I thought had happened to you."

His gaze shifted to Kytan, who took a few shaky breaths before he was able to relate finding him in the water tunnel, and gave an account of Hadlee's heroic efforts to save his life.

Holding back his feelings was impossible. He crushed Hadlee against his chest, leaned down, and returned the kiss she'd given him, tasting the salty tears that ran down her cheek. "I have taken so much from you. I'll never be able to tell you how eternally sorry I am for that. Thank you for forgiving me, and for fighting for my life."

Her arms carefully encircled his neck. She expressed her compassion for the burden of guilt he'd carried for so long, and accepted his gratitude. He held her in a gentle hug, even as he caught the look of sorrow that Taya and Kytan exchanged. Feeling the sting of their pity, he looked away.

Hadlee released her hold, and he reluctantly let her go. He could never tell her all his feelings, but at least she was willing to accept his gratitude, and what she'd done tonight told him she genuinely felt the forgiveness, and friendship she'd offered him, and for him, those were priceless gifts.

Thirty-seven

After only a few hours of sleep, the triumphant conspirators climbed their way out through the lava tube. Reaching the entrance shaft, they stood in the shadows letting their eyes adjust to the sunlight that streamed through the opening before gradually moving into the light, enjoying its warmth.

Ryder blinked up into the sunlight. Shading his eyes, he said, "The sun is past its zenith, so we need to get going. The hardest part of the day is still ahead of us."

He dropped the knapsacks, he insisted on hauling, and adjusted the long coil of rope he also carried, preparing to jump up, take hold of the shaft's rim, and pull himself up through it.

Kytan put a hand on his arm. "Let me do it. You need to take it easy."

Ryder hesitated, nodded, and backed up.

Kytan dropped the multiple knapsacks he was carrying, put his head and arm through the rope Ryder handed him, and adjusted it across his body. He crouched, took a deep breath and leaped.

He let out a whoop, dangling by his hands for a moment in the mouth of the shaft before pulling himself up and disappearing through the opening. A few moments later, the rope dropped through the shaft, and Kytan's head blocked the sun coming through the opening. "Baggage first please."

After all the knapsacks were out, Ryder climbed the rope Kytan had anchored to a boulder. Together, he and Kytan carefully pulled the girls up through the narrow shaft, one at a time.

"I can't tell you how glad I am to be above ground again, and out in the sun," Hadlee said as she sorted through the knapsacks for the ones she was assigned to carry. The others echoed the sentiments collecting the baggage they were responsible to carry.

Ryder settled four knapsacks over his shoulders, and again glanced up at the sun. "Let's go," he said, and took the lead up the steep, jagged steps toward the top of Farlana.

Over the next two hours, the ascent became more treacherous. Ryder paused before tackling the narrow step in front of him. It had jagged teeth like spikes that would require careful navigation. *Thank heaven for the long pants, boots, and gloves the girls made for us. If not for their protection, we'd all be sporting dozens of cuts and scrapes.*

The labored breathing beside him turned him to Hadlee. She was bent over, with her hands propped against her thighs, inhaling deep breaths through her nose and exhaling them through her mouth.

"We need to go single file from here on," he said. "The steps are going to get very narrow, and there isn't any guardrail." He looked at the diminishing distance between the cliff face and the crevasse. "We better tie up."

"Tie up?" Hadlee asked, looking up at him from her bent over position.

Ryder dropped his knapsacks and pulled the hefty coil of rope off his shoulder. "Yeah. Tying us all together will slow us down, but it will also give us a kind of walking guardrail, just in case someone stumbles or misses a step and starts to fall over the edge. Hopefully, with the rope attached to all of us, it will arrest an unexpected stumble, and keep it from turning into a fatal fall."

When they were all roped together, with Ryder in the lead and Kytan in the rear, Ryder went through the relay climbing they would use to keep the rope chain moving. It took ascending several steps, before they learned the rhythm of moving in a relay from step to step.

"This is a bit awkward, and certainly slower, but"—Hadlee looked over the edge of the crevasse—"it's definitely worth it."

Each step toward their goal, added to the conspirators' joy in their freedom, and led to a request for Ryder to sing. He told them he would only sing if they joined him. They agreed, and he taught them silly Boy Scout camp songs. They sang and laughed, enjoying the warmth of the afternoon as they climbed.

When they stopped to eat, on a couple of wider than average steps, Ryder removed the knapsacks he was carrying, and turned to set them on the step above him.

Hadlee yelped, "Your back."

The back of his tunic was bloodstained.

Taya scolded, "I told you, you shouldn't carry any of the knapsacks."

Hadlee leaped onto the step above him and shook her finger under his nose, "Quit being a Boy Scout and listen to your doctor. We can handle your load between us."

"Yes, and we don't need you fainting with the loss of blood," Taya said.

Ryder's expression took on a mulishly quality. "There's nothing wrong with my left shoulder. So I can just sling the bags over that one."

That comment brought on lectures from all three of his companions, but Taya's was the most effective. She drove home their points, making him wince, as she cleaned his back, applied ointment, and tore up his last towel for additional bandaging.

"Alright." Ryder raised his hands in a gesture of surrender when Taya finished. "I'll take it easy," he said, and then muttered under his breath, "At least for a while." When they started climbing again, he allowed the others to carry his burdens.

The climbing got harder as the hours passed, slowing the troop's progress down. When they took a short break, Hadlee began to speculate on the fate of Ateron and Cartu, now that Lowanta was King. "You know I don't approve of slavery," she said. "But in Ateron and Cartu's cases, spending the rest of their lives as slaves would only be just—after all the crimes they've committed."

"I agree, and actually, I'm not sure they deserve that much kindness," said Ryder.

Kytan frowned. "I hope we haven't started a civil war. Who knows how many people might still feel Ateron has the right to be king because of his lineage."

"But Ansuetra's support of Lowanta, and her disappearance, ought to convince even the guards that supported Ateron to rethink their position," said Taya.

"I agree," Hadlee said. "Only Ansuetra would have the power to leave Injanae. And fact she told Lowanta that Ryder was going with her, and he's now disappeared too, should be enough to convince everyone—including Ateron's guards—I really was Ansuetra, and my decrees must be obeyed."

"Let's hope so," Kytan said. "Hey, that makes Pel the heir to the throne."

"I don't think Injanae could have a better one. In the past several months, I've gotten to know him, and I think he is a good man." Ryder, shifted the two knapsacks, he'd finally convinced the others he could carry without inflicting more damage to his injured back, over his left shoulder.

"I have known him for six years," Taya said, "and you are right, Ryder, he is a good man." She stood as they prepared to resume their upward course.

"All in all, I would say we left Injanae in good hands. It's definitely in better shape than when I arrived," Ryder said.

Hadlee giggled to herself.

"What's so funny?" asked Ryder, turning on the step he'd just climbed to face her.

"There are going to be a lot of changes in Injanae," she prophesied. "You know when I was talking to Lowanta, I told him slavery was wrong, and he needed to abolish it."

"How?" Kytan's brows met. "I didn't teach you to say anything about abolishing slavery."

Taya cleared her throat, "You may not have, but I did."

"But you thought we shouldn't try to change Injanae."

"Well, after the argument you and Hadlee had, I thought about the issue. And during the week you and Ryder weren't allowed in the apartment, I taught Hadlee what to say."

"Good for you," Ryder said. "I feel a lot better now about leaving so many good slaves behind in Injanae."

The shadows were deepening into twilight when they reached the ledge that would be their camp.

Ryder looked the shelf over as he pulled off his climbing gloves. "This ledge felt pretty spacious when I slept on it two years ago, but with four of us . . . "

"It will be kind of cramped." Hadlee said, finishing his thought.

With darkness setting in, they hurried to arrange their camp for the night. By the time they sorted and stowed their gear, using the steps above and below the ledge to store their knapsacks and other gear, moonbeams were creeping into the narrow fissure, providing soft beacons of comfort against the blackness pressing in upon them. They diminished the darkness further by lighting one of their last torches. Wedging it in between a crack in the stairs, they had sufficient light to eat a cold dinner of smoked fish and ashcakes, before settling in for the night.

They were largely protected from the wind in the fissure's depths, but the temperature dropped uncomfortably with the darkness. They pulled on their warm alpaca fur coats, and wrapped their blankets around themselves.

Sitting with their backs against the cliff face, huddled together for warmth, Ryder voiced the thought he knew was running through everyone's mind. "I'm afraid it's going to be a long, uncomfortable night."

He reached up, retrieved his climbing hammer from his knapsack on the step above him and two of the long, barbed spikes Kytan had made. He pounded one into the cliff's rough face, knotted one end of the rope—they were all still tied to—and anchored it to the spike.

"These spikes won't hold our combined weight, but they will act as a constraint, keeping us from inadvertently sliding toward the ledge's edge during the night," he said, as Kytan pounded in the spike on his end, and anchored the rope to it.

Hadlee leaned her back against the cold cliff, "I know I won't be able to sleep," she said to Ryder. "Sitting up all night, hundreds of feet in the air, with an abyss only a few inches from my feet, is just a little too unnerving."

"After what you've been through over the past twenty-four hours, I think you'll sleep." Ryder slid his arm around her, pulling her against his side, hoping to make her feel safe, and keep her warm.

"No." She leaned forward. "You don't need me leaning against you, pushing your poor back into the cliff."

"As I told you earlier, there is nothing wrong with my left shoulder or side. Whether or not you let me help keep you warm—and help me stay warm in return—is of course, up to you. But leaning against the cliff is my only option," he said matter-of-factly.

She shivered, the cold air turning her cheeks pink "Well—if you're sure."

"I am."

She leaned tentatively back against his arm. He tightened it around her. She snuggled into his side. "Thanks. I feel warmer already."

The lack of sleep the night before and the exhaustion of the day's climb, caught up with her—just as Ryder had predicted. Before long her head sagged against his shoulder.

Ryder looked over at Taya and Kytan situated on the other side of Hadlee. Kytan's arms encased Taya, her head lay against his chest, and his rested on top of hers. They were a picture of happy contentment.

Envy dug in its spurs.

Closing his eyes, he leaned his head back against the hard face of the cliff, but sleep didn't come. His back throbbed painfully. Holding Hadlee didn't help, but nothing could have kept him from doing it. He resettled his shoulder and tried to relax. *Exhaustion should put me to sleep, not to mention Taya's herbs.* But his brain and emotions just wouldn't shut down. He finally had to admit, *it's impossible to sleep away what might be the last time I get to hold Hadlee in my arms.*

Those first distressing days after they met again, filled his mind. *I fought hard against my feelings for you, Pilot,* he mused, gazing down at her face glowing in the torchlight. *But fighting my feelings was like trying to fight against the pounding force of the falls. I just didn't possess the strength to do it, and after a while . . . I honestly didn't want to.*

The succeeding days and weeks he'd spent with her, wading through pain and grief, finding and sharing forgiveness—even the little joys and deadly danger they'd experienced—intensified his feelings; until he couldn't deny what his heart had tried to tell him from the first moment he'd seen Hadlee MacLean—over twelve years ago. *There will never be anyone that fills my heart like you do, Pilot,* he lamented, knowing each passing moment drew him closer to that final moment when he'd have no choice, but to let her go.

He shifted the pressure on his back, again resettling his left shoulder. *If I tell her how I feel, it's sure to destroy even the fragile friendship we have.* That thought made him tighten his arms around her.

She inhaled a soft, sleeping breath and repositioned her head.

Glad not to have woken her, he couldn't resist lightly kissing the top of her head. He sighed, and stared out into the darkness. *Tomorrow we'll summit Farlana. That means home is only a few weeks away.*

Because their focus for so long had simply been to escape Injanae, he hadn't really thought about what would happen after they were free. *Hadlee will very likely go back to the life she had before Injanae, and just forget she ever met me.* The thought inflicted a wound more painful than Cartu's whip. He backed away from it, and told himself, *she will want me in her life—just as a friend.* That probability came with its own barbed question. *Can I stand to be near her, and be just a friend?*

Gazing down on her face lightly flushed with sleep, he couldn't hide from the answer. *No. Being near her and never being able to give her my heart or have hers in return, would be more than I could endure. It will be better if she does just forget she ever met me,* he decided, enduring the first lashes of grief.

Her head drooped against his chest. She snuggled closer to him, shivering slightly. He tucked her blanket more tightly around her.

It still amazed and humbled him that she had fought so hard for his life. The life of a man she had hated for so many years. *It says so much about her character, her friendship, and the genuine forgiveness she extended to me.* He knew those things were the source of the hope he couldn't rid himself of. *You must be getting delirious if you can hope—even for a single moment—that the daughter of the woman you killed, could love you.* Leaning his head back against the cold cliff face, he closed his eyes, and fought the aching in his heart. *What I want her to feel for me is something from a fairytale. It's that far removed from reality.*

Thirty-eight

Fingers of pale light reached into the crevice. Ryder blinked, surprised he had slept. He yawned and smiled. Hadlee's head was resting against his chest and her arm was flung around him.

How many days do I have left with you? Every step takes us closer to saying good-bye. With that inevitable moment looming ever closer, he wanted to hold on to each moment, and this moment, for as long as he could.

Too soon, the strengthening rays of the sun found Hadlee's eyes through the silky curtain of hair draping her face. Lifting one heavy tress away from her eyes, Ryder smiled down at her.

She smiled back at him. "Hi," she said softly, turned a rosy hue, and took her head and arm off his chest. She looked over at Kytan and Taya. As they began to stir, she whispered to Ryder, "I think there is going to be an engagement announcement very soon. I've seen the ring."

"Have you?" He chuckled, and struggled to his feet.

Sitting up all night in one position made his muscles tight and sore. He stretched and groaned, painfully aware of his lacerated back as he tried to get his circulation going.

"Sleeping on a ledge, tied to three other people, might be an adventure, but it leaves a lot to be desired in comfort." Hadlee covered a yawn, rubbed her shoulders, and reached for one of the food bags.

"We've got a hard day's climbing ahead of us, but we should reach the summit late this afternoon," Ryder said, eating nuts, cold ashcakes, and dried fruit. "Then, it will probably take us about seven or eight days to walk out to the nearest village. We can find transportation from there to Lima."

Kytan and Taya shared a smile. "How long will it take us to get to the United States?" asked Kytan. "Taya and I want to get married as soon as we get there."

Hadlee and Ryder laughed, congratulated, and hugged them.

"We wondered how long it would be before we heard that announcement. Show Ryder the ring, Taya," Hadlee said.

Taya put out her small hand.

Ryder took it, examining the delicate diamond ring she proudly wore on the third finger of her left hand. "It's even more amazing than my arm band," he said, squeezing her hand. "You know, I am looking forward to the very old and hallowed custom of kissing the bride."

"Is that part of getting married in America?" asked Taya, blushing.

Ryder gave her a wolfish grin.

"I don't think I like that American custom." Kytan frowned at Ryder who exchanged a mischievous wink with Hadlee.

"It's not precisely American, probably English," Hadlee said thoughtfully.

"Don't worry brother." Ryder just couldn't help teasing him. "You will still get the girl, but only after all the men get a kiss."

"Stop it, Ryder," Hadlee said, laboring to keep a straight face. "Taya won't want to get married, if you make her believe she is going to get mauled by every man at her wedding."

Taya's horrified expression put an end to the teasing, but it took a while to convince her they were only kidding.

Hadlee gave her arm a reassuring pat. "Honestly, Taya, no one's going to kiss you except Kytan . . . and maybe Ryder—if Kytan lets him."

The morning sun, now bursting above the eastern peaks, filled the crevasse. Taya and Hadlee packed up the food, and everyone reloaded their knapsacks. Kytan checked the rope. Ryder told him to take the lead, and with stiff, aching muscles, they again set off up the stairs.

Late afternoon shadows filled the valley bowl, and were beginning to mask the rugged mountains surrounding Injanae, by the time the climbers could see the end of the stairs. They paused on a small shelf about thirty feet below the top of Farlana to shift positions. Ryder took the lead as the troop resumed trudging up the remaining steps.

The troop cheered when they finally reached the cliff face.

Hadlee leaned back against it. "I thought . . . we'd . . . never make it," she said, trying to catch her breath.

Taya swayed with exhaustion. Kytan's arm went around her as she sagged against him. He wiped the sweat from his face with his sleeve, and blew out a long breath. Taya opened her mouth to add her sentiments to Hadlee's, gulped in a breath, and settled for simply nodding her agreement.

Ryder looked down into the crevasse where the shadows were deepening into blackness and reaching up toward them. Taking hold of the old rope he'd used to descend into the crevasse, he gave it a tug and told the troop, "It would be easier to just climb up this rope. It still looks pretty good, but I'm afraid it's like the rope in the water tunnel, time and the elements have taken their toll, so it wouldn't be wise to trust it."

After a review of how to wear the climbing harness, and clip it onto the rope he would lower, Ryder strapped himself into the harness.

"You really shouldn't be the one doing this," Hadlee said. "You know hauling all of us up will break open your back again."

Kytan put a hand on his shoulder, "It will, you know. Why don't you let me do it?"

Ryder's back throbbed, agreeing with his friends, and letting him know he needed more pain medication, but he didn't want to take another dose until they were settled for the night. He scanned the face of the cliff, and set his jaw.

"We need to be out of this crevasse before the shadows reach us. I would say that gives us less than an hour." He handed Kytan the end of the rope he was attached to and said, "Sorry brother, but you just don't have the experience, and skill I've got to make a technical climb. We will all be on top faster if I do it." He patted Kytan's shoulder and reached for his first handhold.

His progress was slow and inching as he hammered in pitons, attached carabineers, found another crack or bump to pull himself up with, and started the process over again. At fifteen feet, he paused, and looked down.

Hadlee's teeth tugged at her lip, her fingers worried her braid. She called up, "I think this is the scariest part of our escape. There is literally only a thin rope, a few small metal rods, and your skill, between you, and death."

Taya took her hand, her expression as concerned as Hadlee's.

Ryder smiled down at the girls. "Don't worry. I'm very good at this. Besides Kytan is on belay, so I'm safe."

Ten feet later, Ryder pulled himself up, searched for, and secured a toehold and started hammering in another piton. The small knob his foot was on, crumbled under his weight, sending him, and a small shower of grainy pebbles, down the cliff face.

Hadlee shrieked his name.

The rope he was attached to jerked him to a stop after a bone-wrenching drop of five feet. Pain ripped across his back.

Head pointed down, he looked at his friends.

Kytan's muscles bulged with the effort to hold him. Hadlee too, had hold of the rope. She was straining backwards with all her might, her face dead white. Taya stood behind the pair, her hand over her mouth. The fingers of her other hand gripped the back of Kytan's tunic.

"Oops," Ryder called down sheepishly, swinging like a pendulum. "Apparently my skills have slipped some."

He reached for the old rope that hung down the cliff face, righted himself, and secured his position. He felt the rope slacken, and called down, "Are you ready for me to start again?"

"No!" Hadlee abruptly sat down, hugged her knees, and buried her face on top of them.

Idiot, you nearly scared the life out of her, he chastised himself. "I'm okay, and I promise I'll be more careful."

"Go ahead," Kytan yelled.

He gave Kytan thumbs up and started back up the face of the cliff.

Warm blood trickled down his back. "Not again," he said under his breath, fighting the fiery sensation that ran along his lacerations. He pushed the pain to the back of his mind and concentrated, taking his time to be sure of each grip and toehold as he continued to move up the face of the cliff.

When he finally stood on top Farlana, he shouted his victory down to his companions, and watched Hadlee's head come up from her knees. He waved briefly and turned away. With the sun already far to the west, he didn't waste any time pulling up the old rope. After detaching it from the boulder that anchored it, he tied the new one he'd carried up with him in the old one's place. Walking back to the edge, he looked over. "Send up the baggage," he shouted down, dropping the new rope over the edge.

Kytan threaded the rope through the straps of the four food bags, the one remaining wood bag, and their personal knapsacks.

Ryder reeled them in, his back protesting every movement of his arms. He quickly untied the bags. *The sooner everyone is on top, the sooner I can rest.*

He stepped to the edge.

Hadlee was first in the line to follow the baggage up. She looked up at him, her eyes wide with fear.

"Hey, Pilot, you ready for some adventure?" He threw the question at her like a dare, intentionally reminding her of how brave he thought she was.

She lifted her chin, "You bet. Lower the rope."

He grinned and lowered the rope and harness into her waiting hands. She strapped herself into the harness and let Kytan check it.

"I'm ready!" she shouted.

Ryder yelled, "Put your hands at about eye level on the rope and lean back so you are sitting. Your legs and torso should form an L. Then put your feet against the cliff, and walk up the wall as I pull. Got it?"

"Yes!" She leaned back, bracing her feet against the cliff.

Ryder backed away from the edge of the cliff, found a small boulder he could use to brace himself, and began to pull hand over hand. When the top of Hadlee's head rose above the summit, he secured the rope to the boulder, and ran forward. Taking hold of the harness, he lifted her over the top, setting her on her feet.

The peace he had hoped to find when he climbed Farlana two years ago filled him. It felt even more complete than the night on the roof when Hadlee told him about her dream.

Hadlee's smile made his knees go weak. He swallowed, dislodging the lump in his throat and returned her triumphant smile.

She fumbled trying to undo the harness. His hands automatically reached to help. Dropping the harness, he swung her around in a circle—the pain in his back forgotten—threw his head back and shouted, "We are free."

Laughing, she echoed the words.

Their celebration was cut short by shouts from the cliff below them. "Anytime you are ready, we would like to come up too!" Kytan said.

Taya laughed as she walked up the wall. "This is exciting, not like going through that horrible water tunnel," she shouted down to Kytan. She let go of the rope with one hand, waved down at him, and came over the top cheering, joining the freedom celebration.

Ryder threw her into the air like a rag doll, and caught her. Hadlee folded her into her arms, almost squeezing the life out of her. They laughed, danced, and held on to each other.

Lowering the rope for the last time, all three pulled up Kytan. He reached the top complaining the trip up the cliff was too short.

"I would like to try doing a technical climb," he said wistfully.

Ryder responded by jerking him off his feet and dropping him back over the cliff. His gloved hands allowed the rope, still attached to Kytan, to move in a controlled way, through his fingers.

Taya screamed, and Ryder laughed.

Kytan only dropped fifteen feet before the rope pulled taut against the boulder where Ryder had looped it. A somewhat penitent Kytan pulled himself up the rope to the top again.

He and Ryder exchanged wry faces.

Taya scolded, "You two and your antics are going to be the death of me."

"Look." Hadlee saved the men from Taya's wrath by pointing out the majesty of the vista before them with a sweep of her arm.

The conspirators were instantly mesmerized by the grandeur of the saw-toothed peaks surrounding the valley of Injanae. The top of the valley's eastern peak was still brilliantly lit with sunlight that slowly faded into twilight down its jagged face.

The eyes of the group dropped into the deeply shadowed valley. They stood on the edge of the dragon's head in silence. The heavy hand of solemnity pressed in upon them. Each in turn reflected on how their life had been shaped, or changed by Injanae as they gazed down upon it—without regret—for the last time. Clinging to one another, they shared the consensus of never forgetting what Injanae had taught them.

Ryder raised his fists, the others followed suit. "Freedom!" they chorused, their voices echoing along the tops of the peak, exalting in their victory.

"It's already twilight, and we can't go down the mountain in the dark"—Ryder broke the long and joyful group hug—"so we need to find another ledge or ridge on the other side that will protect us from the wind till morning."

They crossed over to the western side of the dragon's scaly head and worked their way south until Ryder spotted what he hoped to find. He led them down a steep, ragged route, across a craggy horizontal face, and into a rocky cleft. The wind immediately ceased to buffet them. The cleft wasn't large, but it was bigger than the ledge they had spent the previous night on, and much better protected.

Kytan and Ryder left the girls to settle in, while they went to look for more fuel for a fire. All they had left was the rope Ryder used to descend two years ago, the remaining half full bag of wood they brought through the water tunnel, and two torches. It wasn't likely, but Ryder hoped they might be able to find some kind of burnable debris, carried up by the wind.

Darkness fell, and they were able to make an adequate fire. "It won't last all night," Ryder said relaxing into the relief of another dose of herbs, and more new bandaging, courtesy of Hadlee's towel.

"No, but after such a hard day, it's nice to have a fire's warmth and cheerful comfort, even for a little while," Hadlee said, as they sat around it, ate hot stew, and listened to the joyful plans Kytan and Taya began making.

As the fire dwindled, they rolled themselves into blankets. The wind dropped, and the stillness of the night closed in around them. Exhaustion from the past two days of strenuous climbing overcame them, and sleep's welcoming arms claimed them.

Thirty-nine

Ryder awoke with a start. He immediately felt the throbbing of his back. Yet, he was sure that wasn't what had stirred him into wakefulness. He shifted, repositioning himself, surveyed the camp, and listened to the sounds of the night.

Nothing remained of the fire except glowing embers. He sat up and put the few sticks of wood still sitting at the edge of the fire ring carefully on the glowing embers. They blazed up enough to warm his hands and give him a better view of his friends, sleeping soundly.

You deserved it, he told them silently, *each of you conquered Farlana without complaint, and I know all of you paid a high price in sore hands, feet, aching muscles, and many painful scrapes.* He smiled with admiration at his exhausted friends.

Wide-awake and restless, he quietly got up, and climbed the short distance to the summit of Farlana. Coming up over the top, he shaded his eyes against the light of the full moon that nearly blinded him.

It was enormous. Hanging in the sky as though it was straight across from him, so big he felt he could reach out and touch the white orb. *The light that rules the night,* he mused. *Something the Lord made.* Mesmerized by the moon's shining face, he followed a moonlit trail to the eastern edge of Farlana.

A profound reverence settled over him. Gratitude swelled his heart for everything the Lord had done for him in the past few months, weeks, days, and even hours. He knelt down on the scaly head of the dragon. Lifting his voice, he poured out his soul to his Heavenly Father, ending with his confession of love for Hadlee. "Please help me find the words to tell her how I feel and the strength to accept whatever relationship she is willing to have with me."

In the wee hours of the previous morning, he'd decided to tell her how he felt. He couldn't stay in the limbo of uncertainty; torn between the impossible hope her forgiveness and friendship inspired, and the despair of knowing how much he'd cost her over the past twelve years—something that might forever limit her feelings for him.

He could face the despair her rejection would bring, and eventually move on with his life—he told himself. Then confessed, "What I can't bear is to let her walk away from me, not knowing if there is any hope she can return my feelings, and then wonder for the rest of my life. No matter how much it hurts, I have to know."

Certainty was sure to bring pain, but also release. He knew only hearing the words of rejection from her mouth could put an end to his impossible hopes, allow him to let her go, and move on with his life.

Coming to his feet, he stood for a long time just gazing at the moon that seemed to move closer to him with each passing minute.

The sound of rocks, disturbed by feet, made him turn.

A vision was walking toward him in the moonlight. A halo of silver-white waves blew out around her shining face. Following a moonbeam path, she gingerly picked her way through the rocks. Captivated, he put out his hand, and went to meet the vision.

Hadlee absently laid her fingers in Ryder's hand, accepting his help over the rocky ground, her eyes riveted on the glory of the moon. He led her to where the edge of the mountain met the sky. They stood side by side on the top of the world, just a little below heaven. Bathed in white light, they silently contemplated the wonder of the moon.

Minutes slipped by before Hadlee finally broke the silence. "Magnificent."

"Exquisite," the deep voice at her side whispered.

She turned to him, but he wasn't looking at the moon. The light from it was so bright she could see the molten gold of his eyes. They were looking at her in a way that made her heart begin to pound. She became conscious that her hand was in his. She began to withdraw it, but he didn't let go.

"I never really told you what made me climb this mountain."

"If I remember correctly, you told me you came to slay this dragon."

"Yeah, but this mountain only represented a dragon I was trying to slay in my soul."

Her brows knit together, "I'm not sure I understand you." When he was silent, she prompted, "Please, I would like to know."

"It's a little strange and complicated," he said, his eyes watching the moon begin to rise above the edge of Farlana. "You know I grew up in Colorado. From the time I could walk, my dad was dragging me up a mountain. He told me it would build character." He laughed dryly. "He was wrong about that, at least for a long time, but after the accident, after I got out of prison—"

She winced on the word, drawing his eyes.

"I deserved to be there, Pilot. It was part of the price of my repentance, and it, along with your dad, my parents, and a great bishop, helped me straighten out my life. So it was a good thing—the best thing that could have happened to me."

Pushing back a long strand of windblown hair that tickled her face, she let her frown inform him that she didn't completely agree with his assessment.

He paused, seeming to gather his thoughts. "After I got out, I started college. It was really hard. In prison I didn't have many choices or decisions to make about how I used my time, what I wanted, or was allowed to do. You know how that feels."

"Yes, I most certainly do." She squeezed his hand with understanding.

"When I started college, no one was making my decisions for me, and I found there were lots of choices and decisions to make—not to mention problems. My need for answers and direction made me start climbing mountains again."

His arm swept the peaks surrounding Injanae, his expression telling her how much he loved them. But to her, they now looked like dark phantoms, baring sharp, angry teeth at the moon they hated for towering over them. She looked away from them and back at the friendly face of the moon that seemed to smile down upon them.

"I found climbing was a good opportunity to have long conversations with heaven. Something about the solitude, and the effort it took, helped me focus and sort through whatever was troubling me. It developed in to . . . I'm not sure what to call it . . . a need, I guess. I began to look for mountains I thought were high enough, or hard enough for each particular challenge I was facing. The mountain became the problem, climbing it brought the solution. And it worked for me, every time—with one exception."

"The accident," she said flatly.

"Partly; I'd made peace with most of it, but there was still one lingering . . . dragon."

"Me," she whispered, with unexpected certainty.

"Your eyes—haunted me." For a brief moment, his face showed the sorrow and anguish that had lived there for far too long. "I'd never seen eyes so clear, so pure . . . so innocent. And I changed them. I watched them take in horror that should never have touched or tainted them. I couldn't rid myself of the anguish and hate I saw in your eyes. They were always there accusing me—not that I didn't deserve it— but at times the torment was like a dragon breathing fire through my soul."

So that's how you have thought of me all these years, as a fire-breathing dragon. She dropped her eyes, and kicked a small rock over the edge of the mountain.

"During my mission, the dragon slept. After I came home, the dragon began to stir, just a little at first. Then a couple of months before I graduated, the dragon came alive with a vengeance, and I knew I needed to find the right mountain."

"I'm so sorry," she said, pushing more small rocks over the edge of the peak with her toe; then suddenly wondered at her lack of fear, standing so close to the edge of the dragon's head.

She became acutely aware of Ryder's strong hand, holding tightly to hers. *Is that why I feel safe?* A small frown puckered her brow, but she didn't try to withdraw her hand.

"You have no reason to be sorry," he murmured. "It was then that I remembered something an old Incan named

Tupac told me in my last area of service as a missionary, in Argentina. While I was there, I learned an Incan dialect from him." He shrugged. "I have a talent for languages."

"You certainly do," she said, thinking of how well he spoke Injanae.

"Tupac could trace his ancestors back over six hundred years. He told me some amazing stories, but the one that stayed with me was about a mountain shaped like the head of a dragon."

"Farlana."

"Yeah, he also gave me the same warning Pucara did about the dragon guarding a forbidden place, surrounded by evil, and that no one who went there ever came back." He shook his head wryly. "I didn't believe it of course."

"I bet you wish you had."

"No, Pilot I don't." He stepped back from the edge, pulling her out of a strong updraft that suddenly burst out of the dark chasm and over the rim of the peak. "My heart told me this mountain was what I needed to finally defeat my dragon. My poor parents thought I was going off the deep end when they asked what they could give me for graduation. They had their eyes on a brand new Ford. " He chuckled. "I told them I would rather climb a mountain in Peru."

"You really *are* nuts," she said, gathering her wind blasted hair with one hand and pulling it over her shoulder. "So you came here to climb Farlana to learn how to slay your dragon."

"Yeah."

"And what did you learn?" She searched his face, while her fingers rotated around her hair, twisting it into a rope.

"When I came over the top, I knew what I had to do."

Their eyes locked.

"I knew I had to find you. That didn't make sense to me at the time. The last thing in this life I wanted to do was look into your eyes again, but I knew it was the answer I sought. When we met again, and I looked into your eyes, I immediately knew why."

"Because I hadn't forgiven you, and you needed my forgiveness to find complete peace."

"Yeah."

"You have my forgiveness, Ryder, and I am at peace."

"But I haven't been—not completely—not until today."

Her face puckered with confusion. "I'm not sure I understand. I thought my dream, and forgiveness, brought you the peace you were seeking."

He tugged on her hand, and they walked over to a large flat boulder and sat down.

"It did, but it didn't totally vanquish the dragon," he said. "What I needed to completely slay this dragon . . . was to climb this mountain with you."

The perplexity on her brow, deepened. "Why would climbing Farlana with me allow you to finally vanquish your dragon?"

He was silent, seeming to struggle for the words he wanted. She waited patiently, wanting to understand.

"When you told me about the baby, and your dad abandoning you, I finally realized how deep the anguish I put in your eyes had become for you. It had become a dragon living inside you. I think that's why your eyes continued to torment me, and why the peace I longed for eluded me. I knew then I would never find peace unless you did. Helping you find peace, and regain your freedom, were the only things that could slay the dragon that tormented both of us."

"You're right," she admitted with growing understanding. "My unforgiving heart, and hidden guilt, was a dragon inside me, tormenting me, giving me no rest."

"We have been fighting the same dragon for twelve years, without knowing it, until six months ago. To me, everything we've gone through, since we met again, has been this mountain, *this dragon.* Climbing Farlana together was like conquering our past, and leaving it behind us, giving us both a new start. Something we needed each other's help to do."

A brilliant smile of comprehension grew on her lips. "Yes!"

"Today, when I pulled you to the top of this beast, and we stood here together on his head, I knew we'd finally slain it, and we were free to pursue futures that would never again be threatened by our dragon. And the joy I felt—I can't express it—but it was freedom and complete peace."

His voice radiated the peace she had felt in her dream. It again filled her heart. "When I learned I was Ateron's prisoner, and would need your help to get out of Injanae, I thought it was the cruelest injustice." She lifted her chin, and met his eyes, "I know now it wasn't an injustice or even an accident that we met again."

"No, it wasn't. Injanae, for all its horror, forced us together, made us face our dragon, and finally find the right swords to slay it."

"Repentance and forgiveness are mighty swords, but I couldn't have wielded them by myself," she admitted.

"And I tried to wield them by myself, and it didn't work—not completely."

"Because we needed not only the Lord, but each other to wield the swords before we could slay this dragon, didn't we?"

"Yeah, we did."

She squeezed his hand, "Thank you for helping me slay this terrible monster. I never could have done it without meeting you again. It would have lingered in my soul and tormented me all my life. It's been so hard—so painful." She brushed the sudden dampness from her eyes. "I'm grateful now that we met, and helped each other climb this mountain, vanquish this dragon, win our peace, and finally our freedom."

He took a deep breath and blew it out, slowly. "So am I—but, I still have one more mountain I need to climb."

Forty

Hadlee's puzzled expression made Ryder feel like the physical torture Cartu had inflicted on his body had been far less painful and infinitely less terrifying than what he was about to do. Sending a prayer by way of the moon, he gathered his courage.

"For years, I thought your eyes haunted me because of my guilt, and that was certainly true. Then I met those eyes again, and knew it wasn't just guilt, and never had been."

Hadlee's hand, resting in his, trembled. He took her other hand, and looked at them. "That night on the roof when you offered me your hand in friendship, I finally admitted to myself that I needed to climb one more mountain." He raised his eyes and claimed hers. "But I don't know if there is a mountain high enough or hard enough on the face of the earth that will solve this particular problem."

"What is the problem?" she asked; the trembling moving from her hands to her voice.

"What I want—may be impossible, but Pilot, I don't just want to be your friend. I want to be . . . your family."

Her face turned to stone. She snatched her hands away and jumped off the boulder. Turning her back on him, she threw the words over her shoulder, "If you're trying to make some sort of restitution by sacrificing yourself to me on the altar of duty, it's unnecessary, I assure you. I don't need or want your sacrifice, your pity, or your Boy Scout chivalry."

He rocked backwards, closing his eyes. Even though the blow was expected, it still landed with the full weight of a knockout punch. His fingers splayed out and pressed against the unyielding surface of the rock, seeking balance, but the blow she inflicted, leveled him. Her words ran without mercy through him. Each one felt like the lash of a whip. They flailed him until understanding came.

His eyes flew open. *Does she really believe all I feel for her is guilt, and that I proposed to her out of some kind of misguided sense of duty?* As careful as he'd tried to be, he was sure he'd given himself away a dozen times or more. *She really doesn't know!* Astounded, he came to his feet. *Somehow, I have to convince her, what I feel doesn't have anything to do with duty, or guilt.*

"Wait," he called, as she stalked back to the west side of the peak.

Her rigid back and forbidding stride, told him there wasn't a chance she would ever want his heart. He gritted his teeth. *Whether she wants it or not, it belongs to her, and always will. I can't let her go until she understands that.*

"Pilot, please"—he chased her down—"there's something you have to understand." Gently taking her shoulder, he turned her to face him.

He was unprepared for her tears.

She averted her face, wiping them hastily away.

His hands shot out, encircling her waist. She gasped when he lifted her from the ground and brought her eyes level with his.

"I needed your forgiveness to find peace, but I need you to be complete. I love you, Pilot, and I have since the first moment I saw you. I want forever with you." He drew her to him until their faces were only inches apart. "If it takes another mountain to prove how much I love you, you name it, and I'll climb it for you."

Forty-one

Hadlee's heart beat wildly. She pressed her hands against his hard biceps, pushing away from him. She searched his face, unable to control the kaleidoscope of emotions she knew was running rampant over hers.

The love shining in his gilded eyes took her breath away, and closed her throat. A tear trickled down her cheek. Her chin trembled, and it felt like eternity passed before she could command her voice.

His face told her it was twice that long for him.

"You don't need to climb another mountain for me." Her chin quivered. *"This mountain will do."*

Her hands moved up along the incredible muscles of his arms.

His eyes searched hers.

She slid her fingers into his windblown hair, pulled his face to hers, and brushed his lips with a whisper of a kiss.

His hands left her waist as his arms encased her.

She pressed her hand against his heart and felt it go still as though it was afraid to beat, afraid to believe what was happening between them. "Mine?" she asked.

His heart came alive with a lurching beat, and then another, until it was beating a hard, erratic cadence under her hand.

"For all time," he said hoarsely.

A heartbeat later, his lips claimed hers in a kiss soft with wonder, almost disbelieving.

She tightened her arms around his neck with encouragement.

His kiss deepened to hope, and intensified with honesty, telling her of all the love he hadn't dared express.

She felt his desire for her trust; his longing for her love— his plead to share eternity.

By the time his lips released hers, her heart harbored no doubts about his feelings. Breathless, she looked into his adoring face, and confessed, "I tried so hard not to care for you. It felt like such a betrayal of my mother."

His face clouded.

She hurriedly continued, "But then, in my dream, after Mama forgave us, she told me I shouldn't let the past rob me of my future. She was looking at you and smiling when she said it." She leaned in and kissed the corner of his mouth.

His dumbfounded expression told her he hardly dared to believe his ears. "Your *mother* gave you her approval of me?"

"Yes," she admitted. "I . . . umm . . . omitted that part when I told you about the dream."

"Why?" The question held hurt reproof.

"How could I tell you that, when I thought all you felt for me was your Boy-Scout duty, and a whole lot of guilt?" She ran the tip of her finger over his lips, sparking a fire in his eyes.

He kissed her teasing finger.

"The only time I even thought you were interested in me romantically was when you danced with me, but then you didn't do anything else. You just treated me like your kid sister."

"You have no idea what that cost me. I knew I scared you that night, if not repulsed you. I backed off because you sent me the unmistakable message you weren't pleased or comfortable being close to me."

She ran the tip of her finger down the gentle crease in his chin and confessed, "I definitely didn't want your interest then. All I wanted was your help to get out of Injanae, and to be forgiven."

"When did you first start feeling differently about me?" He leaned in, kissing her lightly.

Her face pinched with distress. "When you were buried in the tunnel, I had to admit to myself, I cared about you. More than I ever thought I would, or could."

"That scared you didn't it—your feelings, I mean." He pushed a windblown strand of hair out of her face.

"Uh-huh." Her fingers traced the scar at his hairline. "I thought nothing could be worse than the day of the accident, but those hours waiting to know if you were alive were the worst of my life. Well . . . until you drown." She shivered with that memory.

He warmed her with the intensity of a soft, lingering kiss.

Putting her hands on the sides of his face, she confessed, "Letting you out of my arms that night was so hard. All I wanted to do was hold you, and kiss you, and tell you . . .," her voice broke.

"What?" he asked, gently leaning his forehead against hers.

She pulled back, and looked intently into the most incredible eyes she had ever seen, "I love you Ryder Garrison, and I want to be your family too."

Liquid gold glistened in his eyes. He set her back on the ground, took both her hands, and dropped to his already buckling knees. "Then marry me Hadlee MacLean."

Gazing into his handsome face, glowing with hope and love, overlaid with more than a little pleading, she couldn't keep from kissing him. She put her whole heart into it, expressing all the love she'd hidden from him, giving him her heart, making him its guardian, entrusting him with her happiness, promising him forever.

"Does that answer your question?" she murmured against his lips.

Leaping to his feet, he again swept her up into his arms, and whirled her around "Then at your earliest possible convenience, we're going to the temple of your choice."

"Manti—that's where my parents were married."

"Mine too," he said, setting her down.

She reached up and brushed her fingers through his long, windblown hair. "Sing "Only You" for me," she whispered. "And then kiss me again, just to seal the deal."

Wrapping her in his arms, he sang to her in a voice as deep as the love they felt.

Two pairs of soulful eyes smiled at the entwined pair, silhouetted against the moon.

"Wouldn't it be wonderful if someday . . .?" Taya admired the intricate diamond ring on her finger.

"Yes, it would, and I think it will. Someday our two families will be joined together in one. Right now though, they need a chaperone," Kytan said with decision. "Come on." He pulled on her hand.

She resisted. "But, it has taken so long for them to discover their feelings, and admit them to each other. Don't they deserve a little time—"

"No," he said firmly gazing into her eyes. His softened to adoration, making her catch her breath.

"Why?" she whispered, melting under his adoring gaze.

He lifted her into his arms, and gave her a dizzying kiss. Pulling back, he said in a husky voice, "Because I know exactly how he feels."

Forty-two

The moon-struck couples sat around the last dying embers of their small fire, basking in the bright light of the moon, long into the night. Their euphoria was so complete; none of them felt the cold.

Hadlee's hair was a mass of tangles, thanks to the wind on top of Farlana. Ryder sat behind her with a comb, doing what he'd longed to do for months—combing out the tangles, and running his fingers through her long, silver-blond mane. He took his time, deciding he wanted to brush out her hair every night for the rest of his life, and into the eternities.

She urged him to finish.

He reluctantly began braiding her long locks into one thick rope. When he finished, she cuddled back into his arms with a sigh of contentment.

His heart began to pound, and another Cheshire grin spread across his face. *It's a good thing she can't see my face or she might decide she just got herself engaged to an idiot.* His joy went so deep, he couldn't seem to quit smiling, and knew he never would. He tightened his arms, enjoying the feel of having Hadlee's head tucked into the nape of his neck, still overwhelmed by her feelings for him.

Sitting across the fire, Kytan and Taya looked like the other bookend in a matching set.

"I can see we are going to have to set some pretty strict rules of conduct for this trip," Kytan said, leaning his cheek against Taya's head. "There are enough sparks flying between you two," he said to Ryder and Hadlee, "to keep us from ever needing Hadlee's lighter."

"Oh, and it's obvious there are none between you two." Ryder watched Kytan kiss Taya, considering what his brother had said. "I think we only need one rule. As long as all of us stay in visual range of each other, the proprieties ought to be safe, and if anyone sees anything that is getting even remotely close to improper, they're to speak up. Agreed?"

"Yes." Hadlee nodded. "Couples are not to go wandering off together. Taya and I have our reputations to think about you know. We are being badly compromised by traveling alone with you two."

"That's right," Taya said. "Until we are all married, we need to keep some distance between us." She struggled unsuccessfully for a moment before Kytan reluctantly released her from his arms. "Too much contact might get us into trouble."

"Amen." Hadlee tried in vain to loosen Ryder's arms from around her.

"Hey, don't Kytan and I have a say in this?" Ryder asked.

"No," the girls said in unison.

"They are right, Ryder, and we need to listen to them. Besides, you and I know from experience fighting with these two is a losing battle." Kytan sighed, watching Taya move away from him.

"Well, Mrs. Garrison, if I have to let you go, at least I don't have to let you go far."

"I am not Mrs. Garrison yet, and that is exactly why you do have to let me go." She pushed against his arms.

He heaved a soulful sigh, making her laugh, kissed her soundly, and released her.

"You know," Kytan said, getting up and walking over to Taya. "We don't have last names. When we get married will you be Mrs. Kytan?"

"Do we need to have last names to get married in the United States?" asked Taya.

"I don't know," Ryder said thoughtfully, "but if you want to take last names, you could. In many countries the last name of a person is their father's name."

"That's right," Hadlee said. "Like John-son, or in other words, the son of John."

Kytan's dimples sprang to life. "I like that idea. I will take my Father's name as my last name. I am now Kytan Bendarson."

"But I'm not a son, so what do I do? Taya asked.

"You could just use your father's name without adding an ending," Ryder suggested.

"Then that makes me Taya Awtoo." She smiled. "It's a good way to honor our fathers."

"Yes." Kytan returned her smile. "When we marry you will be Mrs. Bendarson."

Her smile took on a wicked gleam. "But until then, you need to move your things over to the other side of the fire."

Hadlee pulled her bedroll over next to Taya's, and they shooed Kytan with his bedroll and knapsack over to Ryder's side of the fire pit.

"This is going to be the nightly arrangement," Hadlee said to the two resigned faces, across the last of the glowing embers. "We have already said prayers tonight, so go to sleep. We have a long climb down tomorrow."

Hadlee rolled herself into her blanket and lay down with her back to the fire. The name, Mrs. Garrison, hung in her mind. She closed her eyes, knowing she wasn't going to be able to sleep. She hadn't thought of the name change she would be making. She hadn't thought of anything beyond her impossible feelings for Ryder. Certainly, she hadn't thought about marriage, because the idea was—*outrageous?*

Pulling her blanket more tightly around her shoulders, she squirmed into a more comfortable position on the hard ground, and tried on the name she had agreed to take, *Hadlee Garrison—Mrs. Ryder Garrison.*

She opened her eyes. The moon was now high in the sky, and far to the west of Farlana. *Was it all just moon madness—our professions of love—his proposal—my response? It all happened so fast—so unexpectedly. Can I really take the name Mrs. Ryder Garrison? Can I truly marry the man who killed my mother?*

Forty-three

Just after dawn, Ryder again stood on the top of Farlana gazing down at the outline of the stone heart he and Hadlee had created beneath the light of the moon. Inside the outline, smaller rocks spelled out their names. A similar one sat near it, with Kytan and Taya's names in it.

"Did you think you dreamed it all?" asked Kytan, making him jump.

He turned to his sneaky brother. "Yeah, I'm still not sure I believe it. It's just so—"

"Right."

"With all my heart, I want it to be."

Kytan cocked his head, "But you aren't sure?"

"I'm dead sure of how I feel, and what I want."

"But . . ."

"It just . . . feels so much like a fairytale, that I'm afraid I'm dreaming. I'm terrified I'll wake up and find Hadlee really doesn't love me, and everything I thought happened last night was only a dream."

"What I saw last night was very real." Kytan's dimples danced.

"It felt real to me too. Still, it's hard to believe Hadlee can love me, and want to marry me, after everything I have cost her."

"That's not the man she sees anymore."

"That's what she told me, after she shared her dream with me."

"So . . . quit doubting yourself—and her. Be happy." Kytan clapped his shoulder, "You both deserve it."

He nodded, and smiled. "Come on. We better start scouting our way down."

With a last look at the monuments they'd created to express the love they felt for the women they wanted to spend forever with, they turned away from the tattoos that would mark the head of Farlana for all time.

Kytan stopped as they reached the lip of the peak. "There are a couple things we need to discuss."

"What?"

"The girls were right last night when they said traveling alone with us was compromising them."

"They were only kidding," Ryder said, but his brows furrowed.

"Yes, but considering we are engaged to them, and how we feel about them, we need to be especially careful."

Ryder nodded. "Yes. We need to be *very* careful."

"We would be wise to limit the number of kisses we give them each day."

"How many do you think we can handle without getting carried away?" Ryder grinned at how specific Kytan was being in making sure things stayed well within the bounds of propriety.

"Didn't last night tell you?"

The smile faded from Ryder's face. "It did, and you're right. I think I can safely handle two."

"So can I." Kytan held out his hand.

Ryder gripped it, making the oath with his brother, with one addendum. "Since all we get is two kisses a day, they get to be good solid kisses, and there's no limit on hand holding."

Kytan's dimples erupted into a laugh, "Agreed."

Withdrawing his hand, Ryder looked down with surprise at what Kytan had left in his hand. "How did you . . ."

Kytan's dimples danced mysteriously. He punched Ryder in the arm, and they left the top of Farlana for the last time.

Wanting to take the easiest possible route down the mountain, they spent an hour reconnoitering. Ryder remembered the mountain from his initial scouting venture the day before he climbed Farlana. He told Kytan they would need to continue to transverse the mountain to the south. The back of the beast's massive neck would offer the easiest course. It extended out a long way on its southwestern flank, making the rocky descent into a challenging downward scramble, with some limited climbing, but at least it wasn't a vertical drop down thousands of feet.

Ryder yawned, as they came back from their scouting expedition. The lack of a good night's sleep over the past few nights was beginning to catch up with him, but his heart was so full of dreams he hadn't been able to sleep. All he wanted now was to get out of the mountains, out of Peru, and to the temple in Manti. He wanted to be married as soon as possible. Where his feet had previously dragged, thinking his days with Hadlee were numbered, now they wanted to move with the speed of light. He'd spent the night planning, and wanted to share everything with his sweetheart, *no my fiancée,* he sighed.

"You know, you're marrying a man who doesn't even have a job," he said ruefully, helping Hadlee climb down a steep rock face.

"Uh-huh," she said, watching her footing.

"I have a degree, and I was offered a job with the State of Colorado, which I was supposed to start as soon as I got back from Peru," he said, sliding an arm around her, to steady her. "I don't suppose my job is still waiting for me, and it might not be so easy to find another one either. I got my degree two years ago, but I haven't worked—at least not at anything I can prove. The gap between my graduation date and landing my first job might prove to be a problem."

Securing her footing at the bottom of the rock face, she informed him, "Then I guess I'll just have to support us. I'm sure I can get a job. I'm a very good pilot." She laughed at his dismay.

"Until we have kids, I suppose it would be alright if you want to work, but I don't intend to let my wife support me."

"Oh. Too proud, are you? Well get this through your head, *darlin'*"—her fingers walked up his chest—"I don't intend to *ever* give up flying. So get used to it."

"I think we're about to have our first fight."

"Oh no, we're not. We've already had our first fight, several times over, if you will recall." She pinched the indentation in his chin.

His lips twitched remembering their little squabbles about his dictates and overprotectiveness.

She gave him her most beguiling smile, "Besides, I won't fight with you about this."

He knew what she was trying to do with her feminine wiles, and he tried not to let her smile sway him, but his insides turned to mush in spite of himself. "Pilot," he said sternly.

"Exactly," she retorted. "You gave me that name because the sky is my solace. You wouldn't take that away from me, would you?" Her eyes soulfully entreated him.

"You're definitely not playing fair." He groaned and looked at Kytan. "I can just see what my life is going to be like."

"It's going to be just like mine." Kytan sighed, dropping off the rock face next to them. "I will never be able to deny Taya anything." He held out his arms to her, "I am under her spell—forever bewitched."

Taya jumped down into his arms from the top of the rock. "I intend to be a very benevolent witch." She gave him the wicked little grin that he confessed always made his heart turn over, and ran her hand gently over the gold ring welded around his neck. "As long as we both know who is in charge, we shouldn't have any trouble." She cradled his face in her small hands.

He rolled his eyes at his laughing brother. "Laugh while you can, Ryder, you are no better off."

"I know. You and I need to stick together, or we will be lost with these two obstinate females." He gave Hadlee a hangdog expression that made them all laugh, then sobered, "But we really do have to think about finding employment. I'm sure my folks will help all of us get started." He tugged gently on Hadlee's braid, "I can't wait for you to meet them, Pilot. I know they are going to adore you—and want to adopt Taya and Kytan. We are going to be one big happy family." He turned to Kytan. "My folks will very likely end up being our first employers."

"Really, what will we do for them?" asked Kytan.

"They own a big ranch, south of Glenwood Springs, Colorado. They run a couple thousand head of cattle that require a lot of ranch hands. While we look for work, better suited to our talents, and get our homes set up, we can work for them."

Concern skidded across Kytan's face. "I don't know much about animals, but I am willing to learn. I especially want to learn all about my new country."

The talk turned to life in the United States. Ryder and Hadlee answered endless questions, while climbing down short rock faces, negotiating narrow transverse crags and picking their way through boulder fields, descending the long scaly neck of the dragon.

As the day wore away, and they got nearer to the bottom of the mountain, Ryder began to feel uneasy. *Hadlee's being far too quiet. She doesn't seem to share the spirit of excitement the rest of us feel.* He looked at her from under lowered lids. *There was something in her eyes too, just for a moment, when I talked about my folks, and meeting them.* An unexpected spark of apprehension flickered to life inside him.

Even with gloves and boots, Hadlee was hand and foot sore by the time they reached the bottom of Farlana. So was everyone else. They found a place to camp and gratefully dropped their knapsacks. With daylight fading fast, and not much in the way of vegetation or timber around them, they quickly fanned out, scouring the area for campfire fuel.

The couples went in different directions but kept an eye on each other. When Ryder and Hadlee were out of hearing distance, but still in visual range of Kytan and Taya, Ryder dropped the knapsack he had slung over his shoulder, to carry back whatever they found, and turned to her.

"Sweetheart," he said taking both her hands, "What's bothering you? You've been kind of quiet and somber all afternoon."

"Have I—I sorry if I worried you. It's just, I feel so tired. Being Ateron's prisoner didn't exactly afford me much opportunity for exercise. What I need is a good night's sleep, and that is very difficult to do without my lovely box springs." She ran a finger over his skeptical brow, deciding not to tell him what was really troubling her, *at least not until I work through it—then I'll tell him.*

She decided the best thing to do was distract him. She did a very skillful job of it, enjoying every moment.

Their scavenger hunt rewarded them with enough sticks and branches from dead grass and bushes to make an adequate campfire, but they were all too tired to linger around it. After eating soup and ashcakes, they wearily rolled into their blankets for the night. Sleep came quickly to everyone but Hadlee.

She wanted to get up and pace, *I need to—badly.* Over the past several months she'd found pacing helped her think. *I simply have to think this out and come to a decision.* She knew she couldn't get up and pace; if she did, Ryder would be sure to hear her and follow. Rolling over on her other side, she looked across the fire pit, hoping he was asleep.

He rolled over onto his stomach, then to his other side, facing away from the low burning fire.

He's probably having trouble getting comfortable because his back is still so painful. Love and sympathy filled her. *If only there was something I could do to ease your pain,* she silently wished, sending that desire from her heart to his, even as a bitter sorrow rose within hers. The soft glow of the waning moon intensified her distress. She closed her eyes against it.

Throughout the afternoon, Ryder had talked on and on about his family. They sounded wonderful, and her heart ached to meet them. Still, when he enthusiastically talked about presenting her to his family, it brought the unpleasant truth she'd managed to banish the night before to the forefront of her mind.

Inhaling through her nose and exhaling through her mouth, she worked to keep from bursting into tears. *I can't take you home to my family, Ryder. They despise you, and I can't bear to let anyone hurt you, especially not them.*

Guilt swallowed her. *I love my aunt, uncle, and cousins. Not that they know it,* she admitted. *I behaved so badly when I was little, blaming them for keeping me.*

During those first years, she'd believed all her aunt and uncle needed to do was tell her father they didn't want her, and her dad would have come and taken her home. She'd hated them for a long time for not doing that.

They probably still believe I hate them. Especially after I ran off to California without a word and didn't contact them for almost a year. That was so ungrateful, so heartless. How can I bring Ryder home now and tell them I'm marrying him? They will see that as my final act of ingratitude and treachery. They won't believe me when I tell them how much I have grown to love them, or how dear they are to me. Marrying Ryder will make those words seem like a lie.

The question came unbidden.

Do I love Ryder enough to choose him over my family?

The answer was instantaneous.

I do. I won't give him up no matter how they feel about him. I just . . . can't.

Guilt for the impending wound she would inflict on her family brought the silent tears she was fighting. She pulled her blanket up over her face as the tears rolled down her cheeks, feeling the stab of an even deeper wound. *How can I tell Ryder I can't take him home to meet my family because they hate him?*

She spent most of the night wrestling with a deluge of unanswerable problems and questions, until exhaustion finally released her.

Forty-four

The thin morning light penetrated Hadlee's blanket, waking her. From under her blanket, she listened to the clatter of pots, and voices talking in whispers, and knew everyone was up. She didn't move.

How long can I keep this from him? I can't burden his heart with this so soon. We deserve to have at least a few days of happiness. I can hide my feelings from him, I did it for a long time, and I can still do it. I do have to tell him before we go home, but not yet—not today. She pulled the blanket from her face, and saw his smiling eyes.

Morning, sleepy head," Ryder said, walking over to her.

She jumped up. "I . . . ah . . . need a moment's privacy. Where should I . . ."

"Around the rocks to your right should do. When you get back, we better set up sanitation rules," he called after her.

"Right." She flung the word over her shoulder and fled to the sanctuary of the rocks. It took only a few moments to take care of her need, but she spent several minutes walking back and forth, fortifying her resolve.

Taya came around the rocks, and stopped. "Okay?"

Yes, I was just coming," Hadlee said, and followed her back to camp.

By mid-morning, they arrived at the place Ryder camped before he climbed Farlana. Like his gear in the cavern, everything in his base camp that was perishable, with the help of animals or elements, was ruined.

Ryder shrugged, "The gear isn't important. All that matters is getting home." He looked to the northwest, at the mountains between them and the trail back to Lima. "It took me five days from where I first saw Farlana, to reach it—and I was moving real fast." He paused, thoughtfully. "I think it will take us at least six or seven, and then maybe another two or three, before we'll come to a road out of the mountains."

As they pushed on, the vegetation became more abundant the lower they dropped in altitude. Ryder found the llama trail he initially used when he left Pucara. Following it would lead them around the bases of the peaks he'd skirted to reach Farlana.

The trail took them through deep valleys, with verdant meadows that beckoned them with lush green vistas.

Taya loved looking at the plants, some she'd never seen. She often lagged behind, pausing to examine, touch, and smell them. When they came across a particularly lovely meadow, she squealed, "Potatoes!"

The meadow was covered in the wild potatoes so prevalent throughout the mountains.

"Our food supply isn't going to last for the next ten days. Especially with the way Ryder eats." She giggled at the face he threw her. "We need to dig up as many of these potatoes as we can carry."

They spent almost two hours digging potatoes, cleaning them off, and stowing them in their knapsacks, before pressing on.

The hiking became easier as they followed the trail that led to the distant peak where Ryder first saw Farlana. All morning a stream ran along the trail beside them. From it they refilled their water bags, washed their dirty clothes and Ryder's numerous bandages, hanging them on long walking sticks to dry as they hiked.

Before the stream veered away from the trail, they stopped beside it for lunch. Pulling off their boots, they dangled their tired feet in the water as they ate.

Eating a handful of nuts and dried fruit, Ryder noticed Hadlee was quieter than she had been the previous afternoon, and when she missed what he said for the third time, he knew something was wrong. Unfortunately the rules of the trip prohibited him from being alone with her to find out what was troubling her. He knew he would have to wait until evening, when they would again go in search of campfire fuel.

The sun was far to the west by the time Ryder led the troop into a thick stand of trees where he'd camped on his journey to Farlana. The flattened grass under the trees marked it as a place animals often slept. Following Taya's suggestion, they collected several armloads of the tall, meadow grass to add to the beds the animals used, making softer beds for themselves.

With twilight expanding across the sky, they spread out again to gather fuel for a fire. Ryder took Hadlee's hand as they moved away from their camp, picking up sticks and putting them into the bag he carried. He took her as far away as the rules permitted, before he kissed her. He'd been dying to do it all day, and did it with tender enthusiasm.

Putting his fingers under her chin, he lifted her face, and looked deeply into her eyes. "What's wrong? You were more distracted today than yesterday." Before she could reply, he put a finger to her lips. "Don't tell me you're tired, I know it's something else. Tell me and let me help."

She stepped back, and turned away. "I'm sorry, but you can't help me with this."

Her rebuff stung like a slap. Taking hold of her arm, he gently turned her to face him. She was struggling to compose her features. He watched her try for her slave-face, but a tear escaped and slid down her cheek.

"I wish you could help, because I don't know what to do."

Her troubled eyes magnified the foreboding building inside him. She came into his arms, her hands moving up his jacket. She wound her arms around his neck, and stood on her toes. His arms tightened, lifting her off her feet. He kissed her again, trying to encourage and reassure her, feeling the tears continue to slide down her face. She returned his kiss, with what felt to him like desperation, clinging to him as though she was afraid to let go.

A rock landed near their feet.

Ryder lifted his head, and set Hadlee down.

Kytan shot him a warning look in the dwindling light. "About time to be heading back," he yelled.

"Soon," Ryder shouted, returning his eyes to Hadlee. "What's the matter, Pilot? You know you can tell me anything. You're my heart. If you're not happy, I can't be either. Tell me, and we will work it out."

Hadlee laid her cheek against his chest. "I didn't want to tell you, not today, not so . . . soon."

His heart lurched. He stroked her hair, waiting for her to get control of her emotions and continue.

She took a deep breath, "I can't go home Ryder. It's the only way. I love you so much. I can't bear to let anyone hurt you, especially not my family. I can't take you home to them. You know I can't. They won't welcome you. How can I tell Mama's sister I'm marrying the man who—"

Ryder stiffened, and she didn't finish that terrible truth.

"I don't care how they feel about you. You're all the family I want or need. It doesn't matter to me if they can't accept us."

Her words were a shockwave of reality that reverberated through him until the wonderful fairytale he was living in crumbled. Its demise forced him to see beyond the blindness of his feelings and desires.

Searching her pleading eyes, he knew he had been deluding himself. He understood what she was saying, and even what she felt. Her family certainly wouldn't welcome *him* as her husband. *How can she possibly bring me home to her aunt? How could I have ever thought I would be allowed to marry her? It's—impossible.*

Her fingers clutched the front of his jacket imploringly. Her kiss still lingered on his lips. *All we need is each other, and I can't live without her. She'll marry me, regardless of how her family feels*, he rationalized. *But, can I live with myself, if she loses them because of me?*

Farlana reared its mocking head, and he realized even being forgiven didn't change the consequences. *I took her family from her. All she has left is her aunt's family. Will marrying me really rob her of them?* The probability wrenched his soul. *Even becoming her family won't make up for losing the only one she has left.* He faced his conscience squarely. *I can't—I won't—cost her another family.*

The promise he'd made on his knees in the forest of Lanka came back to haunt him. *I will pay any price to help her find peace, and get her out of Injanae.* He'd felt in his soul, even as the words came from his mouth, that the price he'd have to pay would be high. *But this price is more than I can bear.*

Her eyes begged for reassurance. He wanted to tell her he would marry her without her family's approval because what they felt for each other would be enough, and his family would become hers.

The words wouldn't come. He had to tell her the truth, no matter what it cost either of them. He tried for his slave-face, and failed miserably. "Pilot, I won't marry you without your family's blessing."

"Don't say that." Her fingers tightened on the front of his coat. "You promised to *be* my family."

"And I want that with all my heart, but if we have to wait to get married, we'll wait. Maybe—given time, your family will see me the way you do."

A bitter scoff answered him. "It took me twelve years to forgive you. What if it takes my family that long? Will you wait for me?"

"Yeah. I'll wait my whole life if that's what it takes," he said, banding her in his arms. "How can I do anything else, when I love you with everything my heart and soul are capable of?"

"And I love you. But it's not right. It's not fair. You've been in too many prisons, for too many years. I won't put you in another one."

"I'm already there." He lost himself in the eyes he would never escape and tenderly assured her, "It's a prison I don't ever want to be free of."

"I know," she said, gently stroking his face. "It's a prison I'm in too."

Another rock bounced near their feet.

Ryder turned to find Kytan striding toward them. He whispered urgently to her, "We're not going to bail out, Pilot. Somehow—we *will* find a way."

She nodded, turning her face away to wipe her eyes.

"Is everything alright?" Kytan asked when he reached them, and then added, "You know you two are about at the edge of our agreed upon permissible conduct."

Ryder was grateful full darkness had fallen, keeping Kytan from seeing his face, and particularly Hadlee's, clearly. "Sorry. We just have a lot of things we want to discuss without you nosy neighbors." Ryder tried for a joking tone, hoping his voice wouldn't reflect the awful reality he and Hadlee now faced. He wrapped his arm around her, she leaned into him, and silently they followed Kytan back to camp.

Forty-five

It was Taya's habit to rise before the sun. In Injanae, there were many chores to do before Hadlee arose. As usual, her eyes opened in the predawn light. She sat up quietly and looked across the still smoldering embers of the fire.

For the third morning in a row, Ryder was gone. She knew he would be back when the sun came up, carrying wood for the fire. She also knew his predawn trips had little to do with gathering wood. Lacing up her alpaca coat against the early morning chill, she couldn't rid herself of the thought; *something is worrying Ryder and Hadlee.*

She and Kytan had felt it a few nights ago when Ryder and Hadlee sat next to the fire holding each other tightly, just staring into the flames. At the time, she couldn't help feeling there was a desperate determination about the way they clung to one another. And they'd stayed up late too, almost refusing to let go of each other.

Taya frowned. During the days, they let Kytan and her go ahead, barely staying within sight of them. She'd turned around to look for them yesterday, just in time to watch them embrace. Then it seemed like they were arguing.

Kytan had seen it too. He told her they needed to mind their own business. The relationship between Hadlee and Ryder was more complicated than theirs. Interfering wouldn't help them solve whatever problems they might have.

Whatever their problems are, Taya decided, *I am not just going to watch their suffering, and do nothing. I love them both too much not to try to do something to help. But first, I have to find out what is wrong.*

After saying a prayer, she got to her feet and moved silently to the edge of the camp. Listening intently, she began moving in a widening circle around the perimeter until she heard the murmur of a voice. Quietly, she made her way in that direction.

Ryder was twenty-five yards from the camp. Screened by a small clump of trees, he knelt in the dew-drenched grass. Not wanting to intrude, Taya knelt down, folded her arms, and listened to him pray in English. Her understanding of English was still limited to the basics, and Ryder was speaking too rapidly for her to make out very much of what he said, but the tone of his voice conveyed his misery.

Something is terribly wrong for Ryder to be so unhappy. She began to pray for him, asking to find a way to help this man she loved so dearly.

Ryder's voice stopped.

Her eyes flew open.

He was sitting back on his heels, his hands clasped together, looking pleadingly into heaven. She jumped up and ran to him, putting her small arms around his neck. He accepted her comfort, laying his head on her shoulder.

She stroked his hair. "What is it, Ryder? What is making you and Hadlee so unhappy?"

He lifted his head from her shoulder, again sitting back on his heels. "I promised the Lord I would do anything to help Hadlee find peace, and get her out of Injanae. When I made that promised, I knew the cost would be high, but I didn't care, not even if the cost was my life."

Taya watched him try to hide his feelings behind a slave-face, but he couldn't manage it and his despair was stark. "I know what the price is now . . . and I'm not strong enough to pay it."

"Why would the Lord expect you to pay anything for helping Hadlee?"

"He doesn't. I set the price—the day I killed Hadlee's mother. The Lord just reminded me of it, but I didn't listen. I couldn't help loving her. I have loved her since the first moment I looked into her eyes. I love her, and—I can't marry her."

"Can't marry her—why?"

"I've already cost her, her own family. I can't cost her the only family she has left. She can't bring me home to her aunt and tell her she is marrying the man who killed her sister." He ran his hand over the back of his neck. "I can't even begin to imagine her family's horror and disgust. If she marries me, she will lose all that's left of her family."

"I don't believe that. You two have been through so much. If she can forgive you, then her family should too. If they want her to be happy, they will have to forgive you."

"Even if they do—or have—that doesn't mean they will want Hadlee to marry me." He took hold of her delicate hands. "I've been praying to find a way to keep Hadlee, but it's not up to me. What I did can't be undone. Even repentance doesn't eliminate some consequences. The consequences of what I did will always follow me, and Hadlee. The final price I may have to pay for the death of Hadlee's mother is—to let Hadlee go."

Taya clung to his hands. "I can't accept that, and neither should you. Give it time. Have Hadlee talk to her family. When she tells them all you have done for her, surely they will thank you for saving her life and bringing her home. If she tells them she has forgiven you, how can they refuse to forgive you too? Don't give up." She searched his face. "The Lord has helped you two through so much. I can't believe it was just so you both could repent. I know how important that was, but what you two feel for each other is so precious, and very rare. Don't let it go Ryder. There has to be a way to win the approval of Hadlee's family."

Ryder's dejected face told her how hopeless he felt that was. "We can't even consider a future together until after Hadlee spends some time with her family. She told me, she has a lot of making up to do because she didn't appreciate them during the years she lived with them. I know they need time with her too. But now, she's refusing to go to them because of how they feel about me. I have to convince her to go home. She needs to let them know how much she loves them, and to accept their love in return. Then, maybe, she can tell them about her feelings for me." He shifted in the dewy grass that soaked the knees of his pants. "It will be up to them whether or not we marry. I won't marry her unless I have her family's blessing. I *won't* destroy her relationship with them. *I can't.* And I'm afraid even if they forgive me, they will never want Hadlee to marry me." Ryder hung his head and rubbed the back of his neck.

Taya put her hands on his cheeks lifting his face to look into hers. "Do you remember what you told me when I asked you how you and Hadlee would get away from the palace the night of the sacrifices? You told me sometimes you just have to go on faith. And remember when Ateron made you leave the apartment after the cave in? You told me to tell Hadlee to have faith. Now I am telling you. Have faith," she said, wiping away the wetness from his face with her fingers.

He hugged her. "Thank you for reminding me that with the Lord's help anything is possible."

"You need to tell Kytan. We are your family too, you know. Let us help and comfort both of you."

"Yes," Kytan said as he and Hadlee came into view through the growing dawn. "It is time you let us help you." Holding Hadlee's hand he led her to them. "I see you two have had the same conversation that Hadlee and I had."

Hadlee's eyes were damp with lingering tears. She dropped to her knees beside Ryder, heedless of the wet grass, and took his hand. "I don't care if my family disowns me. I am going to marry you. Taya's mother gave up her family, and she never regretted it, did she, Taya?"

"That is true, Ryder. She left her family for my father, and was very happy. Even after he died, she didn't regret her decision."

"I won't regret mine either, Ryder. *You are* my family now."

Ryder drew her to him. She laid her cheek next to his.

His voice trembled, "We've talked about this for the past three days. I won't cost you what's left of your family. Unless they give me their blessing—I won't marry you." He pulled his cheek from hers, held her eyes and pleaded, "Go home to them. I can wait. I need to see my family too, and Kytan and Taya have a ton of things they need to do to get settled. I can help them while you're with your family."

Kytan laid his hands on Ryder and Hadlee's shoulders. "That's right. Preparations must be made so Taya and I can be baptized and married. I also need to find work suited to my skills, and find a home for Taya. All these things require time and planning. Taya and I will take care of Ryder for you, Hadlee, while you spend time with your family."

"But I want to be there when you get baptized and married. How can I bear being away from all of you? You are as much my family as my aunt's family is. Why can't I just be part of this family?"

"Pilot, we've prayed over this; you have; I have; we have together—and the answer is always the same. You have to go home. After all these months, your family thinks you're dead. You can't let them go on believing that. Think of the grief they have endured. I know you love them. Don't hurt them because of me. I can't bear that. They need to see you, and spend time with you, and you need that just as much as they do."

Hadlee started to protest.

Ryder put a finger to her lips. "We will let you know when the wedding is. Maybe we can have the baptism the day before, so you can be there for both. It's going to take several weeks after we get home to arrange everything. Please, go home . . . just for a little while. It might even be good for us. Tell your family everything that happened in Injanae. Put in a few good words for me. Soften them up. Maybe you can even change their feelings about me—a little."

Taya took hold of Hadlee's hand, trying to convey her encouragement and support. Hadlee returned her grip, and Taya felt the anguish of the silent battle she fought. It was reflected in her face, and mirrored in Ryder's.

"Alright." The word resonated with forced capitulation. She let go of Taya's hand, ran her finger down the slight crease in Ryder's chin, and met his imploring eyes. "I'll go home."

Forty-six

After twelve days of hard traveling by various means and conveyances, Ryder led the conspirators through the teeming streets of Lima to the American embassy. Their progress was slow due to Kytan and Taya's frequent stops to look at, and examine, wonders they had never seen before. Kytan was particularly captivated by all the automobiles whizzing by.

"Don't worry," Ryder said, taking Kytan's arm and dragging him away from a shiny white sedan parked in front of the embassy. "You can look to your heart's content, and even ride in a car—just not right now."

Kytan followed the others up the steps to the embassy glancing back at the car. "I don't just want to ride in one. I want to drive one," he said wistfully.

Ryder lifted the brass knocker on the embassy's door and let it fall. Hadlee shifted anxiously beside him. He put his arm around her. She leaned against him looking as tired as he felt and every bit as dirty. He smiled down at her. "We will be lucky if they let us inside, considering how we look."

"I wouldn't blame them if they didn't." Hadlee wiped his bearded face with her sleeve, and then her own.

Ryder turned his attention to the door as it opened. He introduced himself, declared his nationality, and requested the ambassador's help.

The man that opened the door, dipped his head with stiff formality, ushered them into the foyer, without comment or question, and asked them to wait while he went to get Ambassador Keeler.

While they waited, the troop admired the wide formal

staircase, the hard wood floor, the high arched, wood framed doorways that led out of the foyer, and the upholstered benches that lined one wall.

Ryder pulled Hadlee over to one of the benches and started to sit.

She grabbed his arm. "No."

He straightened and looked down at his clothes. "I suppose not."

"Definitely not," Taya said, and sagged against Kytan.

A few moments later, Arthur Keeler, a sturdy, silver haired man in his late fifties, whose ramrod bearing and straightforward manners spoke of his military background, marched into the foyer. He looked over the travel-weary troop with shrewd gray eyes. "I am Ambassador Keeler," he said, stepping forward and holding out his hand to Ryder.

Ryder took his hand, introduced himself, and his friends.

A slow smile grew on the Ambassador's face. "I know all about you and Miss MacLean," he said. "I even have your pictures.

"You do?" Hadlee asked, surprised.

The ambassador turned to Hadlee, "Yes, and I've also had the pleasure of meeting your families."

"When—where?" Hadlee asked, reaching out a hand to him.

He took her hand and patted it. "Your aunt and uncle came right after you disappeared. They stayed for a month, trying to learn what happened to you." He released her hand, and turned to Ryder, "Your father has been here twice; the first time by himself, and the second time with your mother. Both times they advertised in the newspaper for information about you, offering a substantial reward." His eyes filled with an old pain. "It was very hard to send your families away without the comfort of knowing what had happened to either of you. But I told them—during their separate visits—that my office would continue to look into your disappearances."

"Forgive me for not being here to greet you," a musical voice said from up the broad staircase. "But Ricardo just told me about your arrival," Everyone's eyes turned to the stairs. Margaret Keeler, the ambassador's wife, hurried down them, neatly dressed in a blue cotton dress, and low pumps. She smiled brightly at the ragged group.

Introductions were again made.

Mrs. Keeler's shocked face looked from Ryder to Hadlee, and back again. "Oh my, you are the two who have been missing for so long." She took Hadlee's hands, "I am afraid your families believe you're dead."

Hadlee's smile wavered. "I hope they won't be too disappointed to find, we aren't."

"I think overjoyed will be understating it," the ambassador said, and fixed Ryder and Hadlee with an almost stern expression. "Where in the Sam Hill have you two been all this time?" He gestured to the arm Ryder had around Hadlee, "And how did you manage to find each other, when no one could find either one of you?"

"My goodness, Arthur, don't start interrogating them here, and now—your questions can wait," Mrs. Keeler said, and gestured at Taya, leaning against Kytan. "Just look at that poor child. She's dead on her feet." Her soft brown eyes ran over the group. "It's obvious they need to sit down. Take them into your study and make them comfortable, while I get them something to eat." She looked at Ryder, "You must be starving."

He grinned.

Walking into the welcoming comfort of the Ambassador's wood paneled study, the worn out conspirators shed their knapsacks, and settled into plush leather chairs. Mrs. Keeler returned with a small army of servants carrying trays of roast beef sandwiches, local fruit, ice-cold milk, and homemade oatmeal raisin cookies. The conspirators told their tale as they ate every morsel of food on the trays.

Arthur and Margaret sat entranced, often slack jawed, and shaking their heads. At first, they seemed unable to believe the incredible adventure the young people described, but the evidence was irrefutable.

They examined the gold bands welded around Taya, Kytan and Ryder's necks.

"I have never seen anything like them, not even among *all* the Incan artifacts I've been shown," Arthur said.

"They are beautiful, but horrible." Margaret shuddered after they told her what they signified.

Hadlee also showed them Ansuetra's jewelry and Ryder's armband. Their extraordinary beauty brought a shower of praise for Kytan's talent, and more questions about Injanae.

The day dwindled into evening before all the Keeler's questions were fully answered. Margaret Keeler's gentle brown eyes watched weariness grow into exhaustion in the young people's faces with each passing hour. It brought out her strong maternal instincts. She took the little group into her heart, and immediately began mothering them.

The conspirators soon learned that this small, frail looking woman had a will of iron that matched the heavy streaks in her light brown hair.

"I won't hear any more arguments about it. You have all been through a great physical trial, not to mention the injuries you and Ryder suffered," she said to Hadlee.

"But Taya—"

"I know Taya is a doctor"—she smiled kindly at Taya—"but I have already sent for Doctor Sanchez, and I will feel better once he has examined all of you."

Following their brief examinations, Doctor Sanchez reported his findings to Mrs. Keeler. "Miss Awtoo is a very good herbal doctor. I have never met anyone whose knowledge of plants and skill with them exceeds hers. The injuries Mr. Garrison and Miss MacLean suffered are healing very nicely, thanks to Miss Awtoo's treatments. They will both have scars, but if they continue with the regiment prescribed by Miss Awtoo, even those will be minimal."

"And Ryder's lungs?" Mrs. Keeler asked, having told the doctor about the drowning incident.

"They are clear and strong." Doctor Sanchez chuckled. "I have always wondered what a titan would look like. Now I know."

"So you're saying there is nothing's wrong with any of them?"

"Nothing that plenty of good food and rest can't cure."

Mrs. Keeler took the doctor's advice and instantly whisked the girls off for long, luxurious baths. By the time their fingers and toes were well pruned, she had procured the basic necessities she felt were indispensable for their immediate comfort. Bathed, and dressed in nightgowns and robes, Mrs. Keeler fed them supper in their room and put them into soft, inviting beds.

Ambassador Keeler detained Ryder and Kytan while he made phone calls to various Peruvian government agencies. The news of a lost culture deep in the Andes was so sensational he was sure the Peruvian government would want to know as much about it as possible.

When he finally hung up the phone, he said, "The minister of Peruvian culture will be here tomorrow right after lunch, along with members of the Incan historical society." He fixed Ryder and Kytan with speculative eyes. "Now that the ladies have retired I want to know more about Injanae and what really happened there."

Ryder and Kytan stayed up well into the evening, eating every bite of the non-stop food Mrs. Keeler plied them with, and answering the Ambassador's questions. They hid their yawns as well as they could, until Mrs. Keeler demanded her husband relinquish the tired men into her care.

The Ambassador looked from one to the other, took pity on them, and stood. "Tomorrow we will begin working on getting you home," he said, clapping their shoulders. "Right now you both need baths and a month's sleep."

Mrs. Keeler led them out of her husband's study, down a hall at the back of the house, and into a large bedroom with twin beds and a connecting bath.

She'd only been partially successful in her quest for night gear, and said apologetically, "Those are for you, Kytan." She pointed to a hastily purchased pair of green striped pajamas folded neatly at the foot of one twin bed, then turned to Ryder. "I'm sorry but these are the best I could do for you." She picked up a pair of bright red cotton pajama bottoms from the foot of the other twin bed and handed them to him.

They were the widest pair of pajama bottoms Ryder had ever seen. He held them up against him. They ended just below his knees and were three times the size of his waist.

"They were all my maid could find," Mrs. Keeler said. "Fortunately, they have a drawstring to keep them up. And don't worry. You will only have to wear them tonight. Oh, and leave your dirty clothes outside the door. I'll have them washed and ready to wear before you get up in the morning."

The corners of Ryder's mouth quirked up. He pressed his lips together to keep from laughing, swallowed, and said, "You have no idea how thankful I am just to be able to take a hot bath, sleep on a real bed and have something clean to put on."

Mrs. Keeler took a small, relieved breath. "Tomorrow morning a tailor is coming to measure you, Ryder, and make clothes and pajamas for you. For now, everything else you both need is in the bathroom"—she looked at Ryder"—including shaving gear."

He smiled through his beard.

She returned it, said goodnight, told them to sleep late, and went out the door.

Forty-seven

Ryder leaned over Hadlee's shoulder as she read the telegram from her aunt and uncle. It contained the same stunned, ecstatic expressions of gratitude his had from his family, and the same anxious desire for her immediate return.

Hadlee brushed away a tear, and whispered. "It's amazing that they are so excited to have me back—after the horrible way I have treated them over the years."

"That's why it's important for you to go home to them," Ryder said softly.

She nodded, but her smile was halfhearted and tinged with doubt.

Ryder glanced at the ambassador, busy with the papers in front of him, leaned in, kissed her lightly, then drew back quickly as Mrs. Keeler entered the room, followed by Taya and Kytan.

"Hadlee, we're going shopping," Mrs. Keeler said, in a no nonsense tone. The prospect of Hadlee and Taya arriving in the States dressed in their Injanaen clothes was—in her opinion—appalling. "I can't send you home looking like rag-a-muffins."

Her husband looked up from working on the travel arrangements for the group, and the papers Kytan and Taya needed to enter the United States. "Good idea. Take the ladies, but leave the men. There's some information I still need from them." He looked down at his papers and then back at his wife, "Oh, and have the girls back before lunch. The Peruvian official will want to talk with Taya."

"Right," she said in a way that made Ryder hide a smile. It sounded so military.

"We can't go shopping," Hadlee said, leaning back against the sofa. "We don't have any Peruvian money."

"No need to worry about that," Arthur said. "Your aunt and uncle, and Ryder's folks, have wired enough money to buy all four of you new wardrobes."

"Let's go." Mrs. Keeler marshaled her troops, and promptly took them off to buy, what she considered, suitable attire.

Mrs. Keeler's enthusiasm for the shopping expedition quickly waned however, when both girls preferred to buy pants and blouses, along with boots and jackets. Seeing her shocked face, they each bought a couple of simple skirts to go with their blouses, and a pair of slip on shoes.

They came back to the embassy just before noon dressed in their skirts to please Mrs. Keeler. Their transformation received a long whistle from Ryder, and applause from Kytan. Both men smiled appreciatively at the close fitting blouses, tightly cinched in waistbands, and the expanse of lovely legs they could see below the skirts.

That afternoon, after the last Peruvian government official left, Mrs. Keeler cornered Ryder and Kytan. "Now that the girls are properly attired, we need to do something about you two." She looked at Ryder and Kytan's long hair and shook her head.

Taya and Hadlee accompanied the men's reluctant shopping expedition and trip to the barber's shop with Mrs. Keeler. Both girls cried a little, watching the long locks—they both loved—drop to the floor.

Kytan's dimples beamed as he looked in the mirror and ran his fingers through his short-cropped hair. But his dimples disappeared when Taya mournfully picked up his long braid and hugged it. He pulled her into his arms and kissed her. She mustered a smile, and his dimples reappeared.

Hadlee retrieved a lock of Ryder's hair too and folded it carefully into a handkerchief. She caught his inquisitive look as she tucked the hankie into her pocket. "At least I'll have a little piece of you near me while we are apart," she said, brushing back the wayward lock of determined hair that always fell over the left side of his forehead, hiding his scar.

"You have to admit, they both look very handsome with their hair cut to the proper length," Mrs. Keeler said, and smiled with satisfaction at the agreement she saw on Hadlee and Taya's faces.

Forty-eight

"But they are the only known members of this lost culture and society. Surely you can understand and appreciate the government's position," said Senor Delgado, the minister of Peruvian culture, to Ambassador Keeler.

Ryder groaned under his breath, stretched his long legs out in front of him, and glanced at the grandfather clock standing next to the door of the ambassador's study. Their argument with the Peruvian government over Kytan and Taya's request to emigrate had been going on for two hours.

The government's interest in Injanae had resulted in an unforeseen consequence. They refused to sign the necessary documents to allow Kytan and Taya to leave the country. Convinced Injanae was a link that would prove to be very valuable in understanding the ancient culture of the Incans; they were adamant that Kytan and Taya remain in Peru.

Kytan staunchly wore his slave-face as he dipped his head in a gesture of respect. "Minister, we have met with all your officials, every day for over a week. Taya and I have willingly told you everything we could think of about our culture, history, government, social structure, religious practices, written language—"he took a breath—"and anything else the Peruvian government has asked. We have even taught the rudimentary elements of our language to your linguists. There is nothing more we can tell you about Injanae." His slave-face broke, and he sent the minister both a frustrated and pleading look. "Please, Senor Delgado, allow us to move ahead with our lives. We want to leave with our friends, and start a new life in the United States."

Senor Delgado pressed his lips together.

The silence of stalemate settled over the ambassador's study. The grandfather clock ticked loudly into the silence, adding to the rising tension in the room.

Ryder rode herd on his growing frustration, not wanting to antagonize the Peruvian officials, but Kytan and Taya's distraught faces stretched his patience to the limit.

Finally, Senor Delgado, who was not an unreasonable or unfeeling man, asked for a private consultation with his associates.

The ambassador rose and ushered the conspirators out of the room. He closed the door behind him and looked into four distressed faces. "I am going to go see if I can call in a favor," he said and left the downcast conspirators standing in the foyer.

Hadlee and Taya sat down on the stairs and watched Ryder and Kytan pace the length of the foyer.

Fifteen minutes went by.

They looked up with hopeful expressions when they heard the ambassador's footsteps.

His grim face told them his mission had failed. "I'm sorry, but it seems Senor Delgado has the last word on whether or not Kytan and Taya will be allowed to emigrate."

The door to the study opened on that disheartening news. Senor Rangel, a minor minister on the board of Peruvian culture, invited them back into the study.

Senor Delgado's face revealed nothing as they took their seats and waited for his verdict. He cleared his throat and addressed Kytan, "If you and Mr. Garrison will lead a government funded expedition back to Injanae, I will recommend that you and Miss Awtoo be allowed to emigrate."

Kytan's face fell.

Taya's head drooped against his shoulder.

Ryder took in a calming breath, but exhaled frustration. "Minister, as we have already explained, it is impossible for any of us to return to Injanae. The people believe Hadlee is their goddess, and that she took all of us with her when she left Injanae. If they learn she is a fraud, and merely escaped the valley using a route we expose by coming back into Injanae, the results could be disastrous."

"Why?" Senor Delgado asked. "Surely someone who knew about your deception has already exposed everyone involved."

"I believe that to be very unlikely," Kytan said. "Our people are very superstitious. I have no doubt, once Hadlee disappeared with us, even the guards who knew about Ateron's plans to use Hadlee as Ansuetra are now convinced she was Ansuetra."

That's right," Hadlee said. "Not even they can explain my unprecedented arrival by parachute, or my mysterious departure. I'm sure all the guards now believe I came, or rather Ansuetra came, to expose Ateron's murders, his unworthiness to be Injanae's king, and to reunite the power of the king with that of the high priest, thus establishing a final and lasting peace."

"If we go back through the water tunnel, and are caught, it would create doubt about Ansuetra's authenticity and the reordering of the kingdom she did. It could tear the kingdom apart and result in civil war," Ryder said.

The minister scoffed.

"Believe me, Senor Delgado, our return would undoubtedly cost not only our lives, but the lives of all those who believe in the deception we put in place in order to escape Injanae," Kytan said.

An idea sprang in to Ryder's mind. He sat forward in his chair, "Besides, you don't really need us to take you to Injanae. I can draw you a detailed map of how to get there."

Senor Delgado lifted an interested brow.

The ambassador handed Ryder pencil and paper. He meticulously mapped out the route he'd followed to Farlana, leaving Pucara out of the scenario. *I wonder how Pucara would feel about my disclosing the location of Farlana to the government when the Incans considered it a sacred, forbidden place,* he reflected as he finished the map.

Senor Delgado took the map and studied it carefully. "The route is very complex. It will be difficult to follow without you as our guide." He paused, and asked, "How did you find Farlana, and the way into Injanae, in the first place?"

The ambassador whispered to Ryder, "I know you don't want to get this Pucara fellow involved, but I believe he is Kytan and Taya's only hope of leaving here with you."

Ryder rubbed a hand over his neck. The promise he'd made two years ago to Pucara, to look him up when he returned, was one he intended to keep. He also wanted Pucara to meet his fellow conspirators.

Senor Delgado and his fellow ministers leaned forward. Their expectant expressions told Ryder the ambassador was right in his assessment. His shoulder slumped with resignation. Reluctantly, he said, "A few years ago, an old Incan, named Tupac, who lived in Argentina, told me about Farlana. He said if I wanted to see the dragon mountain, I should ask his nephew, Pucara, to take me to it."

"So this man, Pucara, knows where Farlana is too, and lives here in Peru?"

"Yes, but he considers it a sacred and forbidden place. I doubt he would be willing to take you there."

Senor Delgado's face fell. "That is bad news for your friends." He shook his head. "If Pucara would agree to take us to Farlana, I would allow Mr. Bendarson and Miss Awtoo to emigrate."

"Is that a promise?" Ryder's gold eyes bore into the minister's brown ones.

Minister Delgado escaped Ryder's eyes, quietly consulted with his subordinates, and turned back to Ryder. "Your friends can go, *if* Pucara agrees to take us to Injanae."

"I will take your hand on that," Ryder said, extending his.

Forty-nine

Pucara lived in Cuzco for most of the year, but it was his custom to spend the last few months of each year in the small village of Callao, ten miles west of Lima. It was the residence of his eldest daughter's family. Ryder felt sure they would find him there. He led the party, which consisted of his fellow conspirators, the ambassador, and six government officials, unerringly to the home of Pucara's daughter.

Astonishment robbed the little Incan man of his normally stoic expression when he was called to the front door. "Ryder Garrison! I never thought to see you again." He took Ryder's outstretched hand, "Didn't you go to the dragon?"

"I did, and you were right, Pucara. The mountain's name is Farlana, and it does guard a great evil, one that held me prisoner—these past two years."

Pucara gaped at Ryder. "I must hear this story. Please come in. Then you can introduce me to your companions."

His daughter's home was too small to hold so many guests, but a spacious, covered patio that looked out over the sea could accommodate the group. Everyone helped move all the chairs the house contained onto the patio. Finding they were still short seats for everyone, Pucara's daughter, Meera, borrowed chairs from her neighbors. They arranged them around a well-used fire pit.

When the fire was burning brightly, Meera, and her neighbors, offered Pucara's guests bread, fruit, cheese, fish, and nuts. It was a lavish gesture of hospitality, and Ryder wondered how much it cost Meera and her neighbors, in this simple fishing village, to provide the banquet they enjoyed.

The cold of the night settled in before every detail of the conspirators' adventure was examined, and everyone's questions were fully answered. With the hour pushing toward midnight, the Peruvian officials finally stood and shook Pucara's hand.

"I will consider your request to lead an expedition to Farlana and send my answer in the morning with Ryder," Pucara said, having already asked Ryder to remain for the night.

The two friends sat alone by the fire pit, after the others left for Lima. They were silent for some time, each lost in their own reflections, staring into the crackling flames leaping into the air, and dancing on the salty sea breeze.

"I understand now why Tupac told you about the dragon sentinel," Pucara said, breaking the long silence. "He saw in you the power to escape the dragon's enslavement and end its evil curse."

"I'm afraid we are going to have to differ on that point. I believe I was sent to the dragon to rescue three people, I love very much, and find healing for an old wound."

Pucara gave Ryder a rare smile. "I can see those you brought out of Injanae are very precious to you, and I am glad you found healing for an old wound. Still, in doing that you have defeated the dragon, and brought back with you an entire culture. The dragon no longer holds the power to enslave those who seek it, nor can the people of Injanae remain hidden any longer," he said with some regret.

"The people of Injanae will be better off when they are exposed to the outside world," Ryder said, holding his hands out to the warming heat of the fire. "Their pagan, sacrificial rites and slavery practices are barbaric. Almost half the people who live in Injanae are oppressed by slavery. Many of them would welcome the chance to leave and be free."

Hypocrite, Ryder thought and grimaced. *Yesterday you argued against going into Injanae, and upsetting that society. But, is that really the best thing for them?*

"That may be." Pucara handed him a woven alpaca blanket to put over his knees. His brows contracted, considering Ryder's points. "But in leaving, they will lose their unique identity as a people. They will melt away into the maze of common Peruvian culture, and be lost, just as the Incans are—to a large extent. In a way, I find that sad."

"I might feel like that too, if I thought there was anything of worth in Injanae's society. And I admit it may have historic value as a link to the Incans. But I think its culture is better off being lost, since it enslaves and oppresses its own people."

"You are right of course," Pucara said. "Still, before the people of Injanae disappear into the world, I believe I will take an expedition there."

Ryder's brows rose. Pucara had seemed very reluctant when the Peruvian official pressed him. "I wouldn't like to think you are doing this just so my friends can leave Peru."

"That is only part of why I am considering the trip," Pucara said, adding wood to the fire.

"And I'm grateful you are willing to consider it at all, but if you decide to go, it would be better to take the expedition only as far as you took me. You don't need to go all the way to Farlana to satisfy the government. As long as they can see it, they can get there with the directions I gave them."

"Yes, but I am intrigued by Injanae, and I would like to see it before its culture is lost."

"I think I need to give you the same warning you gave me, with one slight difference. *Almost,* no one who touches the dragon's scales ever returns. If you go into Injanae, take Kytan's advice. Go with a large, well-armed expedition. You may enter Injanae in peace, but it's unlikely you will be allowed to leave in peace, or any other way. And you must remember there is only one way I know of to get in and out of the valley—besides climbing down a five hundred foot cliff, or landing a pontoon plane on the lake. Strategically it will be very difficult to get a large group of armed men through the water tunnel and out of the pool, before all the warriors in Injanae surround it.

"Then we must do what you did and go through the water tunnel at night so we are in the city before the people arise."

"I wish you wouldn't go into Injanae," Ryder said tasting the irony. "We've changed positions, haven't we?"

"Yes, so now I will tell you that I can take care of myself."

"I hope you can take better care of yourself than I did of myself. Injanae is an interesting place to visit, but you don't want to live there for the rest of your life." Ryder laid his hand on Pucara's shoulder, "I would hate to think of you becoming a slave, and enduring the oppression of servitude like so many of the good people I met in Injanae do."

They again lapsed into their own silent reflections, studying the flames that warmed and lit the night.

Pucara finally broke the silence. "The dragon was not only supposed to protect a barbaric and pagan people, but an ancient treasure too. I wonder if it exists, or perhaps did, at one time."

"The jewelry Kytan made for Ansuetra was of silver. He needed a large quantity of it. The chancellor took him down under the palace to a large treasury full of gold statues, dishes, ornaments, jewelry, coins, and bars. There were also precious stones, cut and uncut. Boxes of fine wood, inlaid with gold and jewels. Armor and furniture inlaid with it too. He was taken through a winding path into the depths of the chamber. The silver he wanted came from an ancient chest. It was black with tarnish, and the objects in it were unfamiliar in design to Kytan. He used a large quantity of the chest's silver. What he didn't use went back into the treasury."

"So there is treasure in Injanae." Pucara nodded his satisfaction. "Then everything my ancestors said about the dragon—in a way—is true."

"And according to Kytan the treasure is vast, but I think the real treasure is the waterfall. Without it, the people of Injanae couldn't live there. It has transformed what probably should be a barren valley into a lush garden, rich in vegetation and teaming with life."

"The opportunity to see those remarkable falls is one of the reasons I want to go, and the passage they hold into an ancient world is certainly intriguing. However, it may also prove to be the passage from one kind of bondage to another. The people who come out of Injanae may find the larger world a very hard place to live. Injanae, despite its evil practices is—for the most part—a safe haven for her people, and has protected them from the evils of our world."

Ryder considered Pucara's opinion, now certain of his own. Even knowing his point of view might cost lives, he replied, "But too many have been denied the freedom and opportunity to choose their own direction in a larger world. I didn't fully appreciate my own freedom until I was condemned to slavery for the rest of my life. I can't tell you how wonderful it feels to be free again," he said, filling his lungs with the briny air blowing in from the sea.

Fifty

The sun was just shooting its first rays of light over Lima when Ryder banged on the door of the embassy. He pushed through it as soon as Ricardo opened it, ran down the hall to his room, threw open the door, and pulled Kytan from his bed.

"What is it?" Kytan asked managing to grab his robe before Ryder dragged him out of the room.

"I'll tell you in a minute," Ryder said, hauling Kytan up the stairs by one arm. He released his hold on Kytan when they reached the girls' bedroom. Grinning, he hammered on the door.

"Are you trying to wake the entire city?" Kytan demanded, slipping into his robe and tying the belt.

"Almost," Ryder said, and stepped across the hall to bang on the ambassador's door.

The door to Hadlee and Taya's room cracked opened. "What's going on?" Taya asked in a sleepy voice.

"Get Hadlee out here—now," Ryder said as he continued to bang on the ambassador's door.

The door flew open.

Ryder came within an inch of knocking the ambassador in the forehead, but managed to arrest his fist.

The ambassador scowled at Ryder. "What in the Sam Hill is going on?"

Hadlee, Taya and Mrs. Keeler all poked their heads out into the hall.

Ryder grinned at all the sleepy expressions and yawns. "Pucara has agreed to take an expedition to Farlana."

The girls and Mrs. Keeler rushed out into the hall. The conspirators wrapped their arms around each other—and the Keelers—in a group hug, laughing and dancing.

The ambassador finally broke the hug. He tightened the belt on his robe and cleared his throat. "I am going to go wake up a few government officials," he said, recapturing the dignity of his office and starting down the stairs.

"This calls for a celebration," Mrs. Keeler said. "And I know just what we should have." She grinned at the conspirators. "Meet me in the breakfast room in twenty minutes."

Ryder and Hadlee laughed with Mrs. Keeler over the priceless facial expressions and exuberance displayed by Taya, and particularly Kytan, as they eagerly ate all-American pancakes with maple syrup.

Their mirth was interrupted by the entrance of the ambassador. He strolled into the sunny breakfast parlor, grinning broadly. "Senor Delgado will be here in less than an hour with the proper government officials to sign your emigration papers," he said to Kytan and Taya.

A cheer went up that could have easily raised the roof.

The ambassador held up his hand and everyone quieted down. "I have more news." He looked at Hadlee "The mail plane will be taking off at noon. The courier who was supposed to be on it needs to stay for a few more days. That means there is a place on it for you. Mara is packing your things as we speak."

The jovial atmosphere in the room evaporated.

Hadlee's face collapsed. She covered it with her hands, leaning into Ryder's shoulder. His arms immediately surrounded her. Kytan and Taya jumped up from their chairs, adding their arms too.

Mrs. Keeler rose as well. "Perhaps we should leave them alone, dear," she said, taking her husband's arm, and leading him frowning from the room.

"I can't go, I can't. Don't' make me leave you," Hadlee said, forlorn. "Or come with me. If all of you are with me, it will be easier to tell my family everything." She slid her arms around Ryder's neck, her expressive eyes pleading with his resigned ones. "Please."

Ryder looked at Kytan.

He nodded, took Taya's hand, and walked to the door, closing it after they went through.

Tightening his arms around Hadlee, Ryder kissed her, and immediately knew he shouldn't have. He was too close to the breaking point, and it only made sending her away harder. *I don't think I can last even one more day before I give in, take her home to my family, and marry her—regardless of her family's feelings.*

His conscience intervened. *If you give in now, you will both regret it. You know you will. She needs her family. It's better if she leaves now,* his conscience insisted. *She needs this time with her family.* Still, what she'd said about all of them going with her, gave him an idea.

He leaned his forehead against hers. "We agreed you need to go home. You know it's the right thing to do."

"Yes, but how can I bear to be away from you, not knowing how long we will be apart? It would be so much easier to tell my family about us if you're with me."

"I hate letting you go too, even for a little while, and I agree I should be there when we tell your family about us. After all, I need to ask them for your hand," he said, kissing that appendage. "Besides, I've been thinking that our lovebirds deserve a honeymoon. They might enjoy seeing the temple and learning more about church history."

Hadlee brightened, "That would be a wonderful honeymoon for them."

"So, if you're planning to fly over for the wedding, what do you say we all come back with you for a week? We can set our honeymooners up in a nice hotel and—"

"You can stay with my family," Hadlee said, enthusiastically, dabbing the corners of her eyes with a napkin.

"Well, I don't know about that, but I think it's going to be important for them to meet me—if they will—and spend some time with me. We need to see if they can forgive me, and maybe take to me . . . a little."

Hadlee put praying hands together. "They will. They have to, after all the prayers I've said—and will continue to say— *they will.*"

"Pilot, I don't want you to be too disappointed if they don't. How we feel about each other is going to be a very big shock to them. We need to take it slow, and if things look favorable, we can tell them about us. If not, I'll look for a place to live, and a job in Salt Lake, so we can work on them."

"Alright, and while you're busy getting everything arranged for Kytan and Taya's baptisms and wedding, I can work on them. They are already dying to know about my adventure, and that means talking about you. By the time I come to the wedding, I'm sure they will want to meet you." She ran her finger down the crease in his chin. "Somehow it's going to work out. It just—*has to.*"

"I hope so. We've been through so much to find each other, and forgive, and be forgiven. We belong together. So keep praying for us, my beautiful, brave Pilot. However long it takes to win your family over, I can bear the wait."

"I love you," she whispered, and kissed him just like she had the night on Farlana.

It came dangerously close to destroying his already faltering resolve. He knew letting her go, even for a little while, was going to be the hardest trial of his life.

The door opened. Taya came in. "Hadlee," she said, holding out her hand, "come with me. It's time to get ready."

Standing on the tarmac of the small airport, Hadlee visibly struggled to hold back the tears building up behind her eyes and in the back of her throat as she commissioned Taya and Kytan. "Take care of him. Keep him busy. Don't give him time to be sad." She kissed Taya and Kytan's cheeks. "I love you both so much, I hate leaving you too."

"And we love you." Taya sniffed, wiping her own wet face.

She and Hadlee embraced. Kytan's arms encircled them, and he assured her, "We will take care of him, and when we get to Colorado we will start planning our baptisms and wedding. It won't be long until we are together again."

Ryder's own struggle with his emotions could only be detected in the rigid line of his jaw and the intensity with which his arms encompassed all of them. They held on to each other in the group hug that had always brought them comfort and courage, until the pilot of the courier plane called to Hadlee.

Kytan and Taya hung back, letting Ryder take Hadlee to the plane, giving them their last moments alone.

Hadlee stood in the doorway of the plane for a moment after she entered, and waved, before disappearing inside it.

Ryder stepped back.

The door closed.

He winced as it latched with painful finality, separating him from his heart. He walked back and stood with Taya and Kytan. Taya waved and wiped her eyes as the plane began to taxi, and then race down the runway.

Ryder's eyes followed it, his face set in the unreadable mask of a slave. Nothing could have conveyed his feelings more clearly. The plane lifted into the air and climbed, circling until it turned north.

I'll see her again, I'll hold her again, I'll kiss her again, he consoled himself, trying to shake the dread he felt. He knew full well, it was a fool's dream to believe he would ever be allowed to marry her. He stood like a monolith, staring at the pinpoint where the plane vanished into the clouds, taking away his heart.

A consoling hand, clapped his shoulder. Gentle arms came around his waist. He absently put his around Taya. "We have a lot to do," he said flatly, still staring at the point in the sky where the plane had disappeared. "We better get going."

They wove their way back through the crowded airport building and got into the American embassy car. The car's big engine roared to life. Kytan immediately dimpled, unable to mask his thrill at being in such a remarkable machine. In moments, they were engulfed in the crowded streets of Lima, driving slowly back to the American Embassy.

Ambassador Keeler was waiting for them when they climbed from the car. He took them into his study, consulted a sheet of paper, and said to Ryder, "By the end of the week, you will be headed home too."

It took a concerted effort, but Ryder forced himself to pay attention to what the Ambassador was saying.

"I have booked your passage on a diplomatic courier plane. I'm afraid you will be doing a lot of hopping around before you get to Denver. It won't be the most comfortable trip, but it will get you there. Your parents have arranged for train passage from Denver to Glenwood Springs."

"Thank you, Ambassador. We couldn't have managed without all your help and kindness. What more can we do for you before we leave?" Ryder was grateful their departure was finally set. Now that Hadlee was gone, he just wanted to get home too.

"Some specialists on Incan tapestries, pots, and art are coming this afternoon to talk with Taya and Kytan. They are bringing samples of Incan artifacts. They want to know if what they have is similar to those in Injanae. They are also interested in how Injanaen pottery and tapestries are produced. Can you tolerate another round of questions?" the Ambassador asked Kytan.

"Certainly," Kytan said. "Taya and I are happy to help in any way we can until we leave. My father ran a very successful textile business, so I should be able to answer the questions on tapestries."

"I am not so sure we will be able to help with the pottery, though," said Taya. "Neither of us have experience in that industry, although we can help with visual comparisons."

"Could I be excused from the meeting, Ambassador? I wouldn't be much help. I don't know anything about the pottery or tapestry making industries in Injanae," Ryder said.

The shrewd eyes of the Ambassador considered Ryder. "Of course." He turned back to Kytan and Taya, "The officials will be here right after lunch."

Ryder went out the door of the embassy, passing the Peruvian officials as they entered, grateful for the opportunity to indulge in the solitude he craved. Not caring where he went, he turned right, wandering through the lanes and the vendor's stalls, fingering the small round object in the pocket of his custom made pants, not really seeing anything.

Hadlee's abrupt departure had been a shock. They'd thought they would have until the end of the week together. *Don't kid yourself. It wouldn't have made any difference—you know it wouldn't have—even if we'd had a few more days, weeks, or months together. I would still be walking around with this gaping hole in my chest, no matter when she left. Darvoe's dagger couldn't have done a better job.* The raw wound of parting pulled him back into that moment.

Dry eyed, they stood near the courier plane, entwined in each other's arms, trying to hold off the sharp pain of the coming separation.

The pilot of the plane shouted for Hadlee to board.

She pulled back. Their eyes locked, speaking a language only their hearts understood. Then there was something else in her eyes. *Defiance?* Ryder wasn't sure until she spoke.

"I'm holding you to your proposal, Garrison. With or without my family's blessing"—her voice rose as the plane's engine roared to life—"we *are* getting married."

He couldn't contradict her. He didn't want to, but they both knew the truth. Their marriage was in the hands of her aunt.

She stood on her toes and whispered into his ear. He leaned down and whispered the words back, then lifted her into his arms. That final kiss conveyed everything they couldn't say over the roar of the plane's engine.

He stayed in the memory of that kiss, clinging to the feelings Hadlee expressed in it, needing the strength of her love to sustain his hope.

The honking of a horn yanked him out of that hope—just as the pilot's final warning to Hadlee had pulled her from him. Again, he felt her tear herself out of his arms and watched her climb into the plane. The anguish of that moment, when the door of the plane closed and locked, separating them, rooted him to the spot, until the car honked again.

He came out of the memory with the realization he was standing in the middle of a narrow, winding lane. He jumped to the side, letting the car speed by, and found himself in front of a jewelry shop. A silver chain hung in the window. He went into the shop and bought it, before continuing his aimless wandering.

What he'd said to Pucara rolled over in his mind. *"I can't tell you how wonderful it feels to be free again."*

The words were a lie.

Farlana's grinning jaws mocked him.

Pucara was wrong. I didn't beat the enslavement of the dragon.

The vision of Hadlee silhouetted against the magnificence of the moon on top of Farlana, took possession of him. A haloed veil of platinum hair blew around her, framing her radiant face. Her silver-blue eyes glowed up at him with such love his heart began to throb. He inhaled the intoxication of her herbal scented hair, felt her arms tighten around his neck, and the softness of her lips on his.

I'm not free, and I don't want to be. No matter what happens, my mind will be haunted, and my heart enslaved by her silver-blue eyes—forever.